If your pulse quickens for ER on Thursday nights, you'll want a dose of Timothy Sheard's medicine... The well-meaning, hard-working hospital folks will warm your heart, while the cold realities of modern medical care will raise your blood pressure and keep you turning the pages.

ROCKY MOUNTAIN NEWS

Sheard...vividly takes the pulse of James Madison University Hospital... This is a really good yarn, if that isn't too old-fashioned a phrase.

HARTFORD COURANT

It's hard putting the book down. I raced through it but hated to see it end... The hospital scenes ring true. For mystery lovers, this one's a must!

CHALLENGE

Lenny Moss and his co-workers bend the rules just enough to figure out whodunnit in this fast-paced, 80-chapter work of fiction.

SUN SPOTS   *Newsletter, Saskatchewan Union of Nurses*

A Race Against Death

Looking for a murder mystery whose hero is a worker instead of a cop? Try this One! While most shop stewards do not get involved in murder mysteries, they solve tough problems at work every day. Now they can look up to a fictional role model—Super Steward Lenny Moss.

PUBLIC EMPLOYEE PRESS MEDIA BEAT

Timothy Sheard provides a delightful hospital investigative tale that grips readers from the moment that Dr. Singh and his team apply CPR, but fail.

MYSTERIES GALORE

Also by Timothy Sheard:

This Won't Hurt A Bit

A Race Against Death

Coming in April, 2010:

Slim To None

(the forth Lenny Moss mystery!)

SOME CUTS NEVER HEAL

A Lenny Moss Mystery

by TIMOTHY SHEARD

PRESS

Printing: January, 2008, by Hard Ball Press
Originally printed by Carroll & Graf, 2002

Library of Congress Cataloging-in-Publication Data
Sheard, Timothy
Some Cuts Never Heal: A Lenny Moss mystery / Timothy Sheard.
ISBN 978-0-9814518-0-0
1. Philadelphia (Pa)—Fiction.   2. Hosptials—Fiction.   3. Lenny Moss.

For my brother Tom,

Gone too soon.

I must down to the seas again, to the vagrant gypsy life,
To the gull's way and the whale's way where the wind's like a
     whetted knife;
And all I ask is a merry yarn from a laughing fellow-rover
And quiet sleep and a sweet dream when the long trick's over.

John Masefield

–ONE–

"Yo, Lenny, come help me move the stiff!"

"Okay, Fred, hold on!"

Plunging his mop into a bucket of soapy water, Lenny Moss ambled across the hall to the opposite room, where he found the old morgue attendant leaning across a battered steel gurney tugging on a sheet.

"I wouldn't bother you," Fred explained, "but I got a big tomato here, and nobody's got time to help me."

"It's the damn hiring freeze," said Lenny. "Everybody's working short."

"You telling me? Every Friday they ask me for overtime; I need time *off*."

Lenny eyed the large mass wrapped in a white plastic shroud as he approached the bed. An unprepossessing man dressed in custodian's blue work clothes and black, steel-tipped shoes, Lenny had thick black eyebrows arching over dark eyes that could change in a flash from impish to deadly serious.

Pressing his hands against the cold, soft flesh, he bent his knees, saying, "Okay, Fred, on three. One . . . two . . . *three!*"

Crack! The cadaver's head made a hideous sound as the two men jerked the body from the bed onto the metal stretcher.

Fred attached a weathered canvas canopy over the stretcher to conceal the body, saying, "Man, this is gonna be one juicy son of a bitch. You got to come down the morgue and see when Dr. Fingers slices him open. Why—"

"Uh, Freddie, I don't mean to cut you off, but I have a shit load of work to do."

"Right-o!" answered Fred, as he maneuvered the stretcher out of the room. "Hey, I got a new joke. Knock, knock."

"*Who's* there?" said Lenny with a groan.

"Ivana."

"Ivana who?"

"I vana hold your h-an-d. . . ."

"Har, har," said Lenny, laughing more from the pain than the humor. "Tell me. Is the supervisor giving you any more grief about your sick time?"

"Nah. Childress ain't said boo to me ever since you won that last grievance."

"Good." Lenny watched the morgue attendant slowly wheel the body away, noting his protruding belly and skinny legs, and recalling the many battles he'd waged to keep Fred's job.

1

Alcoholism was a bitch.

He'd just finished mopping the hall, when Gary Tuttle, RN, asked him to strip the floor in room 709.

"Jeez, Tuttle, I don't have time for that, they have me covering three areas."

"I'm sorry, Lenny, but the floor is disgusting from that GI bleeder. Since the admission was canceled, now is the only time you'll be able to do it."

Grumbling under his breath, he gathered the materials and began the job. He poured out the strong-smelling stripper and worked it into the floor. Once the old wax was removed, he began pouring out a puddle of new wax just as the Central Supply clerk came in carrying an admission kit.

"Ain't there a new patient in this room?" she asked.

"Admission was canceled."

"Nuts," she said. "I ain't got time to come back for the next one. I'll leave the kit." She placed the plastic-wrapped washbasin in the bedside cabinet, then hurried out of the room.

Lenny resumed spreading the sweet-smelling liquid wax with his mop. He'd covered half the floor when he spied his friend Moose Maddox, a dietary aide, standing in the doorway, holding a tray of food. Moose was a tall, muscular black man who had played football in high school and, for a time, tried his hand at amateur boxing.

"Where's the patient?" asked Moose. "I got a late breakfast tray for a Mrs. Blackwell . . . Blakewill . . .something like that."

"Gary says the admission was canceled."

"You sure?"

"Hey, ask him, I'm just the custodian."

"Okay," Moose said, and walked away.

Bending down, Lenny used a putty knife to pry from the floor a piece of gum? Tissue? Snot? It was hard to tell. He poured out more of the wax, inhaling the bubble-gum scent, and thinking it was funny that, after years of working in James Madison University Hospital, he'd actually gotten to like the smell. It wasn't as if he had to deal with the putrid odors that Freddie had. Like rotting flesh. Old blood. Formaldehyde.

Moose stuck his head back in the room. "You were right, the admission's canceled. I left the tray in the pantry just in case. You coming down for morning break?"

"I will if people stop interrupting me."

"Bitch, bitch," said Moose, with a grin. "I'll see you later." He turned and headed down the hall.

After spreading the wax, Lenny set a fan in the doorway to speed up the drying. Next, he placed a yellow sign reading, CAUTION! WET FLOOR beside it. Dropping his mop in the rolling bucket, he stood looking over his work, a nondescript man in work clothes, unnoticed by the doctors hurrying by.

A pharmacy tech came up to Lenny holding a Ziploc bag.

"Damn, " said the tech, seeing the shiny wet floor, "where's the new patient? I got a drug profile I'm supposed to put in the serving drawer."

"Don't jump on my ass," said Lenny, his dark eyebrows furrowed in irritation. "I was told the admission's canceled."

"So how come my computer printout says there's a Mrs. Blackwell *in* the room?"

"Ask Gary, he's the charge nurse. I'm just a simple custodian."

"Custodian, yeah, but, simple? No frickin' way."

As Lenny watched the young man walk away, a mischievous grin erased the irritation from his face. Hurrying to the nursing station, he found Gary Tuttle, RN, accepting a stack of lab reports from the hospital messenger.

"Tuttle, I have a great idea!" said Lenny.

"I'm afraid to ask what you're cooking up this time," said Gary, who leaned back in his chair and folded his arms across his chest. He was a stout fellow with receding, sandy-colored hair and soft features.

"The computer still has that admission coming into seven-o-nine, right?"

"Maybe the patient is scheduled after all," said the nurse.

Celeste, the ward clerk, spun around in her chair. "Gary, I told you, the HMO didn't pre-approve Dr. Fox's admission. That lazy-ass girl in Admissions hasn't bothered to take the name out of the damn computer!"

"*Perfect*," said Lenny. "Everybody thinks there's a patient in seven-o-nine. Central Supply sent up an admission pack, dietary sent a breakfast tray, pharmacy sent a printout."

"*And* . . ." said Gary, eyeing Lenny with suspicion.

"Let's act like there really *is* a patient in the room!"

With a smile like carnival lights, Celeste threw back her head and laughed. She was a tall, smartly dressed black woman who loved costume jewelry. "Oh, Lenny. You've come up with some goofy ideas, but this one's the best. I love it!"

Gary's face was rigid with doubt. "I'm not at all comfortable with this," he said.

"Why not?" Lenny asked.

"We could get in trouble if somebody found out."

"So we'll act dumb."

"Easy for you," said Moose, "we got to fake it."

"Look," said Lenny, ignoring the jibe, "while we've been busting our ass for over a year working short-staffed, the hospital's been operating at a hundred percent capacity. Right?"

"More like a hundred fifty percent," said Celeste, "the way they discharge one patient in the morning and admit another one by noon. Shoot. You know they bill both patients for the whole day."

"Work has been awfully stressful lately," admitted Gary. "All the mandatory overtime . . .the hiring freeze. . ." He looked at the others. Fidgeted. Shrugged his shoulders. "Oh, all right, we'll keep the room empty, at least for a couple of hours."

"I'll fill out a menu for lunch and dinner," said Moose.

"I'll order a consult," said Celeste, turning to the computer.

Looking over the clerk's shoulder at the computer screen, Gary asked, "Whose access code are you using?"

"I got Mother Burgess's own log-on number," she said, giggling.

"Oh, Lord," said Gary, "not the director of nursing."

Lenny clapped Gary on the shoulder. "Be strong, Tuttle. It's just a little joke."

-TWO-

Dr. Martin Kadish, a tall, beefy man in a pinstriped suit, ploughed into Seven South like a big cabin cruiser with the throttle wide open, while the residents and medical students on the transplant service bobbed in his wake, struggling to keep up. Reaching the nursing station, Dr. Kadish told Celeste, "Get me Blackwell's chart, I have a consult. Room seven-o-nine."

He stared impatiently at the ward clerk, his thick lips turned in a frown, while his big, meaty hands opened and closed as though preparing for a wrestling match.

"I'm sorry, Doctor," said Celeste, pretending to look for the chart, "I don't see it. Maybe one of the residents took it down to the patient's room?"

Kadish turned fierce eyes on his team. Each member shook his head under the surgeon's blistering stare. Turning back to Celeste, he said, "Find it. The damn thing doesn't have legs. It didn't walk away by itself. I'll be examining the patient."

While Kadish was speaking to Celeste at the nursing station, Nadia Gonzalez, a portly nurse's aide, went into room 709 to use the phone, knowing that the admission had been canceled. Halfway into the room she stopped, puzzled. A slender, redheaded woman dressed in a Kelly green business suit was lying on the bed, staring at the ceiling.

The perplexed aide approached the bed.

"Miss . . Miss, are you sure you belong here?"

Nadia took one more step, then froze as she realized that the woman's chest was not rising and that her eyes were wide open but unseeing.

Feeling panic constrict her throat, she turned to the door, seeking help, where she collided with Dr. Kadish. She rebounded off the big man. Gasping for breath and unable to speak, she pointed wordlessly at the woman on the bed.

The doctor stepped forward, bent down over the woman, listened for a breath. There was none. He placed his fingers lightly on the side of her neck. There was no pulse.

"Call a code," he said, pointing at the bedside phone.

As a baby-faced intern dialed the hospital operator, Kadish pushed two medical students toward the woman. "There's no ambu bag in the room. You give mouth-to-mouth until anesthesia gets here. You do chest compressions."

Seeing the gaggle of doctors going into 709, Lenny went to the nursing

5

station.

"Hey, Gary, I thought the room I waxed this morning was empty."

"It's supposed to be," said the nurse. "I haven't—"

"Attention! Attention! Code Red, Nursing station Seven South, room seven-o-nine!"

Gary stopped in mid-sentence as he listened to the page operator's overhead announcement. When he realized that the code was on his floor, he jumped from his chair and ran to the crash cart, unplugged it, and set off down the hall at a run.

"I don't understand," said Gary. "The room is supposed to be empty!"

"Well it's full of doctors now," said Lenny, walking hurriedly beside the nurse.

Gary wheeled the crash cart into the room, banging it against the doorframe in his haste. With trembling hands, he pressed the power button on the cardiac monitor, then opened a drawer and fished for the electrodes.

A surgical resident ripped open the woman's blouse and stuck the EKG electrodes onto her chest. All heads turned to the monitor. The rhythm was a jumble of fat, chaotic, ugly complexes.

"V-fib," said Dr. Kadish. "Charge the paddles to two hundred joules."

Kadish glared at Gary as the nurse, stricken by anxiety, fumbled with the dials. Finally, a high-pitched wail announced that the defibrillator was charging. The resident pulled the paddles from the machine and placed them on the woman's chest.

"Clear!" he called, looking up and down the bed. A medical student was pulling the woman's pants down over her knees. "Get off the bed!" yelled the resident.

"Wait!" Gary called out, pulling a tube of conducting jelly from the crash cart. But the resident squeezed the trigger without waiting. The woman's back and neck arched in a grotesque spasm; then she fell limply back in the bed. The smell of burning flesh filled the room.

The rhythm was unchanged.

At that moment Dr. Samir Singh, one of the Critical Care attending physicians, came into the room. He was a bearded, soft-spoken Indian man in a rumpled lab coat and turban. Dr. Singh asked Kadish, "Is this your patient?"

"I've never treated her," said Kadish. "I found her pulseless and apneic. She's in V-fib."

Dr. Singh said softly, "Charge to three-sixty, lubricate the paddles, and shock again."

As the monitor wailed mournfully, building up the charge, Gary looked at Lenny, who was hovering in the doorway. Lenny shrugged and moved on.

The resident shocked again, with the same results.

"Another," said Dr. Singh, staring at the coarse, chaotic rhythm on the monitor.

As the third shock was delivered, an anesthesiologist entered the room with her tackle box. She deftly inserted a breathing tube. A resident jabbed an intravenous catheter into the groin. Dark blood dripped from the opening.

"IV!" he called.

Gary hurriedly spiked a bag of intravenous fluid and connected it to the catheter.

"Give three milligrams epinephrine and continue CPR," said Dr. Singh. He turned to Gary. "Mr. Tuttle, what can you tell me of the patient?"

Gary felt rats gnaw at his belly. "I'm sorry, Dr. Singh, this isn't one of our patients. We were expecting a seventy-year-old patient of Dr. Fox. This isn't her."

"But we must know something about the patient. The reason for admission, at least."

"That's what I'm trying to tell you," said Gary. "I don't think she's a patient at all."

"You mean she may be a visitor or a family member? Someone like that?"

"Yes," said Gary.

"Look for identification. A medical alert bracelet. Something."

Gary searched the woman's clothes for a wallet. Finding none, he scanned the floor, noted a slim attaché case half under the bed. He picked it up, saw a logo on it:: *FALCON PHARMACEUTICALS*. Opening the case, he found a business card that read, *Colleen Creedon, Regional Sales Coordinator, Falcon Pharmaceuticals.*

He silently handed the card to Dr. Singh, who glanced at it as he said, "Shock again, please. And send off labs. Chemistry, toxicology, blood gas. Everything."

"Clear the bed!" yelled the resident, who sent another electric charge through the woman's chest. "We have a rhythm!" he yelled, pointing to the monitor.

"Check for a pulse," Dr. Singh said, studying the monitor.

"I can't feel a femoral pulse," said the resident.

"Run in a liter of normal saline under pressure. Start levophed." Singh was quiet and firm, his cool demeanor belying the anxiety in his heart.

A few moments later the resident called out, "She's back in V-fib!"

"Shock again," said Singh.

The defibrillator howled, the current sparked across the chest, the torso arched and collapsed, but the rhythm failed to convert. Three more shocks, an amp of magnesium sulfate, and injections of dextrose and sodium bicarb made no difference. The chaotic rhythm on the monitor grew smaller, like a dying fire, until it became a flat line. All eyes turned to Singh.

"How long has it been?" he asked, scanning a printout of lab results.

"Twenty-five minutes," said one of the transplant residents, who had been with Kadish when they discovered the patient. "She was already down when we found her, we don't know for how long. Her pupils are fixed and dilated."

Dr. Singh looked to the ceiling, as though he were appealing for heavenly guidance. After a moment's reflection he looked back down at the lifeless figure receiving vigorous chest compressions and oxygen.

"You may stop," he said. "Note the time, please. Thank you, everyone."

The physicians, medical students, and respiratory therapist filed silently out of the room, leaving Gary and Dr. Singh alone with the dead woman.

"I'll clean her up," said Gary. "Will you call the family?"

"Yes, right away. How long can you keep the body on the ward?"

"Well, they have patients stacked up in the ER and Recovery waiting for beds. The hospital policy is two hours, but I'll keep the room blocked all day if I have to."

"Very good. I will let you know what the family says." As he turned to leave the room, Singh stopped and turned back. "You understand, we must leave all the lines in place. This is a case for the medical examiner."

"Even the endotracheal tube?"

"Yes. Everything."

"I understand," said Gary. "I'll just remove the tape and cut it down to the lip."

"That will be fine. Thank you."

Dr. Singh quietly slipped out, leaving Gary with the untidy debris of dying.

-THREE-

Nadia, the portly nursing assistant, came into the dead woman's room, carrying a basin of hot water, linen, and a plastic shroud. Gary had already begun removing the mountain of debris from the bed and the floor.

Drawing the curtain around the bed, they gently removed the clothes, which had been ripped open. Nadia folded them neatly and placed them in a plastic personal belongings bag while Gary dipped a washrag in the hot water, soaped it up, and began to bathe the body.

There were ugly, circular burn marks on the chest above the right breast and along the left flank where the resident had delivered the first electric shock without applying conductive jelly to the paddles. Other than that, the skin was clean and intact, with no signs of trauma or injury. The nails on her fingers and toes were painted a dark red. She wore a slim gold watch and a diamond engagement ring on her left hand.

"You want I should remove the jewelry?" asked Nadia.

"We'll put them in a specimen bag. I'll lock them in the narcotic cabinet until the family arrives," he said.

When the front of the body was clean, Gary pulled it onto the side. The sheet beneath her was stained red from blood where the intravenous catheter was hurriedly jabbed into the groin. As Nadia cleaned the buttocks and posterior thighs, she noted a whitish discharge in the perineal area.

"Looks like she had the woman's troubles," said Nadia, pointing at the discharge.

"It won't matter now," said Gary. "She's past worrying about vaginal infections."

They placed the shroud beneath the patient, removed the soiled sheets, and rolled the body onto its back. They dressed her in a hospital gown. Nadia held the feet off the bed while Gary wrapped the ankles with a roll of gauze. The feet were already cold.

"You want me to tie the hands?" she asked.

"Let's wait to see if the family is coming," said Gary.

He folded the hands over the chest. Although the mouth was open, Gary didn't want to tie the jaw closed with gauze if the family was going to see her. Instead, he pressed gently on the chin with a rolled-up sheet, forcing the mouth closed.

They pulled a crisp white sheet up to her chin, made it trim and straight,

9

and raised the head of the bed a few degrees. Nadia arranged her long red hair neatly on the pillow. Gary saw that the eyes were partly open, as if the corpse were stealing a peak at the world of the living. He squeezed a dab of petroleum jelly into the eyes and pushed the lids closed, sealing them shut.

Nadia crossed herself before carrying away the basin of dirty water and the soiled linen. Gary picked up the trash bag, turned the lights off, and half-closed the window shade, leaving the room dimly lit. He looked back once more at the dead woman, feeling an intense wave of sorrow. And fear.

He thought, *we are in so much trouble.*

At the nursing station, Dr. Singh told Gary that he had reached the mother in Cherry Hill, New Jersey, and that she was coming over as soon as she had notified another relative.

"Please page me when they arrive," said the doctor. "I will speak to them. I do not know what I will tell them, but . . . " He walked slowly off the unit.

Lenny and Moose, who had been drinking juice in the little kitchen across from the nursing station, joined Gary.

"Tuttle, what the hell happened?" asked Lenny.

"I don't understand it. The woman who coded wasn't a patient, she was a drug rep."

"What was a drug rep doing up here?" asked Moose. "There ain't no doctors' offices."

"I have no idea," said Gary, "but I do know one thing: we are all going to catch hell for this."

"How so?" asked Lenny.

"Are you *blind*? We falsified hospital records. We consulted Dr. Kadish. We used Mrs. Burgess's access code. And the woman in the room is *dead!*"

"Gary's right," said Celeste. "There's gonna be an investigation. Heads could roll."

Lenny rubbed his chin, felt the stubble that grew within an hour of shaving. He needed an out. As a veteran union steward, he'd fudged and finessed many a negotiation with a supervisor or an appeal board, but he had never faced a situation like this.

"Okay, here's what we'll do. Celeste, you didn't know the admission was canceled, so you're covered. Gary doesn't know anything about the pharmacy request or the consults. I'll try to find out how the woman ended up in the room."

"What if she didn't die from natural causes?" said Celeste. "Then the shit'll *really* hit the fan."

"It's a medical examiner's case," said Gary. "There will be an inquest. Depositions. We all may be called to testify."

"Let's not panic," said Lenny. "Let's find out as much as we can about her and go from there." He looked into the anxious faces of his coworkers. "The main thing is, nobody talks, everyone walks. Agreed?"

The others silently nodded their heads.

As the group broke up, Lenny felt a heavy weight bear down on him. He asked himself why couldn't he keep his crazy ideas in his head where they belonged. His friends were going to suffer, all because of his sick sense of humor.

Not only that, the bosses were bound to realize that faking the admission was his idea. They would be sure to make him their number one target.

-FOUR-

Mrs. Gertrude Cavanaugh opened her eyes and looked about the room. She saw the stained curtains, the harsh fluorescent lights, the beige cotton blanket. After a moment she remembered that she was in room 712, James Madison University Hospital.

"I must have slept through the whole thing," she mumbled through parched lips. She was a small, nearly bald woman of seventy-eight, with a protruding belly and a bladder that dribbled when she coughed. Mrs. Cavanaugh ran her tongue across the roof of her dry mouth.

"Where are my dentures?" she mumbled. With fingers as gnarled as tree roots, she grasped the bed rail and pulled herself upright. She reached for the blue denture cup on her bedside table, pried off the lid. It was empty.

"Oh, dear," she mumbled, thinking how decrepit she looked without her dentures. "I can't let anyone see me without my teeth."

She reached a trembling hand to the nurse's call button, pressed it, listened for the "Blink, blink" in the hallway. Satisfied, she let go of the button and sank back exhausted in the bed.

If the nurse doesn't find my teeth, I can't go on, she thought. *I just can't go on.*

She felt the minutes pass like days torn from a calendar. Soon, she was sleeping through the winter.

Lost in thought, Lenny absently pushed a dry mop down the corridor.

He wondered why a drug rep would be on Seven South—there were no doctors' offices to visit. He bent down to scoop up a pile of debris and considered the notion that she had been visiting a sick friend or relative.

Going room to room, he asked each patient if they had been expecting a visit from a young redheaded woman. In one room he came upon a burly man sitting in bed with a sour look on his face. A thin woman with mousy brown hair and heavy pancake makeup stood at the bedside holding a cup to the man's mouth.

"Don't be a big baby, Howard, take your medicine!" she said with a voice like fingernails on a chalkboard.

"Not if I have to drink that whole thing," he said, pointing to a gallon jug of clear liquid on the bedside table.

"That nice male nurse Mr. Tuttle told you, it's to clean out your colon so

13

that Dr. Fox can see inside with his instrument. You *have* to drink it *all*."

"I don't like the idea of some guy poking around inside my bowels," he grumbled. "What if something breaks off in there?"

"Nothing's going to break off," she said, pressing the cup to his mouth.

"I don't want to take the test!"

The wife slammed the cup down on the table, splattering fluid onto the floor.

"You listen to me, Howard Stipes. I spent half my life on a table with my legs spread apart bearing you six children, and now it's your turn to assume a compromising position!"

The man watched as she refilled the glass with the bowel prep. Silently, he took the cup in his hand and drank the liquid down.

Lenny said, "Excuse me. Have you had any visitors today?"

"Just *her*," said Howard. "Why?"

"There was a young redheaded woman in a green suit looking for a friend. I thought you might have seen her."

"No redhead's come in here, I'd remember," he said.

His wife glared at him as she poured another glass.

After querying all of the patients, Lenny was satisfied that the dead woman had not been on Seven South to visit a patient. He spied Betty, his housekeeping partner, pushing her cart down the hall. Betty was a middle-aged black woman with gray hair as kinky as steel wool, thick hips, and bowlegs. A figure of Jesus stood on top of her cart among the rags and rolls of toilet paper.

Deciding that he needed and deserved a break, he told her, "I'm going to the cafeteria for coffee. You want anything?"

"No, dear heart. I'm gonna make myself a cup of tea in the kitchen. You take your break. The Lord knows you've earned it."

He hurried off the ward, wishing that he could rewind the events of the morning and start all over. If only life were like a video. Or even better, a DVD.

Dr. Kadish entered the executive boardroom and stood looking over the half-dozen men and women seated around the cherry wood table.

"Good morning, everyone," he said. "Sorry I'm late; there was a code on Seven South."

Roger Lefferts, CEO of James Madison University Hospital, waved him to a chair, saying, "We were about to discuss your unusual proposal, Dr. Kadish."

The chief executive wore a beautifully tailored suit with a silk shirt and diamond tiepin. "I have to confess, it presents us with a number of legal conundrums. Proceeding may be problematic from a medical-legal standpoint."

"Why? Because it's the first time anyone's done it?" said Kadish. "We'll be pioneers."

"I've reviewed the approval notice from the FDA," said Lefferts. "That part seems to be in order. But we're not out of the woods yet."

"I agree with Roger," said Dr. Slocum, the silver-haired chief of staff. "I'm concerned that the public will look on us as publicity-seeking adventurists, not groundbreaking innovators."

"Quadruple-organ transplant has been done on primates in several medical centers," said Kadish. "I've done ten transplants myself in the Basic Science lab. The viability of the technique is well established."

"Then why hasn't it been done on human beings at another medical center?" asked Slocum.

"It's risky, I admit it. But look at the first implanted mechanical device that fully replaced a beating heart. They were extremely high risk cases, but nobody accused those medical centers of recklessness or bad judgment."

Miss Helen Burgess, assistant vice president for patient services, formerly called the director of nursing, cleared her throat. "I'm quite frankly concerned about the status of the donor. How do you propose to find a living donor who can spare a heart, a pair of lungs, a liver *and* kidneys?"

"My ideal candidate is a young adult who is brain dead. We'll transfer the donor to James Madison while still on life support, harvest the organs, then pull the plug."

"I share Helen's concern," said Slocum. "You've got to be sure and pronounce the donor dead *before* you begin the harvest. I want that protocol to be crystal clear, in writing. We don't need some greedy family suing the hospital claiming that we killed their loved one."

"Liability won't be a problem," said Kadish, sensing the tide turning in his favor. "You can be sure of that."

–FIVE–

Humming a hymn and smiling to herself, Betty pushed her housekeeping cart up to the nursing station, where she refilled the paper towel dispenser over the sink. Gary Tuttle was sitting at the counter transcribing medication orders.

"Hello, Gary. How are you this fine day?" she asked.

"Don't ask, Betty, it's been a dreadful morning," he said, reaching for a box of tissues on her cart. He took off wire-rimmed glasses, blew on the lenses, and rubbed them with a tissue.

"Listen," said Betty. "I know you got a lot on your mind, with the visitor dying up here this morning, but that Mrs. Cavanaugh in seven-twelve is crying and carrying on something terrible about her missing dentures."

"I've searched the room but I didn't find them."

"She says maybe they took them from her when she was down the GI lab this morning."

"I called the lab; Tina said they're not there. I suspect that Billy left them on the stretcher when he brought the patient back to her room."

"Well, the poor thing is crying her eyes out. I hope to God you find them, or that devil Joe West will be up here snooping around, mark my words."

"I have a sinking feeling that I'm going to see West, anyway," he said, his face lined with worry.

Placing a hand gently on his shoulder, she said, "I know you're scared about that big mess in seven-o-nine, but don't you worry, Lenny'll fix things, like he always does."

In the executive boardroom, Miss Burgess cleared her throat again, sipped from a glass of bottled water. Her silver hair, swept back in a glistening wave of shellac, glinted in the strong light.

"I have a question about the ten monkeys that you experimented on," she said.

"They were chimpanzees," said Kadish.

"Chimpanzees, monkeys. Whatever. How long did they survive after they had the four organs transplanted into their body?"

"The survival time varied from three to thirty days."

"The best case only lived thirty days?" asked CEO Lefferts. "That doesn't

17

sound like the most promising outcome."

"I could have kept them alive longer, but I euthanized them at thirty days in order to take tissue samples for pathology."

"How many died in a few days?" asked Dr. Slocum. "And what were the causes of death?"

"Two died within forty-eight hours. One from shock caused by bleeding at an arterial suture site. Another died from a pneumothoraxic."

Miss Burgess looked at Dr. Slocum, doubt written on her face. "Two deaths in ten cases. That doesn't sound like a very promising beginning."

Slocum said, "None of the early deaths were due to organ rejection, were they?"

"Definitely not. One of the principles that we have established is that the risk of rejection does not increase with the number of organs transplanted. All of the primate trials were successful from a rejection standpoint."

The CEO looked about the room. "I don't have to tell you how vicious the competition in the healthcare industry has become lately. The state and federal governments are cutting their reimbursement rates for Medicare and Medicaid, the private carriers are demanding restrictive contracts that limit what we bill for services. Our competitors are running breezy, snappy ads on radio and television. The marketplace is brutal. Simply brutal."

"What are our projections for the current fiscal year?" asked Miss Burgess.

"At the rate we're going, we anticipate a shortfall of three to four million dollars."

"I had no idea things were this bad," said Slocum.

"We haven't broadcast the news," said Lefferts. "Once the credit agencies get wind of a deficit, they downgrade your credit rating. Suppliers demand cash on demand or they withhold shipment, and your accounts receivable just spiral out of control."

"Are there no other revenue streams we can tap into?" asked Dr. Slocum.

"If anyone here knows of one that we can get up and running quickly, I'd like to hear about it," said Lefferts. He looked about the table. Nobody spoke.

"My procedure will not only bring in needed revenues," said Kadish, sensing victory, "it will also bring us enormous amounts of publicity and referrals. Other programs will get a boost. Our operating rooms will be running twenty-four hours a day keeping up with the demand."

Casting a stern look about the group, Lefferts said, "The finance department believes that Dr. Kadish's procedure is our best shot at ensuring the hospital's survival."

"How much money will the procedure bring in?" asked Slocum.

"One million dollars," said Kadish. "Cash."

There was a hush in the room as everyone soaked up the size of the payment.

"The money will be paid in full prior to the procedure. I only need to do three or four and it will turn James Madison around."

The CEO looked from face to face, assessing the impact of the million-dollar prize. After a moment he said, "I put it to a vote, which must be unanimous, as you all know, if we're to go forward with this project. Who supports Dr. Kadish's quadruple-organ transplant?"

One by one, the members of the executive committee raised their hands. Miss Burgess finished her bottled water, dabbed a napkin to her mouth, and finally raised her hand.

"Let the minutes read, the proposal is carried," said Lefferts. "Dr. Kadish, you may begin looking for a suitable candidate."

"*Look* for a candidate? I've got him in the ICU with multi-organ system failure. Now all I have to do is locate a suitable donor."

Glancing up from the desk, Gary saw Billy, one of the new transportation orderlies, pushing a patient in a wheelchair up to the station. As the orderly placed the patient's chart on the counter, the nurse said, "Billy, are you sure that you didn't leave Mrs. Cavanaugh's dentures on the stretcher when you brought her back from the GI lab this morning?"

"Gosh, I don't remember seeing any dentures, Mr. Tuttle," he said. "They got us moving so many patients, I can hardly remember one from the other."

"Mrs. Cavanaugh is very upset that her teeth are missing. If we don't find them I'll have to make out an incident report and notify Security."

Billy shifted his weight from one foot to another. He was a long, lean, loose-limbed fellow with a patch of fuzz on his chin. He bit his lower lip trying to remember.

"I don't think I left anything on the stretcher. I remember there was a chart, and her slippers and a robe, but—"

"Brnnng!"

The phone at the station rang. As Gary turned to answer it, Betty pulled Billy aside and whispered in his ear. "Don't say any more, child. You take the patient to his room, I'll go get Lenny."

Billy pushed the patient in the wheelchair back to his room; then he stood at the end of the hall as far away from the nursing station as he could be, and waited.

—SIX—

As soon as Betty found Lenny in the cafeteria and told him about Billy and the missing dentures, he gulped down his coffee and hurried back to Seven South. He found the orderly nervously fidgeting in the hallway by the housekeeping closet.

"Hey, Bill, what's goin' on?" he said.

"Hi, Lenny. Well, see, this patient I took to the GI lab this morning, Mrs. Cavanaugh, she says her dentures are missing, and Mr. Tuttle told me he'd make out an incident report if the dentures don't get found, and me being new and on probation, I don't want to get in no trouble."

Lenny put his hands in his pockets and slouched against the wall. "Did you check the tray under the stretcher when you brought the patient back to her room?"

"I, I think so."

"No, Billy, you're sure. You're sure you checked it because you remember noticing that the tray was dusty, and you were going to ask Betty for a rag to wipe it down when you had a chance."

Billy soaked up the suggestion, nodding slowly.

"Are you okay with that?" Lenny asked.

"Yeah, I can do that." The young orderly still looked anxious. "You think I'll get in trouble for this? I'm still on probation."

"Nah, don't sweat it. The hospital's trying to replace all the full-time transporters with part-timers like you so they don't have to pay benefits. You'd have to drop a patient on his head before they fire you. Go back to work. I'll talk to Tuttle."

He walked down to the nursing station, where he found Gary mixing intravenous medications.

"Say, Tuttle. I just talked to Billy. It doesn't sound like he left those missing dentures on the stretcher, he checked the tray and they weren't there. You sure they're not down in the GI lab?"

"I called Tina and she looked for them, but they're not there."

"Huh," said Lenny. "What did the patient go down for?"

"She had a colonoscopy," said Gary.

Lenny looked puzzled. "Isn't that the test where they stick a hose up your ass?"

"It's a fiber-optic scope, not a hose, but yes, the doctor inserts it through

21

the rectum."

"Well, isn't it unusual for them to take out someone's dentures when they're looking up your butt, not down your throat?"

"You know, I wondered the same thing," said Gary. "They may have a standard checklist and they take out everyone's dentures, regardless of the procedure."

"There'd be a record of that in the chart, wouldn't there?" said Lenny.

"Yes. Let's have a look."

Gary pulled Mrs. Cavanaugh's chart from the rack and flipped through it until he found the GI procedure note. Attached to the note was a vivid color photograph of a long, pink cavern with a ribbed roof. The end of the cavern was lost in darkness.

"Is that the colon?" Lenny asked.

"Yes. Dr. Fox takes a great picture, doesn't he? It's a digital image."

Gary ran his finger down the page until he found the section labeled "Dentures removed." It was not checked off.

"Are the nurses always good about checking something like that off?" asked Lenny.

"Some might forget, but not Tina, she doesn't miss a thing. If I so much as forget to send my patient with a pillow, she lets me know about it."

"So where do you think her teeth are?" asked Lenny.

"I can't imagine," said Gary. "This day is such a disaster, there's no telling what calamity will befall us next."

"Be strong, Tuttle. As long as we hang tough, nobody can touch us."

"I wish I had your confidence." The nurse turned his attention to a pair of women walking toward them. Before they were close enough to hear him, he said softly to Lenny, "Oh, dear, here comes the family."

"You mean . . ." said Lenny.

"They've got to be the family of Colleen Creedon, the drug rep who coded this morning."

As Lenny left the nursing station, Elizabeth Creedon and her sister, Mamie, approached Gary. Both women were dressed in old-fashioned high-buttoned blouses, long skirts, and sensible flat shoes. By the grief in their eyes, Gary didn't have to ask why they were there.

"Where is Colleen?" the mother asked, her eyes wide with fear. "Is she very ill? I was told she was taken suddenly ill. That she was critical!"

"Dr. Singh is the physician in charge of the case," said Gary. "I'll page him for you and he can—"

"She's died, hasn't she," said Mamie, grabbing the edge of the counter as if she wanted to overturn it. "I've been through this before when our father died, I know the signs. Our Collie is dead. Isn't that right?"

Gary felt his throat tighten. He knew that the hospital tradition was for the doctor to inform a family when a patient died, but when the nurses had a good rapport with the family, they sometimes were the ones to break the bad news.

Although he knew neither the dead woman nor the family, Gary didn't have the heart to stall the women. "I'm sorry," he said, rising from his chair and stepping closer to them. "Yes, she expired this morning."

"Oh, my God!" cried the mother. "How could she die? It's not possible!"

Gary stood silently before the two women, feeling useless. And a little guilty.

"You must have her mixed up with someone else," Mrs. Creedon went on. "My daughter is young and healthy and full of life. She *must* be alive!"

The mother became overcome with tears. Mamie put her arm around her sister's shoulder and hugged her. Looking at Gary, she said, "What happened? Did she have an aneurysm that burst or something?"

"I'll page Dr. Singh. He can explain things to you."

Gary dialed the doctor's page number and hung up the receiver. While he stood awkwardly by the phone, the mother asked in a trembling voice, "Will we be able to see her?"

"Yes, of course. I'll take you to the room as soon as Dr. Singh arrives. For now, I think you would be more comfortable in our conference room."

He led the two women to the room, settled them into chairs, and gave them each a box of facial tissues. Then he returned to the station to await Dr. Singh's call.

—SEVEN—

Dr. Elliot Fox sat at a desk in the #1 endoscopy room. Holding the receiver to his ear with his shoulder, he stapled to his procedure note a glossy photo of a stomach ulcer printed by his state-of-the-art digital camera.

"What do you mean, the bay windows haven't been delivered? I'm paying you top dollar to see that the suppliers stay on track."

Fox was a tall, stoop-shouldered man with long fingers and a boyish face topped by a thick raft of prematurely gray hair. He spoke in a soft, controlled voice that was so quiet, the contractor had to ask him to repeat his words.

"If you fall behind schedule, the labor costs come out of your pocket," the doctor went on. "That's what I said, out of your pocket. We have a legal contract, and there are contractors in Cape May who would love to complete this house. Have I made myself clear?"

He wrote an order in the patient's chart while listening to the contractor. "No, that is not sufficient. I want you to call my answering service if they do not make delivery by the middle of next week. We expect to move in by July first. Not one day later."

He hung up the phone, signed off the chart, tucked a gold Cross pen in the breast pocket of his plum-colored silk shirt. As he rose from the desk, he said to Tina, the nurse cleaning the endoscoope, "Enroll this patient in the study protocol. Be sure he gets a follow-up appointment with me in two weeks."

"Okay," said Tina. "Was that the last case?"

"There's a colon on Seven South. You can send for him after lunch."

"What's his name?"

Looking over a packet of three-by-five cards, Fox said, "I don't remember. He's the big baby with the nagging wife. Gary will know who he is."

Fox walked down the hall a short distance to his office. He resisted the temptation to use the sleeve of his lab coat to burnish the shiny bronze plaque on the wall. ELLIOT R. FOX, LESLIE M. BOUCHER. GASTORENTEROLOGY AND HEPATOLOGY.

He entered the reception area, where Myrna, his secretary, was stuffing billing cards in envelopes. She dabbed the gummed flap of an envelope on a bundle of wet gauze in a denture cup and sealed it.

"Are we up to date on the billing?" he asked, walking back to his inner office.

"I'm half-way through May," said Myrna, dropping the envelope onto the mail-out tray.

"Be sure to finish the month. Do you believe Medicare is cutting inpatient reimbursements again? They want us to do everything in the office. It's ludicrous."

"That's the government for you," she said, stuffing another envelope.

He entered his office, closed the door, and settled into his leather chair. Picking up a raft of pathology reports, he stared at them for a few seconds, frowned, dropped them back on the desk. He decided that, with so much stress in his day, he deserved a quarter hour of peace.

He pressed the intercom button. "Myrna, no calls for fifteen minutes."

Retrieving an MP3 player from a drawer, Fox put on a large set of earphones, kicked off his loafers, and leaned back in his chair. As the soothing sound of Mozart filled his ears, he pulled off his socks and curled his toes in the lush carpet. Closing his eyes and losing himself in the music, he decided that life could not be sweeter.

At her desk, Myrna mumbled, "Like I should miss lunch and stay till midnight to finish the billing? Fat chance."

She reached into her desk for a pack of menthol cigarettes and a gold-colored lighter with rhinestones. Stepping into the hall, she called to Tina, "I'm going for coffee and a smoke. You wanna come?"

"I got to clean up the procedure room," said Tina. "It's a solid mess. And then I got to set up for another colon. You go ahead, I'll catch you later."

"Okay," said Myrna, who stuck an unlit cigarette in her mouth as she walked to the elevator. "Be sure to finish the month," she grumbled. "In his dreams."

Answering Gary's page, Dr. Singh entered the ward and went right to the nursing station, where he learned that the mother and aunt were in the conference room. The doctor hurried to the room, knocked softly, and entered.

"I am Dr. Samir Singh," he said, taking each woman's hand. "I am so sorry to have to tell you such terrible news, but there is no easy way to tell you that your daughter has died."

He looked with sadness and sorrow at the crumpling faces of the mother and aunt. Heard the racking sobs as they expressed the pain of a loss that cannot be borne.

After they had cried and dabbed their eyes, and cried once more, he continued.

"I will tell you all that I know, which is not very much. Your daughter was discovered in a patient room in cardiac arrest. We do not know how long her heart was stopped before we could intervene. I think it is most likely that she had been in cardiac arrest for some time, because we were unable to resuscitate her. The heart cannot remain still for more than a few minutes before it becomes refractory to treatment."

Mamie leaned forward, looked intently into the doctor's eyes. "Do you know what made her heart stop?"

"No, I am sorry, I have no idea whatsoever. We will have to wait for the results of the autopsy."

Both women gasped at the word "autopsy."

"Do you have to cut her body open?" asked Elizabeth. "Is it really necessary?"

"I'm sorry, we do. It is required by law whenever someone dies without a medical explanation."

"You said she was found in a patient room," said Mamie. "What was she doing there?"

"We do not know that, either. There are many things that are a mystery to us." Taking Elizabeth's hand, he said, "I will ask the medical examiner to perform the autopsy in such a way that she will look as though she had not been examined."

The mother nodded her head, unable to speak.

After giving her a few moments to absorb the news, he asked softly, "Would you like to see her now?"

Elizabeth nodded her head yes. Mamie took her sister's arm as Singh led the way down the corridor. Seeing them come out of the conference room, Gary accompanied them down the hall.

Inside the room, the two women walked slowly to the bedside as though approaching a freshly dug grave.

The mother grasped her dead daughter's hand.

"It's ice cold!" she exclaimed. "Should she be cold so quickly?"

"It's normal, I'm afraid," said the doctor. "The extremities lose their heat quickly."

They stood silently at the bedside. Suddenly Singh's beeper pierced the silence, startling the two women. He glanced at the number, then stepped to the phone at the bedside.

"Excuse me," he said. "This may be important."

He dialed the number, listened for a moment, thanked the caller, and hung up.

"That was my resident with the initial toxicology report."

The aunt's face showed a puzzled look.

"That is the test for drugs in the bloodstream." As both women opened their mouths to speak, he quickly added. "It is strictly routine in a case like this. I did not expect that the laboratory would detect any drugs which could lead to cardiac arrest, and if fact, there were none."

Both women visibly relaxed.

"The lab has sent the blood out for more advanced tests. These are required by the state whenever there is an unexplained death. Some of the tests are more sophisticated than we can perform here in the hospital."

"Was there any sign that she was, you know, abused?" asked Mamie.

"I saw no signs of injury, but that will be for the medical examiner to determine." He handed the mother a box of tissues, noting that the aunt's eyes were, for the moment, dry. She seemed the stronger of the two, but it had not been her daughter who was lost.

"I will leave you for a moment. Please take all the time that you need at the bedside." Pausing at the door, he added, "Will there be more family members coming?"

"They're all out of state," said Mamie. "Except her fiancé. He should be here soon."

"Then I will go. You can always ask the nurse to page me should you have more questions."

He quietly opened the door and slipped into the hall. As he left the ward he wondered if he should have told them of the one positive laboratory report. But on reflection he decided that his initial decision to hold the information back had been a good one. It would all come out later, at the inquest. For now, let them try to cope with their grief without confusing the picture further.

Time enough for them to learn that their daughter may have been poisoned.

−EIGHT−

If misery loved company, Alfred Desmond Allendale would be forever surrounded by people. But he preferred solitude, which neither added to nor subtracted from his general state of ill humor. His social circle was largely limited to an administrative assistant, a private duty nurse, an accountant, and a trio of lawyers. No one else mattered.

When Allendale's heart, liver, lungs, and kidneys began to fail, Dr. Kadish admitted him to the intensive care unit at James Madison University Hospital. Allendale insisted on occupying the large end room in order to accommodate his personal staff. The room was usually reserved for patients who required isolation, but after a sharp discussion between Dr. Kadish and the head nurse, the room was given to Allendale.

As he entered the isolation room, Kadish looked down on a pale, gaunt old man with an oxygen mask over his nose and mouth. His belly was as swollen as a woman in her third trimester. Because his failing liver had weakened his blood's natural clotting mechanisms, he had large, ugly purple blotches on his arms where he had bled from needle sticks. His lips were cracked and dry, despite the efforts of his private-duty nurse to moisten them with petroleum jelly.

"You better have good news," grumbled the patient.

"Or else what, you'll fire me?"

"Don't think I wouldn't. I may be a sick old man, but there are plenty of other surgeons looking to make a fast buck."

"I'm the only physician in the world who can do the operation you need, Alfred. You know that."

"Hmphh," said Allendale, struggling to pull his blanket up over his bony shoulders. When the private-duty nurse stepped up to complete the maneuver for him, the patient brushed away the nurse's hand. Pulling the oxygen mask from his face, he snapped, "Don't make me feel more helpless than I already am!"

Kadish replaced the mask, saying, "The medical board has given permission to do the procedure."

"It's about time. Have you got a donor lined up?"

"No, but I've sent out word to the emergency rooms in all of the surrounding hospitals. As soon as they get a brain-dead case, they'll page me, and I'll arrange for transfer to our facility."

Allendale pulled the oxygen mask off his face again. "If my heart fails before you find a donor, how do you propose to keep me alive?"

"If I have to, I'll insert a balloon device to support your heart. If that's not enough, I'll put you on cardiac bypass, just as if you were undergoing heart surgery."

"Just remember, if I die, you're out a million bucks."

"I wouldn't throw threats around if I were you," said Kadish.

"They aren't threats, they're the facts of life. Get this thing done, and get it done soon. I may be dying, but I can still do plenty of damage."

Kadish turned and strode out of the room, annoyed that his patient always seemed to get the last word in. At the nursing station he found Dr. Singh writing in a chart.

"Any word on the cause of death of that woman we coded this morning?" asked Kadish.

"No, we are still very much in the dark. The tox screen showed no opiates, barbiturates, benzodiazepines, or any other depressants. There was one most curious finding, however."

"Oh?"

"When the initial tox screen came back negative, I asked the lab to do further tests. They found trace levels of thiocynate in her blood. It was barely detectable, but—"

"Cyanide poisoning," said Kadish. "That's interesting. Was there any sign of recent IV access?"

"Ah, you are considering nitroprussic acid. I had the same thought, but there were no marks indicating intravenous injection, which leads me to believe that the medication was not the source of the cyanide."

"Well, did she present with clinical signs of cyanide poisoning? I don't recall any from the code."

"None whatsoever. What is most puzzling is that the level was extremely low. It was not enough to cause respiratory arrest. Even so, I am going to notify the Philadelphia police. They may wish to investigate."

"It's a shame to send someone so young to the medical examiner," said Kadish. Rising from his chair and looking wistfully into space, as though at an alternative outcome, he added, "She would have made a great organ donor."

In the GI lab, Tina stood at the stainless steel sink cleaning the long, black, serpentine gastroscope. She held it carefully as she ran a brush through it, mindful of the delicate glass fibers and the lens inside the instrument.

She was a middle-aged black woman, thick-waisted, with swollen ankles, and a bone spur in her foot that made standing painful.

Lenny knocked on the open door and entered.

"Hey, Tina, how's it going?"

The nurse flashed him a broad smile. "Hiya, stranger! What brings you down here from seventh heaven?"

"The usual bullshit. Listen, how's the foot?"

"Not too bad. Dr. Primeaux started me on some new pain medicine. It's supposed to not irritate my stomach. If that don't help, Dr. Wagner said he'd cut out the spur, but I don't fancy him opening me up. I seen too many screw-ups when I worked in the OR."

He watched as she gently laid the black scope on the counter and began rubbing it down with alcohol. Lenny shuddered, imagining the thick, glistening black tube snaking down his throat.

"Does somebody really swallow that thing?"

"It's not that bad. We give the patient drugs that make him forget everything that happened. Dr. Fox calls it his 'Kickapoo joy juice.' Most of the time they wake up in recovery and they say, 'When is the doctor gonna start?' They don't hardly believe me when I tell 'em it's all over." She smiled, thinking about the patient's amnesia.

"I guess I shouldn't be laughing," she said, looking Lenny in the eyes. "I heard about that poor woman that arrested up on your floor. Was she a visitor?"

"No, she was a rep for one of the drug companies. Gary told me she worked for Falcon Pharmaceuticals."

"Oh?" said Tina, who stopped wiping down the gastroscope. "What's her name?"

"Colleen something or other. It's an Irish name."

Tina leaned over the counter and hung her head. "Oh, sweet Jesus," she said. "It's Colleen Creedon."

"Who?" asked Lenny.

"Sweet, sweet Jesus, Colleen Creedon." Tina suddenly looked up at Lenny. "And don't you know, she was by here early this morning talking to Dr. Fox!"

—NINE—

Standing beside Tina in the #1 endoscopy room, Lenny gently asked, "You say you saw Colleen Creedon today?"

"That's what I'm telling you. She was back with Dr. Fox in his office with the door shut when I came on duty. Held up the first procedure, they were in there so long."

"So her company sells drugs that the GI doctors use?"

"Uh-huh. Dr. Fox has a bunch of his ulcer patients on a new medication they're studying. He says it's a miracle drug."

Lenny pulled a chair away from the desk and gestured for Tina to sit down. "What was she like?" he asked.

Tina smiled. "She was smooth. She was a real sharp dresser. And she wasn't stuck up, either. She brought us all bagels and cream cheese when we started the drug study."

Lenny listened patiently while Tina described her conversations with the drug rep. Listening was a skill he had developed while trying to solve the endless problems of his coworkers.

When she was done, he said, "Shit, I almost forgot why I came down here. There's a Mrs. Cavanaugh on my floor missing her dentures, and Tuttle is talking about writing up Billy if we don't find them."

"Gary already called down and had me looking high and low, but they're not in the room, I can tell you that for a fact. Besides, we don't pull dentures for a colonoscopy." She gestured toward her bottom. "That's at the other end."

"I was thinking the same thing," said Lenny.

Tina got up and carried the gastroscope to a cabinet on the wall, where half a dozen serpentine scopes hung on hooks.

"Could the dentures be in the other procedure room?" he asked, looking across the hall.

"Shouldn't be, Mrs. Cavanaugh was done in here."

"Do you mind if I look around? Billy's still on probation. He's scared he'll get in trouble if I don't find them."

"Look all you want," she said.

While Tina continued in the first room, Lenny crossed the hall to the #2 endoscopy room. Putting on a pair of latex gloves, he dug through a tall trash bucket. He spied a blue paper underpad stuck together. Having discovered countless missing items in the trash, he peeled the blue pad apart. In it was

33

a thick wad of gauze pads. He felt something hard. Pulling away the gauze, he found the dentures.

"Tina, come check this out!"

The nurse came in, looked at the gauze-wrapped dentures in Lenny's hands.

"Lord, Lord, that's just like Dr. Fox. He must've carried them across the room, and then that new tech Jasmine threw them out without realizing they were there."

"Why would Fox take the dentures out in the first place? He wasn't looking in her mouth."

Tina pursed her lips and folded her arms across her chest. "I don't rightly know," she said. "Sometimes the medicine we give to put them to sleep works too good and we have to call anesthesia. Dr. Fox must have taken the teeth out as a precaution." She reached into a cabinet and withdrew an empty denture cup, adding, "To tell you the truth, that's the only explanation I can think off the top of my head."

Tina rinsed the dentures in the sink, placed them in a denture cup, and snapped the lid down. Writing the patient's name on the lid, she said, "I know Billy will be glad you found them."

"I'm gonna tell him as soon as I get back to Seven South." He looked from the cup to Tina. "What time did you say the drug rep was back with the doctor?"

Tina's face lifted in a sly grin. "You on another case, Lenny?"

"Shit, no. I was just wondering, that's all."

"I came in at seven. They came out of the office around seven-twenty."

"Okay," said Lenny. "Thanks. I've got to get back."

"Say hi to old knobby-knees for me, you hear?"

"I will," he promised.

As Lenny left the endoscopy room, Dr. Fox saw him from his office waiting room. The doctor went in to where Tina was working.

"What did that custodian want? He's not our regular man," he said.

"Oh, that was just Lenny. He found Mrs. Cavanaugh's dentures!"

"Oh? Where were they?"

"Across the hall in the number two room."

Fox stared at the nurse for a few seconds, decided not to pursue the subject, turned, and left the room.

Having finished administering his twelve-o'clock medications, Gary Tuttle entered a note in a chart that Mrs. Cavanaugh was free of abdominal pain following her colonoscopy. He had just signed off to the other nurse in preparation for going to lunch when he felt a steely hand grab his shoulder from behind. Turning, he found himself staring into the cold, shark eyes of Joe West, chief of hospital security.

West was a squarely built man dressed in a navy blue blazer, black pants with razor-sharp creases, and a white shirt starched so crisply it could advertise clothing. He had a small, humorless mouth; dark, deep-set eyes; a low forehead; and a head as square as a block of wood. A pair of handcuffs dangled from his belt.

"I'll have a word with you, Mr. Tuttle."

"Uh, I was about to go on my lunch break."

"It will wait. Follow me."

He led Gary to the Seven South conference room, opened the door, ushered the nurse in, and let the door close behind him.

"Take a seat."

Gary sat down, feeling rats gnaw at his belly. He would give anything to be someplace else. Assist in a code. Bathe a dead body. Help Dr. Fingers perform an autopsy in the morgue. Anything but face Joe West.

"I have a document I want you to explain," said West, sliding an eight-by-eleven inch sheet of paper toward him. It was a computer printout from the Admissions Department. But Gary was so frightened by West's intimidating presence, his eyes couldn't focus on the text.

West stared at Gary, his gaze threatening to dissolve the nurse's composure and reduce him to tears.

-TEN-

Lenny walked up the stairs from the GI lab to his floor, grumbling the whole time about Moose nagging him to avoid the elevator. Ever since he started jogging in Fairmont Park with his friend, he'd been using the stairs to get his legs in shape. Under protest.

The dentures made a rattling sound in the cup as he walked. He thought about going up to Gary and holding the dentures as if they were going to bite Tuttle's nose, Three Stooges style, but he decided the nurse was in no mood for joking. Not with Colleen Creedon's body lying in room 709.

As he emerged from the stairwell onto Seven South, he nearly ran into Patience, one of the X-ray technicians, who was steering her big portable machine down the hall. She was a slim black woman with short hair, a pug nose, and flashing eyes.

"Jeez, Patience, you must be awful strong to push a heavy machine like that."

"Strong enough to whip your butt," she said, steering it within an inch of his feet.

"Hey, careful!" he said.

"Sorry! You got such little feet, I didn't hardly see them."

"Cut to the core," said Lenny, feigning a hurt look, followed by a mischievous grin.

She pushed her machine into a room, where a young man lay in the bed, his leg elevated in traction. Metal rods ran along the sides of the leg. His arm was cast in plaster, and his head was shaved on one side.

Following her into the room, Lenny said, "Need a hand lifting Mr. Silkie?"

"Thank you, Lenny. You hold his bad arm while I pull on his good one and I'll slide the cassette behind him."

She placed the X-ray cassette behind the patient, who settled back onto the hard surface. Then she lined up the machine to send its invisible radiation through his chest.

Putting on a lead-lined vest, Patience backed away from the bed, Lenny following her. He crouched behind her, shielded by her vest.

"Okay, sir, take a deep breath and hold it."

Bleep. She squeezed the button on the control, taking the X-ray.

"Just like a man to hide behind a woman's skirt," she said as Lenny came out from behind her.

Lenny helped her remove the film from behind the patient, which she slid into a compartment in the machine. She made a U-turn and steered the machine out of the room.

In the hall, Patience said, "Thanks, Lenny. I've got to do another film on Seven North."

"No problem," he said, walking beside her down the hall.

"I heard about that poor young woman they found in the bed this morning. They say that she *died*. Is that true?"

"Yeah. They worked on her a long time, but they couldn't save her."

"That's terrible. I wonder what happened to her."

"It beats me, but there's no reason for any of the docs to talk to me about it."

"Are you kidding? *Everybody* talks to you."

As Patience reached the fire doors separating Seven South from its sister unit, Lenny said to her, "Listen, are you doing anything Saturday night?"

"*Doing* anything? I'm doing a lot of things. I promised to braid Takia's hair, and Malcolm wants me to rent him this new Jet Li action movie, and my mother's bugging me to bring the kids out to West Philly so she can see them." She looked into his face. "Why?"

"I just thought we might go out for dinner or something."

She stood with her hands on the X-ray machine, considering his proposal.

"Well, I *did* promise the kids, but if you want, you can come over for dinner."

"Great. I'll bring dessert. What would you like?"

"Surprise me," she said, passing into Seven North. "So long as it's chocolate . . . from Asher's!"

As she disappeared behind the closing doors, he called, "But Asher's closed their Germantown factory!"

"Then you'll have to drive to the suburbs," she called back, and was soon lost from sight.

Lenny returned the dentures to Mrs. Cavanaugh, who immediately put them in her mouth, took a deep breath, and settled back into bed with a contented smile. He decided he better get caught up with his work. Time enough to tell Tuttle that he had found the dentures.

And wasn't it mysterious that they were missing in the first place?

Gary sat staring at the paper that Joe West had placed before him. He was so anxious, he still couldn't focus his eyes properly. For a moment he thought that his glasses must be smeared with petroleum jelly, but gradually the words came into focus.

His problem was that he hated to lie. Worse, he knew that he was no good at it.

West said, "Regarding the unfortunate patient in seven-o-nine, you can see from the Admissions Department record that the patient Blackwell was canceled. The HMO refused to certify the admission. You see that there, do you not?"

Gary nodded his head. "Yes. She's a patient of Dr. Fox." He feared his voice would crack, his throat was so constricted. He wondered if he should spin a tale or feign complete ignorance. Lenny was such a good bullshit artist. He could make up stories off the cuff. Gary hadn't the imagination. Or the nerve. In his mind he repeated Lenny's mantra *Nobody talks, everyone walks.*

"Tell me, then: Did Admissions bring up a different patient to that room?"

"No, not that I'm aware of," said Gary.

"Well I find it curious that this patient who never arrived on your ward had several orders entered in the computer. How do you explain that?"

"I don't know," said Gary.

West slid a second piece of paper toward Gary. The nurse picked it up, saw it was a menu with boxes checked off and the name Blackwell on the top.

"Do you know who filled out this menu?" West said.

"I didn't do it."

"Do you have any idea who did?"

"No."

West slid a third paper toward Gary. It was a pharmacy requisition for Tylenol.

"Do you have any idea how the pharmacy received a request for Tylenol for a patient who was not there?"

Gary stared at the drug request. He knew that fabricating medication orders, even for something as benign as Tylenol, could lead to the State Board of Nursing revoking his license.

"I don't know," said Gary.

"Take a look at this last one," said West, sliding the paper toward Gary. It was the consult to Dr. Martin Kadish. "You may not be familiar with all the computer codes, but the six-digit number in the lower left-hand corner signifies the terminal where the request originated. In this case, it originated from your Seven South nursing station. Do you still maintain that you know nothing about these messages?"

Gary looked intently at the printout. Under the title "Sender" was the name, H. Burgess, the director of nursing.

"Did you ask Miss Burgess about the request?" he said.

"We're not stupid, Mr. Tuttle. It's common knowledge that you people steal access codes in order to send your cute little messages, your dirty jokes and salacious comments about the administration."

Gary felt his face flush. His gut began to cramp up, and his throat tightened. His mouth was so dry, he feared he would croak like a frog if he spoke again. He silently repeated the mantra *Nobody talks, everyone walks.*

West took the papers back. "It's better for you if you tell me now. We know Moss was behind this; it has his foul smell all over it. If you continue protecting him, I'll recommend that a report be forwarded to the State Board. You know what that means. They'll pull your license. If you cooperate, I'm confident we can keep this within the family at James Madison."

West stared at Gary, his dark eyes cold and unblinking. Gary felt as though he were staring into the eyes of his executioner.

After a long moment, Gary said, "I have nothing more to say."

Wordlessly, West stood, opened the door, and gestured for Gary to leave. The handcuffs dangling from his belt brought waves of panic to the nurse

As he walked back to the nursing station, Gary felt the sweat dripping down his sides. He went into the staff bathroom, locked the door, and threw up in the toilet.

—ELEVEN—

When Lenny saw Gary come out of the staff bathroom, he saw that the nurse was pale and shaky.

"Are you okay, Tuttle? You look sick."

A mournful look dragged down the nurse's soft features. "Joe West just left. He was asking about the fictitious patient in seven-o-nine. He knows it was your idea. He said that if I cooperated he wouldn't report me to the state, but if I kept quiet my license would be pulled."

"They always threaten like that. He's trying to make you crack. Stick to our plan and you'll be okay."

"Don't' worry, I didn't tell him anything."

Turning to Celeste, Lenny asked, "Did West talk to you?"

"'Course not. You know I'll call my union rep the first word out of that son of a bitch's mouth. I don't talk, listen, or look at that man without you sitting right beside me."

"Great," said Lenny. Wanting to reassure Gary, he said, "I have a good feeling about this thing. I think we're going to be okay."

At that moment Sandy, an old security guard with a bulldog face and gravelly voice, ambled up to the station. The guard had helped Lenny solve the Randy Sparks murder case, even handcuffing the murderer himself.

"Howdy, all," he said. "I hope you don't have any more excitement on this floor. I'm way too old for it."

Gary admitted that he'd had enough excitement to last him a lifetime.

Lenny asked, "Have you heard any news about the visitor who died on the ward this morning?"

"Just that it's gonna go to the medical examiner," said Sandy. He poked Lenny good-naturedly in the ribs. "You on another case?"

"Shit, no, there's no *case*. I was there when they coded her, that's all."

"Uh-huh. And the little joke about pretending there was a patient in the room—that ain't in the back of your mind?"

"My mind is blank. I stand mute before the court."

Sandy chuckled. "Still and all, if I do hear anything about her, guess it wouldn't hurt none if I run it by you."

"Guess not," said Lenny. "Me, I didn't get a real coffee break this morning. I'm not missing my lunch."

He walked down the hall toward the stairs, wondering, as he often did,

41

why half the hospital acted as if anytime there was a problem, they could always get him to solve it.

As Lenny left the ward, a young man in a rumpled suit, his tie askew, rushed past him and approached the nursing station.

"I got a message about my fiancée, Colleen Creedon. That she's taken ill or something. What's going on?"

Gary rose from his chair and approached the young man. I'm very sorry to have to tell you this, Mr.—"

"McBride. Padric McBride," he said, extending his hand. "Colleen and I are engaged to be married."

"Gary Tuttle. I'm sorry. We worked on her for a long time, we did everything we could, but we weren't able to save her."

Padric stood stock still, numb with shock. He tried to say something, but found he was unable to speak.

"Her mother and aunt are with her in the room," said Gary.

The fiancé continued to stare at Gary as if he were mute.

"Would you like to go down to them?" The young man slowly nodded his head. Gary led the way, the fiancé following a few steps behind, walking silently, like a zombie.

On his way to lunch, Lenny made a detour to the pharmacy, which was in the basement. Entering, he found a huge room as busy as a supermarket on Saturday. Pharmacists were stuffing pills in little Ziploc bags and placing them in delivery trays.

He asked Hector, the pharmacy tech, where Mike was.

"He's down the hall mixing chemo."

"Thanks," said Lenny.

Walking down the hall and around a corner, he knocked and entered a large, brightly lit room. Michael DiPietro was standing at a counter beneath a metal hood that looked like the ones in a commercial kitchen. He had on a full-length plastic apron, a floppy paper hat, mask, and goggles.

"Hey there, Lenny," said Mike, looking up from his work. "How's things?"

The custodian walked up to him. "Not bad, how's with you?"

Signing the label on the bag he'd just filled, the pharmacist pulled off the goggles and mask, revealing a long, lean face with a pointed nose and neatly trimmed mustache. He switched off the vacuum in the hood and stepped over to Lenny.

"Ah, you know how it is: work, eat, sleep, then work some more."

"You still pulling a lot of overtime?"

"I've got to, the kids are eating me out of house and home. Not to mention the clothes they keep outgrowing. It's outrageous. My fourteen-year-old wears a size thirteen shoe, you believe it?"

"Isn't there a drug you can give them that'll stunt their growth?"

"Wouldn't that be nice?" said Mike, grinning. "What brings you down here?"

"If I leave you a scrip', can you have it for me by three-thirty?"

Mike glanced at his watch. "Sure, give it here."

Lenny pulled a piece of folded paper from his shirt pocket, handed it to Mike. The pharmacist opened it, read the prescription. "Got the old crotch rot, I see. You been hanging out on Admiral Wilson Boulevard again?"

"Very funny. Dr. Primeaux figures I picked up some fungus on the job, all the shit we handle."

"He's probably right." Mike placed the prescription in his shirt pocket. "I'll fill it as soon as I get the last chemo done. I've only got one more order to fill. Meet me in the main pharmacy at the end of your shift, I'll have a batch of triple-strength, industrial-grade crotch rot ointment mixed up for you."

"Thanks, Mike. I appreciate it."

Mike's face became serious. "Say, I hear you had a visitor this morning die up on your ward."

"It freaked me out, I don't mind telling you. How'd you hear about it so quick?"

"My friend, in a place like James Madison, news travels faster than the speed of sound. Who was she?"

"Actually, you probably know her; she was a drug rep. She worked for a company called Falcon Pharmaceuticals. Colleen Creedon."

Mike's jaw dropped. He appeared stunned, as though he'd been hit in the head. Hard.

"Jesus Christ, *Colleen*? I can't frickin' believe it. Are you sure?"

"That's what I hear."

Mike stepped away from the hood. "I'm in shock. Total shock."

"Did you see her today?"

"No, I didn't," said Mike, leaning against the counter. "She usually stops in the main pharmacy, but I've been mixing chemo all morning."

Mike's long face seemed to get longer.

"Colleen is—*was*—a wonderful girl," he said. "Very conscientious. She's not like most of the other reps. She'd go out of her way to help you out. And not just to increase her sales, either."

"Had she been ill or something?"

"Not that I'm aware of. She always *seemed* healthy. I never even heard her sniffle with a cold."

"I can't figure what she was doing on my floor. There aren't any offices up there."

"Beats me, unless she planned to meet somebody. A doctor making rounds, maybe?"

"That could be it," said Lenny.

Mike's face was still contorted with shock. "I've got to get back to work. You'll let me know if you hear anything more about what happened to her, won't you?"

"Of course."

Shaking his head sadly, Mike pulled his mask up over his nose and returned to working under the hood.

As Lenny went on to the cafeteria, he couldn't help wondering how well Mike knew Colleen Creedon.

—TWELVE—

"Turn on your left side and relax, Howard," said Dr. Fox.

Howard Stipes grasped the side rail of the gurney and slowly turned over onto his side, saying, "You're gonna put me to sleep, I won't feel anything. Right, Doc?"

"That's right, Howard. You won't feel a thing."

As he gently lifted the long, serpentine colonoscope from the counter, Fox said to Tina, "Give him two cc's of Diazine."

The nurse injected two cc's of sedation into the IV tubing. She glanced up at the clock on the wall, then recorded the dose and time on the procedure sheet.

In thirty seconds the man was snoring loudly.

"Isn't modern chemistry wonderful?" said Fox, smiling. He rubbed lubricating jelly over the end of the scope and gently inserted it into the rectum.

"It sure makes our job easier," she said.

Turning his attention to the video display, he saw the familiar pink, striated cavern of the rectal vault. As the scope moved forward, the vault opened into the rippling folds of the sigmoid colon.

"Did you know that in Japan they don't give any sedation for colonoscopies?" he said, turning the wheel on the head of the scope as he advanced the snakelike instrument through the twisting colon.

"Those little guys must feel no pain," said Tina, checking the patient's chest for a steady rise and fall.

"Mainly they're taught not to complain, I think," he said as he pushed the scope around a corner of the bowel.

In fifteen minutes he arrived at the end of the colon, the ileocecal valve. Slowly pulling the scope back, he examined the bowel a second time.

"Nothing here," he said as he withdrew the long, black instrument from the rectal opening. "Let's do a one-eighty."

"Okay," said Tina. "You want I should wheel him across the hall?"

"No need to dirty up another room this late in the day. Just bring the gastroscope in here and hook it up."

Tina immersed the colonoscope in a tub of soapy water, then hurried across the hall to retrieve the smaller scope used for viewing the stomach. As soon as she returned with the smaller gastroscope and hooked it to the computerized light source, Fox adjusted the digital camera to prepare for pictures.

Turning the stretcher around so that Howard's face was near the scope, Fox inserted a bite block in the man's mouth. He pushed the scope into the sleeping patient's mouth. Spying the opening to the esophagus on the monitor, he deftly pushed the scope down through the rhythmically contracting esophagus.

"No varicies," said Fox. "Have you got a biopsy forceps handy?"

"What for?" said Tina. "You haven't found anything to biopsy yet."

"Howard has a family history of cancer. I want to be ready in case I find something."

Suddenly Howard began to gag. He kicked his feet and reached for the tube. While Fox held the man's hands, Tina quickly injected another two cc's of Diazine. In seconds the patient was again asleep.

Doctor and nurse stared at the monitor as Fox guided the gastroscope along the greater curve of the stomach. The pink, gently contracting walls glistened in the bright light. The opening to the small intestine, the pyloric sphincter, contracted, then opened, like some deep-sea creature expecting food to swim into its mouth. Fox advanced into the duodenum, the first portion of the small bowel.

Tina opened the cabinet on the cart and rummaged for a biopsy forceps. While she searched, Fox played with the buttons on the scope in preparation for taking a photo.

"There she blows," he said. The video displayed a small white patch on the wall of the duodenum, looking much like a fever blister. Fox pressed the button on the camera. The image on the video froze as the camera captured the image. Seconds later, a bright color photo emerged from the printer.

"You want to biopsy that?" asked Tina.

"No, it's just a simple ulcer. We'll put him on the study drug. It'll be healed in a week."

Fox slipped the scope out of the patient's mouth and handed it to the nurse. She immersed it in the basin of soapy water along with the colonoscope.

Sitting at the desk, Fox filled in the procedure note for the colonoscopy, entering "negative" in the results. He placed a copy of the note in the patient's chart, leaving the pink copy for the nurse to file in the GI lab office records.

After taping the photo of the duodenal ulcer to the procedure note for the gastroscopy, he filled in the diagnosis, signed it, and placed it in the chart behind the colonoscopy report.

While Tina ran a brush through the gastroscope in preparation for the sterilizing machine, Fox opened the patient's chart and wrote out orders to start the man on the new ulcer drug. Closing the chart, he tucked it under the sleeping patient's pillow, then strode out of the room. His workday was done. He had earned an afternoon of quiet relaxation.

Tina entered the man's vital signs on the nursing record, keeping one eye on his chest movement to be sure that his breathing pattern was regular. A monitor measured his oxygen level, blood pressure, and heart rate, which were normal.

After completing the check of the vital signs, she wrote a brief note, entered the date at the top of the page, and added her nursing worksheet to the patient's chart. As she placed the nursing note in front of the gastroscope report, she noticed that Fox had entered the wrong date on the form.

She left the date uncorrected, aware that the date on the first report, the one for the colonoscopy, *was* correct. "Ain't my job to fix his mistakes," she mumbled.

A few minutes later, Howard slowly opened his eyes.

"When is the doctor coming?" he asked in a hoarse whisper,

Tina threw back her head and laughed. She told him, "You're all done, the doctor's been here and gone. The orderly's going to take you back to your room in a couple of minutes."

Howard lay back and closed his eyes, relieved that the terrible ordeal was behind him. A short time later, Billy came into the room to wheel the patient back to Seven South.

"Any dentures?" he asked, steering the stretcher toward the door.

"No, Billy, this guy's got all his own teeth. Well, most of them, anyhow." She tucked the chart beneath the pillow and patted the man on the head. "You can take him back to his room."

Billy wheeled the stretcher into the hall and made his way to the elevator.

After running a soapy brush through the two endoscopes, Tina laid them gently in a tank of sterilizing fluid and set the timer for thirty minutes. She covered the tank, wiped down the counter, and rinsed out the sink, glad that the last case of the day was over.

Unless the Gray Fox brought her one of his surprises. She prayed he wouldn't do it. Her foot was aching something awful, and she had missed her lunch. As usual.

After his interrogation by Joe West, Gary had no appetite for lunch. Instead, he made a cup of tea in the little kitchen across from the station and drank it at the desk while he caught up on his notes. He looked up from a chart, found Padric McBride, Colleen Creedon's fiancé standing in the hall, looking lost.

Gary led him to a chair at the nursing station and settled him into it. Then he sat beside him and waited.

"We were engaged to be married," said Padric. "The wedding was to be next month."

"I have her engagement ring and watch locked in the narcotic box," said Gary. "I didn't want them to get lost. I'll give them to you. Okay?"

He unlocked the narcotic box, withdrew the plastic bag with the ring and the gold watch, and gave them to Padric. The young man took the jewelry out of the bag and let the items nestle in the palm of his hand.

"We found this ring in a little antique shop in Manayunk. It's from an estate sale, the man said. It's very old. My wedding ring has the same pattern."

"It's very handsome," said Gary, admiring the intricate floral pattern carved in the ring

The fiancé smiled for a second, recalling their hours together. "I felt that if we exchanged rings that had bound another man and woman together, it would be like we were carrying on for the ones who went before us, even though we had no idea who wore them."

"That is a lovely thought," said Gary.

The young man sat staring at the ring, as though there were a lesson to be learned from examining it. Gary excused himself and went on with his duties, feeling a familiar pain in his soul, as though he had lost someone quite close to him. He almost wished that he could attend Colleen's funeral.

—THIRTEEN—

Dr. Kadish finished his third case of the day, a kidney transplant on a patient with a coagulation disorder whose bleeding had been difficult to bring under control. The patient required large quantities of blood and clotting factors before he ceased hemorrhaging. After sending the patient to the recovery room, there being no bed available in the ICU, where he belonged, he told his team to meet him on Six North, where they would round on the transplant patients.

Riding the elevator to the eighth floor, where many of the doctors had their offices, he passed his secretary, ignoring her, entered his office, and closed the door. He phoned an old friend, a physician he had trained. The man had gone on to specialize in surgical trauma at Samaritan Hospital. After the obligatory chatter Kadish said, "You're a level one trauma center, you get a lot of head injuries, don't you?"

"Oh, we get our share, especially in the winter, with all the ice on the roads. What's on your mind?"

"I'd like you to give me a call if you get a brain-dead patient. I need an organ donor for a patient in the ICU."

"I'd be glad to help, Martin. You know we have to go through the Organ Donor Network—"

"You can call them, too, naturally, but I want to get the first word of a potential donor. I've had extensive discussions with the director of the network. I explained that my patient was critically ill. He's at the top of their list."

"I see," said the trauma physician. "Still, it could be dicey if your patient got special treatment."

"My patient deserves to be first on his own merits. He has multiple organ failure. His liver and kidneys are failing and he's dependent on pressors to keep a minimum blood pressure. Besides, calling me first may be to your advantage," said Kadish.

"Advantage?"

"I was just thinking, when a lawyer refers a civil suit to another lawyer, the referring lawyer typically gets a referral fee. Isn't that right?"

"Yeah . . ."

"It seems only fair that, if a physician refers a patient for organ donor, and if there's a substantial fee involved for the transplant physician, then the referring physician ought to share in the fee, for, say, ten percent. Don't you

49

think that's reasonable?"

"Sharing a fee? That sounds appropriate. What do you bill for this operation?"

"One million dollars."

There was a long moment of silence on the phone. Finally the Samaritan physician asked, "What part of the anatomy were you planning on transplanting?"

"I had four major organs in mind," said Kadish, "but I may take a few more."

Michael DiPietro stood outside room 709 feeling a heavy grief press on his heart. Although he wanted very much to go in and see the remains of Colleen Creedon, he stayed in the hall for another moment, then walked to the nursing station to deliver the afternoon medications.

He dropped off the meds and picked up the prescriptions, not bothering to speak to anyone. As he turned to walk to the elevator, a young man in a gray suit, tie askew, came out of Colleen's room and walked down the hall. Michael walked several paces behind him.

Must be the boyfriend, thought Mike. Keeping a distance between them, he saw the young man stop at the elevator and press the down button. The pharmacist slowed his pace even more.

When the elevator doors opened, the young man stepped in. He held out his hand to hold the elevator for Michael.

"I'm going up," said the pharmacist.

The fiancé let the door close.

Michael decided to take the stairs. He wanted to be alone with his grief.

After the Creedon family and the fiancé had left, Gary paged Fred, the morgue attendant, and told him there was a body to take to the morgue. Fred promised to come right up.

After looking over Howard's post-procedure orders in the chart, he went into the patient's room to see how he was feeling. He heard the sound of flatus coming from the bathroom.

"Are you feeling okay, Mr. Stipes?" he called through the bathroom door.

"I missed lunch."

"I called for a late tray. It should be up here soon."

His wife looked up from a glamour magazine. "Did the doctor find out what's wrong with Howard?" she asked.

"Let me check," said Gary, opening the chart and thumbing through it. He found the procedure note for the colonoscopy, which said that the colon was normal. Turning to the next page, he saw the photo of the stomach ulcer taped to the second procedure note.

"Your husband has an ulcer," said Gary, showing them the photos of the stomach and duodenum. Glancing at the recommendations, he added, "Dr. Fox is starting him on a new medication. It should heal the ulcer in a week or two."

Returning to the nursing station to transcribe Dr. Fox's orders, Gary stopped a moment to admire the doctor's handwriting. Fox wrote in box-shaped letters as perfectly formed as any calligrapher. His eye fell on the date at the top of procedure note. He saw that it was the wrong day. Gary smiled, thinking that the man may be meticulous in his medical diagnosis, but he had his head in the clouds when it came to something as mundane as what day it was.

–FOURTEEN–

Lenny emptied his bucket, rinsed his mop, and told Betty good night. On his way to the time clock, he stopped at the pharmacy to pick up his prescription. He asked Hector, the pharmacy tech, if Mike was around.

"He said he had to run an errand, but he left the medication for you. He told me to pack some condoms with it, but I didn't know if you liked the ribbed kind or the ones with the feather on the end, so I just gave you the medicine."

"Tell him thanks, I'll kill him tomorrow," said Lenny, chuckling as he walked out.

Going down the hall and around the corner, Lenny came to the time clock, which was hung on the wall just past the Housekeeping supervisor's office, the better for the boss to keep an eye on the comings and goings of the staff.

Punching his card, he saw Bridgett, a young woman who worked in the laundry, waiting her turn in line. She had thick makeup on her face and dark glasses. He worried that her husband was beating her again.

He remembered a young woman in the kitchen who had been beaten for years. One day, she didn't show up for work. No phone call. No note. After she missed her third day, the supervisor called her apartment. No answer. He sent a telegram of dismissal, cc-ing a copy to the union.

Lenny spoke to her friends, learning nothing. A few days later, the super for her building went into her apartment after a neighbor complained of a foul odor. The woman had been beaten to death. The autopsy revealed several rib fractures and a punctured lung. The police assumed that the husband was responsible, but he fled the country, and they never found him.

Ever since that incident, Lenny always looked twice when he saw a female coworker on the job wearing dark glasses and too much makeup.

The male and the female attendants with the logo MEDICAL EXAMINER on their windbreakers brought their stretcher down to the morgue. The basement corridor was poorly lit, several of the fluorescent lights having burned out. The floor was littered with debris. Across from the morgue, a construction crew was using jackhammers to tear up the cement floor, preparing to seat additional supports for the ceiling. A new MRI unit was scheduled to be installed in the room above.

Freddie had Colleen Creedon's body on a stretcher by the door of the big refrigerator. The nametag was securely taped to the shroud.

"How're things in Center City?" asked Freddie. "Any grisly homicides come in?"

"Nah, just the usual stuff," said the male attendant. "A drunken husband, wife split his head open. Same old same old."

As they transferred the body onto their stretcher, the woman said, "No knock-knock jokes today, Fred?"

"Nah, I'm feeling punk."

"We all have bad days."

As Freddie watched the pair wheel the body of Colleen Creedon to the service elevator, fatigue washed over him. He had no energy, and he wanted to sleep all the time. The pounding of the jackhammer from across the hall made his head ache. *Hope my liver isn't going out again*, he thought, feeling as wrung out as a washrag used to bathe a body.

Before leaving the hospital, Lenny stopped in at the gift shop to pick up a copy of the Daily News. Marissa, a heavyset Filipino woman, was seated behind the counter.

"How's your husband?" he asked.

"Not so hot." she said in a weary voice.

"What, is he sick?"

"No, retired. All he does is watch TV and drink beer. He makes me crazy."

"Why don't you get him a membership in one of those health clubs?"

"He'd just sit around and watch the women jogging," she said, handing Lenny his change. "It's better to keep him at home, where *I* can keep an eye on *him*."

"Good thinking," said Lenny. "Oh, say, Marissa, do you know where I can buy Asher's chocolate? They closed their factory on Germantown Ave."

"I don't think you'll find any in Germantown. Try one of them expensive gift shops up in Chestnut Hill. They got all that fancy shit out there."

"I will, thanks," he said. He made his way out of the hospital and crossed to the employee parking lot. He got into the old Buick, pumped the gas pedal once and turned the key. He smiled as the old V-8 let out a deep growl. The car had been his father's pride. Together they had tuned the motor, flushed the radiator, and rotated the tires. In the summer when it rained, he and his dad would wash the car, letting the soft rain provide the rinse. His mother would shake her head at the two, their wet clothes clinging to their bodies, but accepted the father-son ritual for what it was: a chance for her husband and son to act like kids.

When his dad died, his mother bought a new Toyota, giving Lenny the Buick.

He drove to the gate, ran his parking card through the scanner, and drove out onto Germantown Avenue. He drove along the cobblestone street, glad that the old trolley had been retired, yet missing its nostalgic look. When it was running, more often than not the trolley ended up blocking the road when it couldn't maneuver around a car that some fool had double parked. But when it ran, it wound its way across the entire city, from the Chestnut Hill suburb in the north all the way to the Tenth and Bigler, in the southern end of the city.

He turned onto Wingohocking Place, a narrow street of two-story row and duplex houses. Several porches were sagging. One abandoned house had been boarded up by the local block club to keep out drug addicts and dealers. He parked on the opposite side of the street with the car facing traffic, Philadelphia style.

Stepping onto the porch, Lenny realized that he was no longer troubled by the silence that greeted him. *Was it really two years since Margaret died?* As the months piled up one after another, he had gradually begun thinking of himself as single, and not as a husband whose wife was away and would eventually come home.

"I'm gonna get a dog," he mumbled, stepping into a small living room crowded with two ancient stuffed armchairs; a sagging sofa covered with an old quilt; and an old, chipped, wooden coffee table. A ceiling-high bookshelf made from old roofing timbers was packed with books, stereo and records, and odd bits of pottery.

Putting on a Sam Cooke CD, he crossed to the kitchen, opened the fridge.

"What's for dinner?" he said to himself. There were several plastic containers with leftovers in them. He opened one, saw the mold growing on meatloaf and mashed potatoes, threw it in the trash, container and all. He tried another; found spaghetti. It *looked* all right.

When did I make that? he asked himself. Monday. He sniffed it, thought it was okay, heated it in the microwave. He took a bottle of Yuengling beer from the fridge, dumped the spaghetti on a plate, and took his dinner to the living room. He read the newspaper as he ate, starting in the back and going to the front. The meal was finished before he got to the comics.

As he cleaned the one dish and fork, he thought about the three women he had encountered that day: Colleen, Bridgette, and Patience. The dead one was a mystery and a problem for him and his friends. Bridgette was another worry—somebody he wanted to save, but he didn't know how. He would have to think about what to do about her.

Since he was a child, his mother had instilled in him the practice of reflecting. "So you don't know what to do *now*. Let it percolate up here," she would say, tapping her temple. "Solutions take a lot of time. Don't be in a rush or you'll fall flat on your face."

She had taken a year thinking about what to do with their house in Philadelphia after her husband died, finally selling it and buying a cottage at the Jersey shore. "We won't have to rent in the summer anymore," she explained. He knew it was really because she hated coming home to the house she had shared with her husband since they were married.

Then he thought of Patience. At least she was alive and normal. With children. He wondered what they would make of him; he had little first hand experience with kids.

No doubt about it, he thought. *Life was a bitch.*

Taking a book from the bookshelf on the wall, he trudged up the stairs to bed. As he washed up, he thought about his old enemy Joe West, the head of hospital security, investigating his little joke. Like Lenny needed to tangle again with the man who had vowed to get rid of him. Permanently.

—FIFTEEN—

Padric McBride sat alone in his car in the James Madison parking lot. Many of the hospital workers had gotten into their cars and driven off. Eventually the lot was half empty.

He looked at the engagement ring with the antique setting and the slender gold watch. He imagined slipping the ring on Colleen's hand, solemnly saying, "I do," and kissing her passionately after Father Lonergan pronounced them husband and wife. Instead, a doctor neither one of them knew from Adam had pronounced her dead.

As he placed the key in the ignition, he realized that there was nowhere he wanted to go. Without Colleen, he had no direction. No purpose.

"Oh, Collie," he said in a hushed voice. "What mischief did you make that you couldn't charm your way out of this time?"

Driving his Lexus convertible along Kelly Drive, Dr. Kadish glanced at the scullers on the Schuylkill River slicing through the water. He took out his cell phone, pressed the speed dial, called the Pennsylvania Organ Donor Network. The phone was answered by a woman with a soft, pleasant voice.

"Hannah Doremus, how may I help you?"

"Hello, Hannah, Martin Kadish here. Listen, that patient I told you about, the one that's going to be a multiple organ recipient . . ."

"That would be Mr. Allendale," said Hannah.

"Right. He's in critical condition. Have you found a suitable donor yet?"

"Not so far, Dr. Kadish. There are over forty other individuals in the Delaware Valley also waiting for major organs. You understand, we have to prioritize based on severity of illness. Your patient—"

"Is in heart failure, liver failure, kidney failure, and has pulmonary edema. If he were any sicker I'd be making out the death certificate."

"I understand your frustration, Doctor. I'm networking in three states. It's difficult. You know how few donors there are."

"How is your daughter doing?" Kadish asked.

"My, uh, daughter? She's fine, thank you."

"You told me that your daughter wants to become a physician. When did you say she starts college?"

"Next September."

"I imagine a full scholarship would be helpful."

"I guess so, yes."

"I'm thinking of undergraduate *and* medical school."

There was a moment of silence on the phone.

""Can I call you back, Dr. Kadish?"

"Of course. Call my cell." He gave her the number.

Punching the END button, he smiled, found a break in the traffic, and downshifted. Accelerating around a lumbering SUV, he decided that, after the operation on Allendale, he'd treat himself to something with a little more sex appeal. Like a Ferrari.

Dr. Singh sat in the ICU nursing station studying Colleen Creedon's lab results. There was nothing there that explained her cardiac arrest. The blood was acidotic, but that was consistent with the anaerobic metabolism during cardiac arrest. The potassium was in the high normal range, expected in an arrest as cell membranes leak electrolytes into the blood. Nothing else jumped out at him, except . . .

There was that one puzzling lab result—the trace amounts of thiocynate, a metabolite of cyanide. The level was not high enough to cause death, or even signs of poisoning, which made the lab finding even more puzzling.

To his limited knowledge of poisons, the trace amounts of cyanide suggested a residual from an earlier ingestion. But how long ago? And what symptoms had she manifested?

He decided to call poison control and find out as much as he could about cyanide poisoning.

Dr. Elliot Fox drove along the tree-lined street, turned into his circular driveway, and pulled up smartly in front of his large, stone house in Chestnut Hill. All his life he had wanted a house with white columns and a circular drive, and now it was his. The renovations had been ungodly expensive, he'd had to fight the contractors every step of the way, but the results were fantastic. The restorations of the porches, slate roofs, and palatial staircase were stunning. He loved nothing more than inviting colleagues to his home for drinks and dinner, knowing their mouths would drop at the sight of the turn-of-the-century mansion.

Stepping out of his Mercedes, he gave the car door a light nudge, and listened for the resonant click as it closed.

There's nothing like German engineering, he thought, patting the hood. *The Japanese did a credible job in engine design, but the Germans had it all over them for a true touring car.*

Walking up broad marble steps, he imagined his wife opening the heavy oak door and greeting him with a martini, dressed in one of those slinky teddies from Victoria's Secret.

Ah, well, he reflected, *perhaps it was too much to ask that his home life would be as satisfying as his business relations.*

—SIXTEEN—

When Lenny punched in at the time clock the next morning, he saw Bridgette standing in line, again wearing dark glasses and heavy makeup. Approaching her, he said gently, "Hi, Bridgette. How're things in the laundry?"

"Hot," she said, punching her timecard and hurrying past him, her shoulders hunched up, as though expecting a painful blow.

Watching the young woman hurry away, he felt helpless. Useless. And angry.

I've got to do something, he thought. *But what? She won't even talk to me.*

He made his way to the locker room, wondering how he could get the young woman to open up to him. In the locker room, he changed to his steel-tipped work shoes, hung up his jacket, and ran a comb through his hair, feeling the bald spot at the back of his head.

Is it bigger? he wondered. He considered letting his hair grow long enough to tie in a ponytail, the way some of the aging, hippie doctors did, but he rejected the idea. He was who he was. It would have to do.

A familiar baritone voice said, "Goodt morning, George Wushington." It was Abrahm Vorchensky, a burly Russian who worked in housekeeping.

"Hey, Abraham Lincoln. How's it going?"

"I am fine, Lennye, but you did not see me. You must have vury much on your mind. Yes?"

"Yeah," said Lenny, tying his shoes. "It's one of the laundry workers. I'm afraid her husband is beating on her, and I don't know how to get her to talk to me about it."

"It is a vury bad man who hits a woman. A coward of a man," said Abrahm. Closing his locker, he added, "But you will figure what to do." The Russian tapped the side of his head with a thick finger. "You will think and think, and then you will know. Lennye Moss, he can fix anything."

Lenny left the locker room, wondering for the millionth time why he was cursed with so many people having confidence in his abilities. He was a union steward, not a magician. He couldn't perform miracles. He couldn't even do a decent card trick.

In the intensive care unit, Gary looked nervously about the nursing station. A green-eyed nurse in green scrubs and white plastic clogs came up to him.

"Are you the float?" she asked.

"Yes," said Gary. "I'm from Seven South."

"Hi, I'm Crystal. I gave you two very stable patients. One of them could go up to Step-Down, but there aren't any beds. The other one is the mother of the chief of urology, so she gets to stay until the cows come home."

"I've never worked in ICU before," said Gary.

"It's all right, I'll be looking over your shoulder. Can you read the monitor?"

"I know what sinus rhythm looks like. Anything else, I'll have to ask you to read it for me."

"That's no problem. Don't get nervous when the alarm goes off; nine times out of ten, it's just artifact. The patient scratched himself or a lead fell off. After you get report from the night nurse and assess your patients, I'll show you where we keep the meds and the IV fluids. Anything you don't understand, just ask me. Okay?"

"Okay."

"Great. Gloria there at B bed will give you report."

Gary walked to the bedside, where a young black nurse with hot pink lipstick and a stethoscope of the same color sat writing her notes. She smiled when Gary approached.

"You have a sweet assignment. My lady in B bed has been sailing all night on a trach collar. She should go upstairs today, but she's a VIP, so they may keep her a little longer."

She went on to report the patient's history and current condition, organizing the information by organ system. By the time she'd finished her report, Gary had a clear understanding of every problem the patient had, as well as exactly what he had to do for her.

The second patient was a bit more complicated. She had undergone a lung resection for a carcinoma two days before. "She's not ready to wean from the ventilator," said the night nurse, "but she's stable enough to go to Step-Down. Just give her morphine and suction her every two hours, and watch her O-2 saturation, she'll be no trouble."

"I understand," said Gary.

"You only need to take their vitals every two hours and record them on the flow sheet. Don't forget to check the blood sugar at ten and two," she added. "Oh, and be sure to tape an EKG strip in the back of the flow sheet.

Chart Review kills us if we don't document the rhythm."

"I will," said Gary. "Thanks a lot."

"You'll be fine," said the night nurse. "Lean on Crystal if you feel unsure of yourself."

She dropped her stethoscope into her bag, gave him a wave, and strode off the unit.

As Gary approached his first patient, he looked across the room at the row of beds, a nurse or a physician busy at each one. He found that he was anxious and excited at the same time.

In the #1 endoscopy room, Dr. Fox held the black, serpentine gastroscope in his hands while Tina inserted the bite block into the old man's mouth.

"Looks to me like you should pronounce the old geezer, not PEG him," said Tina, strapping the block in place. "He must be a hundred years old, if he's a day."

"Has he got a pulse?" asked Fox, bringing the tip to the old man's mouth.

She felt the patient's wrist for a moment and frowned.

"I guess you could *call* it a pulse, but you better do this in a hurry; his heart rate is awful slow."

"All right, we'll work quickly," said Fox.

He rapidly advanced the scope down the esophagus and into the stomach. At the pyloric juncture, he waited for the bottom of the stomach to open. As soon as it did, he advanced into the duodenum.

"What you doin' that for?" asked Tina. "He's getting a feeding tube, not an endoscopy."

"You never know when you'll get a serendipitous finding," said Fox, quickly inspecting the first portion of the small intestine.

Withdrawing from the duodenum, he aimed the tip of the scope at the anterior wall of the stomach. Tina pulled up the man's hospital gown. A pink light lit up the slender old man's abdominal wall.

Hurriedly wiping the lit area with Betadine, she took a long, fat needle in one hand. With the other, she poked the bright spot of the abdomen with her finger.

"ET, phone home," said Tina with a smile.

On the monitor, Fox and Tina observed where the point of Tina's finger was pushing the stomach wall inward.

"Perfect," said Fox. "Stick him."

Taking a deep breath, Tina jabbed the big needle through the skin of the abdomen. The tip appeared on the monitor as it penetrated the abdominal wall and the stomach.

"Feed me," said Fox.

Tina fed a bright blue thread through the needle into the stomach, leaving a portion of the string outside the abdomen. On the video screen she saw the blue thread emerge inside the stomach.

Fox used the gastroscope to grasp the string. He withdrew the scope, bringing the string along with it. Then, with the string running out of the patient's mouth, he tied the end to the PEG feeding tube. "Haul away," he said.

Tina pulled the end of the string that was sticking out of the patient's abdomen. As she pulled, the PEG tube snaked its way down the patient's throat. With a firm tug, the nurse pulled the end of the feeding tube out through the abdominal wall.

As Tina secured the feeding tube and placed a dressing over it, Fox filled out the procedure note.

"It's a pity he hadn't an ulcer," said Fox.

"Don't tell me you were gonna enroll him in the study drug," said Tina.

"Why not, if he meets the criteria?"

"Look at him, he'll be dead by sundown!"

"True," said Fox, "but we'd still get the credit for enrolling him."

As she immersed the gastroscope in a tub of soapy water, Tina said, "We better get him back upstairs before we have to code this old guy."

"Don't worry," said Fox, rising from his chair and stepping to the door. "There's a Do Not Resuscitate order in the chart. We'd just end up sending him to the morgue, instead."

He ambled out of the lab, leaving Tina to clean up and page Billy to return the patient to his final resting place.

—SEVENTEEN—

Walking up the stair and emerging out of breath at Seven South, Lenny cursed his friend Moose for talking him into getting in shape. They were scheduled to go jogging on Saturday. He asked Celeste, the unit clerk, "Where's Gary? Is he off?"

"They pulled him to the ICU. The nursing office left Marianne alone with an agency nurse who looks like she went to school during the Civil War."

"At least she's had battlefield experience," said Lenny. He looked around the station, saw it was empty. "Joe West give you any shit about yesterday?"

"Nope. The bastard hasn't been around, but if I see him, I'll call you first thing."

He saw that his housekeeping partner, Betty, already had her cart out and was going about restocking the patient rooms.

"Hey, Boop, how you doing?"

"No use complaining. The Lord let me live another day, I'm content as I can be."

She tucked a well-worn prayer book into her cart and carried a roll of toilet paper and a raft of paper towels into a patient room. He went to the housekeeping closet and began filling his bucket with hot water, preparing to do battle against the footprints and spills from the previous night, and to gird himself for Joe West's inevitable attack.

At eight-fifteen, Gary read the ICU resident's order for the respiratory therapist. The therapist was to remove the breathing tube from the lung resection patient and place her on oxygen by mask. Remembering that the night nurse had told him that the patient was not ready to wean from the ventilator, and not wanting to make any mistakes, Gary showed the order to Crystal, the charge nurse.

"Christ, is he *crazy*?" said Crystal. "That patient's weaning parameters were god-awful this morning."

She spied the resident at the computer, looking over X-rays. He looked too young to shave, let alone to be the graduate of a medical school. She went over to him.

"Dr. Camacho, did you see Mrs. Millington's blood gas this morning?"

"Of course I did," he answered, not taking his eyes from the monitor.

"The P-O-two was eighty-five. She's ready to be extubated."

"She's not *ready*," said Crystal. "That gas was done on sixty percent O-two."

"*So?*" he said, shifting his eyes to the nurse for a millisecond.

"So? Her predicted P-O-two is over two-hundred. That's a huge A–a gradient!"

"It doesn't matter. Dr. Kadish told me on rounds he wants her extubated and sent upstairs. He's got a train wreck in the OR that'll need an ICU sbed."

"Buy the weaning parameters are all wrong," said Crystal.

"The attending wants the tube out; end of story."

"Well, I'm calling the intensivist. If Dr. Singh says he wants the tube in, it stays in."

Crystal picked up the receiver, dialed the page number of Dr. Singh, and stood by the phone while the resident left the unit.

I have enough headaches with the patients and a float nurse from the wards, she brooded. *Why do I have to put up with high school students pretending to be doctors?*

Crystal beckoned to Gary, who came up to the station.

"I paged Dr. Singh. He's the critical care attending in charge of the unit this month. Until he gives you the okay, disregard the resident's order to extubate. Are you okay with that?"

"I am more than okay," said Gary. "I'm delighted."

Hurriedly writing a note in the chart documenting the call to the ICU attending, Gary smiled in admiration of the ICU nurse's moxie. She was the kind of nurse he had always wanted to be.

He wondered if they would let him work overtime in the ICU on his next day off.

As Lenny rolled the big garbage cart down the hall toward the service elevator, he thought he heard a muffled sob coming from somewhere. He stopped, listened. The sound was coming from the Seven South conference room.

Stepping up to the door, he tapped gently.

There was no answer, but the sobbing stopped.

He opened the door. Nadia, the portly nurse's aide who had discovered

Colleen Creedon the day before, was seated at the table across from Joe West, chief of security.

"*What's the hell's going on?*" said Lenny, stepping into the room.

"This isn't a union matter," said West. "Nobody's accusing Mrs. Gonzalez of any infractions."

"Then why is she crying?"

"I'm conducting an investigation. She isn't entitled to union representation."

"I don't care if you're singing her a love song, she's allowed to have somebody from the union with her."

Lenny stepped closer to Nadia, bent low, and asked softly, "Are you okay?"

She hiccuped, nodded her head yes, then shook it no.

"Mr. West, he ask me if I know anything about the woman in seven-o-nine yesterday. I tell him, no, I don't know nothing. I see her on the bed, I bump into Dr. Kadish, and then I leave the room. That's all I know."

"You didn't explain what you were doing *in* the room," said West. "There was no patient there. *Why* did you go in?"

"I tell him I check to be sure everything is ready for an admission. It is my job to always check the room. Mr. West tells me the police could make trouble with my work visa. He ask me about orders in the computer, but I know nothing about the computer. I only check the rooms."

Nadia pulled a handkerchief from her pocket and held it to her eyes.

"Please don't make trouble for me, sir," she said. "I am a good worker. I do everything they tell me to do. I work always overtime when they need me."

"Why are you badgering Mrs. Gonzalez?" said Lenny.

"It's common knowledge that the employees make personal use of phones in the empty rooms. The phone company bills us on a prorated basis for the amount of local traffic, which is inflated by rampant employee abuse of—"

"Bull *shit!* James Madison pays a flat monthly rate for local *and* area calls. We could talk on the phones all day and all night, the bill would be the same."

"How do you know that?" said West.

"The union reviewed the phone bill last January, it's public record." Lenny stepped closer to West. "I could file an unfair labor practice with the NLRB for this." He turned to Nadia. "You go on back to work, Nadia. If this guy looks at you cross-eyed, you call me in. Okay?"

"Si, thank you, Lenny," she said, glancing at West. Seeing no sign of objection, she stood up and eased her way out of the room.

As Lenny turned to go, West said, "You have twenty-nine days of vacation and twentyfour sick days saved up, Moss. Your termination shouldn't hurt for at least a month, but I have it on good authority that your ward clerk and your charge nurse haven't been nearly as prudent, and they'll have no one to blame but *you* when they get their notice of termination."

West stood up, looked deadpan into Lenny's eyes, and said, "The joke will be on them, unless you want to admit that it was all your doing."

Lenny left the room without another word. As he strode down the corridor, his anxiety grew. West had sounded awfully confident in his threats. But then, the bastard always sounded confident.

He had a sinking feeling that this time it was no bluff.

—EIGHTEEN—

Lenny walked to the nursing station, where he told Celeste about his run-in with West.

"The bastard was trying to intimidate Nadia by accusing her of unauthorized use of the phone. He's hoping she'll cave and dime on the rest of us. "

"I thought that bull with the phone was a dead issue," said Celeste. "You proved it wasn't costing the hospital a penny if one of us makes a call."

"They claim it's wasting company time, not money."

Moose came past the station with the food cart, picking up breakfast trays. When he heard what happened with Nadia, he said, "We need to meet and talk, pronto. Let's take our coffee break in the sewing room."

"Good idea," said Lenny. "I'll meet you there at ten o'clock."

"I'll be there, too," said Celeste. "We need to figure a way to shut down that Joe West before he messes with my paycheck."

"Where's Gary?" asked Moose. "He needs to come down, too."

Celeste explained that the nurse was pulled to the ICU.

"I'll tell him when I pick up their trays," said Moose, then he went down the hall to complete his rounds.

Dr. Kadish was in the ICU making rounds with his team when Crystal called him to the phone. It was the physician in the emergency room at Samaritan Hospital.

"We have a potential donor," the Samaritan doctor told him. "An MVA, came in last night. He's completely a-reflexive."

"Excellent," said Kadish. "Have you run the brain-death protocol?"

"I've ordered an EEG. We need another day at least before we can pronounce him. It's hospital policy."

"An EEG isn't required in Pennsylvania. What about the tissue typing?"

"His blood type matches your donor, I checked with the Organ Donor Network, so I sent off a specimen for tissue typing. They should be running the tests today."

"Well done, my friend. I won't forget your help. Prepare the patient for transport to James Madison."

"Uh, Dr. Kadish, I haven't got permission from the family to donate his organs."

"Well don't waste your time talking to *me*, talk to *them*. If money's a problem, make it clear I'll help them out with the funeral expenses. Christ, I'll get them a gold-plated coffin if it will get them to sign the damn form."

"Okay, I'll get right on it."

"Don't quote any numbers; leave that to me. Just get the body over here as soon as the tissue typing is complete."

Hanging up the phone, Kadish spotted Dr. Singh. He signaled for the ICU physician to join him.

"There's a likely donor for Allendale at Samaritan. I plan to operate tomorrow."

"That is most fortuitous for him," said Singh. "I understand that you are planning to transplant the heart and the lungs, is that right?"

"The heart and lungs," said Kadish, "and the liver and kidneys."

"Really? At the same time? I've not seen that procedure done anywhere."

"We're breaking new ground. Be prepared for a long procedure."

"How long do you anticipate it will be?"

"Twenty-four hours, minimum. It could well run into a second day."

"I will see that there are extra anesthesia attendings and residents on call over the weekend."

"You just keep my patient's heart perfused until I get him on the table, and don't overload him with fluids."

When Singh was out of earshot, Kadish turned to his fellow and said, "Those ICU attendings are wimps. They think a little Lasix and a broad-spectrum antibiotic will cure anything."

He led his team into Allendale's room. The patient had an oxygen mask on. His color was pale, his face more swollen with fluid. He was breathing rapidly through his mouth.

Lifting the oxygen mask from his face, he said, "When . . . is the . . . operation?"

Kadish returned the mask to its proper place.

"As soon as the lab work is complete. Tomorrow afternoon. Sunday at the latest."

"Put it in second gear. I'm dying."

"Nobody dies on my service unless I okay it," said Kadish, winking at his fellow and enjoying his little joke.

Allendale raised an arm, intending to point at Kadish, but he was so weak that his arm slowly drifted down onto the bed. He mumbled something under the mask that no one could hear.

Leaving the bedside without another word, Kadish instructed the fellow to keep a close eye on Allendale's blood gas. If his respiratory failure worsened, he was to get anesthesia to intubate and put him on the ventilator.

Freddie walked into the GI lab to drop off the pathology reports. Handing them to Tina, he said, "No procedures this morning?"

"Not till later. Dr. Boucher's away and Dr. Fox has to see the patients on the floor."

Freddie sat down at the little desk, where he slumped like a sack of potatoes.

"What's the matter with you?" asked Tina. "You feeling your age?"

"Got no energy," he said. "T.G.I.F."

"Maybe you better go see Dr. Primeaux in Employee Health. Could be your liver is acting up again."

"He must be tired of seeing my ugly face, all the times I been down there."

"Not our Alex Primeaux. He's got a heart of pure gold. He's always stood up for your sorry ass. You best go see him." She put her hands on her hips and looked hard at Freddie, letting the silence speak for her.

"I know, I know," said Fred. "Employee Health. I'll get over there soon as I catch up on my work."

"Promise?"

"Scout's honor," said Freddie, holding up a hand in a salute.

"You were never no Boy Scout. You spent your youth in the juvey home."

"Yeah, but I was a model prisoner," he said.

They both laughed as Freddie got to his feet and shuffled out of the room.

—NINETEEN—

Gary was studying the nursing notes that the night nurse had written on his patient. The notes were organized around organ systems, starting with the neurologic. He saw that the format required that the nurse assess every system, even the musculoskeletal, leaving nothing out.

Using the same model to write his notes, he found that he had neglected the urologic system in his examination of the patient. He was kneeling at the bedside examining the patient's urine in the foley bag for color and clarity, when Crystal came up to him.

"How's it going? Are you comfortable with your patients?"

"I think so, yes. I'm just assessing the urine."

"Good. Have you had a chance to check the lab values in the computer?"

"Uh, no, not yet. We don't always call them up on the floor. We mainly rely on the doctors to check the results."

"Big mistake; they miss too much. Come on, I'll show you a few shortcuts."

At the computer station, Crystal brought up the current labs for one of Gary's patients. She scrolled down to the current date, selected "Chemistry," and centered the report on the screen.

"There's your complete SMA-twelve. Abnormal values are highlighted in red. See the bilirubin? It's a little high, but it's coming down. You can right click the mouse over the result and the computer will display what the normal values are."

"Right. I see that."

As Gary went on to review the hematology and blood gas results, he said to Crystal, "I had a visitor die on my floor yesterday."

"I heard about that. Do they know what the cause of death was?"

"No, I don't believe so."

"Want to check the lab reports?" asked Crystal.

Gary fidgeted in his seat. "I don't know. Do you think we should?"

"Why not? She was a patient on your floor, wasn't she?"

"In a sense she was, although we never actually admitted her."

"Type in her name and see what you get."

Gary typed "Creedon, Colleen," waited while the server located the patient's reports. The labs came up on the screen. There were several reports, all from the day she died.

"Check the toxicology tab. We'll see if she had any narcotics in her blood," said Crystal.

The toxicology results were negative.

Crystal pointed to the therapeutic drug levels. It showed a trace amount of thiocynate.

"Is that the same thing as cyanide?" asked Gary.

"It's a breakdown product. Right click on it."

The selection brought up therapeutic and critical values for thiocynate. The level in the patient's blood was extremely low.

"Why would she have cyanide in her blood?" Gary wondered aloud.

"Maybe somebody was trying to poison her," said Crystal.

"If they were, they certainly didn't give her much of a dose. Look how far the level is from the toxic range."

"Well," said Crystal, "if it wasn't the cyanide that killed her, I don't see anything else in her blood that would explain her arrest."

Gary shut down the lab program and checked his patient's medication orders. He mixed an antibiotic and brought it to the bedside. As he adjusted the IV, he began to worry that the police would soon be questioning him. Even though he had nothing to do with Colleen Creedon's death, he felt a rising sense of alarm at facing another interrogation.

He wished that he could be cocky and sarcastic, like Lenny. Or fearless in facing a surly resident, the way Crystal was. He felt that the best he could do was to ride out the murder investigation, helping Lenny as much as he could, and hope that West didn't mess with his license to practice nursing.

Dr. Fox walked quickly down the corridor and entered the hospital pharmacy. Seeing Mike at a table sorting prescriptions, he approached him.

"Say, Mike, can you spare a minute?"

"Sure, Doc. What's on your mind?"

"One of my patients didn't get his study medication for nearly twenty-four hours after I ordered it. The nurse tells me that the night pharmacist had trouble finding the medication. I'm afraid it's the third time in a month."

"I heard about that. Oleg was looking for your drug in the nonformulary section, which is over there . . ." The pharmacist pointed to a set of shelves beside a large vault like cabinet where the narcotics were stored. "He didn't realize Gastronex was a study drug. That puts it in the storeroom in the back."

Mike walked up to a door at the back of the main pharmacy. Through the doorway could be seen a large, dimly lit room filled with rows of metal shelves. Each shelf was packed with boxes, trays, and cartons of medications and intravenous solutions.

"We keep all the study drugs back there in a separate section," Mike said. "You want I should take you back and show you where we keep the Gastronex?"

"I don't think that's necessary," said Fox, "as long as all your staff knows where to find it. That's the principal issue here."

"It shouldn't be a problem any—"

"Yo, Mike!"

Hector, the pharmacy tech, called out from a small glassed-in office to the side of the room. He held a receiver in his hand and pointed to it. "It's Dr. Cuthbert on the phone for you."

Mike rolled his eyes. "My boss," he explained. "Can you wait a minute?"

"Of course. Take your time," said Fox.

Mike went into the office to speak to the department chairman. When he was done, he found Dr. Fox standing where he'd left him outside the storeroom.

"Like I was saying, Doc, we just have to get our staff to understand what drugs are nonformulary and which ones are on a study protocol, like yours. There's a list of study drugs in the logbook. We'll make sure all the shifts review it so they know what's what."

"That's fine," said Fox.

"Anything else I can do for you?" Mike asked as he walked with Fox to the exit.

"No, you've been most helpful. Thank you so much."

"Have a great day, Doc," said Mike. He watched as the slim, soft-spoken physician made his way out of the pharmacy.

Now, why can't all the doctors be as pleasant as him, thought Mike, returning to the stack of prescriptions. *The guy even has such perfect handwriting, I can read his orders.*

—TWENTY—

Birdie sat at her old black sewing machine repairing hospital gowns. The nurses had cut the sleeves when the patients had intravenous tubes in their arms, making it easier to remove the gown, but rendering it unwearable.

Her husband, Moose, sat beside her chewing on a soft pretzel with melted cheese on top. There was a rap on the door. Lenny came in, a cup of coffee in one hand, a bagel in the other.

"Hi, guys," he said, unfolding a beat-up metal chair and taking his place across from Moose.

"Lenny," said Birdie, "did you see the artwork Moose did in that class he's taking at Community College?" She pointed to a printout of a cartoon character, a skinny black kid with a laptop computer that had super powers.

"It's fantastic," said Lenny. "I think he should go to Tyler."

"We got to wait till the money's better," said Moose. "Those art courses at Temple are a lot of bucks."

"How long are you going to wait?" asked Lenny. "Till the kids have gone to college? They'll have grandkids and you'll be wanting to buy them clothes and toys, too."

"The money's not there," said Moose, popping the last of his pretzel in his mouth.

"It never *will* be, Moose, you've got kids. Do it now; don't wait till you're an old man."

"Old like you, that what you mean?" said Moose.

"Yeah, like me."

Celeste came in, opened a chair, and pulled a bottle of water from her bag.

"You sure do like your bottled water," said Moose. "I bet you can't tell the difference from what I pour out of the tap."

"Don't matter if I can or I can't," said Celeste, "so long as I *think* it's healthy. Besides, I learned about all the bugs that grow in the city water the last mandatory inservice program I had to go to. Infection Control gave it. They about scared me half to death. I'll stick with my bottled water, thank you."

She capped her bottle and returned it to her bag. "What are we gonna do about that Joe West?" she asked.

"We're sticking together like glue," said Lenny. "That's the most important thing. West can't touch us as long as he has no one to sign a statement for him."

"We'll be all right," Moose agreed. "But I want to know what you learned about the woman that died."

Lenny told the others that Colleen had visited the GI lab and talked in private with Dr. Fox. He talked about the "miracle" drug Tina had told him they were studying, and he mentioned the missing dentures he had found in the second procedure room across the hall.

"If there was something phony in that study, Fox could have a reason to shut up the rep for the drug company," said Moose.

"I agree," said Lenny, "although Tina didn't say anything like that."

"Would you bite the hand that feeds you?" asked Birdie. "Tina's a good nurse, straight up, but she has loyalty, too, don't forget."

Lenny reported Mike's shock and sorrow over the news of Colleen's death. He noted that the pharmacist seemed awfully broken up for someone he knew only in a professional capacity.

"I hear Colleen Creedon was a real fox," said Celeste. "We all know how you men can be around a sexy young thing."

"I don't know, Mike's been married a long time," said Lenny.

"That's when they get the itch," Birdie said. "Every seven years."

"The only itch I ever got is the one you like to scratch," said Moose. Birdie ignored him.

Lenny finished his account with a description of West's efforts to force Nadia to testify about their activities at the nursing station.

"How are we gonna find out what killed that poor woman?" asked Birdie.

"I'd like to get my hands on the medical examiner's report," said Lenny. "And her hospital chart, too. I don't know how we can do it, but—"

Rap, rap, rap.

A knock on the door stopped him in mid sentence.

Gary poked his head through the open doorway of the sewing room, saying, "Moose told me to come down."

"Tuttle, come in!" called Lenny, unfolding a chair for the nurse. Looking Gary up and down, he said, "It looks like the marks from West's rubber hose have faded." He told the others how West had grilled Gary the day before, threatening his nursing license.

"I haven't heard any more from him," said Gary, "but the charge nurse in the ICU helped me look over Colleen Creedon's lab work. I printed it out. Take a look."

Unfolding the printout, Gary took a pen and circled the category for therapeutic drug levels.

"She had a low level of thiocynate in her blood," he said. "That's cyanide."

"Poisoned!" said Moose. "I knew it."

"Maybe not," said Gary. "It was just a trace amount. It doesn't look like it was enough to kill her. I'm not even sure that it would make her feel sick."

Lenny asked if there was anything in her blood that would explain her death. Gary pointed out that there were no narcotics, tranquilizers, or paralyzing agents. There was nothing to cause a respiratory or cardiac arrest.

"So was she poisoned or wasn't she?" asked Celeste.

"I don't know," said Gary, "but I think it's fair to assume that if she had cyanide in her blood, the police have been notified."

"Of course the cops are on the case," said Moose. "We really got to get our act together. If we find out who poisoned the woman, we'll come off like heroes. Ain't no way West can touch us then."

"That's right, " said Birdie. "We got to find who killed the woman, like we did with Sparks."

"Oh, Christ," said Lenny, "it's déjà vu, the sequel."

"Heh, heh." Moose grinned. "You know you love it."

"Like a shot of penicillin in the ass." Lenny pointed out that there was a gap of more than two hours between when Colleen visited the GI lab and when her body was found on Seven South.

"We need to find out who else she saw," said Moose. "The last person to see a murder victim is usually the one who killed him."

"When did you go to detective school?" asked Lenny.

"He likes to watch *Law and Order*," said Birdie, rolling her eyes.

"It's common sense," Moose said. " She's a drug rep, she probably went to the pharmacy."

"I asked Mike about that," said Lenny. "He didn't see her, but he was in the chemo room. Hector might remember seeing her. I'll talk to him."

Celeste said, "Chances are, she went to Purchasing to talk about when her company was gonna get paid. I'll talk to Emily. Her daughter and mine go to the same modern dance class."

"Great," said Lenny, turning to Moose.

"I'll talk to the cafeteria workers," said Moose. "Somebody might've noticed who the woman dunked her doughnut with."

"That's good," said Lenny. "Here, take this." He handed Moose an article about Colleen from the *Daily News*. "Show the photo around; it might help."

"Yeah, that'll do," said Moose.

"I could read up on cyanide poisoning," said Gary. "I'll try to find out what serum levels produce an illness."

"I'll talk to Fred and see if he can get hold of the medical examiner's report," said Lenny. "Dr. Fingers might have it, her dying in our hospital and all." Standing up and folding the metal chair, he added, "If the cops want to talk to anyone, we follow the same rule. Nobody talks, everyone walks. Agreed?"

All agreed. They threw their coffee cups in the trash and went back to their stations.

—TWENTY-ONE—

Patience wheeled the portable X-ray machine into the ICU, where she asked Crystal which bed Mr. Allendale was in. The nurse pointed to the end room, saying, "It's the guy with the private-duty nurse."

"Why is he in the isolation room? Is he infected?"

"No, he's rich."

"Oh," said Patience, wheeling her machine toward the room.

Entering the room, she saw a frail old man sitting up in bed, his head lolling, his eyes closed. A private-duty nurse sat in an armchair reading a magazine.

"Is this Mr. Allendale?" Patience asked.

"That's him," she said, standing up to help.

At the sound of their voices, Allendale woke up. He looked at Patience, then looked at the X-ray machine.

"Go away! Go . . .away!"

He ripped the oxygen mask off his face, threw the sheet off, and stuck his legs over the rail, trying to climb out of the bed.

"You won't . . . kill...me," he declared, turning gray without his oxygen mask in place. As Patience and the private-duty nurse struggled to get him back in the bed, Crystal hurried into the room.

"Mr. Allendale, no one is trying to hurt you," she said, replacing the oxygen mask on his face. "They're only here to take an X-ray. It's just an X-ray."

Allendale continued to struggle. Crystal picked up the phone and paged the ICU resident STAT, then again tried to calm the patient. He ignored her assurances, again and again trying to pull the oxygen mask off his face and climb out of bed.

"Maybe you better come back later," Crystal told Patience. "I'm going to get an order to sedate him. I'll page you when we get him calmed down."

"Okay," said Patience. "I won't be far away. Just page me when you're ready."

She made a U-turn and wheeled her machine out of the room. As she disappeared from sight, the patient began to stop struggling.

"There, you see, Mr. Allendale," said Crystal, "nobody's going to hurt you. Relax. We're all here to help you."

He looked into her face, seemed to find something familiar and comforting there. He reached up a trembling hand and patted her cheek, saying, "Good . . .girl. Good . . ."

Then he closed his eyes and seemed to fall asleep.

Joe West opened the door to the Housekeeping supervisor's office for Police detective Joe Williams. Inside the office sat the head of the department, Norman Childress, a pasty-faced man in the last stages of middle age. Seated in front of his desk was a diminutive black woman who wore a gold necklace and four earrings in each ear.

After exchanging perfunctory greetings, West pointed to the young woman.

"This is Juanita Childs. She works in the messenger service. She was on Seven South at the time they found Colleen Creedon."

"My friends call me Baby Love," said Juanita, trying to look sexy and cool.

"We're not your friends," said West.

The detective sat down beside the young woman, looked at her for a moment. Juanita squirmed in her seat under his gaze.

"Tell me, Miss Childs, what exactly did you see that morning that pertains to the deceased, Colleen Creedon?"

"I saw the whole thing," she said, perking up at the opportunity to make a good impression. "Gary Tuttle was complaining, like he didn't really want to go along, but Lenny sweet talked him, he's got that silver tongue." To West she said, "You know how he is."

"What did Moss tell them to do?" asked West.

The detective shot him a warning look, unhappy with having the questioning taken over by a security guard.

"Lenny told Celeste—she's the unit secretary—he told her to put orders in the computer like there was a real patient in the room, but they all knew nobody was there!"

"That would be in room seven-o-nine?" said Williams.

"Uh-huh, seven-o-nine."

"What happened then?"

"I couldn't stay around, it would have looked suspicious. She was starting to put in the orders when I left out of there."

"What about the name 'Colleen Creedon'?" asked Detective Williams. "Did anyone mention her name?

"No, sir."

"Did you hear the name 'Falcon Pharmaceuticals'? Did that name come up?" he went on.

"No. I just heard the joke about pretending a patient was in the room. That's all I heard."

"I see."

Supervisor Childress looked at the detective, who indicated he was through with the witness. Childress said, "You can go back to your station now."

"What about my promotion?" she asked.

"I can't announce it now, it would look suspicious. You understand that, don't you?"

"Then when do I get it?"

"I'll interview the other applicants next week. I'll give it some time to look like I'm thinking about it, then I'll give you the position."

"Assistant supervisor for messenger service," she said, lingering over each syllable. "But why do I got to work nights?"

"Somebody has to be my eyes and ears when I'm not around," said West.

"You don't need my ears, you always around," said Baby Love. She turned and sashayed out of the office.

West turned to Detective Williams. "She won't be much help in your investigation, but it certainly makes getting rid of Moss a lot easier."

"Her account supports our view that the victim didn't belong in the room. Not as a patient, at any rate." Rising from his chair, he said, "Do your people require the salesmen to sign in a log every time they enter the hospital?"

"They're issued a day pass at the main entrance each time they arrive," said West, opening the door for the detective.

"I'll need to see your visitor logbook for yesterday. Also her clothes and any belongings she had with her."

"I secured the evidence personally," said West. "It's bagged and tagged in my office."

"I'll page you when I'm ready to inspect it," said Williams. "I want a list of all the departments she did business with."

"I'll get right on that," said West.

"I suggest you start with Pharmacy," said Childress. "I'll show you where the main office is."

As the detective and Childress passed West on their way out of the office, Childress said to him, "You can deliver the disciplinary notices at the end of the shift."

West glanced back at Childress, nodded once, then strode briskly away.

—TWENTY-TWO—

Dr. Kadish's flock of house officers and students was winging its way down the Seven South hallway trying to keep up with the busy surgeon when Dr. Fox flagged Kadish down.

"Martin. I hear you have something big planned for James Madison."

"It's going to get world wide press," said Kadish. "*And* make the hospital solvent for decades."

"Your genius will finally be recognized outside of the Delaware Valley."

"Thank you," Kadish replied. "Oh, by the way, you didn't get a call about that patient of mine that you pegged this morning, did you?"

"The old deaf guy? No, I didn't. Why do you ask? The procedure went perfectly."

"He died an hour after returning from the GI lab. The case may come up next Monday at the M&M conference."

"I gave him no sedation whatsoever. The mortality shouldn't show up in my statistics."

"Don't concern yourself, Elliot. DNRs never get counted. Submit the fee and forget about it."

"Don't think I won't," said Fox. "Excuse me, I have a lot of patients to see. My partner is on vacation."

"Is Boucher in Europe?" asked Kadish.

"No, Cayman Islands."

As Kadish led his team away, Fox entered Mrs. Cavanaugh's room. He sat on the edge of the bed, placed a hand lightly on the patient's hand, and began.

"Muriel? Remember the test I did yesterday, where I looked into your stomach with the long instrument?"

"No, I don't remember it. Not one second, and I'm glad of it. I remember getting on the stretcher, and I remember waking up in my room, and that's all I know."

"I'm afraid I found something that's not good. It's a tumor. That's a growth on the lining of your stomach. We have to remove it."

"A growth you say? You're talking about *cancer*, aren't you? Why is everyone around here afraid to talk plain? I have cancer, you have to take it out. Maybe it'll kill me, maybe I'll lick it. Is that about the size of it?"

"Yes, that's it. You are very brave, my dear. Very courageous."

"No I'm not, I'm old and worn out. All my friends and relatives have died. I've buried my husband and my son. If I croaked in the morning, there'd be precious few to watch me lowered into my grave. Call the surgeon and tell him to sharpen his knives. Let's get this thing over with before I lose my nerve."

"I'll need to do some more tests. X-rays . . .a CAT scan. I've spoken to Dr. Danielle Eisenberg. She's a cancer specialist. She's one of the best; I know you'll like her."

"When is she going to see me?"

"After she reviews the slides from the biopsy. It shouldn't take her long. A day or so."

Mrs. Cavanaugh sat back in the bed and pulled the sheet up to her chin. "Oh, dear," she mumbled half to herself. "I hope this doesn't mean I'll have to give up my martini in the evening."

"I don't see why it should," said Fox, "but we'll let the oncologist advise you on that."

Fox wrote a note in the chart, which he dropped off at the nursing station, then left the ward. A few moments later Gary picked up the chart to put it in the rack. Curious about the tumor in her stomach, he opened the chart and turned to the procedure notes. There he saw the color image of a large, ugly tumor adhering to the wall of the stomach. Gary shuddered, knowing what kind of malignant cells were multiplying and spreading from the mass of dark cells.

He hoped it hadn't spread to the lymphatics, and that the surgeons could get it all.

Detective Williams sat in the office of Dr. Horace Cuthbert, Ph.D., director of pharmacy and chemotherapy.

"This is a criminal matter, then?" asked the director.

"The presence of cyanide raises our level of suspicion," said Williams. "We have a report of a suspicious death from the medical examiner's. We're getting background information at this point."

"I see. Well, you're free to interview any of my staff. We have nothing to hide, I assure you."

Williams asked the director if they stocked cyanide in the hospital pharmacy. Cuthbert assured him that they did not.

"It's a poison with no therapeutic value, not a pharmacologic agent," he explained. "We would have no reason to include it in our formulary."

"None of the drugs you carry have cyanide in them?"

"None whatsoever."

Williams tapped a note into his Palm Pilot with a stylus. He looked up from the screen. "Did she visit the pharmacy the morning she died?"

"Yes, briefly; I checked with my staff the minute I heard of her death. She came in to check on our supply of Gastronex. Dr. Fox is conducting a study of one of her company's drugs. We have to keep meticulous records of how it's dispensed."

"I see. How long did she stay?"

"Five minutes, maybe ten. No more than that. She just asked how the study was going, if there were any problems with the documentation, that sort of thing."

"*Were* there any problems with the study?"

"No, certainly not. Everything was going beautifully. You're welcome to review our records."

"Thank you, I will need to see them. I'll need to see the records of all the Falcon drugs that you carry."

"Certainly," said Cuthbert. "I can generate a printout quite easily."

While the pharmacy director typed in commands at his computer station, Williams said, "I imagine the drug business is very competitive. Is that right?"

"The whole business of healthcare has turned into cutthroat competition."

"When a company wants to promote its product, do they sometimes offer any sweetener for the hospital to carry it?"

"We make all our purchasing decisions on a strict cost-benefit analysis," said the director. "The old days of free trips to Hawaii and luxury cruises for doctors and pharmacists are long gone."

"You're sure about that?"

"Absolutely. Why, six months ago, when Mr. DiPietro wanted to attend a drug conference in New Orleans, he had to pay his own air fare and hotel room. We gave him the days off with pay, of course, but the pharmaceutical companies didn't contribute one nickel to his expenses."

Receiving the printout from Cuthbert, the detective said, "One last thing. Do you know where Colleen Creedon went from here?"

"No," said the director, "I have no idea."

"I'll need to question all of the people who were on duty yesterday morning."

Cuthbert said, "I'll assemble everyone here who worked yesterday."

Once the pharmacy staff was brought into the director's office, Detective Williams questioned each of them about Colleen Creedon's last visit. He asked which members of the staff were the most friendly with the dead woman, and if anyone was known to socialize with her after work. Nobody knew where the woman planned to go after leaving the pharmacy, or if she was close to someone on staff.

As the detective completed his interview, Hector Rodriguez began to feel a growing sense of apprehension. He remembered the way that Mike used to drop whatever he was doing as soon as Colleen Creedon came into the department. How the pharmacist would watch her like a puppy while she met with the director. How he would walk behind her a little too close, as if he wanted to smell her perfume or brush up against her ass.

Picking up a stack of in-house mail that the messenger had dropped off, Hector sorted them according to the recipient, then went to each pharmacist's desk to deliver them. When he got to Mike's desk, which was tucked just inside the storeroom, he noticed a business card tucked into the corner of the big green blotter. The fancy, deep blue lettering that read *FALCON PHARMACEUTICALS* caught his eye.

That's the company the cop was asking about, he thought. Slipping the card out of the blotter, he saw the name Colleen Creedon embossed on the card. He turned it over. There was a note written on the back. *I NEED TO SEE YOU RIGHT AWAY. COLLIE.*

Mikey, Mikey, he thought, shaking his head. *I hope you didn't let your dick do all the thinking.*

Looking to make sure nobody could see, Hector tucked the business card in his shirt pocket, walked back to the main room, and began weighing his responsibilities. *Show it to the cops, or show it to Lenny?*

It was a no-brainer.

—TWENTY-THREE—

Lenny was running the buffer over the floor at the end of the Seven South corridor. He'd set up two yellow CAUTION signs, marking off half the width of the hall. As the machine made lazy pirouettes across the marble floor, he found the rhythm of the machine soothing; it helped him think.

He pictured Bridgette, with her dark glasses and heavy makeup. Imagined the bruises concealed beneath the cosmetics. He felt annoyed that he'd done nothing to help her.

One of the dieticians walked by, a slim young woman with a red leather backpack. Nestled in a mesh pocket on the side of the pack was a liter of bottled water.

Seeing the designer water bottle, Lenny recalled Celeste's story about the mandatory inservice that she had been required to attend, and how the city water was not as pure as it once had been. He thought about water . . . he thought about sitting in a classroom listening to a lecture and being thirsty . . .

What if...

What if the social worker gave a mandatory education program to the laundry workers about domestic abuse? Bridgette would have to attend. It would give her a chance to talk about her problems. Even if she didn't talk, at least she'd hear other women dealing with their issues.

Why not?

Hurrying to the nursing station, he told his idea to Celeste, who was entering medication orders into the computer. The pink and pale blue stones in the rings she wore glittered as her hands hovered above the keyboard.

"That's a great idea," said Celeste, not missing a keystroke. "You gonna bring it to Miss Fabrisio?"

"I think she could go for it," said Lenny. "She's less caught up in the administrative bullshit than most of the other supervisors. She has a big heart."

"She's got a big everything," said Celeste.

Nodding in understanding, Lenny decided to visit the supervisor for the laundry as soon as he finished his work.

Birdie locked up the sewing room and made her way to the Purchasing Department, which was on the second floor. Entering a quiet office painted gray, with half a dozen cubicles laid out like a maze, she went up to the third cubicle.

"Hi, Emily. How're you doing?"

A middle-aged white woman with a cardigan sweater thrown over her shoulders looked up from her computer screen, smiled, beckoned to Birdie to have a seat.

"Everything's fine, except for the crazy thermostat. It's *freezing* in here. We have to wear sweaters in the summer, and we sweat like pigs in the winter."

"At least you can open a window. My little-bitty window up by the ceiling doesn't even open. How's Beth doing with her dance class this year?"

"She loves it, like always," said Emily. "She thinks she's going to be a ballerina someday."

"Mine's the same way. Miss Janet fills her head with all kinds of dreams."

"Well, what would life be like without a dream?"

Celeste settled into a chair beside Emily, leaned forward, and lowered her voice.

"Listen, Emily. Moose and Lenny and me, we're kind of poking around that poor young woman who died yesterday on Seven South. Colleen Creedon. You must have heard about it."

"Of course, it's all we've been talking about. I knew her."

"I figured you would. Your department is the one that pays her company."

"We do pay the pharmaceutical companies. Eventually."

"How do you mean?" asked Birdie.

"Sometimes we hold the check for ninety days. Sometimes a hundred twenty. It's a dirty business."

"The hospital takes that long to pay a bill? Shoot! When *I'm* late paying my electric bill, I hear a whole lot of crap about it, let me tell you."

"James Madison isn't getting paid, either. We bill Medicaid and Medicare for services we provide, and they take six months to pay. A year, in some cases. The insurance companies aren't any better."

"That's terrible."

"Hey, no money in, no money out. It's as simple as that."

"The rumor I'm hearing is the hospital's in deep financial trouble. Is that true?"

"The finance people don't tell us squat," said Emily, "but we hear the same stories down here. I just hope they don't rob the pension fund. Look at what happened at Enron. I'm three years away from retirement."

"I have a lot longer to go than that," said Celeste. Lowering her voice, she said, "Tell me: Was Colleen down here the morning she died?"

"Yes, she was. She came in around nine. I'd just booted up my computer and was sipping my morning coffee."

"Did she stay long?"

"About a half hour."

"Hmmm. Was there anything going on with her? Did she look scared or anything?"

"No, I wouldn't say she looked scared. More like, down in the dumps. Like when a boyfriend dumps you, that kind of look. She wasn't very perky, the way she usually seemed."

"Okay. Thanks a lot, Emily. I really appreciate your telling me all this." Celeste got up to go, adding, "Did the hospital owe her company much money?"

"Fifty thousand or so, nothing out of the ordinary. We were coming up on a hundred days, and her supervisor was asking why the delay."

"Uh-huh."

"But they all have to deal with that. Like I said, no money in, no checks going out."

Celeste bid her friend good-bye, then decided to get a coffee in the cafeteria. If she was lucky, she'd run into her husband. She couldn't wait to tell him what she had learned.

Gary sat in front of the computer at the ICU nursing station. He had updated his nursing notes, entered all the vital signs on the flow sheet, and administered his medications. Although there was a lot of work to do for each patient, he was so used to caring for ten or fourteen patients at a time—not to mention being in charge of the entire ward, thirty-six beds—that after doing everything he needed to do for just two ICU patients, he felt as if he almost had it easy.

He dialed up the Internet connection, selected one of the medical search engines, and entered "cyanide." Scanning a list of articles, he selected one and began reading about industrial exposure as a source of cyanide poisoning.

Crystal came up and looked over his shoulder.

"Well, well. I see we have a detective in our unit."

Looking up at her, he was relieved by the smile on her lips, and went on reading.

Lenny walked quickly down the stairs to the basement. Knocking on the office of the supervisor for the laundry, he heard a husky voice call out, "Come on in to my kitchen!"

Entering the room, he saw Miss Fabrisio, a very large woman, seated at her desk. Her blouse was open at the top, revealing a cleavage of breasts that could succor a small army.

Lenny explained his concern for Bridgette's safety and survival. He told her his idea for a mandatory inservice on spousal abuse. Miss Fabrisio sat looking intently into Lenny's eyes. As she listened, she leaned forward seductively, watching to see if his gaze would fall from her face.

When he'd finished his proposal, she got up, stepped over to Lenny, put a meaty hand on his chest.

"It's employees like you, Lenny, that make James Madison the loving family that is the pride of the Philadelphia health system."

He smelled whiskey on her breath. Although he had learned to keep a poker face in many a hard-nosed negotiation with an administrator or an arbitration panel, Fabrisio's assault on his senses nearly broke through his defenses.

"Thank you," he said, not daring to say any more.

I'll speak to Mae Yeung in Social Service," she continued, pressing closer to him. "I'll ask if she can put the program together by early next week."

"Great. Thanks a lot, Miss Fabrisio," said Lenny, stepping backward in an effort to extricate himself from her grasp. "I've got to get back to my station. Thanks for being supportive."

Moving toward him as he backed away, she said, "Why don't you and I talk some more about your concerns for the women in my department. You could come back to my office after your shift ends . . ."

"Uh, I have a union meeting," he said, feeling for the door behind him. "Besides, I think we should leave the planning to the professionals in Social Service."

She held the door open as Lenny stepped out into the hall, saying, "My door is always open to you, Lenny. You know that."

"I know, thank you," he said, turning and hurrying down the hall.

As he put more distance between himself and Fabrisio, he felt mixed emotions about her. He appreciated her down-to-earth manner, and the fact that she was willing to try and help one of the workers. *But damn,* he thought, *it looked like she wanted to have sex with me right there in her office.*

—TWENTY-FOUR—

Moose approached two dietary aides who were wiping down the tables in the cafeteria.

"Hey, Smooch. Hi, DeeDee. You ladies got a minute?"

They stopped their work and stood together. He held out the newspaper photo of Colleen Creedon that Lenny had given him. "You seen this woman around here lately?"

DeeDee took out her glasses and held them in front of her face. "I don't know, there's so many people coming and going all day. I look at the tables, I don't hardly notice their faces."

"She don't like to wear her glasses, that's why she can't recognize anybody" said Smooch. "They hide her big brown eyes." She took the photo in her hand, studied it a moment. "I seen her," she said.

"You sure?" asked Moose.

"I remember, 'cause she was over there in the corner by the vending machine." The young woman pointed to a corner table set off from the rest.

"Was she with anybody?" asked Moose.

"That's how come I remember. There was this big white guy in a suit. A real sharp outfit it was, must have cost two weeks' salary. Two weeks of *my* salary, anyway."

"I remember them," said DeeDee. "They were talking like they were gonna run out of words."

"Did you hear anything that they were talking about?"

"Not me," said DeeDee.

"Me, neither," said Smooch. "I wasn't that close. I was wiping down the tables up along the windows. Besides, they was sittin' so close, they didn't have to talk loud."

"How close were they?"

"Child, if they was any closer, she would have had extra cream in her coffee."

"Heh, heh," Moose chuckled. "Did the guy have on an ID badge?"

"Not that I could see, but he must have been a doctor."

"What makes you say that?"

"He didn't have one of them suitcases with wheels."

"I got you. No samples, no salesman."

"You got it. Besides that, his beeper went off two, three times. Got to be

93

a doctor if he's *that* important."

Moose thanked them and went back to the kitchen to help load the lunch trays on the line. He was pleased with the way the case was going, and couldn't wait to tell Lenny what he'd found.

He was spooning helpings of mashed potatoes onto the plates, when he saw his wife, Birdie, coming toward him. She had a big grin on her face. He always loved seeing her when she was happy.

As Gary entered vital signs in his patient's flow sheet, Crystal asked him how he was doing. He told her that things seemed to be under control.

"Did you learn anything useful about cyanide?" He summarized what he had read. "It doesn't look to me as Colleen Creedon had the classic signs of cyanide poisoning." He added that cyanide wasn't a medication, so it didn't seem likely that it was even obtained in James Madison.

"We don't give anyone cyanide, it's true," said Crystal, "but cyanide is a breakdown product of one of our intravenous antihypertensives."

"Really? Which one?"

"Nitroprussic acid. It can break down to thiocynate if you give it too long. That's why we have a protocol to run thiocynate levels if we have the patient on it for more than two or three days. We don't want the patient to become toxic."

"That's incredible," said Gary. "How is it administered?"

"It only comes in an intravenous form."

"You can't give it orally?"

"No. The gastric acid breaks it down and the liver metabolizes it. You have to give it as an IV infusion. There's no other way to get it into the blood."

Crystal gave Gary a sly smile, saying, "You really are a detective, aren't you?"

He demurred, but was secretly pleased by her comment. As he walked back to his patients, he heard Allendale's private-duty nurse call out to Crystal. The nurse hurried to the room. Seconds later, she stuck her head out of the room and told the unit clerk to page Anesthesia STAT; the patient was cyanotic.

Gary found the crises erupting around him exciting. Everyone seemed to work together, as if they had rehearsed their parts over and over. Between working in the ICU and finding himself knee-deep in the murder investigation, he was both anxious and happy. In fact, he hadn't enjoyed himself so much since his children were born.

Tired and hungry, Lenny finished a last sweep of the hall. He emptied his bucket in the dirty utility room and hung up his mop. He knew that over the weekend the floor would become streaked and stained, the few custodians on duty stretched out over so many floors and departments. Although the shine would be gone from the floor by Monday morning, at least he was leaving the ward in good shape.

Betty called out to him, "Hey, Lenny, telephone! It's the social worker."

He took the phone.

"Hi, Mae. Did Miss Fabrisio tell you about my idea for a women's inservice?"

"Oh, yes, it's a wonderful idea. I'm going to set up the program over the weekend. I attended a workshop last fall and I still have the syllabus. We'll run the program early next week."

"Great," said Lenny. "Listen, I really appreciate your taking this on. I didn't now what else to do about Bridgette."

"I'll keep an eye on her during the meeting. Perhaps she will be willing to have a session with me another time."

Hanging up the receiver and saying good-night to Betty, Lenny thought that he might have a pretty good weekend, if he could just get away from the hospital without any more people coming to him with their problems.

He walked down the stairs to the basement and made his way to the Housekeeping Department. As he waited his turn to punch out at the time clock outside the office, he saw Moose, who came up to him and clapped his big hand on Lenny's shoulder.

"You gonna meet me at Forbidden Drive tomorrow for our jog in the morning. Right?"

"Yeah, yeah, I'll be there," said Lenny.

"Seven o'clock sharp. Don't be late."

"Cut me some slack, Moose, it's Saturday. I'll be there at eight."

Moose compromised on seven-thirty, then waited for Lenny to punch his timecard so they could walk out together.

Lenny punched his time card and was replacing it in the rack on the wall when he felt something poke him in the back. Turning, he found himself face to face with Celeste. The lovely ward clerk had fire in her eyes.

"That bastard Joe West gave me an unscheduled vacation," she said, handing a letter to Lenny. "It's the permanent kind!"

—TWENTY-FIVE—

Lenny scanned the paper Celeste handed him, with its familiar logo of the Human Relations Department. For years he'd believed that the logo should read Inhuman Relations.

"It says I violated hospital policy on the computer, making false entries and using someone else's ID. How did they find out?"

"West must have a snitch," said Lenny.

"You see anybody around the station that morning we can't trust?" asked Moose. "Think back."

Lenny pictured the scene: Gary was seated at the station, Celeste was at the computer monitor, Moose stood in front of the desk. Gary had a pile of lab reports in his hand that he'd just received from . . .

"The messenger!" Lenny exclaimed.

"You're right," said Moose. "Baby Love came by the station; she was dropping off lab reports just when we were putting the joke together."

"I remember, said Celeste. "She hung around like she was looking for something."

"Trying to be cute," said Lenny. "It's got to be her. She's been bucking for a promotion for a long time. I guess she'll get it this time."

He handed the memo back to Celeste. "I'll grab a grievance form from my locker and take it to Human Relations right away. We'll skip the first step and go right to step two. I'll request a hearing first thing next week."

He stood a moment, watching Celeste, listening. When she said nothing, he asked, "Are you okay with this?"

"Yeah, I'm cool," she said. "I'm gonna get my mom to stay with the kids and go to Atlantic City with my girlfriend. Priscilla has some comps at Caesar's Palace. We'll go down there and have fun." She looked at Lenny. "You should come with us. You work too hard. What do you do for fun?"

He thought about the date he had coming up with Patience. "Actually, I have a date Saturday night."

"Oh, yeah?" said Moose. "You didn't tell me about it."

"Even union stewards have our secrets." Turning to Celeste, he said, "I'll let you know as soon as I get a date for the arbitration hearing. I'm afraid this isn't the kind of charge I can turn around across the street."

"Makes no difference to me," she said, sounding totally blasé. "I know you're gonna get me all my pay back, with interest."

After parting with Celeste and Moose, he fished out a grievance form from his locker, which was overflowing with folders, union newsletters, books, and magazines. He filled in the bare elements, leaving the details for the actual hearing. Signing his name, he took it up to the Human Relations Department, being sure that the secretary there stamped the date and time on the form and gave him the yellow copy.

He was just coming to the front door, looking forward to finally being out of this wretched hive, when he stopped, frozen in place.

"Tuttle," he whispered under his breath. He decided to check with his friend. If West had a snitch who dimed on Celeste, there was a good chance she'd fingered Gary as well. He couldn't leave without finding out about his friend.

Hurrying to the ICU, he saw Gary standing at the station talking with a nurse, a backpack on his shoulder. He waited until the nurse finished talking, then signaled to him as his friend headed for the exit.

"Hey, Tuttle. Are you okay?"

Gary reached into his bag, coming out with a letter with the familiar logo on it.

"I've got a letter in my file," he said, not looking as upset as Lenny had feared.

"I'm really sorry," said Lenny.

"That's all right, I knew it was coming. The part that worries me is what it says at the bottom."

Lenny read the ending paragraph, which stated, ". . . any further infraction or unprofessional behavior may be reported to the state NURSING DISCIPLINE BOARD for review of licensure.

"Why didn't you call me?" said Lenny.

"I'm not in the union, Lenny. I wish I were, I need somebody like you to speak up for me."

"You can appeal it through Human Relations. You have the right to bring a friend for moral support. I'll go with you."

"You will?"

"Of course! The whole thing's my fault, anyway."

'It's the hospital's fault. They pushed us too hard for too long."

"You're right, I'm completely innocent." Lenny looked serious for a moment. "You are going to file a request for appeal with Human Relations, aren't you?"

"Yes, I'll do it right away."

"Human Relations will schedule a hearing in a week. Maybe two, they love to drag these things out. Let me know the date and I'll arrange to go with you."

"I will. Thank you, Lenny."

Finally leaving the hospital, Lenny thought about his friend. Gary might not be the one who held the flag high and led the charge, but he would never turn and run when the bullets were flying.

He was a solid guy. A good friend. Which made Lenny doubly troubled for putting his friend on the hot seat when all Gary ever wanted to do was take care of his patients.

Crystal noted the peak airway pressure reading on Allendale's ventilator. The anesthesiologist had inserted the breathing tube a short time before. She checked the infusion rate of the epinephrine, decided the blood pressure was adequate. She touched his arm, noting the skin was cool and moist.

It really does feel like cold clams, she thought. *Like cold, dead clams.*

The transplant fellow looked at Crystal, worry written on his face. He knew that if Allendale coded, Kadish might give him a failing grade for his rotation, just to blow off steam. He needed to complete his fellowship so he could begin to pay off his crushing debt. Not to mention supporting his wife and two children.

Dr. Singh came into the patient's room and reviewed Allendale's hemodynamics with the transplant fellow and Crystal.

"He is in acute renal failure," said Singh. "His liver is failing as well. His A-a gradient is getting worse. I do not know how long we can ventilate him without producing a pneumothorax; his airway pressures are very, very high."

"I know," said the fellow. "The patient is quite brittle."

"How soon can Dr. Kadish begin the transplant?" asked Singh.

"He is waiting for the donor to arrive. I believe it will be sometime tonight or early Saturday morning."

"His creatinine is three-point-four, but I am afraid he will not tolerate dialysis. His blood pressure is too low."

"Dr. Kadish said that he will have cardiology place an intra-aortic balloon to support him if necessary. We must do whatever we can to preserve the neurologic function."

"If we cannot deliver more oxygen to the blood," said Singh, "I am afraid he will suffer an anoxic stroke. Then there would be little point in proceeding with the surgery, would there?"

—TWENTY-SIX—

Dr. Fingers called Freddie in to his office.

"Listen, Fred. I know you've been putting in a lot of overtime the past few months . . ."

"More like the past *year*. I can't remember the last time I had a whole weekend off."

"I don't like to have to keep asking you, Fred, you know that. It's just that the hospital won't approve a second position. Human Relations is giving me the runaround."

"I know all about that line of bull. The whole hospital's running on a shoestring."

"Be that as it may, I need help with a postmortem Saturday morning. It will only be four hours or so."

"Did you ask Regis?"

"He's already scheduled to work in the laundry."

Fred sank wearily into the chair opposite his boss's desk. He liked Dr. Fingers. The man had stood by him when he was on sick leave for his cirrhosis. Had written glowing letters of support. He even testified at the arbitration hearing to keep his job.

"I want to help you out, Doc. God knows, I need the extra money. It's just, I haven't been feeling too hot lately."

"It will only be for four hours, and that includes the cleanup time."

"You sign my overtime slip for six hours?"

"Of course. Like I always do."

"Okay, I'll drag my ass in here tomorrow, but only for four hours."

"Thank you, Fred, I'm most appreciative." The doctor put on his lab coat, saying, "I'm due for a lecture with the medical students. I'll see you in the morning."

"Right-o, Doc. See you at seven o'clock sharp."

As soon as Fingers was out of the office, Fred looked around the room, thinking, *If I were an autopsy report, where would I lay down my weary head?* Lenny had called and asked him to see if the medical examiner had faxed a copy to Dr. Fingers.

Fred searched the drawers in the office without finding any report for Colleen Creedon. On the verge of giving up, he remembered that the secretary had left early that day and that she was the one who usually checked the fax machine for incoming mail.

Going to the machine, he saw several reports in the tray. He pulled them out, smiling broadly at his own ingenuity. Here it was: PROVISIONAL REPORT OF AUTOPSY ON COLLEEN CREEDON.

He read the report twice. It was not long, and the conclusions were tentative. Nevertheless, they were tantalizing.

"Ain't that some shit," he mumbled as he used the fax machine to make a copy of the report. "Wait'll Lenny reads *this*."

Returning the original report to the tray, he folded the copy and placed it in a legal-size envelope. The clock on the wall showed 4:30 PM—long past the end of Lenny's shift.

He wondered whether he should drive over to Lenny's house and drop it off. It was somewhere in Germantown, he wasn't sure where. He decided to put the report in the housekeeping closet on Seven South. Lenny had told him once about the lock being broken. That way it would be waiting for him the next day he came to work.

Making his way to the closet on the seventh floor, Fred wrote Lenny's name on the front of the envelope; then, just for a laugh, he wrote out a knock-knock joke on the back. He placed the envelope beneath a pair of leather-palm work gloves to be sure Lenny would find them first thing in the morning.

Going to the elevator, he punched the button. Waited. He was so damn tired, he thought that if the elevator didn't come inside of sixty seconds, he'd fall asleep on his feet.

Lenny unwrapped the jerk chicken he'd picked up at the Rib Rack, an old yellow school bus converted into a barbecue joint, and set the savory food on a plate. He licked his fingers, grabbed a raft of napkins, and carried the food into the living room. A bottle of Yuengling beer on the coffee table was already half gone.

Tearing into the spicy chicken, he thought again about the trouble his friends were in. Celeste was terminated; he didn't know if he could win that one. Nadia was worried about her immigration status. She had a green card, but he wouldn't put it past West to try and trump up some criminal charge against her, just to put the screws on and get her to talk.

Moose was all right for now, but Gary was a problem. The letter in his file would be the first of many, Lenny was sure of that. Once Miss Burgess had a nurse in her sights, she kept on firing bullets until the nurse was gone, and the license in jeopardy.

Why do I have to be such an asshole? he thought for the hundredth time, thinking about the practical joke that had created the whole mess. *Why couldn't I grow up loving Ingmar Bergman films instead of The Three Stooges?*

Taking a long pull on his beer, he reflected on how he was always promising to help his coworkers, even when the situation was hopeless. Like he was some kind of a miracle worker. Maybe if he stopped trying to do the impossible, he would get less pleas to solve their problems.

Dr. Fox settled lazily in the Jacuzzi, a glass of champagne at his fingertips. He used the remote to turn up the CD, enjoying Gershwin, a pleasant change from his beloved Mozart.

This was the life. His wife was in the bedroom putting on her best face, his new tuxedo was pressed and ready to wear, and the opera promised to be most enjoyable. None of his wife's Gilbert and Sullivan for him; he was going for the real thing.

What's more, the weather forecast for his golf game on Saturday was sunny and mild.

Mike sat at a counter in the pharmacy, filling prescriptions. It was hard for him to read them, his eyes were tearing and his vision was blurry. Another migraine, and this one was a ripsnorter. A five-alarm fire with explosives in the basement.

He went back to the storeroom, opened a cabinet, removed a box of ergotamine. It was strong medicine. He hated to take it, it required injecting into the muscle, but it was the only thing that would knock it out. He only hoped his vision would hold long enough for him to punch out and drive home. When the headaches were really bad, he had blurred vision.

Home. He suddenly remembered that he wasn't *going* home, he was going to a rented room with a hot plate and a cot for a bed.

He knew he'd screwed up bad this time. So bad that it was hard to tell which pain was worse, the one in his head or the one in his heart. He had screwed up so bad that he would probably never go home again.

Looking about the hotel room, Dr. Kadish decided that the Bellvue-Stratford was still up to his standards. The grand old hotel had been renamed several times, but it would always be the Bellvue to him. The staff still offered the best service and the finest wine list of any hotel in Center City. He would stay nowhere else.

He hit the speed dial on his cell phone.

A familiar voice said, "Pennsylvania Organ Donor Network, Hannah speaking."

"Hannah, Dr. Kadish. Why haven't you cleared the donor for transport?"

"I'm sorry, Doctor, the final tissue typing hasn't been completed. It won't be done until Saturday, I'm afraid."

"I want somebody working on it tonight!"

"It's Friday night, Dr. Kadish. The lab techs don't work at night."

"They will if you offer them double time. I don't care what it costs; send me the bill if you have to. I want the donor cleared and sent to James Madison tonight."

"But—"

"Do you realize how sick my patient is? He's intubated, he's on life support, all his major organs have failed, and he's on pressors to support his blood pressure. The donor *must* be transported to James Madison immediately."

"I understand your situation, Doctor, it's just that the state mandates that tissue typing be completed before we approve a match, and we—"

"I'll hold the procedure until the final results are in, but I need the donor in my hospital so that I can harvest the organs the instant the tissue typing is confirmed."

"Very well, Dr. Kadish, I'll call the lab right away."

"Good. Get the donor transported tonight."

Kadish hung up the phone. He walked to the door of the room, hung the "Do Not Disturb" sign on the outside, then threw the security bolt.

Jennifer Mason, a third-year medical student at James Madison University Hospital, watched Kadish as he selected a bottle of champagne from the refrigerator.

"Is Mr. Allendale going to last long enough to receive his new organs?" she asked.

"He better, or I'll chop off some heads," he said, peeling off the foil cover. As his big hands pulled the cork from the bottle, he studied the lovely woman lounging provocatively on the queen-size bed. Jennifer was dressed in tight black pants, black pullover, and high-heeled sandals. Long blond hair spilled over her shoulders. Her figure was classic; her lips, divine.

"Do you always stay in the honeymoon suite when you're at the Bellvue?" she asked.

"Always, my dear. It has the biggest bed." He poured two glasses of wine. "Did I ever tell you how fetching you look in a scrub suit?"

"No, but I saw it in your eyes when I observed in the OR."

"Did you? My surgical mask couldn't hide my true intentions, I suppose."

"No, Martin. Not with eyes like yours."

She felt a twinge of embarrassment, calling the chief of the transplant service by his first name. But they were off duty, she reflected. Very far off duty.

"Did you happen to bring a set of scrubs with you?" he asked, sipping his champagne.

"No, sorry, I didn't know you liked them. I brought a little nightgown. Shall I put it on?"

"Yes, do."

She picked up her overnight bag and stepped into the bathroom, leaving the door ajar. Savoring his wine, Kadish thought about the pair of leather wrist restraints he had packed in his overnight bag. Some years ago James Madison had banned the traditional leather restraints—the ones with the metal lock and key—replacing them with softer, disposable cotton ones. A lover of classic things, he took a pair of the old leather restraints home with him.

"Tell me, my dear," he said, setting his wineglass on the table and reaching into his bag, "you like to play games, don't you?"

−TWENTY-SEVEN−

The clang of his alarm clock jerked Lenny out of his slumber. He cursed the sound. It was bad enough getting up at 5:30 A.M. for the job, but hearing that annoying sound on Saturday was beyond human endurance

I'm gonna kill Moose when I see him, he thought.

He pulled on an old pair of sweat pants and a T-shirt with a picture of George Washington Carver on it, thick white socks, and an old pair of running shoes.

The T-shirt had been a gift from his freshman roommate at Temple—how many years ago?—because Lenny was always eating peanut butter. The friend had earned his degree, taken education classes, and moved to Seattle, where he was teaching high school. Lenny left college when his father dropped dead of a heart attack in the living room, just a few steps from the phone.

Making a quick cup of cappuccino, he wondered what he would be doing had things gone differently. His mother and her sister had gone out for a few groceries. They weren't gone more than an hour. They found him on the floor, called 911, and gave CPR, but it was no use. His mom always felt guilty about going out that afternoon . . .

Would he be teaching, perhaps, if he'd finished his degree? History. That was his favorite subject. He wouldn't be working in an office somewhere, that would be hell, like Moe or Curly working as accountants. An abomination.

No use looking back, he told himself. Time to meet Moose for their Saturday jog in Fairmont Park.

Stepping out of his house, he looked up at a porcelain blue sky littered with a few fluffy white clouds. "Why couldn't it be raining?" he grumbled, but realized that not even a downpour would stop Moose.

Getting into the car, he recalled a story about his friend that was probably true. One time Moose ran the whole length of Fairmont Park, from Mount Airy to Center City, in a blinding rainstorm.

"Hurricane is what it really was," Moose had said. "I had the wind at my back the whole way. Man, was I flying! My feet hardly touched the ground."

When someone asked him if the wind wasn't working against him on the run back, he answered, "Comin' *back*? You *crazy*? I took a bus!"

Lenny drank his espresso on the drive over to Fairmont Park. The big Buick scattered gravel as he pulled into the parking area along Wissahickon Creek. Moose was there already, his arms extended out to the side, rotating his torso. Lenny cursed as he got out of the car.

Seeing Lenny approach him, Moose said, "Man, when did you buy those sweat pants, in high school?"

"No, I wore them at Temple. I didn't know there was a fashion requirement for this."

"C'mon, stretch out with me," said Moose, bending at the waist and placing his palms flat on the ground between his feet.

Lenny bent forward, groaned, managed to get his fingertips to touch his toes. After several more stretching exercises, Moose announced that they were ready.

"I'll start off easy, like I did the last time. You keep up as long as you can. If you get a cramp in your side, slow down and walk it off. I'll pick you up on my way back. Okay?"

"If I pass out, you'll have to carry me back to the car. I hope you're prepared for that."

Moose ignored his friend as he started down the trail at an easy trot. The ground was deeply rutted from spring runoff.

In minutes the trail descended into a wooded area. Wissahickon Creek burbled and rippled on their right. A father and son sat on a log, their fishing rods extending out over an elbow of water, the sun glinting on the rippling water. On the other side of the creek a wooded hill rose, with rock outcroppings beckoning to child explorers.

"How are you doing with the art class?" asked Lenny.

"Super. I'm doing computer animation. I got my caricatures moving. Next, I'm gonna have 'em speak."

"That's wonderful. You'll be moving to Silicon Valley one of these days."

"Heh, heh. Same day that *you* finish your college degree."

They entered a densely wooded section with branches reaching out to them.

"Guess who I'm having dinner with tonight," Lenny said.

"Who?"

"Patience, from X ray. I'm going over to her place for dinner."

"Hmph," said Moose.

Lenny looked at him, puzzled at the response.

"You don't think it's a good idea?"

"Didn't say that."

They jogged in silence for a few moments.

"Well, what *do* you think?" Lenny asked.

"Ain't for me to tell a man who to get it on with."

"Come on, Moose, I've known you a long time. We were on picket duty together when those goons tried to break up our strike. You can't tell me what you think?"

"Sure I can tell you. I'm just not sure you want to hear it."

"Oh, I see. You're protecting my feelings. Thanks a lot."

They jumped a fallen tree that intruded on the path, then passed an elderly woman walking a little terrier that nipped at them, straining on its leash.

"The thing is," said Moose, "I know you want to get married again. Patience is a single mother, she's got two little kids, she'd like to get hooked up with somebody, too."

"So what's the problem? All of a sudden you don't approve of interracial relationships?"

"It's not what I think that matters, it's what all the ignorant, juked-up sons of bitches on both sides will think that worries me."

"I'm prepared to hear some shit about it," said Lenny.

"Some?" Moose looked at his friend, shook his head. "Lenny, if things *do* get serious between you and her and you get married, you'll adopt her kids. Right?"

"Yeah, I guess so."

"I *know* so. You wouldn't do it any other way. But that's the part you don't get. You can't, 'cause you never been there."

"I don't follow you," said Lenny.

"Once you adopt those kids, you'll never escape the racist garbage that this two-faced town has been dumping on us for two hundred years. Your kids will be *black*, and you won't be able to escape it. It'll hit you in the face every day. Ugly racist shit. And I don't think there's a white man alive—not even *you*—that's prepared for it."

Moose stretched out his long legs and kicked into high gear, making the distance between him and Lenny grow rapidly. His feet seemed to barely brush the ground as he picked up speed, arms pumping like pistons of a hell-bent locomotive.

From over his shoulder he called out, "I'll catch you on the way back. If you get a stitch, walk it out, but *don't stop moving!*"

His legs danced over the ground as light as a butterfly. In seconds he was around a corner and out of sight.

Lenny plodded on, thinking about what his friend had said. He knew that Moose had his best interests at heart. He didn't think his friend was telling him to back off, he was just warning about what he was in for.

But Christ, he thought, *it's only our first date.*

-TWENTY-EIGHT-

Dr. Nelson Fingers, chairman, Department of Pathology, James Madison University Hospital, was pleased to see the body ready on the dissecting table as he came into the room. A few medical students and a pair of residents greeted him. Fingers nodded to Fred, who handed the doctor a circular saw. The doctor flicked on the switch, filling the room with a loud buzz, then he bent down to make a Y-shaped incision in the chest.

"We are fortunate to have this cadaver," he said over his shoulder, guiding the saw up toward the neck. "It's becoming increasingly difficult to obtain permission for an autopsy. Luckily, this old gentleman resided in a nursing home, which had power of attorney. The director is usually happy to oblige our requests, so long as the death cannot be attributed to the care received at *their* facility."

The body was stretched out on its back. A new white latex feeding catheter emerged from the stomach.

Just as Fingers turned off the saw, the teeth-jarring sound of a jackhammer filled the room. Fingers glanced at the door, which a medical student closed, reducing the noise a bit.

"What was the cause of death?" asked one of the residents.

"Heart failure and pulmonary edema," said Fingers.

Freddie placed the saw on a stainless steel table, where it would be available to crack the skull. As he handed the doctor a device for spreading the rib cage, he felt a wave of dizziness come over him. He reached for the wall to steady himself.

"Are you feeling all right, Fred?" the doctor asked, severing the heart from the aorta and vena cava and lifting it out of the chest cavity.

"I'm a little tired, Doc. I'll be all right."

"You can take a break if you need; I can carry on from here." He removed the lungs, then sliced upward through the esophagus to reach the soft palate.

Fred told him he would stay until they were done, but he unfolded a chair and sat, ready to help if needed.

I should have gone and seen Dr. Primeaux on Friday, he thought. The employee clinic wasn't open on the weekends. That meant he would have to drag himself through the weekend. But today was only a half day, and Sunday he'd stay in bed.

Dr. Kadish entered the ICU, walked briskly to the isolation room, his fellow and residents in tow. Picking up the bedside clipboard, he scanned Allendale's latest lab values.

"I see his coags are worse," said Kadish. "So is his blood gas." Turning to the nurse, he asked, "How much epinephrine is he on?"

"Nine mikes," said Crystal. "Shall I increase it?"

"Not yet. Hang another unit of fresh frozen plasma and twenty-five percent albumin."

At the sound of the doctor's voice, Allendale began to thrash about in bed. He bit the breathing tube, occluding it and setting off the ventilator alarm.

"Relax! Don't bite the tube, Alfred," said Kadish.

The patient became more agitated as the blocked breathing tube robbed his brain of oxygen. His eyes bulged as he strained to sit up. The more he felt like he was suffocating, the harder he bit on the tube. He pulled so hard on the wrist restraints that he tore one of the cloth ties. His free hand grabbed the breathing tube. The transplant fellow pounced on the patient like a tiger, trying to keep Allendale from pulling it out.

"Paralyze him, Crystal," said Kadish. "He's not oxygenating as long as he's biting the tube."

"But he's still awake. Shouldn't you sedate him first? It's inhuman to paralyze someone and leave them wide awake."

"His pressure is too low to tolerate sedation. Besides, he's delirious, he won't remember. Put him down. *Now.*"

As the nurse went to draw up the paralyzing medication, Kadish told the fellow, "Get his coags back to baseline; I can't operate with clotting times like this. And tell the team to be ready to assemble at a moment's notice. I'm sending Allendale to the OR in an hour."

"Will do," said the fellow.

"And get Cardiology up here. Have them put him on balloon assist; that will keep his arterial pressure up until we're ready to harvest."

"Where is the donor?"

"He's in the holding area. He'll go in first, we'll harvest his organs, then we'll crack Allendale's chest." He looked hard at the fellow, saying, "You just keep the bastard's pressure up and be ready to scrub. Got it?"

"Yes, sir," said the fellow, furiously writing orders in the chart.

Kadish went to the nursing station, dialed the number for the operating room supervisor.

"This is Martin Kadish. I want rooms five and six ready immediately for my quadruple transplant . . . No, I don't know what time I'll start, I want everything set up . . .Put your people on call, but I want them in the house. None of this driving in from Yeadon. Everybody stays and waits for my call . . . Good."

As he hung up, the unit clerk held another receiver out for him. It was the anesthesiologist who would be caring for the brain-dead organ donor.

"Dr. Kadish? This is Norris Brothers, in the holding area. I was going over the pre-op checklist, and I realized that the family hasn't signed the consent to donate organs yet. We can't proceed without it, as you know."

"I was told that the paperwork was complete. Do I have to do *everything* around here?"

The anesthesiologist waited, knowing this wasn't his problem. It was surgery's obligation to get the consent. For surgery.

"I'll have my fellow track down the family and find out what kind of games they're playing. Sit tight."

He clicked off, turned to his team, his face taking on a dark color as his anger built.

"Which one of you is so brain-dead you didn't get the family to sign the consent?"

The residents looked sheepishly at each other, no one wanting to take responsibility for the screwup.

"Dominick, I told you to get the consent signed when the donor arrived last night. What happened?"

"I don't understand, I went over the form with the family. I gave them the pen, they gathered around. I thought that they signed it."

"Well, apparently they don't understand that they're standing in the way of history. Go and find them and get their name on the paper. Jarvis, you go with him."

As the resident and the fellow hurried away to find the family, Kadish looked at his team, saying, "Doesn't anyone care that we're making medical history?"

Lenny's side was beginning to hurt as he jogged along the trail in Fairmont Park. He slowed to a walk just as Moose appeared on the crest of a hill coming toward him, still going strong. Lenny turned around and walked slowly back toward the parking lot. His friend came up beside him and jogged in place, matching his speed.

Moose asked, "You wanna hear what I found out in the cafeteria yesterday?"

"Of course," said Lenny, catching his breath.

"One of the girls told me she saw Colleen sitting way over in the corner with a tall white guy in a slick suit. She said they were sitting so close, she didn't have to pour any cream in her coffee."

"Any idea who the guy was?"

"Nope, but she figured he wasn't a salesman, on account of he didn't have a bag with him."

"Might be a doctor," said Lenny.

"That's what I figure. Birdie went down to Purchasing. She found out Colleen was in there around nine, nine-fifteen, talking business."

"That's interesting. Was there anything special going on?"

"She said the hospital owed her company money, but it wasn't anything new, James Madison is always late paying bills. They were plenty fast sending me a bill for Birdie's surgery last year, but pay what they owe a supplier, forget it."

"It's the first rule of business: 'Hold the money.' Still, we're filling in her movements that morning. That's got to help."

Climbing a gentle incline, they continued along the trail until they were back at the park entrance.

"That's a great old car," said Moose as they approached Lenny's Buick.

"It's starting to burn some oil," said Lenny.

"You ain't getting rid of it, are you?"

"No, I don't want to do that. But I should take it to somebody and get an estimate for a ring job."

"Take it to Wiggins on Penn Street, off of Belfield. He's good, and he won't cheat you.'"

They stood in the sunlight, the lot beginning to fill with dog walkers and families out with their children. Lenny told Moose how he was going to follow up with the grievance for Celeste's termination, saying he was sure it would have to go to arbitration. "Entering false information in the computer is serious."

"They don't play when it comes to their database," said Moose. "I was lucky, I only got a verbal warning from my supervisor. They didn't put a letter in my file."

"Apparently there's no written policy about filling out a false menu," said Lenny.

"Come Monday morning, there's gonna be a memo tacked up on the kitchen bulletin board warning everybody about filling out menus for patients who don't need to eat. Trust me."

"I'm sure there will," said Lenny. He opened the door to his car. "I wish I had a copy of the autopsy report."

"I thought Freddie was gonna get you a copy."

"I never heard from him, I guess he didn't find it." He got into his car and rolled down the window. "I'll call him when I get home, just to check."

"You going there now?" said Moose.

"No. I have to go to Chestnut Hill and find some Asher's chocolate for Patience."

"That was bullshit, them closing the factory in Germantown," said Moose.

"Wasn't it? Margaret and I used to walk into town and buy their broken chocolate. You couldn't beat the price."

"Or the candy. Best in the city."

"Tell me about it," said Lenny, firing up the big V-8.

Lenny waved good-bye to his friend as he pulled out onto Lincoln Drive. As he headed for Chestnut Hill, he thought about what his friend had said about mixed couples and racism. He asked himself if he really would be prepared for the abuse.

Then he reminded himself that it was only a first date.

—TWENTY-NINE—

While Philadelphia Police detective Williams drove the Impala to the northeast section of the city, he said to his partner, Sternbach, "Read me the ME report again."

As his partner slowly read the report, three things stood out to Detective Williams. First, there was the observation about the right ventricle being "slightly thickened." He made a note to follow up with the doctor in the intensive care unit—Singh—what that meant. The second was the cause of death: "cardiopulmonary arrest, etiology unknown."

"Etiology" had to mean "cause." It's not like the doctors could use simple English. But that wasn't the important thing. The important thing was, the ME didn't attribute the death to cyanide poisoning. It wasn't a drug overdose, either.

Finally, there was the pregnancy. The blood type of the mother and the fetus were different.

"We have to check the blood type of her fiancé. If it's not consistent with the baby, we'll need to check her business associates at Falcon, and maybe some of the people in the hospital."

"West can get the blood types from the hospital employee files. We might need a court order for the drug company if they get fancy with their privacy," said Sternbach.

Williams hoped that the fiancé turned out to be the father; it would eliminate one line of inquiry. That would require him telling the poor bastard that his wife-to-be was pregnant—a double loss. Well, it couldn't be helped; the information had to come out some time.

"You want to see the pharmacist first, right?" said Sternbach.

"We're halfway to Logan anyway," said Williams. "After we see DiPietro we can cut over to Glenside and see if the fiancé is home."

"You're on," said Sternbach. Williams drifted around a city bus and began passing cars, weaving around them in a fluid motion, like water around stones. He loved going faster than anyone else on the road.

Lenny parked his car in Chestnut Hill and looked in the windows of the classy gift shops and food emporiums. He was always amazed at how much somebody was willing to pay for a loaf of bread if it had a few herbs and nuts thrown in.

He found a shop that carried Asher's chocolate, bought a pound. Paying the bill, he felt a pang of regret, thinking of the days when he and Margaret had walked to the old chocolate factory on Germantown Avenue and bought hurt chocolates at half price. It had been the best buy in Philly, for the best chocolate. She and the factory were gone. The best he could do was to honor the dead and move on.

On the way home he stopped at a traffic light, looked at his face in the rearview mirror, decided he needed a haircut. He ran his fingers over his chin, realizing he hadn't bothered to shave that morning. He looked like crap.

For several years he'd wanted to treat himself to a real shave from a barber, with the hot towels and the lather and the straight razor. He decided today was the day. He cruised into Mount Airy and stopped at his favorite barber, a young Italian American who was following in his uncle's footsteps. The young man loved classic cars, so he and Lenny always had plenty to talk about as he clipped and snipped.

As he settled into the barber's chair, he felt the steaming towel press against his face. The last two days' tension began to ebb away. He felt so good, he decided that he'd even let the barber clip his nosehair and around his ears.

While Lenny was in the barber's chair, Patience was in the Superfresh market. Takia, her six-year-old daughter, was pushing the cart, while Malcolm, the seven-year-old, was hanging on the front of the cart, making sounds of motor engines and crashes.

Stopping at the meat section, she picked up a roast beef, saw the price per pound. It was a little high, but it would give her leftovers she could use for sandwiches and soup. Even a stew.

She placed the meat in the basket. Takia saw it.

"Can't we have hot dogs?" she asked.

"No, no hot dogs for dinner. We have a guest coming."

"Can we get pizza from Giovanni's?" asked Malcolm, eyeing the roast beef with disdain.

"We had pizza last night," she said. "Friday night is pizza night, not Saturday."

She pushed the cart down to the produce section, wondering if Lenny liked to eat collard greens. She decided to play it safe; she would serve baked potatoes and a tossed salad. And greens for the children.

Fred was feeling weak and wobbly. There was a fuzzy region in the edge of his vision that wouldn't come into focus. His mouth was dry, and when he stood up after sitting for a few minutes, the room seesawed, as though he were on a little boat being tossed from wave to wave.

I'm glad I don't have any more work today, he thought. *Any more bodies come down, Doc Fingers is gonna have to do the setup himself.*

He was on his way to the cafeteria, feeling that a cup of tea and some toast might perk him up, when the light in the corridor seemed to dim.

Something wrong with the power, he thought. He walked unsteadily, keeping close to the wall so he could reach for a firm surface if the dizziness got worse. All of a sudden, he felt an iron hand grab him by the shoulder, anchoring him in place.

As the iron hand slowly turned him around, he found himself staring at Joe West.

"You've been drinking again, Gopie. You know what that means."

"No, Mr. West. I haven't had a drop in over a year. Honest!"

West sniffed around Fred's mouth. The breath was pungent and fruity, like a sweet wine.

"I can smell it on your breath, don't bother denying it. This time your ass is mine. I'm terminating your employment, effective immediately."

"But I've been straight, I swear to God! I go to my meetings, I work the program. Ask Dr. Fingers. Ask Dr. Primeaux. You got me all wrong."

"I'm sick and tired of your lame stories. That pesky friend of yours Moss won't be able to bail you out this time. You're history. Now come with me."

West dragged Freddie to the elevator, roughly shoved him into it, and rode with him to the first floor. From there he led him by the arm to the main entrance.

Standing on the top of the marble steps, West growled, "I want you off hospital property. You can come back on Monday to clean out your things, *if you're sober.*"

As Fred stood at the top of the stairs, West added, "If you fall and break your neck on the steps, don't come crying to me. Nobody's going to pick your sorry ass up. Now get out."

He watched as Fred reached for the railing and slowly eased himself down the stairs. He continued to watch until the man had crossed to the employee parking lot, gotten into his car, and driven through the gate. Only when the car had turned onto Germantown Avenue and passed from sight did West reenter the hospital.

There was a gleam of satisfaction in his eyes, the closest thing to a smile that he would tolerate.

—THIRTY—

Dressed in scrubs, paper boots and cloth cap, Dr. Kadish tied a mask loosely around his neck and stepped out of the surgeon's locker room. At the entrance to the OR he struck the metal plate on the wall with his fist. As the electric doors swung open, he read the sign with the giant red letters: STOP! RESTRICTED AREA! SCRUB ATTIRE MANDATORY.

He smiled as he passed into the inner sanctum, his private domain. His fiefdom. The entourage waiting within at the nursing station made him think of humble servants welcoming royalty. Which he was, to be fair. In his mind it would not be inappropriate to hear the sound of trumpets as he entered. Perhaps, after the breakthrough surgery, he could convince the head nurse for the OR to find a more appropriate musical selection for the CD player. Something with trumpets.

Kadish spied the cardiothoracic surgeon, Dr. Louis Defreres, and his physician's assistant at the long sink, scrubbing up to their elbows. As Kadish joined them at the trough, he said, "Louis, remember to keep plenty of cardioplegia in the chest. I don't want the donor to end up with a stone heart."

"I told you that I can keep the thing beating the whole time it's out of the chest if you wish," said Defreres. "The heart will be fine. So will the lungs. It's up to you to keep them from being rejected."

"I'm using Falcon's new immunosuppressant. There will be no rejection in my patients."

An orderly came out of OR Room 5 and came up to them, saying, "Excuse me, Dr. Kadish. Anesthesia wanted you to know, the donor's on the table. They're prepping him for harvest."

Kadish tore open a Betadine sponge packet, wet it, and began vigorously lathering his hands, wrists, and arms. Once he was done, he stepped into the operating room.

As the other surgeons joined him in OR Room 5, Kadish looked at the youthful, naked body laid out on the table. The surgeon looked around him, then said in a solemn voice, "Gentlemen, prepare yourselves. Today we make medical history."

Freddie drove slowly down Germantown Avenue, the cobblestones rattling his old Chevy Celebrity. He drove cautiously, knowing he wasn't in the best of shape.

I'm a solid mess, he thought. *I'm gonna take my sweet time today.*

As he drove, he imagined the look on Lenny's face when he read the knock-knock joke scribbled on the envelope in the Housekeeping closet. It was his best one yet. He chuckled, thinking of his friend's reaction.

Sure is getting dark awful early, he thought. *Must be a storm coming in.* The white lines in the road were blurry. He had trouble seeing the traffic lights overhead.

Squinting his eyes and leaning forward, he peered through the windshield, trying to make out the street signs and the dividing markers in the center of the road. But everything was so blurry, the light was so dim. And why did his hands feel like they were asleep? Like they didn't feel the wheel in his hands?

He heard a horn sound. It was loud and persistent.

What's that, somebody want to pass me? he wondered, peering into the rearview mirror. But his eyes wouldn't focus on the mirror, so whatever was behind him was a mystery.

He looked out through the windshield, saw a car directly in front of him skidding and swerving to his left. He jerked the steering wheel to the right and tried to jam on the brake, but he hit the accelerator instead.

A large, fat tree with branches reaching up to the sky came rushing at him.

What's that tree doing in the middle of the road? he thought just as his car hit the tree head-on.

His vehicle had no air bag.

He was wearing no seat belt.

—THIRTY-ONE—

The ambulance came screaming into the entrance at James Madison University Hospital, the red and white dome light swirling. As the big vehicle jerked to a halt, one of the paramedics threw open the back doors. By the time he'd released the stretcher from its floor anchor, the driver was around back ready to help lower it onto the pavement.

In seconds they were running through the big glass doors as Freddie lay strapped to a board, blood saturating the thick bandages wrapped around his head and his abdomen.

In the ER, Dr. Leanne Robinson and nurse Napoleon Pearl had the first trauma room ready. They scanned the portable monitor, reading at a glance the heart rhythm, oxygen level, blood pressure, and pulse while simultaneously releasing the straps so they could transfer the patient from the stretcher to the ER bed.

"He's got no breath sounds on the left side," said the first paramedic. "I tubed him at the scene, didn't get any blood from the airway. Pupils are sluggish, but he withdraws from pain."

While the physician listened to the chest with her stethoscope, Napoleon cut away the dressings on the abdomen, the better to assess the wound. Bright blood began to run out from under the bandage, dripping onto the floor. He pressed more dressings onto the bleeding area, but still it oozed bright red blood.

"Maybe he's on a blood thinner," said the doctor, noting the stream of blood.

"I don't think that's it," said the nurse. "He has liver failure; his clotting times are probably off."

"He does?" asked Dr. Robinson as she inserted a large IV catheter into Fred's groin.

"Yeah, he's an old alcoholic," said Napoleon, taping down a thick wad of bandages.

Dr. Robinson drew off a syringe of blood and handed it to Napoleon. Then she pressed on Fred's abdomen, feeling for an enlarged and hard liver.

"Be sure and type and cross him," she said, shining a penlight into Fred's eyes. "And get a blood sugar while you're at it."

"Gotcha."

After Napoleon filled several blood tubes and sent them off to the lab, he squirted a drop of blood on a plastic strip and stuck it in the glucometer. A minute later, the instrument's alarm sounded.

"Damn, it's over eight hundred. The machine can't even read it."

"You mean the glucose is off the scale?" asked Robinson.

"Yup. I'll get the insulin. How many units do you want?"

"He must be in DKA. Give him fifty units of regular insulin IV push."

"Okay," said Napoleon, hurrying to the fridge to retrieve the insulin. As he returned and drew up the dose, repeating the number 'fifty' to be sure he'd heard the physician right, she began unwrapping a cut-down tray in anticipation of having to insert a chest tube. Patience was already pushing the portable X-ray machine toward them.

"You want me to call the ICU and see if they have a bed?" asked Napoleon.

"We may have to send him to the OR for an exploratory lap; let's work on the unit bed later."

"I hope he makes it," said the nurse. "He's one of our own."

The doctor looked blankly at Napoleon.

"Don't you know who he is?" he said.

"No. Who is he? A hospital administrator? Someone on the board of directors?"

"He's Freddie," Napoleon explained. "The hospital morgue attendant."

Dr. Kadish stood at the head of the OR table gazing down at the young, robust body of the organ donor, like a priest before his flock. There were no scars on the donor's skin, only the small lesion on the side of the head where the neurosurgeons at Samaritan had tried to relieve the pressure on the brain by drilling a burr hole.

Thankfully, the effort had failed.

With a nod from Kadish, Dr. Defreres, the cardiothoracic surgeon, and his assistant made the first incision, cutting along the breastbone with an electric knife. The smell of burning flesh filled their senses.

In short order they split the long breastbone with a saw. The physician assistant secured a metal clamp to the side of the table and placed the metal teeth in the middle of the bone. With Defreres separating the breastbone with his hands, the assistant secured the clamp and began to turn the screw, prying the chest open.

They clamped off the vena cava and the aorta, leaving the pulmonary artery intact to keep the heart and lungs connected. They sliced through the vena cava and aorta and snipped the thick, ropelike nerves, of which there were several branches.

Once the heart was free, they went on to the more difficult process of disarticulating the lungs, which had more arterial and venous connections than the heart. The work was arduous, but made easier by virtue of their not having to preserve the other organs in the chest. The body was disposable.

As the heart surgeon worked in the chest, Kadish and his fellow worked in the abdomen, tying off arteries and veins, snipping nerves, and pulling the bowel out of their field of view. The deep purple liver glistened in the harsh fluorescent light.

Dr. Kadish smiled behind his surgical mask as he worked. His large hands were deft and accurate. He could almost work in the dark, his fingers were so sensitive, his movements so sure. He told one of the residents to go into Room 6 and check on Allendale. A moment later the report came back that the recipient was hemodynamically stable on cardiac bypass and ready for the surgeon.

After six hours of painstaking work, the team had all four organs removed from the donor. The heart and lungs floated in a bath of iced saline, the liver and kidneys nestled in a separate bowl.

Kadish looked one more time at the hulk that had been a man in a coma several hours before. The chest and abdomen gaped open. Blood mixed with saline half filled the cavity. The anesthesiologist had turned off his ventilator, the breathing tube having no lungs to inflate.

The transplant surgeon told the fellow to release the clamp at the chest, close the wounds, and sew them up. The body was bound for the morgue.

Removing his gloves and donning a new pair, Kadish led his team across to the other operating room. Following behind him, two circulating nurses carried the bowls with the organs as though bringing precious gifts to a royal wedding. Or a holy birth.

Taking a scalpel in hand, Kadish prepared to make the first incision in Allendale's abdomen, then stopped, his hand hovering above the skin. He turned his intense eyes on Jennifer, the third-year medical student, who was standing at the foot of the table.

"Would you like to make the first incision, my dear?" he asked. "It will no doubt prove to be historic."

Jennifer blushed, the color rising to her scalp. She hoped that the mask and cap would keep the others from seeing it. She stepped between two residents and stood beside the surgeon. When she took the scalpel in her trembling hand, she nearly dropped it.

"I'll guide you," he said. Kadish stepped behind her and brought his long arms around her slender waist. He gently grasped her hand and guided it to the lower end of the breastbone; then he applied pressure as the blade cut through the skin.

For just a moment, he recalled a similar position he had assumed the night before; then he turned his full attention to the project at hand.

—THIRTY-TWO—

Lenny pulled up to a narrow row house in East Mount Airy. It had a little postage stamp garden in front, and a welcome mat in the shape of a cat on the tiny front porch. He approached the door and rang the bell, his hair newly cut and blown dry, and no five-o'clock shadow on his face. He even wore a button-down shirt and slacks with pleats.

A little girl with mocha skin and big molasses eyes opened the door.

"Are you the *mailman*?" she asked

"No, I'm Lenny. I work with your mom in the hospital."

"*Too* bad," she said, closing the door in Lenny's face.

A moment later Patience opened the door. She stepped aside to let him in.

"I'm sorry, Lenny. Ever since my daughter got a book in the mail from her grandmother, she thinks any stranger at the door is the mailman again."

"Kids. They have wacky imaginations."

She led him into a carpeted living room with a glass-topped coffee table and plastic covers on the armchair and sofa.

"I'm just making the salad. Have a seat," she said, indicating the sofa.

"What can I do?" he asked, following her into a narrow Pullman kitchen.

"Would you rinse the lettuce and spin it?"

"Of course."

He ran water over the head of lettuce, pulled apart the leaves, and put them in the spinner. He ran water into the spinner as he turned the handle; then he shut off the water and spun the leaves dry.

A little boy came into the kitchen. His hair was cut so short, he seemed to be bald.

"I'm Malcolm!" the boy announced. He held out his hand to Lenny, who shook it.

"I'm Lenny!" said Lenny, drying his hands on a towel.

"Wow, your hand is hard!" said Malcolm, feeling the calluses on Lenny's palm. "Wanna see my turtle?"

"Sure."

Without looking at his mother, Malcolm grabbed Lenny's hand and led him out of the kitchen. Lenny glanced back, saw a nod of consent, and followed the boy up the stairs, the sister close behind them.

They entered a tiny corner room that had been carved out of a larger bedroom. The boy walked to a small a desk. Books were neatly arranged along the back. Holding up one end of the row was a small aquarium.

The child reached into the aquarium and pulled out his turtle, which immediately pulled in its head and legs. He held the turtle up close to Lenny's face.

"He pulls in his head when you pick him up. It's 'cause he thinks you want to eat him."

"I *am* very fond of turtle soup."

Malcolm pulled his hand away.

"But I only eat the soup that comes in a can," Lenny went on. "I'd never make soup out of a pet turtle." He held out his large hand. "Can I hold him?"

"O-kay," said Malcolm, casting a suspicious eye on Lenny.

Lenny let the turtle nestle in his hand. He gently stroked the hard shell. "Come out, come out, wherever you are."

Suddenly Lenny felt something wet. The liquid ran through his fingers and onto the floor.

"Oops, sorry!" said Malcolm.

"It's all right," said Lenny, laughing. "If you had any idea the kind of junk I get spilled on me at work. Blood and guts and ever worse. "

He returned the turtle to the aquarium.

"I better wash up. Where's the bathroom?"

Malcolm pointed down the hall. As he stood at the bathroom sink washing his hands, Lenny felt a tug on his pant leg. Turning around, he saw Takia, standing with an armload of dolls.

"Wanna meet my dollies?"

"Sure!"

He followed her to another small bedroom. Takia lined up her dolls along the head of her bed and began explaining who each one of them was. Malcolm came in to join them.

As Takia introduced her last doll, Patience came into the room. "Time for dinner."

Everyone trundled down the stairs. They were soon seated around the dining room table. Patience asked Lenny for his plate, which she piled high with slices of roast beef, a baked potato, candied carrots, and corn bread.

"Do you like greens?" she asked, passing him the butter dish.

He said he did, so she added a generous helping of boiled greens. Then she served the children and herself.

"We're goin' to the zoo tomorrow!" said Malcolm, scooping a big spoonful of candied carrots into his mouth. "Wanna come with us?"

"Don't talk with food in your mouth," said his mother.

The boy swallowed his food, then opened his mouth wide. "I ain't got no food in my mouth!"

"Then put some in it. And don't talk street in this house. Say, 'I don't have any,' not, 'I ain't got no.'"

The children attacked their roast beef while Lenny and Patience talked about the hospital. She offered him a second helping, which he declined. She offered none to the children.

Lenny suspected she was saving it for leftovers. He imagined the great sandwiches he could make with them.

Fred's blood ran out from his abdomen, staining the sheet crimson. Napoleon hurriedly spiked a new unit of blood and hung it. He milked the tubing to speed up the drip, but it wasn't fast enough for him, so he wrapped a blood pressure bag around the unit and pumped it up, replacing the drip-drip-drip with a rapid red stream.

"What's his pressure?" Dr. Robinson asked.

"Eight-six over fifty," called Napoleon. "I have epinephrine at ten mikes."

"He doesn't have the clotting factors," said the ER physician. "That liver is going to be his death. Let's get some fresh frozen plasma and a unit of cryoprecipitate."

"Right away," said the nurse, scribbling the order on a pair of blood bank request forms. "Is surgery going to see him?"

"I talked with the chief resident. It took half an hour for him answer me; they're all in the OR watching Kadish's big production."

"They going to explore Fred's abdomen?" asked Napoleon, entering vital signs on his flow sheet.

"Not with a blood pressure like his. The fellow said, 'I must have a mean arterial pressure of sixty or above to do surgery.' Like I don't know that."

Napoleon spiked a fresh liter of normal saline and replaced the empty bag that was hanging with the blood. He glanced at Fred's face, the mouth distorted by the endotracheal tube, blood oozing from his nose and mouth. He knew what the outcome was going to be, and cursed himself for coming in and doing overtime.

—THIRTY-THREE—

When the dinner plates were picked clean and the last drop of gravy was soaked up with corn bread, Patience told the children to help clear the table. They carried their plates into the kitchen. Then they went into the living room, turned on the television, and plopped down on the rug a few feet from the screen.

"Don't sit so close!" their mother called from the kitchen. The children crawled backward like a pair of crabs until they reached the sofa.

When Lenny stepped to the sink and offered to wash the dishes, Patience pulled him away.

"I'm just going to put them in to soak," she said. "You can clear the rest of the table."

He brought the glasses and silverware into the kitchen. After that he took an extra sponge and wiped down the table. When he was done, Patience brought a tray of coffee into the dining room. They sat and drank their coffee and talked, while the children sprawled on the living room carpet, staring at the TV.

He told her about his efforts to help Celeste and Gary at work, cursing quietly under his breath at his foolish joke about keeping the bed occupied by a virtual patient.

"If it weren't for me, they'd be enjoying a nice weekend, instead of worrying about where their next paycheck was coming from."

"Don't blame yourself, Lenny, it's not *your* fault that Childress and the rest of them can't take a joke."

"It's not?" asked Lenny, sipping his coffee and looking utterly miserable. "Then why do I feel so *guilty?*"

"*And,*" said Patience, pouring him more coffee, "why can't I get those kids of mine to feel the way *we* do?"

After nearly eight hours of meticulous work, Dr. Kadish and his fellow lifted the liver and kidneys out of Allendale's abdomen and placed them in a large stainless steel basin. The discarded organs would go to the surgical pathology department for examination. Dr. Defreres had already removed the heart and lungs, leaving the chest cavity strangely empty, like the engine compartment of a car without its motor and transmission.

Bright red blood flowed through the long, clear tubing of the bypass machine, keeping Allendale alive. The anesthesiologist sat by his ventilator, which was on standby, waiting for lungs to ventilate.

As Kadish and his assistant irrigated the abdominal cavity, Defreres signaled to the circulating nurse. She wheeled a cart over to the table. In the cart was the basin with the new heart and lungs floating lazily, like jellyfish, in iced saline.

"I have your plane ticket to Stockholm here, Martin," said the surgeon. He and his PA slid a plastic sheet beneath the organs. Using the sheet as a hammock, they slowly lifted the organs out of the water. With exquisite care, they brought the hammock to the chest. After lowering the sheet into the cavity, Defreres used his hand to hold the organs in place, while the assistant carefully pulled the sheet away.

Kadish's eyes moved from the readings on the monitor above the anesthesia machine to the surgical site. He glanced at the pump technician.

"Up the flow a bit, Tony," he said.

"Yes, sir," said the pump technician, a young man with a ponytail and John Lennon style rimless glasses. He increased the flow of blood slightly, watching the numbers on the monitor as he did so. He gave the surgeon a thumb's-up. The anesthesiologist watched the progress carefully, poised to resume ventilating the patient as soon as he had a pair of lungs to oxygenate.

The PA began to suture the trachea to the new lungs, while Defreres began connecting the aorta to the aortic valve.

"Pressure is ninety over fifty," called the anesthesiologist.

"O-two sat is adequate," said Kadish. "Ninety will do until the liver is in situ. Have you hung the second unit of fresh frozen plasma?"

"The second unit is almost complete," said the anesthesiologist.

"As soon as it's done, repeat the coagulation study. I don't want any excessive post-operative bleeding."

While he waited for the anesthesiologist to prepare a blood tube for the coagulation test, Kadish stepped away from the table, clasped his gloved hands together, and watched the cardiac team working in the chest. He glanced at Jennifer, winked, returned to watching the heart surgeon, impatient to take his turn.

Napoleon saw Fred's monitor go flat line even before the alarm sounded. Cursing, he called to Dr. Robinson, lowered the side rail of the stretcher with a crash, entwined his fingers, positioned the heal of his palm on Fred's breastbone, and began pumping.

The abdomen was enormous, bloated with blood and fluid. Everything they ran into him just emptied into the belly. Knowing the outcome was inevitable, the physician told Napoleon to go through a single round of drugs, "just for the record."

The nurse knew it was cover-your-ass time; you never knew when a family member would bring in a shyster lawyer or the Department of Health to review the chart.

Besides, they couldn't do Fred or anyone else harm —with his liver disease, he wasn't much of a candidate for organ donation anyway.

As she carried their dirty coffee cups into the kitchen, Patience told Lenny, "No, you can't do the dishes, thank you." She came back into the living room and stood looking down at the children. "Time to get ready for bed," she said.

"But Mom!" said Malcolm. "Can't we see the end of the show?"

"No! You can brush your teeth and get in your pajamas. Now get up there!"

"But—"

"I'm not playing with you, Malcolm. *Now!*"

The boy slowly got up and followed his sister up the stairs.

"They're great kids," said Lenny, settling down on the couch.

"They get on my last nerve sometimes," she said, sitting beside him. "Especially on Friday. But, yeah, they're okay,"

She put an Ella Fitzgerald CD in the stereo and adjusted the sound low. Lenny was just telling her how much he liked Ella when he spotted Takia standing on the stairs.

"Mama, will you read us a story tonight?"

"No, I have company. You can read to yourself."

"Aw, pu-leeze!" she said.

Malcolm silently came down and stood behind her sister.

"I'll read them a story," said Lenny, turning to Patience, "if it's okay."

"You really don't mind?"

"No, I'd like to."

Patience looked at him doubtfully.

"Really."

"All right. You read them a story, and I'll do the dishes."

Takia led Lenny upstairs and into her room. She picked up her dollies from the bed and placed them on a dresser, making room at the head of the bed. Lenny pulled off his shoes and settled into the bed.

Malcolm settled in beside Lenny while Takia went to a little bookshelf. She came back to the bed carrying a thick volume of Harry Potter, which she held out to Lenny, a look of pure innocence on her face.

"Wait a second," said Lenny. "This book is a zillion pages long!"

She shrugged her shoulders, returned it to the shelf, and selected a slim book, *Good Night, Moon.*

"This one's *easy* to read," she said.

"Good. I have trouble with the big words."

With the children nestled on either side of him, he began to read. Takia stuck a thumb in her mouth and leaned into him to better see the pictures. Malcolm leaned in from the other side, wrapping his small hands around his arm.

When he was finished with the story, the two children cried in unison, "Read another!"

"Okay, one more, but that's all you're gonna get."

This time Malcolm selected a book about a little black boy who hid his grandfather's false teeth. He laughed at the picture of the old man, toothless, struggling to eat corn on the cob.

As Lenny read the story, Patience stood in the doorway and silently watched them. A wave of emotions rose up inside her. She felt warmth and affection for Lenny, and at the same time, a pang of regret for the past three years, when her children had only her to read to them.

Her swirling mix of emotions was further complicated by a twinge of fear: What if this kind and gentle man would never come to her house again?

—THIRTY-FOUR—

"How is the suturing coming?" asked Kadish, looking over the cardiac surgeon's shoulder.

"Just fine; I'm nearly done."

Defreres and his assistant were finishing the last sutures for the lungs. The heart was already connected to the aorta and the vena cava. Pulling his hands out of the chest cavity and tossing the needleholder onto a tray, Defreres told the anesthesiologist, "You may ventilate now, but keep the airway pressures low; you don't have the chest wall to support the lungs."

The anesthesiologist connected the ventilator to the breathing tube and punched a button. The machine came to life, the new lungs puffed up, the heart lying quiescent between them.

"Nice work, Louis," said Kadish, watching the lungs expand and contract. "Warm up the heart and establish a rhythm, then get him off bypass, I'll begin work on my end."

While the PA irrigated the heart with warm, sterile water, Kadish signaled to the transplant fellow, who brought the second stainless steel basin to the OR table. Using another plastic sheet, they lifted the new liver and kidneys and gently slid them into the abdominal cavity, just as Defreres had slid the heart and lungs into the chest.

"Now comes the hard part," said Kadish, looking at Defreres. Ignoring him, the cardiac surgeon studied the heart, noting the rhythmic contractions and detecting no abnormalities in the wall motion.

"We have normal cardiac function," he said. "I'm taking him off cardiac bypass."

Signaling to the pump technician, Defreres removed the big catheter that had been delivering blood to the aorta. Holding the catheter in his hand, he looked up at the clock. It was nearly two in the morning.

"You're in for a long night," he said.

"If you get tired, you can sleep in the on-call room," said Kadish.

The heart surgeon chuckled. There was no way he was going to let Kadish take all the glory. He already had the lion's share of it, anyway.

When Lenny finished reading the second book to the children, Patience told them, "Okay, lights out."

Seeing the serious look on her face, the children didn't argue. Takia settled into her bed, while Malcolm jumped down and raced to his room. He dove under the covers at the foot of the bed and burrowed his way to the head, emerging with a fat grin on his face.

Patience tucked them in their beds and kissed them goodnight. Lenny waved goodnight to them from the hall; then he followed Patience downstairs.

Turning off the lights in the kitchen and dining room, she settled into the sofa in the living room. Lenny sat down beside her, wondering if it was time for him to go.

"Thank you for reading to them," she said. "They really like you."

"I enjoyed it."

She gave him a doubtful look.

"Really, I did. Maybe it's because Margaret and I never had kids. We wanted them, but she got sick with the cancer, and then it was too late."

"I remember the last time she was in the hospital," said Patience. You were so broken up, but you didn't let her know it. It tore me up to see her like that."

"It's funny, I never noticed you. Everybody was supportive, but they were mainly a blur in the background." He looked into her face. "I never knew you were there."

Patience smiled, saying nothing.

"Do you read to them every night?" he asked.

"Yes, every night. Sometimes, when they've been bad, I feel this voice inside me threatening to say, 'No stories!' But I didn't get read to very much when I was a child, and I want them to have something they can depend on."

"Why weren't you read to?"

"I was the oldest of seven. My dad worked twelve-fourteen-hour days, six days a week. Sometimes all week long. My mom worked, too, even when she was pregnant. By the time I was six, I was changing diapers and feeding the littlest one. The kids kept coming, and I kept working harder and harder. My mother had her hands full; she didn't have time to read to me. She was depending on me to read to the others as soon as I learned my alphabet."

"That's a tough way to grow up. My brother and I loved being kids. We got in trouble all the time, which drove my dad nuts, but my mom always forgave us."

"So did mine. Not that I got in trouble very often."

Spying a children's book on the coffee table, Lenny said, "Come on, I'll read you a story."

"Excuse me?"

"Come on, just for fun. Besides, I love this book. It was one of my favorites when *I* was a kid."

"I don't know, Lenny, it seems weird."

"Just one story," he said, picking up the book. "Now, you sit back and get comfortable . . ."

Dr. Alex Primeaux sat with Dr. Robinson, the ER physician, as she filled out the death certificate for Fred. Napoleon was behind a drawn curtain, wrapping the body.

"Ah can't believe he's gone," said Primeaux, his southern accent becoming more accentuated with the emotions churning inside him. "Ah just can't."

"He was in DKA, Alex," said Robinson. "I'm sure it contributed to his losing control of the car."

"Did the police say what happened?"

"He was driving erratically along Germantown Ave. He crossed lanes, then he swerved to avoid the oncoming traffic and ran into a tree." Signing her name at the bottom, she added, "No seat belt."

"After all the work we did getting him sober and fighting the cirrhosis. All the hospitalizations, all the relapses, he had to die like this." Primeaux felt tears threatening. "I blame myself."

"Why do you say that?" asked Robinson.

"Fred's last blood sugars had been mildly elevated. I asked him to come in for a glucose tolerance test. He kept putting me off. He said he was too busy at work. Ah should have insisted."

The ER doctor saw a nurse signaling to her from across the room. Picking up her stethoscope, she said, "Don't be too hard on yourself, Alex, you did your best. Nobody could ask for more."

Primeaux crossed to the curtains that concealed Fred's body. Taking a deep breath, he parted the curtains and entered. Napoleon was just about to close the shroud around the face.

"You want to say good-bye, Doc?" the nurse asked.

"Yes, thanks."

Alex approached the body, peered down at the face, now slack and discolored. Blood saturated a dressing on the forehead. The eyes were closed. He was grateful for that, not feeling that he could look his friend in the eyes, though they could see him no longer.

"I'm sorry, Fred," he whispered, touching his hand to Fred's forehead, "I'm truly sorry." He wanted to say a prayer, but didn't believe; wanted to turn back time and treat the diabetes before it got out of control.

Choking on grief, he turned wordlessly to Napoleon, nodded his thanks, and passed back through the curtains.

A few moments later, the nurse took the body to the morgue.

—THIRTY-FIVE—

As Lenny opened the children's book and began to read, Patience settled slowly back on the sofa. "*The Runaway Bunny*," he said, "by Margaret Wise Brown."

Lenny's voice was quiet. Soothing. As the words flowed gently from his mouth, her skepticism slowly gave way to acceptance. She began to relax. The words were rhythmic and comforting. She closed her eyes to listen more closely, finding contentment in the simple story of a mother's love.

When he finished the story, Lenny put down the book and looked at her. There were tears in her eyes.

She looked up at him with a face that was open and vulnerable.

"How did you know?" she said, wiping her eyes with the sleeve of her blouse.

He smiled. "Us union stewards get special training in childhood development."

She smacked him on the chest. "I'm serious. How did you *know*?"

Lenny shrugged. "I didn't know it would mean *that* much to you. I just had a feeling you'd enjoy it."

Patience sat up, put her arms around his neck and kissed him gently. Drawing her head back, she said, "Okay, you can spend the night."

"Huh?"

"You *do* want to sleep with me, don't you?"

"Well, sure, but–"

"There's just one thing you have to promise."

"O-kay."

"You have to leave before the children wake up in the morning. It's not that I'm embarrassed or anything, it's just that I've known you for years, but they only met you today." She looked into his eyes. "Is that all right?"

"Fine," he said.

She stood up, took his hand, and led him upstairs. After peeking into the children's rooms and confirming that they were asleep, she led him into her bedroom, silently closed the door, and drew back the cover of her bed.

Kadish and his assistant began the painstaking work of connecting the renal arteries and veins. It took nearly two hours, using fine sutures. Once the vessels were attached, Kadish ordered the arteries to be unclamped. As blood entered the kidneys, one of the connections began to leak, filling the abdominal cavity with blood.

"Clamp it off!" he ordered, lifting the leaking artery in his fingers to examine it, "and check the coags again."

Once he had repaired the leaking artery and been assured that the bleeding times were within acceptable limits, Kadish began the most difficult part of the operation: connecting the liver. With its many arterial and venous branches, restoring circulation to the new liver would require many hours of work.

He had just begun suturing the first small artery when the anesthesiologist called out, "Blood pressure is down—seventy over forty."

"Get the pressure up," said Kadish, "I can see his viscera turning dusky already."

"He's on a hundred percent oxygen," the anesthesiologist said. "I'm giving him neosynephrine and albumin."

"Do you want him back on bypass?" asked the pump technician, sitting on a stool near the foot of the table.

"Not yet," said Kadish. "Let's see how he responds to pressors."

Kadish and the fellow continued suturing as fast as they could in the cramped space of the abdominal cavity. Loops of colon had been pulled away and secured with clamps. As the blood pressure improved, the tissues in the cavity began to grow pink.

"O-two Sat is ninety percent," said the anesthesiologist.

"Keep it there," said Kadish, driving the needle through the silky artery. "What's the pressure?"

"Pressure is eighty-six over forty-eight. Pulse, one-fifty-two."

"I told you I want a systolic of ninety! I don't want to lose these organs because you can't perfuse them." He looked up from his suturing, glanced at the pump technician. "Be ready to go back on pump," he said. The technician gave him a thumbs-up sign.

Kadish called for suction. The scrub nurse sucked out blood and fluid from the abdominal cavity, clearing the visual field. He took a fresh needle and thread and began suturing another vein.

The anesthesiologist read out the hemodynamic values at five-minute intervals. The blood pressure slowly rose, the oxygen level remaining above ninety.

"His pressure is stabilizing," said the anesthesiologist.

"Don't let it fall again," growled Kadish.

Six and a half hours after placing the donor liver and kidneys in Allendale's abdominal cavity, they were connected and ready for a blood supply. Kadish ordered the fellow to unclamp the renal and hepatic arteries. When the clamps were removed, the patient's heart rate suddenly plummeted, triggering the alarm on the monitor.

"Christ!" yelled Kadish. "What's wrong with your heart?"

"It's not the *heart*," said Defreres, stepping up to the table and calmly squeezing the heart with two hands. "You must have released toxins into the blood when you unclamped the liver."

The anesthesiologist administered atropine. Defreres removed his hands from the heart and let it beat on its own. The blood pressure rose until the systolic reached a hundred.

Once he was satisfied that there was no bleeding from the suture lines in the arteries and veins, Kadish ordered his fellow to close the abdomen. While the fellow was using sutures to bring the abdominal walls together, the cardiac surgeon released the clamp that had been holding the ribs apart. He used a staple gun to wire the breastbone together.

""What's his latest blood glucose?" Kadish asked.

"Two-ten," said the anesthesiologist.

"Be sure the nurse in the unit does hourly glucose checks," he said to the resident. To the anesthesiologist he said, "Start the antibiotics as soon as he gets in the ICU."

When the wounds were fully closed and dressed, they transferred the patient to a bed in preparation for the trip to the ICU. Kadish told the team, "Once we've got him settled in the ICU, I'll catch a quick shower and a shave, then I'll speak to the press. What time is it?"

"Just past seven," said one of the nurses.

"Not bad. That's under twenty-four hours."

As they wheeled the patient in the bed out to the hall, the anesthesiologist asked. "Dr. Kadish, did you say that you notified the press already?"

"I had my secretary call them this morning. I expect international coverage."

—THIRTY-SIX—

Lenny awoke Sunday morning refreshed and relaxed, having driven home from Patience's house some hours before and gone back to sleep. He glanced at the clock on the bedside. 8:20 a.m.

Christ, he thought, *I never sleep late!*

It had been a long time since he had slept so soundly, and awakened feeling so good. He slid out of bed, walked to the bathroom, brushed his teeth. He gargled musically, then spit into the sink with satisfaction.

Downstairs in the kitchen, he poured milk over a bowl of Rice Krispies, noting, as he had done many times before, that the cereal didn't snap and crackle the way it did when he was a child. But, then, neither did he. He was finishing the cereal when he heard the doorbell ring.

"Damn Born Agains," he mumbled, going to the door. "Every fricking Sunday . . ."

Opening the porch door, he saw a familiar, unwelcome sight: Police detective Joe Williams.

"Morning, Mr. Moss. Got a minute?"

Lenny wished he was dealing with a Jehovah's Witness hawking the *Watch Tower*.

"I guess so." Lenny led the detective into the living room. Williams sat in the stuffed chair, Lenny on the sofa.

The detective cast his eyes around the room, noting the piles of newspaper on the floor and the old quilt covering the sofa, doubtless concealing the worn fabric beneath.

"You still keep a nice place," he said,

"You're not going to tear it up again, are you? The maid's on vacation."

"No, no search warrant this time," he said, referring to the time that the police searched Lenny's house as part of the Randy Sparks murder investigation. At the time they had a suspect in jail and were ready to close the case, but Lenny and his friends were investigating other suspects, interfering with the case.

Williams leaned forward, looking and sounding serious.

"I'm investigating the death of Colleen Creedon," he said, taking out a sleek new Palm Pilot with a stubby antenna.

"Nice Palm," said Lenny. "That's the wireless model, isn't it?"

"Yeah. It's great for getting faxes and reports while I'm in the field."

"Those things are pricey. Is that my hard tax dollars at work?"

"I have a friend gets it for me wholesale," said Williams. He selected a file and scrolled through it. "I understand that the room they found her in was reserved for an admission, but the patient was canceled. Is that right?"

"Yeah, that's right, the admission was canceled. Some problem getting HMO approval."

"Do you have any idea what the victim was doing on your ward?"

Feeling the detective's intense gaze, he wasn't sure he could bluff this man.

"I haven't any idea what she was doing on Seven South."

Looking hard at Lenny, Williams said, "I know you've got a special status at James Madison. You're the guy everybody talks to. You get all the dirt. You must have heard *something*."

"Not really," said Lenny, putting on his poker face.

"You were there when she was discovered. What did you see? What caught your eye?"

Lenny's mind went back to the moment when he'd seen Kadish and his crew go into his "empty" room. Then the page operator announced the code, and Gary rushed down the hall with the emergency cart. He stood outside the room watching, wondering what was happening.

"I don't know much. I saw the docs go into the room, I heard the page operator call the code, they worked on her a long time, she ended up dead."

"You knew the room was empty. Is there, like, a sign on the door saying, 'Empty Room' or 'Admission Canceled'? Something like that?"

"No, it looks just like any other room. There was a WET FLOOR sign in the doorway that they ignored."

Williams wrote WET FLOOR SIGN in his Palm.

"And you haven't learned anything more about her since Thursday? Nobody shared their observations with you?"

"Nothing useful," said Lenny.

Williams snapped the lid down on his Palm, looking unhappy.

"Look, Mr. Moss, I'm trying to catch a killer. Is it too much to expect a little cooperation?"

"Last time around you arrested an innocent man. If a bunch of us at the hospital hadn't come up with the right guy, Regis Devoe would be on death row."

"I told you then and I'll tell you now, bring me evidence that points in a direction, I'll gladly go down that road, no matter where it takes me."

"Yeah?"

"Yeah."

Lenny weighed the value of claiming ignorance against the value of trading information. It was a tough call, but there were things the detective might know that he would have trouble finding out.

"If I give you something, you've got to return the favor. Can you live with that?"

"Depends on what you've got. So long as what I tell you doesn't compromise my investigation, I'll consider your questions."

Lenny hesitated, recalling his own advice to the others that "Nobody talks, everyone walks." Then he thought of how he might turn the situation to his advantage.

Lenny told him about the traces of cyanide in Colleen's blood, which Williams already knew about. He pointed out that Colleen Creedon had been in Dr. Fox's office around seven that morning, and that Fox was involved in a drug study that Falcon Pharmaceuticals sponsored.

"Why do you think there's a connection between the study and the death?" Williams asked.

"I don't know there is one," said Lenny. "I just think it's worth looking into."

"Okay, I'll check out the drug study. What else?"

Lenny decided not to mention the missing dentures that he had found in the Number 2 endoscopy room. They didn't have anything to do with the murder, though they were suspicious. Besides, he had to hold a few cards close to his chest.

"She visited the Purchasing Department. The hospital owed her company money. She got there around nine-fifteen."

"I spoke to them already," said Williams. "What else?"

"Colleen Creedon was seen in the cafeteria getting very friendly with one of the doctors."

"Which one?"

"I don't know his name—"

"Give me a break," said Williams.

"Really, I don't, but I'm working on it. When I find out who it was, I'll tell you."

Williams continued to give Lenny a skeptical look.

"Hey, I've been off Saturday and Sunday, give me some time. As soon as I get back to work I'm sure I'll find out more."

"All right. I'll check back with you in a couple of days. In the meantime, here's my card. Call me if you learn anything important."

As the detective stood up and stepped toward the door, Lenny said, "Wait a minute; you haven't answered my questions."

"What's on your mind?" said Williams, standing in the doorway.

"For starters, did Colleen Creedon have any medical problems?"

"None that we're aware of," he said.

"What was the cause of death? The Medical examiner did the autopsy, didn't he?"

Williams looked hard into Lenny's eyes. "The report is provisional. The cause of death has not yet been determined."

Lenny said, "When you get the final report, will you tell me what it is?"

"When I get it I'll tell you, *if* it doesn't compromise the investigation."

"Fair enough," said Lenny, holding the door open for him. "By the way, who do you suspect?"

"You're number one on my list!" said Williams as he passed out to the sidewalk. He got into his unmarked police car and drove off, burning a little rubber as he accelerated away.

—THIRTY-SEVEN—

Kadish sang in the shower of the surgery on-call room. He covered his body with a generous amount of strongly scented soap and rinsed with scalding hot water. Finishing with his shower, he hummed a tune as he shaved at the sink. He put on a fresh scrub suit and a crisp white lab coat that had been specially laundered and pressed at his own expense.

He rode down to the first floor and walked briskly to the auditorium, where the hospital Public Relations Department had set up for the press conference. Dr. Defreres and his cardiac team were already there. *Fair is fair,* thought Kadish. *Let him ride my coattails, as long as I'm the one with my name on the Nobel Prize.*

Roger Lefferts, the hospital CEO, was seated beside the public relations coordinator. Miss Burgess, the director of nursing, and Dr. Defreres were seated beside him. The area directly in front of the stage was crowded with cameras and lights. Behind them in the seats were more journalists than James Madison had ever attracted. There were representatives from the television, radio, and print media. Reporters from Europe, Asia, South America, and Africa were there, along with all the usual American broadcasters.

Kadish stepped confidently up to the lectern, grasped it with his big hands, looked directly into the cameras in front of him as if looking at his destiny. Lefferts stood up, remaining behind him, as did the others.

"Pioneers, in every field, have always faced controversy. Even condemnation. I am no different. Some in the press, and some in my own field, have criticized our proposal to transplant four major organs at one time—the heart and lungs, liver and kidney. It is a breakthrough surgical procedure. It is unprecedented in the annals of surgery. And it is the first in a whole class of organ transplants that will revolutionize medical care.

"I must say, before talking in detail about what we have done, that our work could not have gone forward without the consummate skill of my colleagues, Dr. Defreres and the others on the cardiothoracic service, and of my own transplant service, in this immensely complex procedure.

"Just as important, I would not have the confidence to proceed with this pioneering work if not for the exhaustive research and the rigorous clinical trials which Falcon Pharmaceuticals has conducted in developing their newest class of antirejection drug, Imunox. All of the other products currently on the market are more likely to weaken the patient's immune system, which leaves them vulnerable to infection. But Imunox is much less likely to exert this effect, and it is only by virtue of its unique properties that I felt we could pursue this groundbreaking surgical procedure.

"Finally, I can report to you that the patient who underwent the quadruple-organ transplant is in the intensive care unit, that he is in critical but stable condition, and that he is following the anticipated postoperative course, with no unexpected complications.

"I will now entertain questions."

A dozen voices called at once, "Dr. Kadish! Dr. Kadish."

The surgeon pointed to an attractive brunette reporter. "Yes, my dear?"

"Dr. Kadish, we have heard reports that your patient is not awake. Has he suffered a stroke or some sort of damage to his brain?"

"Absolutely not. My patient was given general anesthesia for nearly twenty-four hours. It will take him many hours to metabolize the anesthetics and to excrete them through the kidneys. It may be twenty-four hours before their effects wear off."

A second reporter asked, "Do the new organs appear to be working? Are his kidneys producing urine, for example? Are his lungs delivering oxygen to the blood?"

"All four of the donor organs are functioning. He has not yet made a prodigious amount of urine, but that is expected in the acute phase of organ transplant. We measure urine function by blood chemistry, specifically by the B-U-N and the creatinine. Those values are within the normal range."

Kadish answered several other questions. He assured the press that the patient was accepting the new organs and that nothing unexpected had occurred. When asked what the patient's chance of survival was, he pointed out that in a new, extremely complicated surgical procedure such as this there were no prior cases on which to base a statistical probability. He nonetheless expressed his opinion that the patient had a very good chance of surviving, and he expected to see the patient walking the halls and chatting with the press within a week.

After ending his remarks, he turned the microphone over to CEO Lefferts. Lefferts spoke about the courage and forward thinking of the James Madison leadership, which made it possible to perform the breakthrough surgical procedure, led by Dr. Kadish and his team.

The CEO went on to describe plans to expand the transplant service to include harvesting and transplanting every one of the body's organs. He speculated that someday it might even be possible to transplant a human brain and central nervous system, although he admitted that there were many technical details that had to be worked out.

Lefferts ended his remarks by declaring that Dr. Kadish's procedure put James Madison University Hospital on the cutting edge of surgical services.

Seated in the last row of the auditorium, silent and pensive, sat Dr. Alex Primeaux, family practice physician and director of the employee clinic. He was not as confident as Roger Lefferts that the radical transplant procedure would turn out to be a boon for mankind. He had more mundane medical concerns, such as diagnosing and treating chronic diseases before they killed the patient, as had happened to his friend Fred Gopie.

After throwing a load of dirty clothes into the washing machine, Lenny called Celeste.

"Hi, it's Lenny. Did I wake you? You sound sleepy."

"No, I was just fixin' to go to bed. Me and my girlfriend went to Atlantic City yesterday. We was up all night. I just got in the house not ten minutes ago."

"Go ahead, Celeste. So, how do you feel? Are you down about the termination?"

"Not really. I'm not worried, 'cause I know you're gonna beat it, just like you did with Regis."

"That was a special case. Besides—"

Bleep.

"Excuse me," said Lenny, " I have another call. Hold on." He clicked over.

"Lenny? It's me, Moose. We got trouble."

"I have got Celeste on the other line. Let me sign off with her. Hold on."

He clicked back, apologized to Celeste, explaining that Moose was on the other line and that he had a problem to discuss.

"If it ain't one thing it's another," said Celeste. "I'll talk to you later."

"I'll call back," Lenny promised, then he clicked over to Moose, wondering what the bad news would be this time.

—THIRTY-EIGHT—

Lenny heard the phone click, asked his friend Moose, "What's going on?"

"It's Freddie. He crashed his car yesterday on his way home from the hospital. Lenny, he's dead. He died in the ER."

"Oh my God, *Freddie*? That's terrible. He was doing so great! He was working the program, he was going to his meetings. What the hell happened?"

"That prick West fired Freddie. Said he was on the sauce again, drinking on the job. He kicked Fred out of the hospital on his ass."

"And he let Fred drive home, knowing he was drunk? That's fucking unbelievable," said Lenny.

"I don't believe Fred was drinking. I mean, he was sober for a whole year. Why start back now?"

"His blood work will determine what happened," said Lenny. "Anyone in an auto accident gets a blood alcohol level; it's standard procedure."

"Can you find out about it?"

"I know a nurse in the ER, I'll call him. I'll get back to you when I know more."

He called the emergency room at James Madison, asked for Napoleon Pearl. Lenny and Napoleon shared a love of jazz, although Napoleon preferred the later Miles Davis, while Lenny thought the early work was stronger and cleaner.

"Nate? It's Lenny."

"What's shaking, man? You on the job?"

"No, I'm home. Listen, were you on duty yesterday when Freddie was there?"

"Yeah, I assisted with the code. He was fucked up good. Trauma to the face, spinal cord injury, internal organs. His heart stopped before we could get him up to the ICU. Too much internal bleeding. His blood was thin from the liver disease."

"Jesus fucking Christ, this is terrible. Freddie was doing so great. He hadn't had a drink for over a year. I can't believe he started drinking again."

"He didn't. His blood alcohol was zero."

"I knew it!" said Lenny. "But if he wasn't drinking, why was he in a fatal accident? Did somebody hit him?"

"It was his blood sugar. It was over eight hundred. He was in DKA."

"DKA. What's that?"

"Diabetic ketoacidosis. His pancreas wasn't making enough insulin. He couldn't metabolize the glucose in his blood, so his body switched to another form of metabolism. It made him acidotic. It would have fucked up his vision and his concentration."

"Son of a bitch! Moose told me that Joe West fired him because he thought he was drinking, but Freddie wasn't drinking, he was sick!"

"That's the bottom line, brother. West killed old Freddie when he canned him instead of bringing him here for treatment, no doubt about it."

Lenny squeezed the receiver so hard his hand began to cramp.

"He's going down for this, Nate. If it's the last thing I do, I'm gonna nail that bastard to the wall and let every victim of his sadistic methods have a piece of him."

"Save one for me, man. I'll wait in line."

Lenny hung up. He felt sick. His hands trembled with the anger and the sadness. He and Fred had been through so many battles together, not just to save his job. Fred had always come through for Lenny when he needed somebody to give out union leaflets, or walk a picket line late at night, or volunteer at the annual Christmas party. Many a year he'd been a drunken Santa, but always a sweet, good-natured one. He'd never let Lenny down.

Lenny decided that things were getting too complicated. He needed to get a handle on events. Even in a simple grievance, there were always facts that came out later, after he did some digging. The accused rarely told the whole story. The witness, intimidated by the supervisor, often failed to exonerate the accused employee in the hearing, fearing that he would become a victim of West's anger.

His mind began to sort and prioritize the things that had to get done. There was the funeral—he would make some calls and see that a collection was started on Monday, unless Betty was doing overtime this weekend. If so, she'd be passing an envelope around already.

He had to contact Freddie's family to ask what they needed. There would be food platters to bring to them, flowers for the funeral, cars lined up to take coworkers to the ceremony.

Then there was the incident itself. Lenny wanted to nail West this time. That meant that he had to interview witnesses to the incident, obtain Fred's lab reports, talk with Alex Primeaux about Fred's medical condition. Alex had treated Fred for years in the employee clinic.

Maybe I should leave it to the family to get a lawyer, he thought. But he knew he couldn't leave it alone; he was too angry. He wanted justice. He wanted revenge. A lawyer couldn't get down in the muck and mire with the workers the way he could. As usual, it was up to him to root out the facts and try to get a little justice.

Sitting on the edge of the bed, Mike felt the walls of his rented room closing in on him. *What have I done?* he thought. *How could I have been such a fool?*

He didn't believe that his wife would ever take him back. Not after he'd walked out on her over Colleen.

I've screwed everything up, he reflected. *Everything.*

The migraine pounded his head life a pneumatic pile driver ripping through his skull. He wondered if the headaches were God's way of punishing him for his sins. He felt that if he could just find a little relief from the migraine, he might be able to figure out what to do. But it pounded and pounded on his brain.

He thought about how much he had needed Colleen. Of the joy she had brought him. The euphoria. The ecstasy.

He remembered how he felt every time she came into the pharmacy. He could almost smell her perfume. Hear her laughter, like wind chimes singing. He could feel her full, wet lips devouring his, her fingers caressing him with maddening tenderness.

But she was dead. And for his folly, he was dead as well. Dead to his family. Screwing up at work. The police focusing on him, sure to arrest him. Soon he would exchange his cheap rented room for a jail cell.

What was the use of going on?

The headache beat him mercilessly. He was half blind from the pain.

He opened the box of ergotamine, took another syringe. With trembling hands he broke the neck of the ampoule of medication and filled the syringe. Rather than inject the muscle, as he had done before, he decided to inject it right into his bloodstream. It would either cure him or kill him, he didn't care which.

Using his belt as a tourniquet, he injected the ergotamine directly into the large vein in the crook of his elbow.

His head exploded in depth charges of pain and flashes of light. He felt as if his head had been blown open. He fell back on the bed, moaning. The last thing he remembered was darkness wiping away the flashes of light.

—THIRTY-NINE—

As Lenny carried his clean clothes up from the basement, he considered calling Patience. He wanted to tell her what a great time he had the night before. But that sounded stupid. He was thinking of the whole evening, not just going to bed with her. Malcolm and his turtle, Takia and her dollies. Reading to the two of them, that was so much fun. He'd go back just to hang with the kids, even without the sex, although the sex *had* been great.

He hoped that she had enjoyed it half as much as he did.

He decided to put off calling her until he'd tracked down Freddie's family and worked out how he could help with the funeral plans. He packed the espresso machine, made himself a double, frothed the milk, and poured a tall cappuccino. This was going to require some serious mental acuity.

After some thumbing through the phone book and sweet-talking the phone operator (humming the Jim Croce song "Operator" while put on hold), he located Freddie's brother, whose first name turned out to be Terrence. Reaching Terrence on the phone, Lenny quickly learned that the brother was an alcoholic who was *not* on the wagon.

"Hi, I'm Lenny. I was a friend of Freddie's," he said. "I'm real sorry to hear about what happened to your brother."

"Them's the breaks," said Terrence. "When your time's up, it's up. Nothin' the fuck you can do about it . . . Up is up."

Freddie's death hadn't brought him the gift of sobriety, that was certain. Lenny asked the brother about the funeral arrangements, explaining that he wanted to help.

"Why is it my job? I don't have two nickels to rub together. Call his sister, Florence—she's all high and mighty, church deaconess or some shit. She'll tighten you up."

After a good deal of haggling, Lenny managed to get the brother to find the sister's address and phone number. He thanked the man and hung up.

It's always the women who handle a crisis, he thought.

Florence, the oldest of the siblings, turned out to be a serious, devout woman who had helped raise Fred when his parents divorced. Although it was only one day since Fred's death, she had already arranged things with the funeral home. The minister from her church would handle the service. He would be buried beside his parents.

"Freddie spoke of you quite often," she told Lenny. "You were a good friend to him, and we thank you for all your kindness."

"He was a great guy," said Lenny. "I'm really going to miss him."

"Well, he's gone home to his heavenly Father. We can't feel sorry for him, he's with the Lord."

Making no comment on the afterlife routine, which grated on his nerves, he asked what day the funeral was set for.

"Burial will be on Tuesday, at one in the afternoon."

"I don't mean to be critical, but does it have to be so soon? I'm just thinking about his coworkers. It doesn't give people much time to arrange for the time off."

"Our church believes that the body should not be allowed to remain unconsecrated for more than three days. It must return to the earth from which it was formed."

"I appreciate your belief. Can everyone in the family get here in time?"

"Oh, yes," she told him. "We don't have a large family. There's a cousin coming down with his wife from New York, and my sister came up from Baltimore already. Oh, we'll all be there, I assure you."

He learned the name and address of the church where the service would be held, offering to send flowers. He explained that it was a union practice to take up a collection for the family of a coworker. Florence told him she deeply appreciated any help they could offer; the money would go to help pay for the burial.

With the funeral plans set in motion, he said good-bye, feeling a new pang of worry. There wasn't much time for him to collect money for flowers, or to organize people to cook platters of food for the family.

And how in hell was he going to get the bosses to allow half the hospital staff to take off from work and attend the funeral at one o'clock?

He made a few more calls to coworkers, starting with a return call to Moose. Birdie agreed right away to cook a big batch of fried chicken—she was a great cook. A laundry worker agreed to start taking a collection Monday morning. A technician in the microbiology lab offered to make up flyers and give them to the messengers to post around the hospital.

He noted the time, figured Betty would be back from church by now, dialed her number. He smiled, hearing her voice answering the phone, saying, "The Lord bless you on this day of prayer."

"Hi, Boop, it's me."

"Hello, dear heart. What can I do for you?"

He told her about Fred's death and filled her in on the funeral plans, ticking off the people he had reached so far. She promised to help collect money and to organize friends to cook for the family.

"But I don't see how we can go to the funeral with them having the service at midday," she said. "What church did you say she attends?"

When he told her the name of the church, she said, "Well, they're Christians, to be sure, but they're almost *Hebrew* the way they read the Old Testament. Still, all churches lead to God, so what does it matter?"

"I guess so," said Lenny, not sharing his friend's views on religion. "I just hope we can all find a path to the church in the middle of a workday."

"But we have to go. This is a very important service, Lenny, you understand that. We have to have the time off to attend. I could never forgive myself if I did not pray over Fred before he goes to his final resting place."

"What do you think is driving me crazy? I can't see Mr. Freely giving so many people time off. It might set a precedent that the hospital would regret."

"Well, then we'll just have to convince him of the righteousness of our need," she said.

He rang off, called a few more coworkers, then decided to go out for a few groceries. The fridge was bare. He didn't even have any beer.

-FORTY-

Patience was ironing the clothes in the kitchen, while Malcolm did school work at the kitchen table.

"Mom," said Malcolm, "when is Lenny comin' back?"

"You like him, don't you," she said, hanging up a set of scrubs and placing another shirt on the ironing table.

"He's nice. He likes my turtle!"

"He likes you, too," she said, feeling a rising warmth in her chest.

The boy looked out of the corner of his eye at his mother. "Can we have pizza tonight?"

"Sure. Pizza is fine," she said, letting the iron glide smoothly over her hospital uniform.

"For *real?*" he said. He was about to blurt out that it was Sunday, not Friday, then thought better of it. Instead he leaped off his chair and went running into the living room, calling, "Takia! We gonna have pizza tonight!"

"Oooh," said Takia, "Mommy's in love!"

Patience smiled, hearing her daughter sum up the situation in one simple phrase. Of course it was foolish to describe her state of mind with such *extreme* words. One night doesn't make a relationship. But she had known Lenny for several years. Had watched him suffer as his wife withered and died from the cancer. She had taken many of the X rays herself.

He was a good man. A decent man. A family man. It didn't matter to her that he was white, that he wasn't a hunk, that he didn't drive a sexy car. He was a loving man who enjoyed children. Hell, deep down he was a child himself, in a lot of ways. Not in the way that mattered most, though. In that way he was fully grown.

Lenny was in his kitchen tackling the dishes, the radio set to KYW, the all-news station.

"This medical bulletin just in: Dr. Martin Kadish, noted transplant surgeon at James Madison University Hospital, has successfully completed the world's first quadruple-organ transplant."

He stopped rinsing a dish and turned up the volume.

"Here is Dr. Kadish, speaking at a press conference given this morning at James Madison Medical Center."

Lenny listened intently to the doctor. He had no doubts about what the operation was about—publicity for the hospital. More revenues. Bigger fees for the attending physicians.

He wondered what the hospital was going to do with all that money.

He was struck by the arrogance of the man, who promised that the organ recipient would be "up on his feet in a matter of days." Lenny didn't know much about medicine, but he knew that somebody who received four organs at one shot was going to take a very long time to recover.

Something else caught Lenny's attention. Kadish mentioned the name of a drug he used to prevent organ rejection. Imunox. He mentioned it twice in one press conference. Lenny wondered if it was common for doctors to tout the manufacturer of a drug in a procedure like this. It struck him as odd, like a product placement.

He'd have to stop in at the Employee Clinic and ask Alex Primeaux about it.

He also noted who the maker of the antirejection drug was: Falcon Pharmaceuticals. It was obvious that the publicity from the radical operation would give the company enormous positive publicity.

Lenny wondered what role Colleen Creedon had played in the affair.

Elliot Fox sat in his recreation room. The children were out with their mother at miniature golf. He flicked on the television, a large flat panel suspended on the wall. The crisp high-definition digital image burst on the screen like an Impressionist painting.

A close-up of Martin Kadish came into focus, a repeat of his morning press conference. As Fox listened, the camera pulled back, showing the CEO, Roger Lefferts, seated beside the cardiothoracic surgeon, Dr. Defreres. Fox saw someone else seated at the end of a row of chairs, someone he recognized from past conferences: the area marketing representative for Falcon Pharmaceuticals.

When Fox heard Kadish praising the research and efficacy of Falcon's antirejection drug, he smiled. *Well, I guess they didn't get wind of the CDC report on the problems with their plant in India.*

He wasn't very subtle, Fox noted, but subtlety wasn't a surgeon's bailiwick.

The image switched to a close-up of the local news department's medical reporter, a slim woman with cascading hair and full lips.

Some Cuts Never Heal

She probably has a B.A. in biology, he mused. *Or English.*

The reporter spoke with unbridled optimism about the future of transplant surgery. She conjured up images of new organs bringing people back from the dead. Since the use of embryonic stem cells to grow new organs was decades away, said the reporter, doctors would continue to have to rely on organs from donors. And since the rejection problem had been all but solved by the new drugs coming onto the market, organ transplant was the wave of the future for nearly any organ in the body.

Fox took out the newspaper clipping from Friday's *Inquirer*. He stared at the picture of Colleen Creedon, wondering if the authorities would ever determine what had been the cause of death.

—FORTY-ONE—

On Monday morning, after punching his timecard outside the Housekeeping office, Lenny went to the locker room, where he put on his steel-toed work shoes. His Russian friend Abrahm was seated on the bench, polishing his shoes.

"Goodt morning, Lennye. I have heard the news about Fred. It is terrible."

"West murdered him, son of a bitch. The funeral's tomorrow."

"Do you want I should help collect money for the family?"

"Yeah, that'd be great."

"I will ask the transportation people, yes?" said Abrahm, carefully putting his can of shoe polish, rag, and brush in a Ziploc plastic bag and returning it to the shelf in his locker. His black work shoes were as shiny as a mirror. "And I will go to the switchboard."

"That's a good idea; everyone forgets about the operators."

"Yes. They are invisible. Nobody sees them. Who else you want me to talk to?"

"You stick with the operators and the transporters. I've got plenty of others helping me. Thanks."

Abrahm stood up, shook his head, and walked to the door, muttering, "Terrible . . . a terrible thing."

Slamming his locker door, Lenny climbed the stairs from the basement to Seven South. He was so angry, he didn't even notice his fatigue when he finally reached his floor. He walked to the end of the hall and opened the door to the Housekeeping closet, which was unlocked, the lock having broken a year ago. Maintenance, even more short-staffed than Housekeeping, hadn't gotten around to replacing it.

In the cramped room, he reached up to a high shelf for his leather-palmed work gloves. Beneath them was a sealed business-size envelope. Taking the gloves in one hand, he held the envelope with the other, scrutinizing his name, which was scrawled across the front in a shaky script.

He started to put the gloves down on Betty's cart in order to open the envelope, when he felt something slender and hard inside one of the gloves. Puzzled, he pulled open the glove and looked inside.

The tip of a very large and very ugly needle was pointing out toward him.

"What the fuck," he mumbled, stepping out into the hall. "Hey, Boop, come look at this!"

Betty came into the room from the hall, where she already had her Housekeeping cart ready for the day. She bent close and looked at the malevolent needle.

"Lord God almighty, how did that evil thing get inside your glove?"

"I don't know. I just found it there, pointing *out*."

Betty gripped Lenny's shoulder and squeezed it tightly. "Dear heart, the Devil is in this, make no mistake about it. You weren't stuck, were you?"

"No. I felt something hard when I picked up the glove, so I looked inside before I put my hand in."

"Thank the Lord you were careful." She retrieved her well-worn Bible from its place on a shelf, pressed it to her chest, closed her eyes, and began to pray. "Our dear God in Heaven, father of Jesus Christ, protect us from the evil that is walking among us. We humbly beseech you, dear Lord, gird us with your holy love, and keep us from harm. Amen."

When she was done, Lenny felt a wave of affection for her partner. Although he had no faith in spirits or other supernatural things, having been an atheist since he was twelve, he knew that Betty's efforts were heartfelt, if misguided.

"I'll take it to Tuttle and have him check it out," said Lenny.

Putting on latex gloves, he carefully carried the needle down the corridor to the nursing station, where Gary had just come on duty. Betty walked alongside him.

"Hey, Tuttle, what do you make of this?" said Lenny, holding the needle under the bright fluorescent light at the station.

"Hmm. Where did you pick that up, on the floor in a patient room?"

"It was inside my work glove. The tip was pointing out. At my hand."

"My God, were you stuck?"

"No. I felt it in the palm when I picked up the gloves; otherwise I'd have been pricked for sure." Placing the needle on the counter, he asked, "Can you tell me if it's been used?"

Betty looked on, concern etched in her face.

"Easy enough," said Gary.

Carrying the needle into the medication room, he laid it in the bottom of the stainless steel sink. Then he took a new disposable needle and syringe, spiked a vial of sterile water, and filled the syringe. Removing the small disposable needle, Gary connected the syringe to the large, lethal-looking one that Lenny had found in his glove. He pointed the needle into the sink, turned his face away to protect his eyes from a splash, and pressed on the plunger.

A long, black, rubbery strand of clotted blood squirted out of the needle.

Gary looked at Lenny, shaking his head in horror. "God only knows what that blood is infected with. If you had been stuck . . ."

Lenny looked into the sink. "What kind of needle is this, anyway?"

"It's a spinal needle. They use it for a lumbar puncture. It's so thick because the needle has to be strong enough to penetrate the spinal cord."

"Who would use it? A neurologist? A neurosurgeon?"

"Yes, they use them quite often, but almost any physician can do a spinal tap."

Gary lifted the needle and syringe from the sink and stepped toward the sharps container. He hesitated, looked at Lenny, who nodded his head, then dropped it into the container.

"Are the needles easy to get?" asked Lenny.

"Very easy. We stock them in disposable trays in the clean utility room. You don't even have to sign for them."

"So anybody could find it. A doctor. A nurse. A security chief . . . "

"Joe West?" asked Gary.

"It doesn't exactly have his stamp on it. He's more the in-your-face, I'm-gonna-pound-you-to-a-pulp kind of guy. But maybe he's learning subtlety in his old age."

As they stepped out of the medication room, Moose came up to the station. Gary filled him in on the incident with the needle, then turned to Lenny, his forehead creased with worry.

"Lenny, I hope you're taking whatever information you've found and turning it over to the police."

"Funny you should say that, Tuttle. I had a nice sit-down with a detective Sunday morning. We exchanged information. It was great."

"I know how the cops work," said Moose. "It was more like *he* wanted information out of *you.*

"I tried to keep it a two-way street. I told him some things, he threw me a few crumbs."

"But aren't you frightened by this threat to your life?" asked Gary.

Lenny considered the question.

"I should be scared to death, I guess, but for some reason, I'm not. I'm pissed. *Really* pissed. First Joe West fires Celeste and gives you a letter, then he kills Freddie, then somebody puts a giant needle in my glove. I'm sick of all the abuse."

"You ain't lyin'," said Moose.

"When I find out what asshole has been fucking with me and my friends, I'm gonna fuck him up good, cops or no cops, and West is gonna be number one on my list, the bastard."

"You and me and a whole lot of others," said Moose. "I'd like to strap him down and do surgery on him with a knife from the kitchen."

Looking at his friends, Gary said in a solemn voice, "If it's all the same to you, I'd like to be there just to be sure that he gets no anesthesia."

Lenny was turning to go when he suddenly slapped himself in the side of the head.

"Wait a sec, I forgot about the envelope!"

"How's that?" asked Moose.

"Under my work gloves there was a business envelope with my name on it."

"It might be a warning from the person who planted the needle," said Gary.

"There's only one way to fined out," said Lenny, reaching into his back pocket and pulling it out. He held it in his hands while his friends looked over his shoulder, everyone wondering what would be in the mysterious envelope.

—FORTY-TWO—

Tearing open the envelope and removing a sheet of paper, Lenny recognized the glossy paper and the slightly blurred font as a copy made on a fax machine.

"It's a preliminary report from the medical examiner on Colleen Creedon," he said.

Gary and Moose looked over his shoulder as they read it together.

"Good Lord, she was three months pregnant," said Gary.

"No surprise," said Moose. "You know there's got to be sex in shit like this. That's what makes men crazy."

"I've been thinking the same thing," said Lenny. He pointed at an entry on the report. "Tuttle, the mother and baby have different blood types. What does that mean?"

"There's nothing unusual about that. The baby inherits its blood type from one of the parents. Since it's not the same as the mother's—"

"It's got to be the same as the father's."

"That's right," said Gary. "She wasn't married; she was engaged to a man named Padric McBride. I gave him her engagement ring."

"Interesting," said Lenny. "I wonder what type of blood the fiancé has."

"No way you can ask him, is there?" said Moose.

"I don't see how." He pointed to the end of the report. "It says here, cause of death: cardiopulmonary arrest, etiology unknown. That means they don't know what caused it?"

"That's correct," said Gary. "She stopped breathing and her heart stopped beating, but they don't know what precipitated the arrest."

As Lenny stuffed the paper back into the envelope, he noticed writing scrawled on the back of the envelope.

"What's that on the back?" asked Moose, pointing at the writing.

"I don't believe it," said Lenny. "It's one of Fred's knock-knock jokes."

"Let me see," said Moose, plucking it out of his friend's hand. He read the joke silently, then broke out into a broad grin. "It's good. It's real good."

"Let me hear it," said Lenny with a groan.

"Okay, I'll read it straight through." Moose cleared his throat. "Knock, knock . . . Who's there? . . . Lenny Moss."

Lenny waited for Moose to finish the joke. When he realized that there was no more to read, he said, "That's *it*? That's the whole joke?"

"Heh, heh. That's all he wrote."

Lenny shook his head in bewilderment.

"Don't you get it?" said Moose. "Freddie figured, with you in the joke, he didn't need a punch line."

"Oh, like I'm some kind of walking gag?"

"No, it's not like that. You're the man who gets the job done. We don't need any more."

Lenny shook his head, unable to fathom the meaning of the joke, if there even was any.

"We've got to tie up our plans for Freddie's funeral," he said. Abrahm is going to the transporters and operators for donations. Moose can cover dietary. I'll ask Lottie to take care of Central Sterile and the OR."

"Regis is covering the laundry and the storeroom," said Moose. "You know he and Freddie were tight."

"Good man. I'll order a big flower display on my credit card and we can figure out the bill later. Let's meet at the sewing room at twelve and see where we stand." He looked at his friends, adding, "If I can just get permission for us all to go to the fricking funeral."

"What's the problem?" asked Gary. "The service is after work, isn't it?"

"That's just it. The family is having it on Tuesday, in the middle of the day, and I have my doubts that the administration will let us take time off."

"But surely they'll see how important it is to all of us," said Gary. The nurse looked at his friends, saw the skeptical look on their faces. "Won't they?"

Brrnng! Brrnng!

Alfred Desmond Allendale heard the sound of an alarm as he felt himself sinking down into black, frigid water. He felt the chill of the icy waters penetrate his body. At the same time he felt his lungs fill with water, bringing on the terrifying sense of suffocation.

His blood seemed to become sluggish from the cold. He felt his bones become brittle and threaten to shatter. He shivered violently, his muscles aching from the violent shaking.

He sank deeper and deeper. From overhead came a different sound: *Whoosh! Whoosh!* He thought it must be the props of a large ship passing on the surface.

The feeling of cold and suffocation brought him to a state of abject terror.

He flailed with his arms and legs, trying desperately to swim up to the surface, but his limbs seemed to be tied to heavy weights.

He thought, *They're trying to drag me down! My enemies have conspired to have me killed!*

Mad with fear, he strained to kick his legs, but they were pinned somehow. Feeling his body sink faster and faster, he asked himself, *Is there no end to this ocean?* Will I never *hit the bottom?*

-FORTY-THREE-

Dr. Martin Kadish stood impassively, listening to the transplant fellow's report. With each set of numbers, he pictured how the different organs looked inside Allendale's body. He saw their gray color, their swelling tissues. He could already anticipate the look of the cells on the pathology slide after they were removed and sliced for microscopic inspection.

The physician watched as Allendale struggled feebly against the four-point limb restraints. A bite block in his mouth was smeared with blood where he had bit his lip. *Better to bite the lip than bite through the endotracheal tube,* he thought. *Having to reintubate him would be a disaster.* The constant oozing of blood told him that there was no need to measure the bleeding parameters, the coagulation time was way off.

Which meant that the liver was failing . . . Which meant the body was rejecting the organ . . . Which meant that the likelihood of recovering was quickly approaching zero.

"I had the nurse give a hundred twenty milligrams of SoluMedrol," the Fellow continued. "I—"

"I wanted a gram of SoluMedrol, not a hundred-twenty milligrams," said Kadish.

"Uh, did you say a *gram*, Dr. Kadish? As in, a thousand milligrams?"

"Christ, are you *deaf*? Give him a gram of SoluMedrol, two more units of fresh frozen plasma, a unit of cryoprecipitate, and ten units of platelets."

"Yes, sir," the Fellow said, hurriedly scribbling the orders in the chart. He left to notify the nurse.

Dr. Singh came into the room and approached the bed.

"Dr. Kadish, good morning. I see that Mr. Allendale is in acute organ rejection."

"He can't be in rejection, I have him on the latest anti-rejection drug. It's a perfect agent. Did you see the chest X ray this morning?"

"Yes, I did. I saw some vascular congestion, but it appears to be more of an effusion pattern to me. That would suggest—"

"It's not an effusion, its congestion! Those idiots in Anesthesia loaded him up with so much crystalloid, they've put him in pulmonary edema."

"He is anuric and his coagulation studies are abnormal. Do you not think he is in hepatic failure as well as renal failure?" asked Singh.

"It takes a day for a donor liver to begin functioning," said Kadish, ignoring the remark about the nonfunctioning kidney. "Look at how long he was on the table, over twenty hours. He'll turn around." Facing the transplant resident, he asked, "Have you given him Lasix?"

"Yes, I ordered one hundred milligrams. He made only fifteen cc's of urine."

"He may have to be dialyzed until he gets over the acute phase," said Kadish. "Call the renal fellow, tell him to get his ass up here right away."

"Yes, sir, right away," said the resident.

"I do not believe that he can sustain a viable blood pressure during hemodialysis," said Singh. "You realize that, surely."

Kadish pulled himself up to his full height. Towering over the smaller physician from India, he said, "I intend to do whatever I have to do to get my patient over the acute phase of this procedure. And I'm sure as hell not going to let anyone withhold treatment and scuttle this breakthrough procedure."

Singh looked into the surgeon's surly face. Rather than answer him with logic and science, he turned and walked off the unit. From the first day of his medical career, coming into the hospital as a young intern, he had made a vow to never lose his temper with a colleague. After practicing ten years as a critical care physician, he was not about to let a pompous surgeon ruin his inner tranquillity.

Dr. Danielle Eisenberg had beautiful hazel eyes. Her face was plain and her figure, forgettable, but her bright, lustrous eyes were brimming with compassion and wisdom.

She knocked on the open door to Mrs. Cavanaugh's room, entered with a smile.

"Mrs. Cavanaugh?" she said in a quiet voice.

"Yes," said the old woman, pulling herself up to a sitting position. "Who are you?"

"My name is Dr. Eisenberg. I am a cancer specialist. Dr. Fox asked me to see you."

"I've been expecting you, Doctor, but I thought you were going to see me over the weekend."

"I'm sorry if there was a misunderstanding," the doctor said, standing beside the bed. "I had to wait for the pathology report to come back from the laboratory. That takes a couple of days." She glanced at a chair by the wall. "May I sit down?"

"Of course. There's no need to be so formal, Doctor. I'm just an old woman, worn out and not good for anything."

The doctor could see that this elderly patient had a lot more savvy than she let on. She suspected that she was going to enjoy caring for her.

Eisenberg asked the patient about her medical history: when she first noticed a change in her dietary habits; what kind of abdominal discomfort she had; how much weight she had lost.. She inquired about any family history of cancer.

"I think my grandmother had cancer. They didn't talk about it much back in those days. We don't talk about it much today either, for that matter. I don't know of anyone else, but I don't have much family."

"Are you married?"

"I was. I'm a widow. I've been alone for nearly twenty years. My son died twelve years ago. He was a wonderful man. He was very loving and dependable."

"Have you no other relatives, Mrs. Cavanaugh?"

"Oh, there's a cousin or two scattered around the globe. You know how these young people like to move around, chasing some foolish dream. But there's nobody in the world who cares about me."

The physician explained that since the CAT scan showed a degree of lymph invasion, she would be ordering chemotherapy before they sent her for surgery. She explained how the medication worked and what side effects it would produce. When asked if the chemotherapy would make her vomit, Eisenberg promised to order an antinausea medication that would ameliorate most of the nausea.

"Will I lose my hair, Doctor? I haven't any teeth, I have a leaky bladder, and my eyes are poor. Will I have to go bald, too? That would be terrible if I lost my hair."

"You will probably lose some of your hair, but it will only be temporary. The nurse will help you select a wig, if you like. The Rehabilitation Department has catalogs with wonderful selections of wigs and scarves."

When the doctor finished her interview, she wrote a note in the chart. As she got up from her chair she asked, "Are you sure you don't have any more questions for me?"

"I do have one, yes," said Mrs. Cavanaugh. "Will Medicare pay for the wig?"

The doctor promised to speak to the social worker and get the answer to her soon.

−FORTY-FOUR−

Regis Devoe was delivering the morning linen to Seven South floor. As soon as he'd loaded up the linen closet, he found Lenny, who was emptying the trash buckets overflowing from the night before.

"Hey, man, we're gonna go to Freddie's funeral, aren't we? No way I'm gonna miss his service. No way, Jose."

Lenny tossed a pair of bulging trash liners into a big wheeled bucket, turned to his friend. The young black man was a bundle of pent-up anger. Broad shoulders, muscular arms, eyes crackling with electricity.

"I'm ready to walk out, sure," said Lenny, "but we have a contract. We can't just ignore the language."

"Fuck the contract. Freddie was special. He was family."

"I loved the guy, same as everyone else, even with all the ups and downs he put me through. Kind of like somebody else I know."

Regis shrugged his shoulders, ignoring the bait.

"We got to get off. We *got* to. It was Freddie, man."

"I'm gonna talk to Childress and some of the other supervisors. If they don't give us the okay, I'll talk to Freely in Human Relations."

"That little—"

"Don't even say it, Regis. We've been through it before."

"Yeah, all right."

"The thing is, we can only walk out if we have everybody together. Our strength is in our numbers. One or two guys talking tough will just get fired."

"What should I do?"

"Talk to the workers in linen. And hit up the store room, too. Get them to see that we can all go to the funeral if we stand together. It's the only way."

"That's what you *always* say."

"That's because it's always true."

Regis slapped Lenny a high five, then he grabbed his linen cart and pushed off for Seven North.

After leaving Mrs. Cavanaugh, Dr. Eisenberg went to the nursing station to write out her orders. She found Gary seated at the desk.

"Gary, any questions about my orders?" she asked, placing the chart in front of him.

He scanned the physician's orders, grateful that he could read them without difficulty. The chemo was so powerful. Ever since an oncology fellow misplaced a decimal point, and a nurse on Seven North gave a fatal dose to a patient, he was extra careful with chemo drugs. That was why he liked working with Dr. Eisenberg. She always went over her orders with the nurse.

He pointed to the order for antinausea medication. "Wouldn't an intravenous route have a more rapid onset?"

"Not necessarily. Remember, seventy percent of the venous return from the rectum bypasses the liver. The first pass goes right to the receptor cells in the brain."

"I see what you mean," said Gary. "I only asked because I saw that memo from Pharmacy asking us to replace intravenous meds with less expensive routes."

"I got that memo, too," said the doctor, rising from her chair. "The Pharmacy Committee can rant and rave all they want about reducing the cost of drugs, but I will never, *never* order an oral or a rectal medication if it's less effective than an intravenous."

After the doctor left, Gary signed off the medication orders and dropped them in the pharmacy pickup tray. A few minutes, Hector, the pharmacy technician, came rolling up to the station with his medication cart.

"Hey, Gary, I got your delivery," he said. Placing a bag stuffed with medications on the counter, he added, "You seen Lenny around?"

"He should be out on the ward."

"I'll find him, thanks."

The young pharmacy tech pushed his cart down the hall, glancing side to side looking for Lenny. He found him removing trash from a patient's room.

"Yo, Lenny. What's shakin'?"

"Hi, Hector," said Lenny, dumping bulging plastic trash bags into a large bucket. "Is Mike on duty today?"

"Nah, he called out sick. He's got the migraine again."

"No surprise, all the shit we've been dealing with."

Hector stepped closer to Lenny, lowered his voice. "I hear you and Moose are looking into that drug rep that died last week. That right?"

"Yeah, we're poking around. Did you see her in the pharmacy the morning she died?"

"I sure did. She came, I don't know, quarter to eight, eight o'clock? I remember it was before I left on my first delivery rounds."

"I'm getting the feeling that this was a woman people tended to notice," said Lenny.

"Hey, she dressed to show it off, but it was very tasteful. Classy. She was the kind of women guys like me dream about."

When the young man made no sign of moving on, Lenny asked, "Something on your mind?"

"Tell you the truth, I'm kind of worried about Mike."

"Oh, why is that?"

"Ever since he went to this big drug conference in New Orleans about six months ago, he's changed. He's not the same old Mikey."

"Who was he, Tony Bennett?"

"No, I mean he's like distracted. He made a couple of mistakes filling prescriptions. Mike *never* screws up a script. *Never.*"

"Do you know if Colleen Creedon was at that conference?" asked Lenny.

"Yeah, I think so."

Lenny waited while Hector weighed what to say next. Years of representing people in trouble had taught him the value of patience. He knew that the truth was often the last thing to come out of a coworker's mouth.

Hector said, "What if a guy knew something about somebody he liked that made his friend look bad? Should he spill it if he's talking to somebody he trusts?

"That's hard to answer. Sometimes the cops use incriminating evidence to put the wrong guy behind bars."

"Like they did with Regis."

"That's right. And sometimes the friend is guilty." Seeing the uncertainty in Hector's eyes, Lenny added, "I often find that, when the *whole* truth comes out, ugly or not, it usually leads to the real criminal."

Hector slowly pulled out his wallet, withdrew a business card, handed it to Lenny.

"I found it on Mike's desk. I was delivering the mail, and there it was, tucked into his blotter. I wouldn't go through his desk, it's just . . ."

"It caught your eye, you picked it up."

"Yeah, that's right, it caught my eye. When I saw the message on the back, I figured it would be bad if the cops got it, at least, before you saw it."

Lenny read the name on the front: Falcon Pharmaceuticals, Colleen Creedon, sales representative. He turned the card over, saw the note scribbled on the back. *Must see you right away. Collie.*

"What do you think?" Hector asked.

"I think if Mike had something to hide, he would have torn up this note into a million pieces."

"That's just what I was thinking!"

"Which leads me to believe that it probably has nothing to do with Colleen's murder."

'Man, I feel so much better," said Hector. "I'm glad I brought it to you."

"Well, you still need to keep this just between the two of us. All right?"

"Sure, Lenny, you know I don't talk. My lips are wired shut." As the young man grasped his pharmacy cart and prepared to leave the ward, he said, "Oh, listen, what's the story with Freddie's funeral? I hear it's in the middle of the day."

Lenny explained how he was trying and get permission for people to go, but it was unlikely that the administration would give them the time off. Hector grew more and more angry.

"The hospital's so damned tight-assed. Hiring freeze. Part-timers. Suspensions. It can't go on like this, Lenny. I can't take it."

"I know, Hector. Everyone feels the same."

As Lenny watched the young man wheel his pharmacy cart away, he couldn't help but feel that the way the pressure was building around the hospital, it was bound to end up in an explosion. And explosions meant a lot of people would be hurt.

—FORTY-FIVE—

Dr. Fox stopped Martin Kadish in the hallway and slapped his friend on the back, saying, "You've certainly put James Madison on the medical map. I hear that *Time* magazine is going to put you on their cover next week."

"Don't believe the hype," said Kadish, "although I did send them a press kit."

"Your triumph is bound to spill over to every department. There will be more admissions, more referrals . . ."

"More for everybody," said Kadish. "Yes, I think the hospital's financial status will be assured for years. Decades, even."

"You've got a free trip to Stockholm, Martin. I have no doubt in my mind."

Kadish shrugged off the suggestion, even while a satisfied smile lifted his thick lips. At the thought of receiving the Novel Prize for medicine, his mind wandered to an image of a gorgeous Swedish woman making him feel welcome in a deluxe hotel suite. Perhaps she would be a physical therapist, with long, supple fingers.

The prize itself might very well be an afterthought.

Mae Yeung, one of the hospital social workers, came up to Lenny on Seven South. She was a tall, slender young Asian woman wearing a tailored suit and carrying a slim red leather attaché case.

"Hi Lenny. I just wanted to let you know, the inservice on domestic violence for the women in the laundry is set for tomorrow at seven-thirty."

"That's great, Miss Yeung. I really appreciate your setting this up for me."

"Oh, please, it's my pleasure." She took his hand. "It was a very loving thing, your suggesting this inservice. I wish we had more men like you, Lenny."

He mumbled a few self-effacing words, then broke away and explained that he had a lot of work to get done. As he walked away, Mae Yeung reflected on some of the ways that Lenny was special. She noted that, of all her non-Asian coworkers, he was one of the few who pronounced her last name correctly, saying "ye-ung," rather than "yung."

A one of a kind, she reflected. It had been so sad when his wife died, right here at James Madison University Hospital. At the time she wished that she had been able to do something to help him. Yes, he was a special kind of man.

And he was single.

After catching up with his work, it was time for Lenny to ask about getting time off for the workers to attend Fred's funeral. Among the many supervisors, he decided to start with Childress in the Housekeeping office.

Might as well start with the biggest hard-on, he reasoned.

Going to the basement office, he found the supervisor at his desk, speaking to somebody on the phone while scrolling through a document on his computer. He wore the usual sour look on his face, set off by crooked teeth and pasty skin.

"What do you want?" growled Childress, hanging up the phone.

"I've come about the funeral for Freddie."

"What about it?"

"It's tomorrow at one o'clock. Everybody wants to go. I think the Housekeeping staff should be given time off to attend."

"Who the hell is going to run the hospital if they all take off?"

"It's lunchtime. I was thinking you'd extend their lunch break an extra hour."

"Are you crazy? They can have their forty-five-minute lunch break and not a minute more!"

"But the church is in East Mount Airy. It's a good fifteen, twenty-minute drive each way."

"You think I can give time for every Tom, Dick, or Harry who croaks?"

"Freddie was different. Everybody loved him. He worked here for close to twenty years. Everybody felt for him when he was drinking, and they rooted for him when he almost died from liver failure."

"Cry me a river," said Childress.

"They only want an extra hour."

"Forget about it. You tell your people if they're late coming back from lunch break they get written up, and if it's their third infraction for the year, they'll be suspended."

"That's a load of crap," said Lenny.

"And if anyone calls out sick they better have a doctor's note or I dock him a day's pay."

"There's no provision in the contract for a one-day absence. You can't demand a doctor's note unless it's two days in a row, or a day tagged onto a holiday."

"I can smell a pattern when it stinks up the department. If they call in, they pay the price."

Lenny felt a burning desire to remind Childress of the role that Joe West played in Fred's death, but he decided to try another tactic before bringing out his heaviest ammunition. Besides, he'd learned that if you back a mad dog into a corner, he just gets more vicious.

"I'm taking this to Mr. Freely in Human Relations," said Lenny, turning and stepping out the door.

"You go see him!" called Childress. "And you ask him how he's going to replace all the people I just terminated when he's got a hiring freeze in place!"

Gary finished transcribing Mrs. Cavanaugh's doctor's orders. Curious about what type of cancer had been diagnosed, he turned to the lab section and read the pathologist's report. It was an adenocarcinoma, a very aggressive form of cancer.

He briefly glanced at the colonoscopy report, which was negative, the photo showing rolling folds of pink bowel. Turning to the gastroscopy report, he stared for a moment at the photo of the tumor. It was an ugly, brown, misshapen mass protruding into the stomach, like the face of a vicious animal pushing through a veil.

He found his eye passing over the date at the top of the form. Something about it tickled his brain. He turned back to the pathology report. The date was a day earlier than the gastroscopy.

That's odd, thought Gary. *Why would the pathologist date the specimen a day before it was collected?*

If the specimen had been collected late in the day of the procedure, it would have sat in the lab refrigerator overnight, and then be examined the following day. But that would make the date of the pathology report a day *later* than the gastroscopy. The opposite was the case.

Then he recalled how Fox had entered the wrong date on Howard Stipes's procedure note. He decided that the physician had his mind on more important things than his calendar.

—FORTY-SIX—

Moose carried a plate of hush puppies down the corridor to the Medical Records Department. Stepping in, he scanned the busy department. Nobody looked up. Ringing phones were ignored, faxes were printing out documents. A doctor at the desk was asking a clerk why "they" couldn't find a simple chart he had been requesting for two days, while the clerk kept repeating that the chart was not in the records room.

"How do you sort your charts?" he asked. "By zip code?"

"I'm sorry, Doctor," said the young woman, "the patient was discharged two days ago. If the floor didn't send it down, Medical Records can't be held responsible for its whereabouts."

The doctor scowled at the clerk, standing his ground.

"Would you like me to page you when the chart arrives?" asked the clerk.

"Will you actually *do* it?"

"Excuse me?"

"People down here say they'll page me and they never do."

"I can't speak for anyone but myself, Doctor, but I can assure you that when the chart arrives I will call your pager."

"Fine," said the doctor, writing his page number on the chart request.

As the doctor exited the scene, Moose went up to the young woman.

"Hey, Tiffany. Got time for a break?"

"*Break?* You *crazy?* I haven't even had my coffee, and it's supposed to be my day off."

"That's a shame," said Moose. What are you gonna do with all that overtime money?"

"Ha! Money. I'm gonna buy clothes for my little boy that his father won't cough up the money for, but let's not get on *that* subject." She looked at the plate of hush puppies in his hand. "Yum, yum. Are those for me?"

"Nobody else."

"What do you want?"

"Do I have to want something?"

"You're a man, you want something."

She saw Moose's face turn crestfallen. "It's okay, Moose, I know you're all right, Birdie is always telling me what a good husband and a good father you are. What can I do for you?"

He looked over her shoulder, indicating that they needed privacy.

"Come on back to my desk," she said.

They filed through a crowded warren of cubbyholes, past tables piled with mounds of charts, and a water cooler with an empty water bottle on top. Reaching her desk, she brought a chair over for Moose, who set the plate of food on her desk and sat down.

"Me and Lenny are looking into that drug rep that died up on Seven South last week."

"Yeah, I heard about it. The cops haven't arrested anyone yet, have they?"

"No, not yet. We're worried they'll find a patsy, like they did with Regis Devoe, so we figured we'd nose around ourselves."

"Okay," she said, eyeing the hush puppies but not wanting to take a bite until she knew what was being asked. "What do you want from me?"

With a deadpan face he told her, "I need a copy of Colleen Creedon's chart."

"Jesus Christ," she said, pushing the plate toward Moose. "If I get caught helping you, Joe West'll chew me up and shit me out his ass. Besides, how am I gonna get it out of the department?"

"You could put it in that great big purse of yours. It holds enough for a weekend."

"Honey, when I go away for a weekend, I only need an itty-bitty bag for my nightie and my perfume." She sat brooding, not looking very encouraging.

Moose said, "You know Lenny filed a grievance over the mandatory overtime the hospital wasn't paying, don't you?"

"Yeah, we talked about it at the last union meeting."

"He's busting his ass trying to make things better for you."

"I know, but . . ."

"Don't you think you could help him out this one time?"

"There's no way I'm giving you a copy of a patient chart—that's strictly confidential material. End of story."

She pulled the plate of hush puppies closer, peeled away the clear plastic wrapping, took one up in her hand. Her fingernails sparkled with diamond-like jewels in a swirling pink background.

Taking a bite, she said, "Did I tell you the po-lice called and told my supervisor to make them a copy of somebody's chart?"

"What patient?"

"That's confidential, too, I can't tell you. The supervisor told me to do it, but I been so busy, I haven't got to it yet."

Moose hung on each word.

"Now, if I was to accidentally press the number "two" on the copy command of the copy machine in that room over there . . ." she pointed to an adjoining room, "and if I made myself an extra copy by mistake, I'd probably throw it in the trash bucket beside the machine."

Moose nodded his head.

"When you gonna be using the copy machine?"

"Soon as you get out of my face and let me eat my hush puppies!"

Chuckling, Moose stepped out of the office. He went to the gift shop, bought a *Daily News*, walked back to Medical Records, taking his time. The office was still busy, two doctors at the desk asking for old charts, phones still going unanswered, clerks rummaging through stacks of charts.

He passed unnoticed into the copy room, bent down by the trash bucket, acted as though he were retrieving the newspaper from the trash. He found an unmarked manila envelope buried deep in the trash. He slipped the envelope into the middle of the newspaper, then made his way out of the office.

With the newspaper tucked under his arm, he walked to the sewing room to stash the envelope, feeling as happy as a newborn bird spreading its young wings for the first time.

—FORTY-SEVEN—

In the Pathology Department, Dr. Fingers was having difficulty concentrating on the slide that he was viewing. He took his eyes away from the microscope, reached for a raft of tissues, and wiped his face. His thoughts were of Freddie, and the manner of his death. A blood sugar over eight hundred. It was a tragedy. An abomination. Someone ought to have to answer for it. But who?

He felt a twinge of guilt run through him, like a spasm in the right colon. He wished he had been more attentive to Fred's health. In retrospect, the signs were there. The frequent urination, the thirst, the fatigue. Fingers had assumed it was all due to the cirrhosis. The symptoms were consistent with an old alcoholic with hepatic-renal failure.

When you hear the sound of hoofbeats, don't immediately think of horses.

He recalled the classic epigram from medical school. In Fred's case he had thought of the kidney, not the pancreas. Of alcoholism, not diabetes.

If only he'd paid more attention.

Poor old Fred thought that staying off the booze by itself would make him healthy. It wasn't enough. Fingers thought about that Neanderthal, Joe West. Why hadn't the hospital gotten rid of him years ago? He was a menace.

Which is probably why they keep him, he realized.

The doctor read Colleen's autopsy report again. He wondered about that odd finding, "mild thickening of the right ventricle."

Why was it thickened? She could have used drugs. Injecting drugs can bring on bacterial infection in the heart. But there was no mention of needle marks. Rheumatic fever as a child? A stenotic mitral valve? Pulmonary hypertension would increase the resistance against the right ventricle. The problem was, diagnosing a dysfunctional valve or pulmonary hypertension was next to impossible unless the heart was beating. These were functional abnormalities that were difficult to diagnose in a cadaver.

And there was that trace of cyanide in the blood. It wasn't enough to kill the woman. It probably didn't even produce symptoms in her. But the unborn child—might the cyanide have been given to produce congenital defects in the baby?

The findings were very curious indeed.

The medical examiner listed the cause of death as cardiopulmonary arrest, etiology unknown.

Fingers wondered.

Gary dialed the phone, sat back in his chair at the nursing station. After two rings, a voice on the other end said, "Toxicology. Muhammad speaking."

"Hello, Muhammad, this is Gary Tuttle on Seven South."

"Yes, Mr. Tuttle. What can I do for you?"

"I wonder, could you tell me something about how you measure cyanide levels in the blood?"

"I will do my best. What exactly do you want to know?"

"We had a patient recently who had very low levels of thiocynate in her blood. Is that a measure of cyanide?"

"Yes. Thyocynate is a by-product of cyanide."

"I see," said Gary. "Well, could the thiocynate come from another chemical other than cyanide? From a medication, for example?"

"Yes, of course. It is a metabolic by-product of several chemical compounds. Nitroprussic acid, for example, breaks down to thiocynate. Some compounds in industry—metal plating for one—give off cyanide, but we do not have such compounds in the hospital."

"Nitroprussic acid is a blood-pressure drug, isn't it?"

"Yes. It is a potent intravenous medication. What was the thiocynate level in the blood?"

"It was fifteen," said Gary.

"That is extremely low. Such a low level would indicate that the patient received a small amount of cyanide, in my opinion."

"What if somebody gave her very small doses of cyanide over an extended period. Would that produce a level in this range?"

"Oh, yes, most definitely. It would not be a fatal dose, you understand. I suggest that you speak to a poison specialist for that information. I am just a simple technician."

Gary thanked Muhammad and hung up. Although he hadn't learned how Colleen Creedon had been poisoned, at least he had narrowed the range of possibilities. That was something he could report to Lenny.

At eleven-thirty, Lenny was coming out of the stairwell into the hospital lobby when he felt his arm caught in an iron grip. Turning, he saw the shark eyes of Joe West staring at him.

"Childress told me you want to take your people out of the building to a funeral. On company time."

"We're a sentimental sort. You wouldn't understand."

Releasing his grip, West brought his face so close to Lenny, the custodian was afraid that the security chief was going to turn into Hannibal Lechter and bite his face off.

"Just be clear on one thing, Moss. I will write up any employee who leaves the facility on company time and remains out beyond their approved lunch period. They will be cited for being off site during their work period, and they will be disciplined for stealing time."

"'Stealing time'? What is this, an episode of *Star Trek*, the prequel? If somebody's late coming back from break, you dock them and counsel them, *if* it's their first offense. The language in the contract is cut and dried."

"Only if they punch out for their break. If they don't punch out, they're trying to get the hospital to pay them for time when they're out of the building. We've made that issue clear in a dozen disciplinary actions."

"Which the union has grieved. The arbitrator hasn't ruled on this issue."

"*I'm* the rule. You go out, you're off site without permission, you get written up. Period."

West abruptly turned and strode away, as if on his way to check the hospital's defensive perimeter. The clinking of the handcuffs on his belt rattled Lenny, who had no desire to lead his coworkers into an ambush.

—FORTY-EIGHT—

Just as West strode down the Seven South hall and disappeared into the stairwell, Patience approached Lenny.

"What did the pit bull want?" she asked.

"He's carrying on about us taking time off from our shift for Fred's funeral. Talking about disciplining anybody going over their lunch break."

"How are you going to fix things?"

"Fix things? Why does everybody always think that I have some kind of magic wand I can wave over the executive suite and make things right?"

"Because, my dear," said Patience, wrapping her arm around his and walking down the hall with him, "you never give up. You're as bad as my kids when they want to stay up late and watch a movie."

"It looks to me like you have perfect children."

"Perfect devils is more like it. My problem is, they have me outnumbered two to one."

"So you need an ally to even the score."

She pulled her head back and eyed him with suspicion. "Those kids could bend you around their little fingers without even breaking a sweat."

"It's more likely their mom who'll do that," he said.

She pulled her arm away and looked serious. "If you think you're gonna get lucky again with a line like that, you're crazy!"

Lenny raised a single eyebrow. He looked down at her lovely face, decided now was not the time to discuss romance.

"As I was saying, West is threatening to discipline anyone who takes extra time for Freddie's funeral. I'm going to take it to Mr. Freely in Human Resources. Sometimes he's sympathetic—at least if it means saving the hospital's public relations."

"You want me to go with you? I'm not a union representative or anything."

"That would be great. Do you have time?"

"*No*, of course I don't have the time. We've got a stack of requests in the department, and everyone's expected to work a double shift again. They can take their short-staffing and shove it. Let's go."

After Lenny explained the situation to Freely's tight-lipped secretary, they were ushered into his office, where they found the slim, slightly built man seated in a large brown leather chair that was too big for his slender frame.

With his handlebar mustache, paisley vest, and bow tie, he looked like a member of a barber shop quartet, which in fact he was.

Lenny made his request for extra time off so that the workers could go to Fred's funeral. Mr. Freely pointed out that they were already short-handed in virtually every department. "We can barely maintain our level of service with the people we have. It would never do to send hordes of them packing off to an afternoon affair."

"It's not an 'affair,' it's a funeral," said Lenny. "And you're short staffed because of the hiring freeze. That's not our fault."

"Be that as it may, Mr. Moss, we must work within the restrictions of our existing labor pool." He glanced at Patience. She cleared his throat, unused to talking to administrators.

"Mr. Freely," said Patience, "maybe you don't understand. We *loved* Freddie. We supported him when he was in a coma and nearly died in the ICU. I remember, I took his X rays. When he went to AA and stuck with it, we were so proud of him. He was one of us. We have to pay our respects."

Freely silently calculated the benefits and risks to the hospital's morale if he continued to deny the request.

"Here is my decision: I will allow the employees to combine their morning break with their lunch. That comes to a full hour, but they *must* go to the funeral in shifts, just as they do for their regular meal break."

"But that barely gives us time to get in a car, drive to the funeral home, go in and say a prayer, and then come back to James Madison," said Lenny. "We won't be able to participate in the service."

"Surely you don't want the hospital becoming seriously backlogged. That is what would happen if everyone took the time off simultaneously. It would produce gridlock in every department. Don't you agree?"

"But half the staff will miss the service," said Patience.

"I'm really very sorry," said Freely. "My heart goes out to your people, but I just can't oblige your request. It would set a precedent. Every funeral, bar mitzvah, and wedding would bring requests for time off. It would spiral out of control."

Lenny studied Freely's eyes. He considered proposing that the workers owe the time; a sort of time return in reverse. But it would be a Herculean effort to keep track of all the workers who took off, and very few of them were likely to stay over on the job to make up the time owed.

Rising from his leather chair, Freely said, "The one hour will have to be enough to pay respects, and then get back to work. I can't allow James Madison to be stripped of its workforce. I'm sorry."

Lenny walked with Patience back to the main lobby, his dark eyebrows furrowed in worry.

"I didn't think he'd go for it," he said. "It could have set a precedent. They hate setting precedents."

"You gave it your best shot, Lenny. Don't beat yourself up." Pausing in the lobby, she said, "What are you going to do now?"

"Moose and I are gonna have lunch in the sewing room and talk about things. You want to join us?"

"I'd love to, but Radiology is swamped. I'm transporting patients as well as shooting their X rays."

"That's all right. I'll let you know what we discuss."

He watched her walk off toward the Radiology Department. He liked her slim figure and the way she walked, fluid and silky. He recalled her taking him by the hand and leading him upstairs to her bedroom. It had been a long time since he had felt loved in that way.

As Patience entered the Radiology Department, she thought about Lenny's face. It was his eyes that she liked the best. They were warm eyes. Trusting eyes. They weren't the eyes of a man who was running a game. They were the eyes of a man who wanted to connect.

She smiled as she picked up a request and signaled to a waiting patient to follow her into the X-ray room, thinking how lovely it would be if he stayed all night and long into the next morning.

—FORTY-NINE—

Alfred Desmond Allendale pulled fiercely on his restraints. *Am I a prisoner?* he wondered. *Have I been kidnapped? This must be about money, it's always money. They want my millions! They've gagged me, that's why I can't make a sound, the bastards! I've got to get up . . . Get out . . .I've got to . .*

He heard the sound of alarm bells going off. The noise was painful in his ears.

What was that, a security alarm? The police must be here. The FBI. They've come for me!

Desperately pulling on his restraints, unable to move arm or leg, he silently screamed, *In here! . . .I'M IN HERE!*

At the patient's bedside, Crystal noted Allendale's rapid heartbeat and the low blood pressure. The cardiac output was up, but the vascular resistance was profoundly low. Septic shock. The worst number of all, though, was the temperature. Allendale's core body temperature, the measure of his arterial blood, was only ninety-seven degrees. Allendale was so sick he couldn't even raise his temperature to normal level, let alone run up a fever.

Dark red blood oozed from his nose and mouth, the blood unable to clot because the liver wasn't making clotting factors. His skin oozed yellow fluid as the serum leaked from the tiny capillaries, spilling into the tissues and leaking out through the skin. The white sheets were stained yellow and red.

After sending the nurse's aide to get the warming blanket, Crystal paged Dr. Singh to tell him the latest parameters. She prepared herself for a long shift without a lunch break. She'd be lucky to get five minutes in the bathroom.

Dr. Kadish stepped into the office of Roger Lefferts, James Madison's CEO. The surgeon admired the dark wood, plush carpeting, and crystal lamps. He thought, *The man has excellent taste. For an administrator.*

Lefferts waited for Kadish to settle into a plush chair before beginning.

"Martin, I'm concerned about your patient's condition. I've heard reports that he hasn't awakened from the operation. That he's in a coma."

'He's not in a coma, he's sedated. It's a residual effect of the anesthesia. His pulmonary function isn't optimal, true, but there's no indication that he has suffered any damage to his brain."

"If we can't give a positive report to the public it will look bad for the hospital. I understand that new procedures such as yours are inherently risky, that the first cases may not survive for long periods of time. Nevertheless, if the patient doesn't wake up, if he dies immediately following the surgery without ever accepting the new organs, you'll have a lot of trouble convincing the hospital's Internal Review Board to give permission for another quadruple transplant. It won't help the hospital's reputation, either."

"We have to be prepared for some criticism, Roger, you knew that going into this thing. I told you that the postoperative course would be rocky. There's nothing unexpected in Allendale's condition."

"I hope you're right," said Lefferts, pouring a glass of mineral water into a crystal goblet. "When will he wake up enough to communicate with you?"

"You can't predict this sort of thing. I hope that his pulmonary and his renal status improves over the next few days, but they may not. It's possible I won't be able to extubate him until the postmortem."

"*What?*" said the CEO. "Is he doing that badly?"

"He's doing as well as anyone can reasonably expect. He may recover, he may not. We're navigating in uncharted waters here."

"Developing innovative new procedures is one thing, that's well and good," said Lefferts, "but if there is even the slightest appearance that the procedure was ill-conceived, that financial reward was any part of our decision-making process—"

"The animal research is a matter of record, I've covered our base there, don't worry." Kadish looked at his watch, stood up. "I have patients to see. I'll keep you abreast of Allendale's condition. If there's any change for the worse, I'll give you a call."

Standing but not offering his hand, Lefferts said, "You have got to keep the poor bastard alive for at least seven days. Ten would be even better. If you don't, the press will eat us up. That will erode our client base."

"I'm doing everything I can. I can't perform miracles."

"And he must get out off the breathing machine so that he can make a statement to the press. That is very important."

Kadish stepped to the door, paused, looked back at the CEO.

"I'm a pioneer. I need courageous explorers around me. If you don't have the guts to take the hard knocks, there are plenty of other medical centers who do."

He turned and walked out.

"Yo, Moose!"

Smooch, a dietary worker, came up to Moose, who was working on the food line reading menus and filling the plates with the proper food items. As each tray rolled by him on the conveyer belt, a dietary worker dropped an appropriate item onto the tray: a carton of milk, a cup of coffee or tea, a slice of bread and tab of butter.

"What's up, baby?" he said, looking up from a tray of meat loaf and smiling at the cafeteria worker.

"I was watching the news last night, and they had a thing about that big-time transplant they did here."

"Yeah . . ."

"It's that doctor, the one that done the surgery," she said.

"Kadish?"

"That's him. He's the guy."

"What guy?"

"He's the guy I seen in the cafeteria with that lady drug salesman that got herself killed."

"Really. You sure?"

"Sure I'm sure. She just about had her tongue in his fly. It was him, all right."

"Heh, heh. Thanks, Smooch. I'll tell Lenny as soon as I see him."

He turned back and scooped a helping of roast beef onto a plate. Moose was so happy with the news, he dipped into the serving tray and gave the patient a double portion.

"Your chemo's here," said Hector, placing on the counter a thick plastic bag with a large label reading,

DANGER: HAZARDOUS MATERIALS.
DISPOSE OF IN PROPER CONTAINER.

Gary placed the medication in the refrigerator. He decided to give it after lunch. That would give Mrs. Cavanaugh a chance to get her lunch down before she lost her appetite.

He called the cafeteria and asked to change Mrs. Cavanaugh's diet to a light lunch. The low-fat food would empty from her stomach more rapidly, leaving less food to vomit in case she became nauseous.

"Will cottage cheese and a fruit platter be all right?" asked the dietary clerk.

"That will be fine," said Gary. "And tea, no milk."

"Tea, no milk. I'll send up a wedge of lemon with it."

"That will be great. Thanks."

Gary placed the thick bag of chemotherapy with its bright orange warning label in the fridge that was labeled NO FOOD ALLOWED ONLY FOR MEDICATIONS.

He hated to give chemotherapy, it was such a toxic medication. Just handling the intravenous bag put him in danger of developing a blood disorder, were the medication to come in contact with his skin and be absorbed.

He considered that perhaps a disease as insidious and remorseless as cancer needed a treatment that was equally bad.

—FIFTY—

Brrang! Brrang!

Allendale's ventilator alarm was loud enough to be heard all the way down at the other end of the ICU. Rushing to the room, Crystal saw that the patient was fiercely biting the breathing tube, preventing the ventilator from forcing air into his lungs, and setting off the alarm.

"Mr. Allendale, you have to stop biting the tube, you're cutting off your airway!"

Allendale thrashed wildly in the bed. He shook his head back and forth, separating the flexible oxygen tubing from the breathing tube in his mouth. The nurse hurriedly put on latex gloves and reconnected the tube, calling out, "Somebody draw up some Dyazine! I need to sedate this man!"

Allendale strained at his wrist restraints, pulling so hard that the veins on his neck bulged and his face turned purple, the ventilator shrieking all the while: Brrannng! Brrannng!

The patient's lips were turning blue; his face, ashen.

"*I need that Dyazine!*" she cried.

A resident rushed into the room. He reached for an ambu bag hanging from the wall, disconnected the ventilator, and began manually ventilating the patient.

"There's a lot of resistance," he said. "I can hardly get air in him."

"He's bit through the endotracheal tube!" said Crystal. She yelled out to the desk, "We have to reintubate. Page anesthesia STAT!"

A second nurse came running into the room with a syringe filled with sedation. She screwed the syringe into the port on the IV tubing and injected one cc. Then she watched the monitor to see how much the blood pressure would drop.

"Don't worry about his pressure, I'll dial up his epinephrine," said Crystal. "Give him more sedation."

With the second dose of sedation, the patient began to calm down. His limbs relaxed and he stopped biting the tube.

"He's ventilating much easier," said the resident.

Crystal pulled apart the patient's lips and inspected the tube. She could see the tear in the soft plastic where Allendale had bitten though the soft plastic.

Moments later a young anesthesia resident rushed into the room carrying his tackle box. He was a baby-faced Korean man with a perpetual smile on his lips. As soon as he saw that it was Allendale, Dr. Kadish's quadruple organ transplant, his smile washed away.

"You bag the patient, he be okay," said the young resident. "I get Dr. Singh." He hurried out of the room to call his supervisor.

Moments later, Dr. Singh came in. He asked the anesthesia resident for the fiberoptic scope. The young resident pulled it out of his tackle box and handed it to the attending, who ran the scope through a fresh endotracheal tube. He ordered the resident to untape the leaking tube and remove it.

As soon as the old tube was out, Singh placed the tip of the new one in the patient's mouth. Peering into the lens of the scope, he advanced the scope, searching for the opening to the trachea.

"Suction, please," he said. "There is a great deal of laryngeal edema and bleeding. The visual field is obscured."

Crystal looked up at the monitor.

"His O-two sat is eighty-five," she said.

Singh used a suction tube to remove some of the blood. He found the trachea and advanced the tube past the vocal chords.

"O-two is eighty," said Crystal. "Seventy-nine . . . seventy-eight."

In seconds Singh had the new tube in place. While Crystal delivered large volumes of oxygen with an ambu bag, the resident listened with his stethoscope for breath sounds, carefully going over all the lung fields. The smile returned to his face.

"Tube is good," he said. "Don't need x-ray." The resident helped Crystal tape it securely in place. They reattached the ventilator. The oxygen level slowly rose. It did not reach ninety.

"His color is still poor," said Singh. "Let's get a blood gas. I'm going to increase the PEEP." He stepped over to the ventilator and began to adjust the dials. Crystal looked at the doctor with new anxiety.

"Aren't you worried about a pneumothorax?" she asked. "I don't think the patient could survive a collapsed lung."

"I know it is risky," he said, "but if we do not improve his oxygenation, his donor organs will not survive." Completing his adjustments, he stepped back, looked at the patient, and added, "I do not believe he will survive, no matter what we do."

—FIFTY-ONE—

Moose and Gary were sitting beside Birdie in the sewing room when Lenny came in with a sandwich and a cup of coffee. "That Freely is a fricking pain," he said, putting down his coffee and opening a battered folding chair. "He won't give us any more time for the funeral than our regular lunch hour combined with the morning break."

"That's a whole lot of nothin'," said Moose, "but it's just the first round. You got to be ready to go the distance. That's why I've been dragging your sorry ass out to Fairmont Park, to get you in fighting shape."

"I don't mind going toe to toe with West or with Freely," said Lenny, "I just wish we had more information. There's a lot of stuff the police can get their hands on that we can't."

"We got the medical examiner's report," said Moose.

"Yeah, but it doesn't give us the cause of death."

"Can I see that report again?" asked Gary.

Lenny handed it to him.

Gary pointed out that there were no needle marks on the body, other than the one in the groin where the resident had inserted the central venous catheter. "I was trying to discover how the cyanide was introduced into her system," he explained. "There's a blood pressure medication that breaks down into thiocynate, just as cyanide does, but it's only given intravenously. You can't give it by mouth, the stomach acid breaks it down."

"Moose told me about the poison," said Birdie, holding up a sheet to decide if it was so small that it had to be made into pillowcases. "I was thinking maybe the cyanide was supposed to cause a miscarriage, not kill the mother."

"Will cyanide do that?" asked Lenny, looking at Gary.

"I don't know. I didn't see anything about it in the articles I read. If it doesn't cause an actual miscarriage, it's possible that it was given in order to hurt the baby."

"Why would a father want to do that?" asked Lenny.

"You know why," said Moose. "Jealousy. Revenge. He could be a psycho. Could be lots of reasons."

"Poisoning a woman to make a defective child—that's a sorrowful thing to happen to a mother," said Birdie.

"I remember when you lost your first baby," said Lenny. "Moose was afraid you'd never get pregnant again."

"We got to be dealing with one sick motherfucker, do something like that," said Moose.

"Well," said Lenny, "we have to find out who the intended victim was, the mother or the baby. It's a shame we don't have her hospital records. They might shed some light on what happened."

"Heh, heh." Moose grinned as he unfolded the *Daily News*, pulled out the manila envelope, and handed it to Lenny. "Take a look at what I found in the trash."

"Holy shit!" said Lenny, recognizing the hospital logo on the paper, "it's a copy of her chart!" He looked at Moose with wonder and admiration. "You're my hero, Moose."

"Patient records are strictly confidential," said Gary, anxiety now deeply rooted in his face. "If you get caught with something like that, it's grounds for immediate dismissal. There may even be criminal charges." Seeing that Moose and Lenny were unfazed, he added, "I understand that it's cool to be blasé in the face of danger, but this is serious. You could both end up in real trouble."

"Life ain't worth a damn if you don't take a few risks," said Moose. "That's why I spent time in the ring. I knew I could get hurt. I only left when our kids were born."

"I'm not making light of your concern, Tuttle. We'll hide the stuff as soon as we take a look at it."

Lenny read a few lines, struggling over the sloppy handwriting as well as the unfamiliar language. After trying with marginal success to comprehend the first page, he said, "I'm no nurse, I can't read half this stuff." He turned to Gary, put a puppy-dog look on his face. "Tuttle, do you suppose you could . . . "

Gary stared at Lenny for a minute. Finally he sighed, pulling his chair closer. He read the doctor's notes aloud. They described the cardiac arrest and the efforts at resuscitation in cold, clinical detail.

"Any mention of something that could have caused the arrest?" asked Lenny.

"No, nothing like that," said Gary. "Besides, her toxicology report was negative." He reminded them that the level of cyanide was so low that it could not have caused the arrest.

He went on to read the nursing notes, which supported the doctor's observations. There was no sign of trauma or prior illness, except for the vaginal infection.

"Doesn't that mean she was getting some on the side?" asked Moose.

"Not necessarily," said Gary. "We would have to know what the organism was, and if her fiancé gave it to her."

"I bet he was cheatin' on her," said Birdie. "Lots of women get AIDS from their boyfriend or husband, and they never even go outside the house."

"I'm afraid we're going to have to talk to the fiancé at some point," said Lenny. "I just don't know how I can get him to talk to me."

"You'll get him to open up," said Moose. "Trust me. Everybody talks to you." Moose took a sip of black coffee. "We got to find out who gave her that poison."

"Let's go over who she saw that morning," said Lenny. "We know she visited the GI lab at seven in the morning. She was in talking with Dr. Fox with the door closed. Tina said it held up the first procedure. She left around seven-twenty."

"Where'd she go then?" asked Moose.

"The pharmacy. Hector saw her around quarter to eight. She left about eight-thirty."

"I found out she was in the Purchasing Department a little after nine, right after Emily opened the office. She stayed there about a half hour."

"Did she say anything to Emily about a problem?" asked Lenny. "Was anybody giving her trouble?"

"She didn't discuss anything unusual. The hospital was slow paying her company, but they were always slow. Money's tight, or so they say."

"The hospital loves to cry poverty," said Lenny. "They have money stashed in all kinds of funds." He washed down a mouthful of sandwich with coffee, then added, "I heard that Mike DiPietro has gone through some changes ever since he came back from a drug conference in New Orleans."

"That's sin city," said Birdie. "I heard he left his wife. They say he's living in some rooming house somewhere. You think there's a connection?"

"Colleen Creedon went to the conference, too," said Lenny. "Besides, I can't help thinking that a pharmacist might know a really sneaky way to poison someone. Some formula that's almost impossible to detect."

"Michael DiPietro kill somebody?" said Gary. "That's absurd. There is no way he would be involved with something like that. Mike is as decent a human being as you will find on this earth."

"There's more, Tuttle. I found a note that Colleen Creedon wrote that was tucked in the blotter of his desk. It said, 'I have to see you right away.' It could be nothing, it could be trouble."

"Did you ask him about it?" asked Moose.

"I couldn't, he's out sick."

"Love can make a man do crazy things," said Moose. "I know, I married Birdie."

She smacked him in the back of the head, then smiled as she fed another sheet through the sewing machine.

-FIFTY-TWO-

Finishing the last of his sandwich, Lenny said, "Maybe Gary's right. Maybe we shouldn't look at Mike as a suspect. He didn't even see her that morning, he was mixing chemotherapy drugs down the hall."

"I'd like to know what she and Dr. Fox was talking about behind that closed door," said Birdie.

Lenny told them what he knew about the study drug that Fox was working with in the GI lab. "He's getting paid for the study. I don't see that giving him a motive to kill her."

"Maybe there was something phony in his results," Moose. "If she found out, she might've threatened to expose him, so he kills her to keep her quiet."

"Speaking of Dr. Fox . . . " said Gary, looking at his friends.

"Spit it out, Tuttle, you're among friends."

"It's probably nothing, but I was looking at the procedure notes from the GI lab on Mrs. Cavanaugh—you remember, the woman who was missing the dentures?"

"Sure," said Lenny.

"Well, the date of the pathology report on her stomach ulcer was one day, but the date on Dr. Fox's procedure note when he took the biopsy was for the following day. She couldn't have gone to the GI lab that day, there was no order to make her NPO, and no nursing note that documented her going down for the procedure."

"He could've just got the date mixed up, couldn't he?" said Birdie.

"Normally I would think that was the reason and just ignore it. But Dr. Fox made the same mistake with another patient. He's normally very meticulous. Not just with his writing, but with all his orders."

"A wrong date doesn't sound like much," said Lenny. "I can never remember what day it is myself."

"Remember how you asked me why somebody would remove dentures on a patient who was having a procedure on the colon?"

"The hose up the ass, of course I remember. I figured Dr. Fox looked down her throat the same day, but I didn't have an idea why Tina would hide it from me."

"The date on the pathology report can only mean one thing," said Gary. "They did both procedures on the same day, probably during the same visit to the GI lab."

"Why, Tuttle. You're becoming a regular Columbo," said Lenny. "Now if somebody could tell me how I'm going to get Tina to tell me what the hell's going on down in her department . . . "

Moose said, "That's gonna be a problem, Tina is nothing if she ain't loyal. She's been with Dr. Fox for years."

"She might be loyal," said Birdie, "but she's still a A-One nurse. She'll do what's right. I know she will."

Moose sat back in his chair and folded his arms across his broad chest. "Forget about Fox. I'm putting my bet on Kadish," he said.

"Why is that?" asked Gary.

"'Cause he was up close and personal with Colleen Creedon before she died." He described the intimate scene that Smooch had related in the cafeteria.

"I bet ya she was carrying his baby," said Birdie. "Those high-and-mighty surgeons think they can get into anybody's pants they take a fancy to."

"Being flirtatious doesn't mean that she was having an affair with him," said Gary. "I was struck by something in Dr. Kadish's press conference."

He explained how Kadish made a big deal about the antirejection drug that he used, even naming the product and the company. "The reason it caught my eye is, I heard one of the transplant residents say that there were problems with Falcon Pharmaceutical's plant in India. A batch of the antirejection drug was impure. He didn't understand why Kadish was using it."

"The company greased his palm," said Moose. "Now it's payback time."

"I don't know," said Lenny. "If I were making medical history, I'd sure as hell use the best drugs on the market." He threw his empty coffee cup in the trash, glanced at his watch. "It's obvious that we don't know enough about the dead woman's comings and goings."

Lenny looked around, saw that Gary was lost in thought.

"Earth to Tuttle: Are you with us?"

"I'm sorry," said Gary, returning his focus to Lenny. "It was something you just said: 'We don't know enough about the dead woman.' I just remembered . . . "

"Remembered what?" said Lenny.

"During the code, when Dr. Singh asked Kadish if Colleen was *his* patient, he said that she wasn't his patient. But he didn't tell him that he knew her."

"And he must have recognized her, she sold him her company's drugs. Way to go, Tuttle!"

"I told you," said Moose, "my money's on Kadish. He's dishonest, and a pig."

"We have to keep on digging," said Lenny.

"What about Fred's funeral?" asked Birdie. "How much money have we got collected so far?"

"I don't have a total," said Lenny, "but I know it's close to two hundred already, and there are several people still collecting."

He stood up, looked at his friends. "We'll pool all the money in the morning. Then when it gets close to lunchtime, we'll get as many workers together as we can in the main lobby and walk in on Freely. We'll demand that he give us the time off."

"How many people you think you can bring with you?" asked Moose.

"As many people as loved Fred," said Lenny.

"That'll do it," said Moose, smiling in anticipation. Even Gary relaxed some. As the group prepared to return to their stations, Lenny said, "I just wish I knew what Colleen Creedon was doing on Seven South."

"I don't know," said Birdie. "Maybe she was coming to see you."

Mike kneeled on the bathroom floor of his one-room apartment, dry-heaving. He hadn't been able to eat anything all day. A glass of water was all he'd been able to get down. His head throbbed as though he'd been beaten with a baseball bat.

He was sure he had a cerebral aneurysm that was about to burst.

Good, he thought. *Let it happen. Let me stroke out and die in this crummy bathroom. It will be a relief.*

He thought about Colleen. Beautiful, seductive Colleen. With her laughter like Christmas bells. Her lips like caressing fingers. Her sweet, mouth-watering breasts.

Then he thought of his wife and his three children, and how much pain he had caused them when he left.

What did I do? What was I thinking? I'm such a fucking idiot. I've screwed it all up. My whole life is a screwup.

He didn't care if his head exploded in a burst of blood. He'd rather die than face all of his gutless failures.

—FIFTY-THREE—

Dr. Kadish scowled as the transplant resident reported on Allendale's condition.

"The patient is anuric; he failed to respond to two hundred milligrams of Lasix. The B-U-N is ninety-five, the creatinine is three point five. His—"

"Why is his O-two sat eighty-nine?" barked Kadish.

"His chest X ray shows pulmonary edema and bilateral infiltrates," the fellow replied. "If he is in acute rejection—"

"Show me the film," said Kadish.

An intern quickly pulled the film from a folder and handed it to Kadish, who held it up above his head, using the fluorescent light to read it.

"This isn't rejection of the lung, this is fluid overload. I told Anesthesia not to flood him with saline." Handing the film back, he said, "What did the Renal Service say?"

"I'm sorry, Dr. Kadish, I don't believe they've examined the patient yet."

The surgeon's face darkened. "I want Renal to see him *now*, and I want him dialyzed in an hour. An *hour*, do you understand?"

"Yes, sir, I'll call him right away."

Kadish's beeper went off. He looked down at his belt, saw Elliot Fox's office number on the beeper display.

"Excuse me," he said. "Get the fluid off his lungs. I'll be back shortly."

He went out to find a phone that would give him some privacy.

Stepping into the Employee Health Clinic, Lenny looked at the familiar stained ceiling tiles and the peeling plaster where water had run down through the walls.

He spotted Margie, a plump, battle-worn nurse who ruled over the clinic appointment book.

"You know why I love this place?" he said. "It makes my house seem like a palace."

"You must spend a lot of time in Nashville," she said. "What brings you down to my witch's den? Are you feeling sick, or have you got somebody looking to go out on disability?"

"Neither. I was hoping you could help me with a little, uh, research." He put on his sweetest, most guileless look, sat down on a plastic chair that tipped to the side under his weight. "If you help me, I'll promise not to sue when this chair collapses and I topple over, hitting my head."

"Brother, if you fell on the floor and busted your head, Joe West would probably write you up for damaging the furniture and causing a hazardous spill."

"I guess you're right." He looked about the room, saw there was nobody near, leaned closer to Margie. "I need to know the blood type of three employees," he said, pulling a piece of paper from his shirt pocket and handing it to her. "Do you think you could take a little peek in their charts and get that for me?"

The old nurse cast doleful eyes at Lenny, made a "tsk, tsk" sound, and clasped her hands together as if invoking a prayer or a promise.

"You realize you're asking me to violate patient confidentiality. I took a solemn oath as a professional nurse about that, not to mention that Joe West has eyes in the back of his head and snitches everywhere."

"I know it's kind of touchy, but—"

"*Touchy?* I only have a year and two months until my *full-pay* retirement. Let me see—did I leave anything out?"

"You forgot the Declaration of Independence and the Port Huron Statement."

"Mmm, I guess I did."

"So," said Lenny, smiling and beginning to see hope in his entreaty, "can you help me out?"

"Give me the names," she said, holding out a pudgy hand.

He placed a neatly folded piece of paper in her hand.

"I'll need ten minutes to pull the charts," she said, "Why don't you disappear? It wouldn't look right if somebody nasty came in and saw you looking over my shoulder."

"Is Alex in?"

"Yeah, he's in his office, filling out *government forms*. You can rescue him from terminal boredom."

"Thanks. I'll just poke my head in."

He rose carefully from the plastic chair and ambled over to Dr. Alex Primeaux's office, which was kitty-corner to Margie's desk. With a light tap and an invitation to "Come awn in," he opened the door and entered the doctor's office.

"Hey, there, Lenny Moss," said Alex Primeaux, rising from his chair. "Mighty nice t' see your face."

"Don't get up, it's only me," said Lenny.

Primeaux was a family practice physician who covered the Employee Health Clinic. He was sitting at an old oak desk cluttered with files, a rumpled corduroy sports coat draped over the back of a battered leather chair. His gentle voice had a southern accent that became more pronounced when he became excited.

"Park yourself down and set awhile."

Once Lenny was seated, the doctor asked what he could do for him.

Lenny explained that he was investigating the death of Colleen Creedon, and he wanted to know if a very small amount of cyanide would induce an abortion. Having collaborated before in the investigation of a young resident physician's murder, Lenny felt confident that the doctor would help him again.

"That's a tough question, I don't rightly know," said Primeaux, "Ah don't remember it ever being used for that purpose, but I'd be happy to look it up for you. I'll go through my textbooks, and if that doesn't do it, I'll go online."

"That would be great. Thanks. I'd also like to know if a small amount of cyanide could be used to cause the baby to be malformed."

"You think the cyanide might have been given to cause congenital defects?"

"Something like that."

"My, oh, my, this person sounds like pure evil." He looked pensive for a moment, contemplating an act that was beyond his imagination. "I'll do a search just as soon as I get done with these wretched forms."

"That's great, Alex. I can't thank you enough."

"It's mah pleasure." The doctor rose from his chair and shook Lenny's hand. "I guess I'll see you at Fred's funeral tomorrow."

"I hope so. The administration is giving us grief about taking time off from work at lunch time."

"Why'd the family schedule it for midday?"

"It has something to do with their beliefs. They're one of those Christian fundamentalist groups. They have very rigid notions about life and death."

"Well, it takes all kinds," said Primeaux.

Lenny left the good doctor to his forms and returned to Margie. The nurse had a piece of paper folded in half in her plump hand. She held it out to him. Then, as he reached for it, she jerked her hand away.

"You still owe me from the last time I helped you, Lenny."

"This is like when you double your bet."

"And what do I get for my sacrifice?"

For once, he was out of words. But after a moment's reflection, his imagination rallied.

"If I ever marry again—and that is a very iffy kind of if—I'll ask you to be one of the bridesmaids. How's that?"

"Well, that will be an honor." She handed him the paper, holding it a little more firmly than she had to just to let him know he wasn't' getting away with everything. "I'm gonna hold you to your promise," she said.

"Oh, I know you will," he said, pocketing the paper and stepping toward the door.

"You aren't seeing anybody special, are you?"

"Nope. It's just me and my ragged old house."

"I'll put the word out that you're interested. There'll be women coming up to Seven South by the busload. It'll be like Atlantic City on a Friday night."

"Gee, thanks, I can hardly wait," said Lenny as he escaped out the door.

As soon as he was back on his ward, he stepped into the Housekeeping closet, closed the door, and took out the paper Margie had given him. He read the blood types.

Martin Kadish—Type A positive.

Elliot Fox—Type AB negative.

Michael DiPietro—Type A negative.

He felt a twinge of regret. He had hoped that the pharmacist would be removed from the list of suspects. But he knew from years of representing his coworkers that half the time they earned their place on the boss's shit list. Defending the good and the bad with a hundred percent effort came with the territory. The saddest part about Mike being on the list of suspects was that it could get him the death penalty.

—FIFTY-FOUR—

On Seven South, Gary removed the bag of chemotherapy from the fridge, placed it on top of the computer monitor, where the heat would raise it to room temperature. He would never administer the chemotherapy cold, it would constrict the vein, increasing the chance of damaging the inner lining of the vessel.

While the chemotherapy medication warmed up, he took a suppository for nausea from the fridge and carried it to Mrs. Cavanaugh's room.

"How are you feeling today, Mrs. Cavanaugh?" he asked, entering the room.

"I feel like yesterday's burnt toast," she said. "Are you here to give me my chemo?"

"In just a few minutes. I want to give you the medicine for nausea first. It's a suppository."

"You're bound to take away my last bit of modesty, aren't you?"

'I'm sorry, Mrs. Cavanaugh, but that's what the doctor ordered for you." He drew the curtain around the bed. "Would you mind turning on your side?"

"Oh, all right. Just be careful of my hemorrhoids, they're very sensitive."

"I will," said Gary. Putting on a pair of exam gloves, he peeled back the blanket and lifted her hospital gown. She was wearing old, threadbare cotton underpants. Pulling them down just enough to expose her anus, he saw protruding hemorrhoids. He squirted an extra dollop of lubricating gel onto the bullet-shaped suppository.

"Here we go," he said, gently inserting the suppository into the rectal vault. "All done."

He pulled her panties back up, restored her gown, and pulled the sheets up to her chin.

"When will you give me the poison?" she asked.

"I'm going to wait for fifteen minutes or so for the medicine to take effect, then I'll hang the chemotherapy. Can I get you anything else?"

"No, I suppose not. Unless you have a little gin and an olive."

Lenny used the pay phone in the patient lounge to call Mike at his new apartment. The phone rang a dozen times. No answer, no answering machine. He hung up, worried about his friend. Was he really home sick with a migraine, as Hector said, or was he staying out of sight?

He didn't want to believe that the hapless pharmacist could do something as crazy as kill the woman he loved. But Hector's description of Mike making mistakes and mooning over Colleen Creedon were worrisome signs.

He wanted to drive out and visit Mike, but his plate was awfully full. He had to keep an eye on the money being collected for Fred's funeral. Everybody loved Fred, so the workers were being generous in their donations, but two years before, a union member collecting for a funeral mysteriously "lost" the cash. The same worker showed up a week later with a very expensive leather coat that she said came from Santa Claus, which didn't help assuage his suspicions.

He was glad he had Moose and Birdie and Regis and Abrahm to help him. And Tuttle was really getting fired up. They were solid people. He trusted them with his life.

Kadish stood outside Allendale's room flanked by his fellow, residents and medical students. Facing him was Dr. Juanita Butero, one of the renal attending physicians. She was a small, quiet woman who kept her eyeglasses perched on the top of her head, pulling them down to the bridge of her nose when she read a chart or examined a patient. She was backed up by her own crew of physicians in training and a dialysis nurse.

Jerking his thumb in the direction of the failing patient, Kadish told the renal doctor, "My fellow tells me you're dragging your heels on the dialysis. If you *don't* dialyze him, he'll die from acute renal failure."

"Brought on by rejection of your ill-conceived organ transfer," the renal attending replied.

"Look at the creatinine. Do I have to draw you a picture? You *have* to do the dialysis!"

Dr. Butero transferred her glasses to her nose and glanced at the flow sheet, noting the intravenous infusions and the patient's vital signs. She asked, "Why is he on sedation?"

"He was delirious this morning. He bit through the ET tube. Anesthesia had to reintubate."

"I'm very concerned about his blood pressure. If he drops his pressure during the treatment we will have to stop it. That's assuming that he even tolerates the first exchange, which I think highly unlikely."

"He's on epinephrine," said Kadish. "You can just dial up the infusion and maintain his pressure."

"I'm familiar with basic pharmacology, thank you," said the renal attending. "I only want to be sure that you understand, if Mr. Allendale's pressure drops and we cannot maintain it with pressors, I will order the nurse to abort the treatment." Raising her glasses again, she added, "I do not want this death showing up on my quarterly statistics."

"Just get two liters of fluid off and let *me* worry about his survival," said Kadish.

He turned and led his team away, leaving the kidney doctors to try and place a large-bore double catheter that would allow them to connect the dialysis machine to Allendale's vascular system. The dialysis nurse began setting up her machine.

Gary carried the bag of chemotherapy into Mrs. Cavanaugh's room. Approaching the bed, he saw a middle-aged woman sitting stiffly in a chair beside the bed. She stood and moved her chair back out of the way without speaking. Gary thanked her as he hung the medication on the IV pole.

"I have your first dose of chemo," he told the patient. "I'm going to run it in very slowly, and I want you to put on your call light if you feel nauseous or light-headed. Okay?"

"If I do get sick to my stomach, can I have some more of that medicine you gave me?"

"Yes, I'll have another suppository handy, just in case."

The old woman settled back in her bed. She had an old afghan, frayed and needing repair, which she pulled up over her chest.

The nurse reached down and examined the intravenous site in the patient's arm. Satisfied, he began the infusion.

The visitor sat in her chair and watched, never saying a word.

—FIFTY-FIVE—

Lenny made a quick run through the ward with a dry mop, sweeping the floors. As soon as he was done, he called to his Housekeeping partner, "I'm going on a break, Boop. Cover for me?"

"Like I always do," she said.

He hurried down the stairs to the third floor. Arriving at the GI lab, he found Tina in the recovery room setting up the patients who had completed their studies for lunch. She opened up cartons of milk and unwrapped sandwiches.

"Hey, Tina," said Lenny. "You got a minute?"

"I had a feeling I'd be seeing you again," she said, no smile on her face this time.

The nurse scanned her charges, saw that everyone had their dentures in their mouths, napkins tucked under their chin, and tea bags removed from their cups of hot water.

"I made coffee," she said. "Let's go back into the office."

He followed her to the office, passing Myrna, who was using a Dictaphone to transcribe doctors' reports.

"I don't have any more cases scheduled," said Tina, pouring a cup of coffee. She offered a cup to Lenny, who declined the offer. "Dr. Fox is off seeing patients." She settled into a chair at the desk. "What's bothering your brain this time?"

"Do you know anything about Colleen Creedon attending a big drug conference in New Orleans about six months ago?"

"Sure I know about it, it was down in New Orleans. Dr. Fox went. Matter of fact, they paid his whole expense. I hear he even flew first class. They served champagne and caviar and the whole nine yards."

"Is that common, a company paying a doctor's airfare and all?"

"Oh, sure, they do that all the time. Dr. Fox was on a panel. They talked about these new drugs coming out for ulcers and colitis and such. Dr. Fox talked about the great results we're getting with Falcon's new medication. Even though the study is only ninety percent finished, it's obviously a great drug."

"That's interesting." said Lenny. "And Colleen Creedon went because her company's product was getting a lot of promotion. Is that it?"

"That's what makes the world go round, Lenny. You know that as well as me."

Myrna came into the room, greeted Lenny and poured herself a cup of coffee. He looked from the secretary to the nurse, unsure if he should continue the discussions.

Tina said, "You can talk in front of Myrna, she and I are soul sisters. Ain't that right?"

"We sure are, all the bullshit we have to put up with," said Myrna.

"Something else has been bothering me," said Lenny. "Those dentures I found last week of Mrs. Cavanaugh's?"

"What about them?" said Tina, shooting a glance at Myrna.

"Is there a chance that Fox did two procedures on the same day? You know, one down the throat, one up the ass?"

Dropping a spoon of sugar in her coffee, Tina looked into the cup as she stirred it, not looking at Lenny.

"Well, see, it's like this," she said, still not looking up. "Once in a great while we do double up on a patient. We call it a 'one-eighty,' on account of we turn the stretcher a hundred eighty degrees so we can go from examining the colon to the esophagus."

She continued stirring her coffee, offering no further explanation.

"The reason I ask," said Lenny, noting Tina's evasiveness, "Gary looked at Mrs. Cavanaugh's nurse's notes. He said there's nothing about her going down to the GI lab on the day that the procedure note says she was examined."

"Maybe the nurse forgot to put it in her notes."

"There would be an order from the night before to make the patient NPO, and there wasn't. Gary checked that, too."

"That Gary Tuttle is a darn good nurse," said Tina. "I always said that about him."

Myrna looked at her coworker, sadness in her eyes. "I never liked what they were doing. You know that, Tina."

"I didn't like it no kind of way either. That's why my notes always had the correct date on them. Those are *legal documents*. No way I'm losing my nursing license by falsifying the date of a procedure, just so the Gray Fox can make a couple of extra bucks."

"Is that what it's about? Money?"

"Dr. Fox said it was better for the patient," said Tina. "It wasn't *about* the money."

"What *was* it about?" asked Lenny, a note of impatience in his voice.

"See," said Myrna, "it's like this. Medicare won't pay for two GI procedures on the same day. They're afraid we'd be cheating them, billing for two procedures when we only did one."

"I get it. You claim that the procedures were done on different days so you can get the government to pay the two bills."

"There's a whole lot more to it than that," said Tina. "Each time we scope a patient, we have to put him to sleep with IV sedation. That's dangerous. They could stop breathing, or drop their blood pressure. If we can do both procedures in one trip, it's better for them."

"Plus we can sometimes discharge the patient a day earlier," said Myrna. "That saves on the length of stay. It all helps the hospital's bottom line."

"Hold on," said Lenny. "Supposing that there are legitimate reasons for making a false claim. Do you think Colleen knew about the doctor's little scam?"

"I don't see how she could," said Tina.

"I don't either," Myrna added. "Falcon Pharmaceuticals would have no knowledge of our billing practice or our doubling up on procedures. They were only interested in the *upper* endoscopies, not the colons."

"So Colleen Creedon wouldn't know about your problem getting paid by Medicare and the altered exam dates?"

"No," said Tina, "I'm sure she didn't. She had to keep really precise records for her company. If there was anything wrong, even a wrong date, she'd have asked me about it right away."

"Is there any way we can tell for certain?"

Tina rose from her chair. I'll get the logbook from the drug study."

She hurried back to the lab, returning with a large, leather bound notebook with the embossed image of a falcon in flight on the cover.

"This is where we record the study patients. It's where Colleen got all her information." Showing him the entries, she said, "Lookie here. There's nothing in the log about anybody getting two procedures. Just the upper."

"Does the drug rep ever look in the patient's chart?"

"Oh, no," said Myra. "That would violate patient confidentiality. They only get the reports that we send them."

Lenny sat quietly for a moment, processing the information.

"How much did Falcon pay Dr. Fox for enrolling a patient in a study?" he asked.

"A thousand dollars," said Myrna. "I know, I handle all the invoices."

"The patients all had ulcers, there was no question about that?" said Lenny.

"They had ulcers, all right," said Tina. "I saw them on the monitor with my own eyes."

"And the drug really did the trick?"

"We did follow-up endoscopies on all of the study patients, it's part of the protocol, and all the ulcers healed up. Listen, I been in the business going on twenty years, I know an ulcer when I see one."

Lenny stood up to go. "One last thing. Are you sure Fox didn't leave the GI lab the morning Colleen was killed?"

"He was here *all* morning," said Tina. "We had a full schedule. Except for a phone call from his wife that he took in his office, he was with me the whole time."

Myrna stuck a menthol cigarette in her mouth, even though she couldn't light it until she was outside the building. "There's one thing you're missing," she said to Lenny.

"What's that?"

"Dr. Fox wouldn't want to see Colleen dead; it would be like killing the goose that laid the golden egg."

Tina tossed her coffee cup in the trash, got up to return to the lab. "I keep telling you, Lenny, Dr. Fox is a wonderful doctor. You've got to look for the killer someplace else."

As Tina and Lenny walked out of the office, they were surprised to see Dr. Fox in his inner office, reading a report. Reaching the hallway, the nurse looked at Lenny, a question in her eyes.

Lenny shrugged. In a whisper he said, "I thought you said he was out seeing patients."

"That's what he told me he was doing. Do you think he heard us?"

"I hope not. If he did, we'll be on his shit list till hell freezes over."

—FIFTY-SIX—

Sandy was manning the security desk in the main lobby when a salesman in a sharp suit and with a jaunty air came striding up to him.

"How are you today, my good man?" asked the salesman. "Kurt Lessing, senior marketing representative for Falcon Pharmaceuticals. I'm here to see Dr. Martin Kadish."

He whipped out a business card, gave it a little snap with his hand, and handed it to the old guard.

Sandy held the card at arm's length and read every word out loud. Then he looked at the salesman's valise, which had *FALCON PHARMACEUTICALS, INC.* embossed in gold letters on the side.

"I'll have to call up and see is he expecting you," said Sandy.

Confirming the appointment with the doctor's secretary, the old guard reached into his desk and came up with a day pass. He filled in the salesman's name, dated the pass, then gave it a little snap as he handed it to Lessing, a twinkle in his eye. "Put it on your suit jacket so it's easy to see," he advised.

Lessing peeled the back off the pass and slapped it on his crisply pressed jacket. As he was just turning to go, the guard reached out and grabbed his arm.

"Say, you got a minute for an old security guard?"

"Uh, yeah, I guess so. What's on your mind?"

"Our department's been helping the police investigate the death of one of your salespeople."

"You're talking about Colleen Creedon. She was a wonderful young woman. We've been cooperating with the police to the fullest extent, naturally."

"The reason I brought it up, one of our best people is in the middle of the investigation. I know that he'd appreciate talking to you, if it's not too much trouble."

"No trouble at all," said Lessing. "Where can I find him?"

"He's bound to be on Seven South. You just take the main elevator to the seventh floor, go to the desk, and ask for Mr. Moss."

"Moss, you say?"

"That's the guy. Leonard Moss."

As he watched the salesman walk toward the elevator, Sandy picked up

221

the phone to tell Lenny that he was going to have a visitor. With sheer will-power he suppressed a broad, happy smile until the salesman had entered the elevator and disappeared.

Dr. Fingers got off the elevator and made his way to the Seven South nursing station. Spotting Lenny sweeping in a patient's room, he said, "Excuse me, have you a moment?"

Lenny came out to the hall, asked what he could do for the doctor.

"I'd like to attend Fred's funeral. Can you tell me the time and the location of the service?"

"Sure, I'll get you a flyer," said Lenny. "It has all the information on it."

"That would be most helpful," said Fingers.

Walking with the doctor to the Housekeeping closet, Lenny retrieved a flyer. It had a grainy photo of Fred in the middle of the page. The heading read, "HOMECOMING FOR FREDERICK GOPIE."

Looking over the flyer, Dr. Fingers said, "He was a good man, our Fred. He was not without his flaws, but he was a solid, loyal worker."

"I liked Fred a lot, even with his horrible jokes."

"Yes, they weren't very funny, were they? Still, he kept things in our department light. In pathology, that is a valuable asset."

"I guess that's why he kept making up jokes," said Lenny.

The two grew silent, recalling their lost friend. Lenny looked at the man, noted the tie with the stains on it, the wrinkled collar, the faint odor of formaldehyde.

"Listen, Doc, you mind if I ask you something?"

"No, I don't suppose so," said Fingers.

"I was wondering if you had an idea about what was the cause of Colleen Creedon's death."

The doctor's face lost all trace of sympathy.

"The autopsy results are not public knowledge until they are read into the record at a public hearing. I can't discuss them with you."

"I'm not asking you to tell me what's in the autopsy report. I just figured that you pick up information here and there, and you might have some idea about why she died."

"Suppose that I have given her death some thought. Why should I speak to you?"

"I don't know. Maybe because you want to see justice done?"

"I have faith in the police," said Fingers. "Don't you?"

"Yes and no. Look how quick they arrested Regis for Dr. Sparks' murder—an innocent man, remember that? Now I hear the police are sniffing around one of our pharmacists."

"How can you be sure he's not guilty?" asked Fingers.

"It's true, I can't be sure, but I want to see that the right man is arrested."

The pathologist recalled the many times that Lenny had fought like a pit bull to try and keep Fred from being terminated. Everyone had said it was a hopeless case, that Fred deserved to be canned, that he would never quit the bottle.

But Lenny won by bringing in dozens of employees to testify on Fred's behalf, himself and Alex Primeaux included. The arbitrator had been so impressed, he granted the union grievance, shocking the hospital's lawyers.

Dr. Fingers decided that this pesky custodian deserved a little help.

"I may share an idle thought with you, but on one condition—that it goes no further."

"I'll take it to my grave, if you'll pardon the expression."

"Very well." The doctor moved off to a corner, Lenny following close beside him.

"The county pathologist found a slight thickening of the deceased's right ventricle. The final pathology report isn't back yet, but I strongly suspect that it will not find evidence of infection, which would be one explanation for a thickened heart muscle."

"Okay, if it wasn't an infection, what was it?"

"She may have had a problem with her mitral valve."

"*May* have?"

"You see, some diseases are functional. Disorders of a working muscle group do not always show up on an autopsy, since the muscles are not functioning under pressure."

"I got ya."

"In the case of disorders of the heart valves, when the heart is at rest, the disease has to be advanced before it is apparent on autopsy."

"Tell me this, Doc. If Colleen did have a functional disorder, what would that have to do with the cause of her death?"

"Well, usually when a patient has a chronic heart disorder, he learns to compensate. He avoids strenuous exercises, say, or chooses not to vacation in the Rocky Mountains."

"Because they can't handle the added stress," said Lenny. "And when they do stress out, they collapse. Right?"

"Exactly. Think of the athlete who collapses on the field and dies. He often has a heart disorder that he ignored."

"Or his coach did," said Lenny.

"Perhaps. In the case of Colleen Creedon, if she did have a functional heart disorder, and if she were stressed beyond the endurance of her cardiovascular system, it could be a cause of death."

"And it wouldn't show up on an autopsy?"

"That's right. Once the heart is stopped, the dysfunction disappears, and the cause of death along with it.'

Lenny thanked the doctor. He reaffirmed his promise to keep the source of information private, then returned to his duties.

—FIFTY-SEVEN—

Lenny had just returned to sweeping the patient rooms when he was called on the overhead pager to come to the nursing station. With a frustrated sigh, he ambled down to the station. A man in a suit carrying a black leather bag held out his hand to him.

"Mr. Moss? Kurt Lessing, Falcon Pharmaceuticals. I'm pleased to meet you."

Lenny wanted to let out a groan, but kept it inside. Sandy's phone call suggesting that he pose as a member of the security department was way beyond anything he had done before. This lunacy was bound to get him fired, if not put in jail. Unfortunately, the old guard sent the salesman up to Seven South before Lenny could stop him. He saw no way to get out of the subterfuge.

He shook Lessing's hand, eyeing the man, and noting the diamond stick-pin in his flamboyant tie.

"I am . . . that is, I *was* Colleen Creedon's supervisor."

"Nice to meet you," said Lenny.

"I was signing in at the front desk and the guard down there said that the hospital Security Department was assisting the Police Department investigate poor Colleen's death."

Lenny looked about the station, saw a medical student reading a chart and a part-time unit clerk buffing her nails.

"We should find some place more private," he said. They walked across the hall to the little kitchen, which was empty.

"Like a glass of juice or coffee?" Lenny asked.

"No, I'm fine. The guard didn't say that you were working undercover. I must say, the costume is very effective. It's totally convincing."

"Thank you," said Lenny.

"How is the investigation going? Are you making progress?"

"It's early, yet, but I believe it's going very well."

"That's great. How can I help?"

"You could start by telling me about Miss Creedon. Was she a good employee? Was she reliable? Were there any problems with her work?"

"Oh, she was the best in the business. Colleen was a natural-born salesperson. She took to sales like a duck to water."

"Did she?"

225

"Oh, yes. By her third year with the company she'd broken every one of our sales records."

"Did that create any jealousy among the other sales reps?"

"Not really. You see, each rep has a territory, so there's no poaching on one another. If one rep does well, it doesn't bleed off sales from another."

"I see."

"When it came to handing out awards, there might have been a little grumbling, but we were all delighted with her record. Anyone who boosted the company made it better for the rest of us. We all have stock options."

"That must be an effective motivator," said Lenny. "Tell me about the study that Dr. Fox was conducting."

"It was the final stage in our clinical studies. We'd done several animal and human trials. This was the final one before we receive FDA approval."

"And there were no problems with the study. Nothing unexpected?"

"No, not at all. The efficacy of our product is unparalleled. And as to side effects, we've had absolutely no report of serious adverse reactions. It's a great drug."

"I'm glad to hear that," said Lenny. "So, you're confident that Colleen never had any problems with the study, is that right?"

"That's correct. She was on budget and on time. The only extra expense she ever put in for was a repeat study for one of her patients."

"Oh? Why the repeat?"

"Apparently one of the study patients was an old contrarian. He wanted a second opinion, despite the fact that we showed him photographs of his ulcer. We weren't obligated to pay for another physician to examine him, but as a humanitarian gesture, we okayed the expense."

"That is very generous. Do you know what the results of the second study were?"

"We'd have no way of knowing; they weren't part of our study. We just paid the bill and wished him well."

"Okay." Lenny wondered how far he could string the salesman along. Feeling that he was on shaky ground, he decided it was better to cut things short rather than drag it out and get caught in a lie.

"I appreciate your taking time out of your busy schedule to speak to me," said Lenny, leading the salesman out of the kitchen. "It would be best if you kept this conversation strictly confidential. You understand, it is a murder investigation."

"I understand completely. My lips are sealed."

Lessing shook Lenny's hand with a firm grip, flashed a million-dollar smile, and then strode briskly off to make his appointment with Dr. Kadish.

As he watched the man leave, Lenny decided that he would add Sandy to his death wish, after Moose, for making him use the stairs and go jogging.

Abrahm approached Lenny, who was emptying his bucket in the dirty utility room down the hall from the nursing station. Holding out a bulging envelope bound by rubber bands, he said, "Lennye, I have collected much money. You want I should give it to you now?"

"This is great, Abrahm. Why don't you hold on to it until the morning. I'll get a pay envelope and put everyone's donations together."

"Good. There is some coin change I will make into bills. The donations are going well?"

"Yeah. Regis has money for me. So does Moose and Birdie. I talked to Fred's sister. I know she'll appreciate it."

"Did you get the okay for us to go to the funeral?"

"Freely is jerking me around. He claims he can't run a hospital without all the staff being on duty."

"We should just go. We walk out. They cannot stop us if we stand together."

"That's my thinking. There's a good chance Freely will give in if we march into his office with twenty or thirty workers and demand he let us go. He isn't like West. He hates a confrontation. It's just . . . "

"Just what, Lennye?"

"It's just that we have a contract that forbids us from walking off the job. If I support an action like that, I'll be removed as union steward. They'll probably fire me, too. I know it's selfish to think about myself, but . . . "

The burly Russian clapped a hand on Lenny's shoulder, saying, "Do not worry yourself. We will go with you, everyone in our department. We will make them let us say good-bye to our friend, and no one will be punished. Not you, not me, not anyone."

Buoyed by his friend's encouraging remarks, Lenny went to the Housekeeping closet and put away his equipment. He bid good night to Betty, then took the stairs down to the Housekeeping office to punch out. He would have liked to go home, have a cold Yuengling and some leftovers, and chill out, but he needed to talk to Mike in person. That meant driving out to Logan and finding his apartment.

Walking down the stairs, he still worried that his coworkers would face disciplinary charges for going to Fred's funeral. He knew that the best chance of getting away with it was for everyone to stand together, like they did in the old days when they built the union, with everyone fired up and hanging together.

Everyone loved Fred. More importantly, everyone hated Joe West for kicking Fred out of the hospital when he was sick and unsteady, and not drunk. If there was ever a chance to beat West, this would be it, if they all just stood together.

Walking toward his car in the employee parking lot, he pictured the scene of carloads of workers arriving at the funeral home and joining in the service. A worrier by nature, he saw a new problem rearing its head as he pulled his car out onto Germantown Avenue: Once they started to party after the service, how was he going to get all those workers to go back to work?

—FIFTY-EIGHT—

Kurt Lessing knocked on the open door of the transplant office. When the secretary saw him, she smiled and beckoned him to come in. He strode up to her desk, flashing a broad smile.

"That's a lovely perfume you have on today, Cindy. Is it a new brand?"

"I'm not wearing any perfume, you smooth talker."

"You're just naturally sweet," he said, reaching into his leather bag. He took out a shiny, elegant pen, held it out to her. "This was made by Cross, it's got a lifetime guarantee. I'm supposed to give it to a physician, but . . . "

The secretary smiled, leaned forward to study the raised lettering on the pen that said *Falcon Pharmaceuticals*. "It's lovely."

"If you promise me you'll take it home and never let Dr. Kadish see it . . . "

She scooped the pen out of his hand, pulled her purse out from a drawer, and dropped it in, clicking the purse closed with a conspiratorial snap.

"So," said the salesman, "is the big guy in?"

"Oh, he's in, all right," she said, "but this might not be the best time to talk to him."

"Why is that?"

"He's in a foul mood. His famous patient's not doing very well."

"He's always in a foul mood," said Lessing. "I'll just have to brighten his day."

As the secretary announced his presence over the intercom, he winked at her and sauntered down the hall to the office

When Kadish saw the salesman, he growled, "Shut the door behind you."

"We're getting great press coverage on your case, Dr. Kadish. There are journalists here from London, Paris, Tokyo. It's incredible."

"The press can bury you as well as make you," said Kadish, leaning back in his big leather chair. "I'm afraid they're going to cut us up when Allendale dies."

"Things are going that badly?"

"Between you and me, I could start the autopsy."

Lessing pondered the implications of an early death. Failure was bad press. It could bring a retreat in Falcon's stock price. Maybe even a downgrade by Standard + Poor's.

"If the patient dies, you chalk it up to the risk of a bold new procedure," said Lessing. "It's not a problem by itself."

"Any postoperative fatality is a problem."

"There is one thing that worries me," said Lessing.

"What?" snapped Kadish.

"It wouldn't look good if Allendale died from organ rejection; it would cast a negative light on our product. That's bad for business."

"You can't fake an autopsy report. Not when the ME is reviewing the organ pathology. They do microscopic examinations, for Christ's sake."

"Still," said Lessing, "there's talk that he could have had a stroke. Is that right?"

"There is a risk of a cerebral even during long-term cardiopulmonary bypass," said Kadish. "And he was on bypass a lot longer than a bypass."

"I was just thinking that if there was some way that you could be sure that Allendale dies from a stroke and not from organ rejection, it would draw attention away from our product."

Kadish pursed his thick lips, half closed his eyes. "I have a neurologist friend who owes me a big-time favor. I'll get him to examine Allendale. When the time comes, he can support my determination of the cause of death."

"I can't thank you enough for your support," said Lessing. "Falcon is very appreciative."

Standing, Kadish pulled on his lab coat. As he scooped up his keys, Lessing said, "You know, I was glad to hear there's some progress in the investigation of Colleen's death."

"Oh, really?" said Kadish. "I've been too busy with my case to follow the news."

"I was talking with one of your security people just a little while ago; he filled me in on things." Lessing grabbed the sleeve of Kadish's lab coat, adding, "It was funny, though, he was wearing a custodian's uniform, like he was supposed to be *undercover.*"

Kadish stared at the salesman. "What was the name of this 'investigator'?"

"Moss. Funny name. Funny guy. He was quite complimentary about you, though."

"Me? What did he say?"

"He mentioned your groundbreaking surgery and the use of our antirejection drug. He was quite knowledgeable."

Kadish frowned, chewed his lip. He didn't know if Lenny Moss was just flailing around in the dark, or if he knew something. He decided he better not take any chances, there was too much to lose.

As soon as the salesman was out of his office, Kadish closed the door and picked up the phone, telling the page operator to get Joe West. When the chief of security answered, the doctor told him how Lenny Moss had tried to get information from the Falcon salesman by posing as an undercover security guard.

"Do you mean the salesman was dumb enough to fall for that crap?" asked West.

"He was skeptical, but apparently that Moss is slick; he must have put up a good story. I want you to get rid of this guy, permanently."

"Don't worry," said West. "I've got the termination papers drawn up. I'll just fill in the blanks and serve the papers on him."

"Well, I want it done today. The longer that pest is walking the halls, the worse it's going to be for James Madison."

Kadish hung up without saying good-bye, thinking he had left the security chief on the line, but West, the master of the fast exit, had already pressed the disconnect button on his phone.

While the doctor was on the phone, Lessing went back to the surgery office to say good-bye to Cindy. He perched on the edge of her desk, letting his leg brush against hers. "Do you like champagne?"

"Of course I do, if it's French. Why?"

"Oh, I know this new restaurant down in Center City. I thought you might like to sample their fare. Say, next Friday?"

Cindy pulled a leaf off a sticky pad, scribbled her phone number on it, and handed it to him.

"You can pick me up at eight. And it better be a nice car."

"It's a Lincoln," he said, pocketing the number. "And the leather seats are as soft as a down comforter."

Regis Devoe was loading a linen cart to take up to the wards for the last delivery of the day. The sheets were still warm from the big automated ironing machine. He was glad the summer hadn't hit, the temperatures in the laundry room got ridiculous.

He thought about putting in for a transfer to the morgue. Having filled in for long stretches when Fred had been sick, he found that the work was partly revolting, partly fascinating. The formaldehyde smell was the worst part. He didn't want to bring the odor home, especially if Salina got pregnant again. But she was nursing their first baby, and she had no intention of carrying another baby inside her so soon.

As he wheeled the cart toward the door, he heard a muffled sound. Looking around, he saw Bridgette seated at a table in the corner, folding linen. She was trying hard to hold back tears. He walked over to her.

"Hey, Bridge. You hurtin'?"

She wiped her nose on the sleeve of her scrub suit, looked briefly at Regis, then looked down at her work.

"I'm all right," she said.

"That's good. You probably got a cold, is all."

He went back to his cart and wheeled it out of the room. As he made his way to the elevator, he thought he would tell his Salina about Bridgette. He didn't know what to say when a woman was getting knocked around. Maybe Salina could call her up and talk to her. He knew what he would do if he ever ran into her lowlife husband. He just didn't know how to talk to her.

Yes, he would talk to his wife. If anybody could convince a girl to stand up for herself, it was his Salina.

Joe West ran his finger along the rack of time cards in the Housekeeping Department until he got to Moss, L. Pulling it out, he confirmed that Lenny had punched out and was gone.

It was disappointing; he wanted to take care of the pest as soon as Dr. Kadish called, but it also gave him time to look over the contract. He wasn't sure how to cite the employee for impersonating a security guard, but he was confident he would find a work rule somewhere.

It would have to be a major transgression. A three-day suspension wouldn't do. He was going for termination.

—FIFTY-NINE—

Crystal looked at the blood pressure reading on Allendale's monitor as the low-pressure alarm sounded. Shaking her head, she increased the infusion rate of the epinephrine. She noted that the dialysis nurse had seen it as well.

The transplant fellow, having been told to stay in the room throughout the procedure, asked the dialysis nurse how long the patient had been on the treatment.

"Eight minutes," she said dryly, appealing to Crystal with her eyes. Crystal shrugged, as if to say it was up to the physicians to kill the patient, there was nothing the nurses could do about it.

"If the mean arterial pressure does not reach at least sixty I can't dialyze him," she said. "It's too dangerous to put negative pressure on his vascular bed. He'll code."

The fellow frowned. He didn't want to be blamed for the treatment failure. At the same time, he didn't want to be Kadish's whipping boy. He could only take so much abuse.

"Can you lower the flow any?" he asked.

"It's already at the minimum."

The pressure alarm sounded again.

"Can't you shut that thing off?" asked the doctor, referring to the alarm.

"No, I can't," said Crystal, "It's going off for a reason. Why don't you give the order to stop the dialysis?"

"It's okay," said the dialysis nurse, punching a button on her machine. "Dr. Butero told me to quit if I can't maintain a systolic of ninety or better. I can't, he won't, end of story."

Relieved that he didn't have to be the one to make the decision, the transplant fellow walked to the station to page Kadish and tell him that the dialysis had failed. Secretly, he was glad. Allendale never had a chance of surviving the quadruple transplant. The whole thing was a grab for money and publicity; everyone in the department knew it.

Everyone except Kadish. He believed his own press reports.

Lenny aimed the Buick for the Logan section of town and eased back in the bench seat. He had the rear windows lowered, sending a fresh breeze through the cabin, while the radio played cool jazz on the Temple University station.

"Someday I've got to get a better sound system for this old car, he mused. *Subwoofers and all that.*

He had a good sense of the city streets, having grown up in Philly, a small town that didn't know where to stop sprawling. Years of visiting workers of every ethnicity in every section of the city had deepened his knowledge. He realized he could get a job as a cabbie if Joe West ever succeeded in getting rid of him.

He crossed Fifth Street on Lindley and found himself in a neighborhood of sagging porches and broken windows, sinking foundations and shrinking hopes. Built over a landfill, some of the houses were sunk to the doorway. A few were abandoned. In others, the owners held on, trying to get a little compensation from the city.

He pulled up in front of an old brick house with a dented aluminum storm door. There were five buzzers beside the doorway, the names written in fading ink. Lenny found the button for DiPietro, pushed it. He didn't hear a buzz from inside.

Probably broken, like everything else around here.

He knocked on the door. A Spanish woman with a kerchief over her head looked out from a first-floor window.

"Who you looking for?" she asked.

"Mike DiPietro. I'm a friend of his from the hospital. Is he in?"

The woman eyed Lenny's custodian's uniform, saw his name embroidered on his shirt, decided he probably wasn't trouble.

"I don't know if he in or out, but you can go up and see."

He heard a buzz, pushed open the door.

"Third floor rear," she called as the aluminum door slammed shut behind him.

Climbing the dark, unlit stairs, he found Mike's door, knocked, waited.

Form inside came a muffled voice. "Who is it?"

"It's me, Lenny."

A lock turned, a chain rattled, the door opened. Mike stood in the doorway. He was unshaven, dressed in cutoff jeans, old leather slippers, and a t-shirt bleached a hundred times too often.

"As I live and breathe," said Mike, "Lenny Moss, what a surprise. Come in."

Lenny walked into a shabby room, saw the sofa bed open and unmade, a hot plate and tiny fridge on a table in a corner. Flies flitted around a plate of half-eaten food.

"You don't look too good," said Lenny. "Hector says you've been sick."

"It's the damn migraines," said Mike, tapping his head. "I've had them for years. They get better, they get worse. You know, like life."

"Tell me about it."

Lenny studied the man's long, gaunt face. He saw lines of fatigue etched in his cheeks, or were they lines of worry? He also noticed the tremor in Mike's hands as he grasped the plate of food and carried it to a tiny sink.

"I was worried about you," said Lenny.

"I'm okay. I took my medicine Sunday night, and it hit me hard. I had to sleep it off."

"What are you taking, Percocet?"

"No, ergotamine. It's an old treatment, but it's still the best, at least in my case." He ran water over the dishes, saying, "Can I get you a cup of coffee?"

"Thanks, that would be great."

Lenny winced as he saw Mike take out a jar of Wawa brand instant coffee, but said nothing. Mike ran water into a saucepan and set it on the hot plate. Then he spooned some coffee into a cracked mug, took a can of condensed milk from the little fridge, and set them on a plastic picnic table.

Once the coffee was made, the two sat facing each other across the picnic table on white resin chairs.

"Mike, have the police been out to see you?"

Yeah, they were here on Saturday. They woke me up from a deep sleep. I was so groggy, I didn't remember where I was for a couple of minutes."

"Do you mind if I ask you about this? Moose and I are sniffing around Colleen Creedon's death. We want to make sure the cops don't arrest the wrong guy."

"Yeah, like me, right?"

"That's it."

"They asked me the kind of crap that cops always ask. How well did I know Colleen? Did I see her the morning she died? Did I have a romantic involvement with her?"

"Uh-huh. " Lenny sipped his coffee, concealing his concern. He waited, only to meet silence. He had learned from many an interview with a reluctant coworker, if he gave the guy enough time, he often coughed up the story. But Mike wasn't talking.

"Listen, remember that time you didn't come back from vacation on time and I got Human Relations to tear up your suspension?"

"Sure I do, I'll always be grateful for that."

"Well, now I need your help. I don't know what the hell I'm doing in this murder investigation, and I won't get anywhere if you don't fill me in."

"Anything I can do to help, I'll do it, Lenny. Anything at all."

Lenny wondered how far to push the man. Mike looked like he was on the edge, his hands trembling, his eyes bloodshot. He decided to push . . . gently.

"Mike, I know you didn't have anything to do with the woman's death. But the thing is, I need to find out everything about her that I can."

"Why come to me? We just knew each other professionally."

Lenny paused, reached into his shirt pocket. He came up with Colleen's business card with the note on the back saying I NEED TO SEE YOU RIGHT AWAY. He handed it to Mike.

"This was on your desk. It's from Colleen. You want to tell me about it?"

Mike left the business card lying on the table, as if he were afraid to touch it. He just sat silently gripping his coffee mug with two hands, looking as if he would fall apart any minute.

-SIXTY-

Mike let his cup of coffee go cold, having lost his taste for food or drink. Or living. He looked across the table at Lenny.

"I never saw that note before," said Mike. "Honest to Christ, it's news to me. On my desk, you found it?"

"That's right. So you're saying it isn't addressed to you?"

"It doesn't have my name on it, does it?" he said, finally picking up the card and turning it over.

"No, it doesn't," said Lenny. "Could it have anything to do with the time you spent with her in New Orleans?"

"New Orleans?" said Mike, appearing baffled.

"That's right. A drug conference. You, her, a hotel . . . booze, music. Do I have to draw you a picture?"

"Okay, so I went to a drug conference. That doesn't prove anything."

Lenny leaned forward, looked hard at Mike. "I'm trying to help you, Mike, I'm your friend, remember? I know you were mooning over Colleen Creedon for months, *and* that you left your wife after going to New Orleans."

"Yeah. So?"

"So if you dick me around, I'll end up going in circles, and the cops will have a big jump in the investigation. They're a mile ahead of me already."

He watched to see what effect his words were having, deciding to pause and let it all sink in.

After a long moment of silence, Mike said, "You want to know did I go down to New Orleans hoping to sleep with Colleen Creedon. Right?"

"That's right."

"I probably would have left home even without the trip. I was never the kind of guy to sleep around on my wife. You know me, Lenny."

"Yeah . . ."

"But, Christ, I used to get a hard-on every time she came into the department. There was something about her that drove me *nuts*. I was like a stray dog smelling a bitch in heat."

He pushed back from the table on his chair, as if he needed room to be able to tell his story.

"Maybe it was chemistry. Maybe it was a midlife thing, I don't know. But I never wanted any woman as bad as I wanted her. Not even with all the cute little pharmacy students coming through every year on their rotation."

"How far did it go?"

Mike stood up. He swayed a moment, grabbed the table for support. His face was pale and sweaty. He looked like he'd been drunk for a week straight.

"Are you all right?" asked Lenny.

"No, I'm not all right, I'm a fucking mess."

He carried the mugs to the sink and began to soap them up. His hands trembled as he held a cup under the running water. Steam rose from the sink as he rinsed the mug, but he seemed not to care how hot it was.

"We danced the light fantastic," he said softly, the steam rising about his face.

"How's that?" asked Lenny, not sure he'd heard the words clearly.

"We danced."

"That was it? That was the whole deal?"

"I can still smell her hair. I can still feel her body melting in my arms."

Mike turned from the sink, folded his arms across his chest. "She took me to her room and played with me, the way a cat plays with a mouse before she bites its head off, but I didn't care. She could have killed me right there; I would have died happy."

A wistful look cam on his face, then it faded, replaced by sorrow and pain. "I should have died, all the pain I've caused my wife, my kids. My friends. I should be dead and buried in an anonymous grave, with nobody to mourn for me."

"Come on, Mike, spare me the melodrama. You fell in love, you went a little crazy. It happens all the time. You don't have to crucify yourself for it."

Mike looked at the palms of his hands. "Crucify. Yeah. They knew how to punish a guy in those days." He rubbed his hands together. His eyes glistened, threatening tears.

Lenny rubbed his chin, felt the stubble that was always there, thought about the case.

"Was Dr. Kadish at the conference?"

"He sure was, the bastard. The second night he and Colleen weren't at the dinner lecture. They missed the third night, too. When I got back to Philly, I couldn't get her out of my mind. I waited in the pharmacy every day for her to visit. I called her, I left messages at work, but she didn't call back."

He turned off the running water, dried his hands on a filthy towel. "She never let me touch her again. She wouldn't even shake my hand at work."

"Why did you move out on your wife if the affair wasn't going anywhere?"

"After Colleen, everything else seemed pointless. I didn't want to hear about day care and bills. Homework. I wanted to be that mouse again. I wanted her to tease me and make me crazy again. I never gave up hope she'd give me another night, until she was dead."

He sat down again at the table, his shoulders sagging, his eyes still wet.

"You've go to believe me, Lenny, I had nothing to do with Colleen's death. I *loved* the woman. I worshiped the ground she walked on. I couldn't do anything to harm her. It's unthinkable. Impossible."

"I believe you, Mike, for what it's worth. The problem I have is, the cops see the cyanide in her system, they look at you, a pharmacist. You were jilted. You've been acting crazy."

"Of course I'm acting crazy; I've ruined my life and stabbed my wife in the heart!"

"Maybe she'll take you back."

"Who would want me?"

"Don't be so negative. A lot of couples have overcome problems like this. I see it happen all the time."

"Yeah, sure. Even if I *could* patch things up at home, what am I gonna do about the police?"

"That depends."

"On what?

"On whether we can find another suspect the cops will buy, because you've got READY-MADE CONVICT stamped all over you."

Crystal was at the foot of Allendale's bed writing down his vital signs when she realized she'd have to change the numbers—his heart rate was dropping rapidly. The complexes on the heart monitor were growing wider as well. Cardiac arrest was seconds away.

She yelled to the nurse at the station to call a code and bring the crash cart, then she went to one of the intravenous pumps and opened the door. As the alarm on the IV machine joined the cry of the cardiac monitor, she squeezed the bag of epinephrine, forcing a bolus of medication into the patient's bloodstream.

Seconds later the second nurse came in with the crash cart.

"You need the board?" she asked, pulling the CPR board from the cart.

Crystal looked at the monitor, saw that the heart rate was still dropping.

"Yes, I do." She stepped to the bed, put her arms around Allendale's shoulders, and lifted. "I just don't want to be the one pushing on his chest. That wound is going to open up and somebody's going to fall in."

As the two nurses worked the board under Allendale's torso, the first in a troop of physicians, respiratory therapists, supervisors, and medical students entered the room. It was an army bracing for battle.

Crystal wished that this one time she could switch sides.

-SIXTY-ONE-

After leaving Mike, Lenny aimed the big car for home, driving out Lindley across Broad Street and past Wister Woods. Turning onto Germantown Avenue, he thought about Mike and his obsession with Colleen. He tried to imagine the pharmacist becoming so angry that he planned to murder the woman of his dreams, but the scenario didn't play. A man might act out of anger, he reasoned, but that would be spontaneous. Unplanned.

Colleen's death had all the appearances of a carefully planned murder. That suggested that the killer was someone who saw danger approaching and had time enough to eliminate it. Or he was in place to catch a big payoff, but Colleen was standing in his way.

Lenny didn't see how Mike fit into either of those categories. But he had to admit, he didn't have a clue who did. Fox was working with her on a promising new drug, and Kadish used her product to pull off some breakthrough procedure. But what, if anything, did that have to do with her death?

He had no idea.

Like I know how to be a detective, he chided himself. When he was young his mom would tease him. "Mr. Know-So-Much," she called him, because at the dinner table, when a current topic came up, he always had an opinion on an issue.

His dad had enjoyed debating with his son. He would listen thoughtfully during dinner, stroking his chin and nodding at Lenny's run of ideas, dabbing a napkin to his lips. Then he would pull a leg out from Lenny's shaky structure, making it come crashing down.

And then they would have dessert.

It all turned out to be training for Lenny's union duties. Years of negotiating on behalf of his coworkers had taught him that very few people were saints. Some of them really did steal from the hospital. Or slept on the job. Or punched time cards for somebody else who had left work early.

Lenny might become frustrated with the foibles of his coworkers, but he still took issue when the punishment didn't match the crime. Termination was unacceptable. He called it cruel and unusual punishment. In his mind, it was never justified, unless the worker was a threat to the patients, because termination could break up a family. Put them out on the street. Drive a man to drink.

If they weren't lost in the sauce already.

He turned his mind back to the murder investigation. He realized he needed to know more about the victim. All he knew was that she was an ardent sales rep who probably used her sex appeal to boost her sales. Nothing out of the ordinary there.

Mike felt that she had toyed with him. Was she a cockteaser? Maybe she used men more than they used her.

That line of thought was fine, but it still didn't lead to any suspects. He needed to speak to the person who had intimate knowledge of the victim. Someone really close to her.

The fiancée.

But how the hell was he, a hospital custodian, going to get him to talk to him?

Dr. Singh stood outside of Allendale's room, flanked by the ICU residents and medical students. Kadish faced him, backed up by his transplant team. Singh pointed at the patient through the glass partition, saying, "Look at the patient, Doctor. He is a-reflexive. His pupils are fixed and dilated. His coagulopathy is intractable. His heart is only beating because it is in a bath of concentrated catecholamines. You must pronounce him "dead;" there is no possibility that he will recover."

"I admit the prognosis is poor," said Kadish, sounding cool and clinical. "Any first-year medical student can see that. But I'm not ready to give up on him just because of a little bradycardia—"

"Are you saying that *asystole* is just a form of bradycardia? That cardiac arrest is merely a very *slow* heart rhythm?"

"Let's not be pedantic," said Kadish. "The point is, he has a blood pressure, he has a pulse. Ergo, he's alive."

"His brain is not functioning and it never will," said Singh, growing heated. "What's more, he is rejecting all of the organs you gave him."

"You cannot make that determination without examining tissue samples under the microscope."

"The autopsy will just be a pro forma affair," said Singh. "There can be no doubt of the acute rejection. His kidneys are making no urine, his lungs are not transporting oxygen to the blood, his liver is not making clotting factors, and his heart is unable to support his circulation without massive amounts of stimulants."

"I'm preparing him for liver dialysis," said Kadish. "We have the new machine ready to go. Since he was unable to tolerate hemodialysis, we will use hemofiltration to remove excess fluids."

"He doesn't have enough pressure to create a flow through a filter!" said Singh, on the verge of losing his temper. He paused to collect himself. "As attending physician for the ICU this month I have the authority to consult Neurology to undertake a brain-death examination. If you are unwilling to let this poor man finally die, I will have no choice but to bring in a neurologist and have him pronounced."

"He's already been seen by Neurology," said Kadish. "This is *my* patient, and no preening intensivist is writing a single order in *my* patient's chart as long as I have privileges in this hospital."

"Then I will call Dr. Slocum myself and ask him to intervene."

"Call him. See if I give a damn. This is my patient. You will not go near him, or I'll have Security throw you out of the unit."

Turning his back on Singh, Kadish told his team to remain at Allendale's bedside twenty-four, seven. They were to take shifts around the clock and physically block any physician not personally authorized by Kadish to treat the patient.

It took all of Singh's training and self-discipline not to curse Kadish in front of his colleagues. Instead, he turned and walked away, deciding it was best to go to his office, collect his thoughts, and speak to Dr. Slocum, the chief of staff. Surely, thought Singh, the old man would see that further treatment was futile.

Arriving at his office, he pondered what to do. Gradually he came to see that even without the phone call to Slocum and forcing a death pronouncement on Kadish, nature was bound to take its course. Probably before the night was over.

Perhaps it was best to let sleeping dogs lie, and let dying men fall at their own speed.

"Daddy, could you help me with my homework?"

"Sure," said Moose, putting down his copy of the *Daily News*. He followed his daughter, Patrice, into the little room off the kitchen where they had the computer set up. She had a book open on the scanner.

"I need to put this picture into my report," she explained.

"Okay. Did you give the picture a file name?"

"Oh, sorry, I forgot."

Moose showed her how to save the scanned image with an appropriate name so that she could find it later with the search program.

"If you keep the file size small, it'll be easier to move around in the computer. You see?"

"Uh-huh," she answered, using the copy command to put the picture on the clipboard.

Good," said Moose, looking over the page of the report. "Now put the cursor where you want to insert the photo, then hit the paste button.

"I know," she said, watching as the text opened itself up to make room for the photo. "But it's upside down!"

He showed her how to open the image-rendering tools. After a few misses, she was able to grab the curving handles on the image and spin the image around until it was upright and centered on the page.

"You can shrink it, too," Moose reminded her.

"I *know*, Daddy, I'm not a little child."

"Heh, heh." He pulled back and looked at his daughter. "You are getting awful grown up. Are you eighteen yet?"

She smacked him on the chest, saying, "You know I'm only twelve, but I'll be thirteen this summer!"

Standing up, he said, "You all right to work on your own?"

She nodded her head, already busy on another part of her project. He went back to the dining room to finish his paper.

-SIXTY-TWO-

"Morning, Boop," said Lenny as he came onto the ward at six-thirty in the morning. "How're you doing?"

"Good morning, dear heart," she answered. "The Lord smiled upon me when I awoke this morning. I can't ask for anything more." She piled rolls of toilet paper and bundles of paper towels into her cart, adding, "But you look troubled. Somebody been messing with you again?"

"No, I'm okay. Everyone wants to take off for Fred's funeral. I just don't see how I'm going to get the administration to let them go."

"God will show us the way," she answered. "He wants us all to celebrate Fred's journey home. Trust in Him, all will be well."

He went to the Housekeeping locker, took out a dry mop, and had just started sweeping the hall when he ran into Moose, who had come to pick up the menus for the late admissions. Moose asked about the funeral plans. When Lenny told him that it didn't look like Freely would be changing his mind about people going to the funeral, Moose balled up his fists.

"We're still goin', ain't we?" asked Moose.

"I don't know. They want to replace every full-time worker with part-timers. Walking off the job might give them an opportunity to terminate a lot of workers. They'd save a billion dollars in benefits. I'd like us all to go, it's just—"

"What do you mean, you'd 'like' to? That's not what your dad would have said. He'd be saying, 'Shut it down! Walk out! Spit in their eye!' That's what he'd say if he were alive."

"Those were different times, Moose. There was more militancy in the unions. More fight-back spirit."

"We're the same workers and they're the same bosses. Nothin's changed."

Lenny put a hand up to his face, felt the rough stubble that was always present, even an hour after shaving.

"Maybe I'm being selfish, Moose, but if I lead a walkout that the union hasn't authorized, they'll pull me off the stewards' committee. I won't be a rep anymore."

"They can do that?"

"Yeah. It's in the contract." He stepped through the double doors into Seven North. "I don't want to sound like the union *has* to have me for a steward, but I think I do a *little* good for the rank and file."

245

"Don't give me that humble pie, man, it's bullshit and you know it. We need you on the front line. Nobody's takin' you off the union leadership. It's just like when they found the woman dead on your unit. We all hung together, and that's what all of us are gonna do if the union president tries to mess with you."

"The only way that we can force the administration to give us permission to go is if we get a really strong turnout for the funeral. If we can pull fifty, sixty people and all go together to Freely's office, I think he'll back down."

"Back down? He'll beg us to let him come to the service." Moose jabbed his friend in the arm, a grin on his broad face. "Don't worry. We're gonna have a hundred workers behind you. We'll have Freely making a donation for the family."

Lenny nodded his head slowly, encouraged, as always, by his friend's enthusiasm and support. "Okay. We march on Freely's office at twelve-thirty. He hates confrontation. He'll have to give us the time."

"That's the way to do it. Now what about the murder investigation?"

"I'm gonna talk to Tina again about Dr. Fox. I'll get with you when you bring up the breakfast trays."

"I'll catch you later," said Moose, who hurried off to finish his rounds.

Crystal looked at Allendale's bloated body, still attached to the ventilator, still not completely dead, and shook her head in disgust. Blood oozed continuously from his mouth and nose. His eyes were so swollen with fluid, they were just slits in a puffed-up face. There was blood in the endotracheal tube, blood in the urine tube, and bloody fluid running out of puncture wounds in the arms.

She knew that Allendale should have been taken off life support the night before, after he coded. Although they had restarted his heart and achieved a minimal blood pressure, his pupils were fixed and dilated, the brain was gone. Dr. Singh was ready to pronounce him dead and shut off the epinephrine infusion, which would drop his blood pressure and stop his heart in about a minute, but Kadish still had a resident watching over the patient, making sure that Singh didn't take measures into his own hand.

Kadish wanted to string out the illusion of life as long as possible, and politics ruled the hospital. The longer his patient "lived," the better his "breakthrough" procedure looked. They could claim the quadruple transplant was a limited success.

And they say nurses are bitches?

She hung another unit of blood, adding the blood bank slip to a thick stack of slips piling up in the bedside chart. They must have given him over fifty units of blood, platelets, frozen plasma, albumin, cryoprecipitate. It was crazy. Money down the drain. They were transfusing a corpse.

She realized the bottom line was public relations, big time. It all added up to new surgical cases coming in, more money in the hospital's bank account.

A man wearing a white lab coat over a brown suit walked up to Crystal. She thought he looked familiar, but couldn't place him. He certainly wasn't one of the physicians on the transplant or critical care service. Still, she knew she'd seen him before.

The man looked through the glass doors at Allendale in the isolation room. He said without looking at Crystal, "He's not progressing very well, is he."

She thought it was an odd phrase, "progressing very well." Nobody in the hospital talked like that. It was amateurish. Fake.

She stood directly in front of the man, spread her feet like a linebacker ready to rumble, looked him dead in the eyes and said, "Can I see your hospital ID, please?"

"Uh, sure," he said, fishing in his pockets. When he ran out of pockets, he said, "Gee, I seem to have left it in my locker. I'll be right back."

As the man hurried out of the ICU, Crystal suddenly remembered where she'd seen the man. He was a reporter on one of the local TV stations.

She picked up the phone and called Security.

Dr. Fox stepped into the GI lab, where Tina was setting up a scope for the first procedure of the day.

"I have a family emergency," he told her. "I have to be out of the hospital for a while. I've asked Dr. Amankwah to do the two colons we have scheduled. The fellow will handle the uppers."

"You're letting a surgeon do your colonoscopies?" she said, not believing she had heard him correctly.

"Yes. He's very good. I left his page number with Myrna. Just call him when you're ready to start."

"Okay." She gently coiled the scope on the portable cart and attached it to the light source. "Is one of your kids sick?"

"It's personal. I'll tell you about it when I come back."

He turned and walked out of the room. Tina stepped into the hall and watched the slim figure with the stooped shoulders and the prematurely gray hair. She noticed that at the end of the hall, instead of turning right and going to the elevator, he entered the stairwell. That was not his habit.

"He must be in a powerful hurry," she mumbled, stepping into the office. "Hey, Myrna, do you believe this? Dr. Fox is letting a *surgeon* do colons in the lab today!"

Myrna threw a memo in the copy machine and punched the print button, saying, "I know, isn't it crazy? I don't even know how I'm going to bill it."

"Screw the bill," said the nurse. "I want to know what the Gray Fox is up to!"

"You and me both." The secretary removed the copies and began to stuff them into inter-departmental envelopes.

—SIXTY-THREE—

Mae Yeung introduced herself to the half-dozen women from the linen room as she passed out handouts to the women from the laundry seated in a small circle in the employee lounge.

"Good morning, girls! My name is Mae Yeung. I am one of the hospital social workers. I've asked you all to join me today for a discussion of abuse against woman." She paused a moment, looked at each woman's face, letting her words sink in, then continued.

"I know that this is a subject that is hard to talk about. I'm going to go around the room, and I want everyone to introduce yourself, and then I'd like you to tell me how your significant other treats you. All right?"

The women fidgeted in their chairs, looked down at the floor.

The social worker turned to the woman seated beside her. "Sadie, why don't you begin?"

Sadie, a middle-aged white woman from South Philly, cleared her throat.

"My old man don't knock me around much," she said. "He spends a lot of time in the bar with his buddies. When he comes dragging his ass home, he usually falls asleep on the couch."

Several women nodded their head, recognizing the story.

"Sometimes he can't get up the stairs," she continued. "Fact is, he can't get much of anything up, all the drinking he's done."

Smiles and laughter sprinkled the little group.

"Is he verbally abusive?" asked Mae.

"I guess that depends on what you call 'abusive.' Sometimes he says I'm a pain in his backside. Or a ball and chain 'round his neck. It's not sweet talk, I know, but it's not as bad as some of my friends get."

"Thank you for sharing," said Mae. "Lisa, what's your mate like?"

"My old man used to knock me around, but he don't do it no more, he ran off with some young thing last year. He left me with two kids, but we get by."

"Is there a new man in your life?"

"I have a friend, yeah. Marlon. He's kind of old. He has a wife, but he lives with me."

"How does he treat you?"

"All right, I guess. He doesn't hit me or anything. He falls asleep a lot after dinner. Like I said, he's kind of old, but I'd rather have old and sleepy than young and mean, know what I'm saying?"

"Mmm, those sound like hard choices," said Mae. "It seems like you've chosen to be safe." She turned to the next woman in the circle, saying, "What about you, Bridgette?"

Bridgette sat hunched over, her arms crossed, her hands tucked into her armpits, as though she were cold. She stared at her lap.

"Bridgette? Would you like to share your thoughts, even if it's just about what Sadie or Lisa was talking about?"

"They don't have nothin' to do with me. My old man don't come home drunk."

"That's a good sign. How does he treat you?"

"He all right," she said, not looking up.

"All right. What would you say is good about how he treats you, and what would you say is not so good?"

"Well," said Bridgette, collecting herself, "sometimes he tells me I'm pretty. And he jumps my bones a lot, 'cause I'm so hot and sexy. He tells me that lots of times."

"That's good. He gives you affirmation for your sexuality. Is he always loving in the way that he treats you?"

"No, not all the time."

"What is he like when he's not so loving?"

The other women held their breath. They had seen the heavy makeup and the dark glasses, had noted the days when she spoke to no one, keeping to herself, as if ashamed. Or scared.

Sadie reached over and put her hand on Bridgette's arm. "It's okay, honey, you're with friends."

Bridgette cleared her throat, looked at Mae. "A couple of times he did kind of get mad," she said.

"What happened?"

Tears slid down Bridgette's cheeks. She clenched her hands and hunched down in her seat.

"I guess I got myself made up too pretty. Roland said I was making eyes at a dude in the club, but I wasn't making eyes at nobody. I was just being nice."

"What did Roland do?"

Bridgette put her hand to the side of her face, as if touching a fresh wound.

"When we got home he about knocked my teeth out with the back of his hand. I thought he was gonna kill me, but he didn't. He just slapped me around a couple more times, then he was rough with me."

'Rough . . . " said Mae.

"You know, rough. In bed." She began to cry.

While Sadie held one of Bridgette's hands, Mae clasped the other. Leaning closer and speaking softly, she said, "You don't have to risk dying, dear, in order to be loved."

The other women added their assent. They encouraged Bridgette to get out of the relation. The more they encouraged her, the more she cried.

Crystal withdrew two amps of epinephrine from the glass ampoules and injected the medication into a small bag of normal saline. They were using up a bag every two hours—an ungodly amount of Adrenalin. It was the only thing keeping Allendale's blood pressure high enough to even pretend that the patient was alive. If you called an arterial blood pressure of seventy over thirty-five "living".

Walking up to the intravenous pump at the head of the bed, the nurse noticed that the date on the tag stuck to the IV tubing was three days old. According to hospital policy, all tubing in the ICU was to be changed every other day to prevent bacterial contamination of the line.

Crystal knew that she didn't have to change the tubing on Allendale's epinephrine; his case was an exception. If she put the IV pump on hold for a minute, stopping the infusion, his blood pressure would rapidly drop to zero. He would suffer another cardiac arrest, almost certainly a fatal one.

She looked about the room, saw that the transplant resident who had been ordered to watch over the patient was on the telephone talking to his girlfriend. He was supposed to watch out for doctors writing unapproved orders, not nurses doing their job.

Crystal decided that the patient was at risk of acquiring a bloodstream infection if she left the old intravenous tubing in place. It was better to change it.

Pressing the "hold" button on the pump, she told herself that, after all, she was only following hospital policy.

—SIXTY-FOUR—

Dr. Eisenberg knocked on the open door and entered Mrs. Cavanaugh's room. As she approached the patient, she saw a middle-aged woman sitting in a chair in the corner knitting a shawl.

The doctor held out her hand to the woman in the chair, saying, "Hello, I'm Dr. Eisenberg. I'm caring for Mrs. Cavanaugh."

"I'm Judy, her daughter," said the woman. Holding up her knitting, she said, "Mom, you like the colors, don't you?"

"It's not my favorite blue. I like a robin's egg blue. You know that."

"They didn't have that at the craft store."

Mrs. Cavanaugh sighed, threw a look at her daughter as if to say, "Why can't she ever get it right?"

Eisenberg looked at the shawl. "I think it's lovely. Is it for your mother?"

"Yes, it's almost finished. I hope she'll wear it."

"You can put it over my head when you bury me."

The doctor pulled a chair over to the bedside and sat down. As she did, Judy put down her knitting.

"You two want to talk. I'll go have a cup of tea."

"It's all right with me if you stay," said the doctor.

"No, I'll go," said the daughter, standing up and hurrying out of the room.

Once they were alone, the doctor said, "I thought you had no family."

"We're estranged. We haven't talked in years. She drops me a card on my birthday and on Christmas. That's about it."

"Then you hadn't told her about your cancer?"

"No, but she heard the nurse asking me about my chemotherapy."

"It's very lucky for you she found out."

"I don't see why, I have enough to deal with already."

"Well, I'm sure it's a comfort to have someone close to you when you're receiving chemotherapy." She opened the chart and glanced at a lab report. "How are you feeling? Are you tolerating the medication all right?"

"It's not too bad. I got a little sick to my stomach, but I kept my food down."

That's very encouraging."

"How many more treatments will I have to have?"

"Six more."

"Six?"

"Yes, You'll receive two more doses in the hospital, then you can come back as an outpatient and have them done in our chemotherapy unit. Will your daughter be able to drive you to the hospital?"

"I suppose she'll have to."

"It sounds to me like you have some issues with her regarding your independence. Perhaps you're uncomfortable reaching out to her and asking for help getting to the clinic. Is that it?"

"No, that's not it. She's a *terrible* driver."

Ding!... Ding!... Ding!

As the alarm on the cardiac monitor chimed, Crystal reached up and pressed the one-minute silence button. Having turned off the intravenous pump in order to hang a new bag of epinephrine with new tubing, she had slowly and methodically hung the new bag and restarted the pump while the blood pressure drifted down to zero.

Stepping out of the room, she called to the nurse at the desk, "Lydie, would you call a code please?" The other nurse picked up the phone and dialed the code operator.

The transplant resident who had been told to watch over the patient leaped up from the nursing station, where he had been on the phone, and ran toward the room.

"*Shit*, is Allendale coding again? *Shit*, Dr. Kadish is going to kill me!"

The Resident hurried to the room, behind a nurse pushing the crash cart. The nurse broke open the cart and whipped out two syringes of Adrenalin. Tossing one to Crystal, she assembled the other and quickly injected it into the patient's IV tubing. Crystal gave the second right after her.

Crystal calmly and methodically pulled on a pair of gloves, disconnected the ventilator, attached an ambu bag, turned up the oxygen flow to the bag, and began to squeeze the bag. The resident began pressing on the patient's chest, asking, "What happened?"

"He bradied down and dropped his pressure," said Crystal. "He's already on maximum doses of epi and Dopamine."

As the resident increased the speed and pressure of his chest compressions, Crystal told him, "Do you really have to work so hard? You're trying to revive a dead man."

254

Sandy ambled down the Seven South corridor, glancing into the patient rooms as he walked. The walkie-talkie squawked on his belt. Seeing Lenny washing an empty bed, he went into the room.

"Yo, Lenny. What's goin' on?"

"Hi, Sandy."

"How's it look for the funeral? You think Human Relations will cut you some slack?"

"The only thing he agreed to was we could combine our morning break with our lunchtime."

"That's not near enough time to join the service. We can't pay our respects."

"Tell me about it," said Lenny, running a wet rag over the side rails and headboard.

"I thought I better tell you, Joe West said in morning report we had to write down the time and the name of any employee who leaves the building today, and write up when they come back, too. Even if they punch out, we still got to make a record."

"He's a cold son of a bitch," said Lenny, pulling the mattress up and washing the bed frame beneath it. "I'd like to see him put away for what he did to Fred."

"You and a couple hundred others. But my friend on the force tells me nobody in the DA's office is talking about charging him with anything over Fred's death. It would make the hospital look bad."

"Of course. We have to preserve the good name of James Madison." Finished with the bed, he carried his bucket out to the corridor and took up his mop.

"Thanks for giving me the heads up," said Lenny.

"Ain't no big thing," said Sandy. "How's the murder investigation going?"

"Not great. We haven't really come up with a motivation. Without that we're shooting in the dark, plus we don't really know *how* she was killed."

"I thought she was poisoned. Cyanide, right?"

"She had traces of it in her blood, but supposedly it wasn't enough to kill her, although it might have been enough to hurt the baby."

"She was *pregnant?*" said Sandy.

"Yup. We're not sure who the father is. That's something else we have to get a line on."

"Well, you keep digging, I know you'll get it done. Just don't forget, I want to be there to put the cuffs on, just like I did with the Sparks murder."

"I promise, Sandy, if there's any way to bring you in to make the arrest, I'll do it."

With a broad smile lifting his hound dog face, the old guard continued with his rounds.

—SIXTY-FIVE—

After cleaning the empty beds and removing the trash from the patient rooms, Lenny saw that it was nearly nine. He signed off to Betty and made his way to the GI lab, where he found Tina cleaning a pair of scopes at the sink.

"How ya doing, Tina?" asked Lenny.

"I'm waiting for a surgeon to come do a colon, but he's in the OR. Dr. Fox left early, he had a family emergency."

"Is it okay if we talk? In private?"

"If you have to," she said, laying the scope out on a towel on the counter. "Come on back to the office and have some coffee."

They walked through the office to their little lounge area, where Myrna was sitting with a woman's magazine and a cup of coffee. The secretary saw him eye the coffeepot.

"You want some?"

"Please!"

As he took the cup and settled into a folding chair, he said to Tina, "I'm still wondering about the drug study Dr. Fox was working on with Colleen Creedon."

"Why you always picking on Dr. Fox? He's a very dedicated physician. And he's the best in the business. Do you know that he has the highest percentage of positive endoscopic exams of any gastroenterologist in all of Philadelphia? Let me tell you, when that man says you got an ulcer or colitis or whatever, you can take it to the bank!"

"I'm not questioning his skills," said Lenny, "I'm just trying to figure out if there's a connection between him and Colleen Creedon's death."

"Why would there be?" she asked.

"Well, he was getting a thousand bucks for looking at the patients. Money's a good motivator."

"That was for doing *two* endoscopic examinations," said Myrna, "plus three office visits, a complete physical, and a ton of paperwork!"

"That's not a lot?" asked Lenny.

"We make more money on an inpatient procedure than we do with a study patient," said Myrna, "when you factor in all the labor hours involved, he's doing better billing Medicare than doing the study for Falcon."

"*See?*" said Tina. "It ain't about the money. Dr. Fox was helping to prove that the drug really worked and was safe. He was making a contribution to medicine."

"Then there was nothing suspicious about the drug study?"

"I've seen the results with my own eyes," said Tina. "Pictures don't lie."

Lenny sipped his coffee, wondering if pushing Tina more would just make her more defensive, or break through her story.

"If everything was kosher, how come one of his patients went to Women and Children's for a second opinion?" asked Lenny.

Myrna shot a questioning glance at Tina. "Tell him," said the secretary.

Tina's face turned sad.

"So somebody went and had another doctor look in his stomach after Dr. Fox did the upper," she said. "He was just ornery, that's all. It wasn't no big thing."

Myrna poked the nurse in the arm, saying, "If Dr. Fox is innocent, nothing bad will come from your telling Lenny."

"I don't like to go behind the doctor's back," said Tina. She put her coffee cup down, repositioned her hips on the chair, cleared her throat. "We did an endoscopy on this old coot two-three weeks ago."

"You looked in his stomach?" Lenny asked.

"That's it. He had an ulcer, so we put him on the study drug and Myrna scheduled him for a follow-up upper in two weeks."

"To document that the ulcer had healed," explained Myrna.

"Okay," said Lenny, noting Tina's guarded body language.

"This old guy was a real pain in the butt. He asked questions about every-thing. Why did we do this, why did we do that. He wanted to know why we put him to sleep for the procedure, how did he know we weren't doing some experiment on his body."

"The man's been watching too many *X Files*," said Myrna.

"Prob'ly so," said Tina. "Anyhow, any of the patients that get conscious sedation, we have to call them up at home the next day, make sure they're feel-ing all right. It's a state requirement. He wasn't in, but I did get a hold of him late in the afternoon on the day *after* that, and he told me he went to Women and Children's and had *another* upper endoscopy done over there."

"The insurance carrier wanted to get out of paying for it," said Myrna. "They knew from the patient that we'd done the same procedure just the day before, and they were questioning the medical need to repeat it."

"In the end they gave the okay for the procedure," explained Myrna. "Falcon paid the full cost of the one we did here, so there was no double bill, and he *did* have the symptoms of a gastric ulcer."

"What did the old guy tell you when you reached him?" asked Lenny.

"He said the doctors at Women and Children's told him he didn't *have* an ulcer. They said his stomach was perfectly normal!"

Lenny looked into Tina's face. "How could somebody have an ulcer on one day and no ulcer on the next?"

"It beats me," said Tina. "I saw his ulcer on the monitor as plain as day. Dr. Fox took pictures of it."

"Can I see the photo?" he asked.

"Sure, the files are all together. I'll go get them."

She opened a file cabinet, withdrew a thick folder. Rummaging through it, she soon found the patient's chart.

"Here you go, Arnold Dortman. His name's as dumb as he is." She opened the chart to the procedure note, pointed at the photo. "See, there's the ulcer, as plain as the nose on your face."

"Don't get personal," said Lenny.

"We started him on the study drug and scheduled him to come back for a repeat in two weeks to document that the ulcer was all healed up."

"Why did he go to Women's? Did he say?"

"I don't think he ever believed us when we told him he had an ulcer. He thought he had heart trouble, but the cardiologists cleared him and sent him to *us*. I think he was just a suspicious old coot."

"But how could the second study not find the ulcer if it was really there?" asked Lenny.

"Listen, the whole GI tract has lots and lots of folds in it. Maybe when they looked, the ulcer was hiding in one of the folds and they missed it."

"That doesn't sound likely," said Lenny. "They must have known your doctor told him he had an ulcer. They'd be trying extra hard to find it, wouldn't they?"

"I guess they would," agreed Tina. "It don't make no sense to me no how."

Myrna said, "Lenny, do you really think that Dr. Fox could have killed Colleen?"

"I don't know what to think. I just know it's suspicious, this guy who has an ulcer and then he doesn't." He tossed his coffee cup in the trash and stood up. "I have to get back to my floor, Joe West is gunning for me."

As he turned to go, Tina said, "Hey, Lenny, we're going to Fred's funeral, aren't we? I hear it's at one o'clock."

"We don't have permission from Freely. The plan is for as many of us as possible to meet in the main lobby at twelve-thirty. We'll march on his office and demand to be released."

"The way Joe West killed poor old Fred, letting us go is the least they could do," said Myrna.

"Unfortunately, when you back a mad dog in a corner, he usually doesn't wag his tail and let you pass."

—SIXTY-SIX—

When Lenny returned to his ward from the GI lab, he saw Nadia, the nurse's aide, who beckoned to him from the room where she was making beds.

"Oh, Lenny, I am glad you are here. A man called. He wants you to go to the morgue right away. He say it's urgent."

"The *morgue*? That's not my area; what the hell is he talking about?"

"He say Mr. Childress himself wants you with the mop and bucket. They spill something nasty, I think, and they need it cleaned up right away."

"Jesus Christ, as if I don't have enough work to do in this fricking place. I'm filing a grievance for unfair working conditions. This is ridiculous."

He pushed his mop and bucket along the hall to the service elevator and rode down. Arriving at the basement, he pushed his bucket past the room where contractors were remodeling a section of the storeroom. The loud rat-a-tat-tat of a jackhammer bombarded his ears. Knowing that the outside contractors did not enforce safety regulations as vigorously as did the hospital Maintenance Department, he checked out the workman on the jackhammer as he passed. The sound was loud enough to wake the dead. Happily, the workman was wearing protective earpads.

Not that the James Madison maintenance men were angels. He recalled how they used to take a piss into the floor drains in the machine shop, rather than walk up a flight of stairs to get to a toilet. That was disgusting, especially when somebody tried to unclog one of the drains with a Roto-Rooter. He broke the pipe, which was old and brittle, spilling urine and dirty water through the ceiling tiles into the room below.

Arriving at the Pathology Department, he recalled the many jokes Fred had forced on him over the years. The bouts with alcohol. The battles to keep his job. Dr. Fingers and Dr. Primeaux testifying for Fred and writing letters of support. All to be destroyed by that bastard West, and diabetes.

Death was a bitch.

Lenny saw a slim doctor with mask and gown cutting up an organ on a counter, bloody fluid running down into the sink.

"You got a spill I'm supposed to clean up?" asked Lenny.

"In the fridge," said the doctor, pointing to the walk-in refrigerator where they stored the dead bodies.

"Shit," said Lenny, "I might have known it would be in there."

Opening the thick, insulated door, Lenny stepped in to assess the situation. Suddenly he felt a terrible pain in his skull as a hard object came crashing down on his head. Shoved roughly into the cold storage room, his knees buckled and he fell to the floor.

The last thing he remembered was the how filthy the floor was.

Gary stopped his medication cart in front of Mrs. Cavanaugh's room. Going in to give her the twelve-o'clock medication, he saw the shawl that her daughter had knit in the trash. He picked it up, held it out for the old woman to see.

"Excuse me, Mrs. Cavanaugh, did you mean for this to go in the trash?"

She turned her face away from him, clamped her mouth shut, the way some patients did when they refused to eat.

"Your daughter was knitting it, wasn't she?"

"Hmmph." Mrs. Cavanaugh still refused to look at him or to answer.

Gary pulled a chair over to the bedside, sat down, looked at the old woman. He saw many things. A woman with cancer, fearful for her life. A patient who'd been through surgery and experienced pain every time she coughed or got out of bed. A mother with a conflicted relation with her daughter.

He sat quietly for another moment. He wanted the woman to accept her daughter's offer of assistance and support, but he was not sure what to say. Finally he told her, "Your daughter hasn't give up on you. How about if you don't give up on you?"

Casting weary, tearful eyes on him, she reached out a hand and grasped Gary's arm with gnarled fingers, squeezing him so hard that it hurt.

"I don't understand why she came. All the times I turned her away. Why does she come back? What does she want?"

"I don't know," said Gary. "Perhaps she wants to be your daughter."

She released his arm, settled back into bed. Gary handed her a little cup with her pills in it. She took them in her mouth, swallowed them with a sip of water, then looked up at Gary again.

"Thank you, Mr. Tuttle."

He left her to continue his rounds.

Moose was really looking forward to the confrontation with Freely over Fred's funeral. He stopped in at the sewing room, where he found Birdie going through torn sheets. Those that were strong enough she sewed up and sent to the laundry. The ones that were threadbare she made into pillowcases or tore into rags for the housekeepers.

"Hey, baby," he said, striding into the room.

"Hi, Moose. We still meeting in the lobby at quarter to twelve?"

"We got to, Human Resources hasn't given us extra time. We're all gonna march on Freely's office. We're gonna push him till he gives in."

"Good. That's such a dirty deal, telling us we can't go to Fred's service, and it was their Joe West that killed him!"

"West is gonna pay, it's just a matter of time. I'm going up to Seven South and see how Lenny's doing, I'll see you at twelve," he said, opening the door to go.

"I'll make some more calls. 'Bye," she said, and blew him a kiss.

–SIXTY-SEVEN–

"What the fuck," mumbled Lenny, lifting his head off the cold floor of the morgue refrigerator. His face was icy and numb; his head, aching. He rolled over and pushed himself up to a sitting position. In a moment his head began to clear and he realized where he was.

"This is fucked up," he said. "I'm freezing."

He grabbed the edge of a stretcher and pulled himself to a standing position, the throbbing in his head growing worse. He reached for the handle, a round plate on a shaft, and pushed it in, then he pressed on the door. The door didn't budge.

"Fucking A," he said. Placing both hands on the cold metal door, he bent his knees and pushed with all his strength. The thick, insulated door did not give a millimeter.

He pressed and pulled on the latch. It was obviously disconnected, since it offered no resistance to his pressing it.

He banged on the door with his hand.

"This is not funny!" he called. "This is fucked up!"

He continued banging and hollering, but nobody came to his assistance. Then he recalled the rat-a-tat-tat of the jackhammer just down the hall and the workman with the earpads on, and a sense of foreboding came over him.

He yelled and banged on the door with all his might.

Moose emerged from the stairwell onto Seven South grinning and eager to talk to join up with Lenny. It was almost twelve. Time to get ready to go in the ring.

He walked the length of the hall, glancing side to side at every room, looking for his friend. No sign of him. He went to the Housekeeping locker, found it empty. Going to the nursing station, he asked Gary, "Where's Lenny? He's supposed to meet me, like, now?"

"I don't now, Moose. I haven't seen him since I went to the pharmacy to pick up a STAT order."

He crossed through the fire doors to Seven North, where Lenny also was assigned. Betty was there with her cart.

"You seen Lenny?" he asked her.

"No, dear heart, not for a while. Is something wrong?"

"I don't know. I'm supposed to meet him here so we can go over the plan before meeting everybody in the lobby."

Betty looked at the clock on the wall, saying, "He didn't tell me where he was going. Sorry."

Lenny felt himself getting sleepy. He thought he'd read somewhere that when people froze to death, they got very drowsy and just drifted off. Maybe it was something he saw on the Discovery channel. It was supposed to be a peaceful death. No pain. No terror. Just blissful sleep.

He told himself, *Get a hold of yourself, Moss! You're too young to die. Besides, you've got a killer to uncover.*

He stepped over to a stretcher, saw that the corpse was resting on a sheet. Rolling the body from side to side, he wrestled the sheet free. It was wet with an ugly brown fluid. Grimacing, he folded the sheet so the wet portion was more or less away from his body, and he wrapped the sheet around his shoulders and chest.

Next he eyed the plastic shroud wrapped around the corpse. It was secured with a lot of nursing tape. Too much to unroll without tearing it. And it would be full of fluids. Realizing that he would quickly freeze to death if he got wet, he left the shroud untouched.

He examined the door, looking for a hinge to take apart, but the door had external hinges. The inner aspect was smooth.

Hoping to distinguish the noise of his banging from the workmen down the hall, he tried rapping on the door with the handle of his paint scraper in a Morse code kind of pattern, using the handle of his paint scraper.

BANG!BANG!BANG!

Bang . . . bang . . . bang . . .

BANG!BANG!BANG!

The sounds didn't really mimic the 'Save Our Ship' signal of three short beeps, three long beeps, then three short ones again. He alternated banging with the handle and scraping with the blade, which produced a longer, more accurate sound.

BANG!BANG!BANG!

Scrape . . . scrape . . . scrape . . .

BANG!BANG!BANG!

Nobody came to open the door. His efforts seemed to be falling on deaf ears.

"What are you, deaf out there?"

His earlier sense of foreboding was blossoming into outright terror. The goose bumps that he felt on his arms were not just from the cold.

"LET ME OUT OF HERE, I'M FREEZING MY ASS OFF!"

He repeated his SOS maneuvers, alternating them with baleful howls, thinking that if someone heard a dog in the building, they would think it odd and come to investigate. "OW-WOOOO!" he called out. "OW-WOOO!"

As the cold penetrated to his bones, he used his steel-tipped shoes to kick a staccato rhythm on the metal-lined door, trying to work up a reggae beat.

Tap. Tap. Tap-tap-tap. Tap (two, three, four).

Tap. Tap. Tap-tap-tap. Tap.

He repeated the kicking, the beating with the scraper, and the calling out, varying the tempo, increasing the volume, as long as he could. But the cold was sapping his strength. His hands and feet were numb. He couldn't feel his toes inside the shoes, just like when he was a kid and his dad kept him and his brother out too late sledding in Fairmont Park, and he got frostbite. His mother warmed his feet in a bucket of warm water, while feeding him hot chocolate and berating his father, who predicted the boy would keep all of his toes.

Lenny had the terrible thought that he would die in the fridge and be buried frozen stiff. A wave of fatigue washed over him. The floor, cold as it was, looked so inviting. He wanted nothing more than to curl up on the floor and sleep.

To sleep, he thought. *Perchance to freeze.*

-SIXTY-EIGHT-

Moose checked the staff toilet and the conference room on Seven South looking for Lenny, without success. He went to the nursing station and asked Gary if he knew where his friend was, but the nurse had no idea.

He went back down the hall going into the patient rooms, calling Lenny's name. In one room he came upon Nadia, the nursing assistant, who was sitting with an elderly patient, feeding her.

"You look for Mr. Lenny?" she asked.

"Yeah, you seen him?"

"He had to go down to the morgue. They had a spill. He went down a long time ago."

"How long is that?"

"More than an hour, I think. Maybe two, even."

Moose returned to the station and told Gary what he had learned.

Gary looked at Moose, worry rumpling his face.

"Perhaps I'm being an alarmist," he said, "but in all the time I've worked here, no one has ever pulled Lenny or Betty to the morgue. They have other housekeepers who cover down there. Besides which, it shouldn't take *that* long to clean up a spill."

"I agree. It smells rotten. We better go down there and check it out."

They walked together toward the elevator, Gary telling the other nurse that he would be right back. Moose pointed out it was quicker to take the stairs.

As they descended, their alarm grew. By the time they had reached the third floor, Moose was taking the steps three at a time, while Gary worked hard to keep up.

In the basement, they heard the sound of drills and hammering, then the staccato of a jackhammer. Passing Dumpsters loaded with debris, they hurried on down a dimly lit corridor to the pathology lab, which was empty. They passed Dr. Fingers' office; the door was closed, the light off inside. No Lenny.

At the end of the hall they saw the sign on the wall: MORGUE. Approaching the big refrigerator, they saw a mop and bucket.

Moose ripped open the heavy metal door. He saw Lenny, curled up in a fetal position on a metal stretcher, covered in a dirty sheet. His lips were blue, as was his nose. His eyes were closed. Moose couldn't tell if he was breathing.

"Gary, check him out!"

Rushing in, the nurse stumbled over a cadaver on the floor. Catching his balance, he reached Lenny and placed his fingers lightly on the motionless figure's neck.

"He's got a good pulse. It's slow, but strong."

"Lenny! Hey, man, open your eyes, it's Moose!"

Lenny slowly opened his eyes. He seemed to have trouble focusing. He lifted one hand from where he'd tucked it in his armpit beneath the sheet, reached out to touch Moose's face.

"Mm-mm-Moose, am I dead?"

"No, man, you're with the living. Let's get you out of this box."

They lifted him to a sitting position and eased him down to the floor. With teeth chattering, Lenny wrapped his arms around his friends and let them help him out of the morgue.

"Jesus Christ, you're cold!" said Moose, wrapping his big arms around his friend.

"I thought I was back in this apartment me and my brother had," said Lenny. "It was so cold my waterbed froze."

"He's suffering from hypothermia," said Gary. "We have to get him to the emergency room. They can wrap him in a warming blanket and monitor his heart."

"My h-h-heart is hunky-d-d-dory," said Lenny between chattering teeth. "What time is it?"

"It's just twelve," said Moose.

"I have to see Freely. It's almost time for the funeral."

"But Lenny," said Gary, "if your core body temperature is below ninety-two degrees, you're in danger of suffering serious arrhythmias until you warm up again."

"Fuck my core body temperature," said Lenny. "I want to nail the bastard that locked me in that fucking box!"

"But—"

"No buts, Tuttle, we're going to the lobby."

—SIXTY-NINE—

By the time Lenny, Moose, and Gary reached the main lobby, there was a crowd of workers milling about. There were nurses and aides from the operating room and recovery dressed in lavender scrub suits and crisp white lab coats. Critical-care workers in green scrubs and pastel-colored lab coats stood among them. Transporters in pale blue scrubs mingled with maintenance workers in navy blue work clothes, their belts laden with tools. Abrahm, in navy blue work clothes, stood with several custodians.

Patience rushed up to Lenny, her face lit up with excitement.

"Regis and Birdie are going floor to floor calling out the troops," she said. "I went around my department and invasive procedures. There are a lot more on the way." She touched his arm. "Why are you so cold?"

"It's a long story. I'll tell you later," said Lenny.

"Didn't I tell you?" said Moose, looking out over the crowd. "Ain't nothin' stopping us. Not the morgue. Not Joe West. Not nothin'!"

"Morgue?" asked Patience, looking at Lenny.

"Somebody hit Lenny on the head and locked him in the morgue," explained Gary. "I wanted him to go to the emergency room and get checked out, but . . . "

"I agree," said Patience.

"Forget it," said Lenny. "It's time to have another chat with Freely."

Walking quickly toward the entrance to the executive suite, Lenny ripped the door open so hard that it banged against the stop on the wall. The crowd of coworkers followed him down the thickly padded corridor.

Coming up to Freely's outer office, Lenny, Moose, and Patience walked in and approached his secretary, a prim, middle-aged woman wearing bifocals, a white blouse buttoned up to the chin, and a haughty air. She looked past Lenny, saw that the corridor was choked with workers.

"We're here to see Mr. Freely," said Lenny.

"He's not available, he had an interview," said the secretary. "You'll have to make an appointment—"

"We don't have time for no appointment," said Moose. "Our friend is about to be buried, and we don't want to miss the funeral. We want to see Freely *now!*"

The workers behind him started to speak out. The rumbling swelled, like a crowd at a demonstration. Curses and threats blended with passionate entreaties.

The heavy oak door to Freely's inner office opened. The director of Human Relations stood in the doorway, his mouth open, as he stared at the crowd filling the outer office.

"What is the meaning of this?" he said, his voice shaking.

"We're all going to the funeral, and nobody's gettin' docked!" said Patience.

Regis stepped forward, adding, "And nobody's punchin' no damned time clock, neither!"

Lenny turned his head to survey the crowd behind him, then faced Freely again.

"Mr. Freely, Freddie was one of our own. He was family. Families go to funerals. We have a right to go, and we have to go on company time."

"I don't know, Lenny, the rules are quite clear—"

"The whole fricking administration took the afternoon off for Dr. Simon's service last year," said Birdie. "I bet they didn't have to make up no time for that!"

"They didn't come back to work 'cause they was all crocked!" said Lottie, from Central Stores.

Laughter and curses rose from the crowd.

"Just give us time enough to attend the service," said Lenny. "That's all we ask."

"It's awfully difficult to run a hospital when we're missing most of the staff," said Freely.

"We all get a lunch break. We're only talking about extending it," said Lenny.

Freely looked again at the crowd of workers. There were so many that they packed the outer room and still occupied much of the hall.

"Well, I suppose we could make an exception this one time. As long as the union doesn't use it to set a precedent."

"I promise you, this is a once-in-a-lifetime thing. Freddie was special."

"Very well," said Freely. "I'll give everybody a double lunch break. That's a full hour and a half, but no more. And no drinking!"

A cheer went up from the crowd. Everyone turned and filed out of the room, clapping each other on the back, smiling and laughing. They were being let off the job, and it was all on company time!

They poured out of the main entrance and hurried to the employee parking lot. Engines roared, doors slammed, voices raised in celebration. They were going to the service. They were going to enjoy good food and drink. With toasts and testimonials they would celebrate the passing of their hard-drinking, good-natured, cat-with-nine-hundred-lives friend. The guy who carted the dead bodies to the morgue, who helped Dr. Fingers cut them open, and who cleaned up the smelly mess when the job was done.

Freddie, the morgue attendant, was making his last trip to the cold locker.

Martin Kadish stood in the doorway of Allendale's room and surveyed the wreckage. When the code was announced over the intercom, he'd hurried to the ICU. Dr. Singh wanted to stop the resuscitation efforts after a single run through the ACLS protocols, but Kadish insisted on three full sets of medications.

When the staples in Allendale's chest had pulled loose and his long incision begin to open, blood ran out in torrents with every chest compression. Kadish considered cutting all of the staples and doing open-heart massage, but it would have been useless. The organs had failed. There was nothing to support the circulation and oxygenation.

As soon as he gave the signal, the team gratefully stopped. Now only Crystal and a nurse's aide were in the room, their plastic gowns and gloves splattered with blood. Even their white shoes were stained red. Towels and absorbent pads had been thrown on the floor to cover the pools of blood.

The alarm on one of the intravenous pumps sounded. Crystal walked to it and turned it off. She threw a glance at Kadish, her face and body language saying it all.

The surgeon turned and walked away. He had to prepare for the press conference.

In the pharmacy, Michael DiPietro heard the code called overhead. He stopped filling prescriptions for a moment. The announcement made him think of the day that Colleen Creedon had died, and that memory stabbed at his heart as sharply as an electric shock sent across a fibrillating patient's chest.

He had failed so many. Betrayed the ones who loved him. He'd been a fool for love and an idiot for pleasure. Now he seemed to be the Police

Department's number one murder suspect. Not that the detective who came back to his room had admitted it was a murder investigation. A "suspicious" death is what he had called it.

He thought, *If the cops knew what I knew, murder would be the least of their concerns.*

—SEVENTY—

Lenny pulled up to the church, a converted row house with a simple wooden cross above the door. BROTHERHOOD IN CHRIST read a hand-painted sign on the double doors.

Moose, Birdie, Patience, and Betty piled out of the car and walked up broken cement steps to the little church. Other workers from James Madison had already arrived.

As they came up to the front of the little church, Celeste came out of the doorway, saw Lenny, and came over to give him a big hug.

"What was that for?" he asked.

"That was for doing such a great job. Look at all these people coming off of work to pay their respects to Freddie, all thanks to you."

"I had very little to do with it, believe me," said Lenny.

"It's true," said Moose. "My man was chillin' right up till it was time to leave for the service."

He explained how Lenny had been locked inside the morgue refrigerator. Then he told her about the march on Freely's office and how the Human Resources administrator backed down.

"I knew you'd beat those bastards," said Celeste, "just like you're gonna get me my job back."

"Your arbitration may be a little tougher, but I'm like Fred. An optimist."

Together they entered the church. An elderly black man in a crisply ironed black suit greeted them in the vestibule. He shook hands with each one as they entered, giving a copy of the service, with a photo of Fred on the cover.

IN CELEBRATION OF FRED GOPIE'S HOMECOMING read the bulletin in large, ornate letters.

"Welcome to our home in Christ," he said. "God is good. God is with us."

Betty paused to exchange words with the man. He told her his name, Brother Reginald. She praised him and his church, for which he was deeply appreciative.

Inside the narrow building, simple wooden benches took up half the room, metal folding chairs, many of them bent and rusting, taking up the rest. The altar was a small platform made from plywood over wooden pallets.

Lenny spied a middle-aged woman who was directing another lady carrying a platter of food. Thinking she was Fred's sister, he went over to her.

"Hi, I'm Lenny. Are you?"

"I'm Florence Carter. I'm Fred's sister. You must be Lenny Moss, how pleasant to make your acquaintance."

"I'm sorry for you loss," he said. "These are some of Fred's coworkers. Moose and Birdie. He works in dietary, she's the hospital seamstress."

"Bless you, welcome to our home in Christ," said Florence.

"This is Patience Sinclair. She works in X ray."

"We all loved your brother so much," said Patience. "He was very special to us. We'll miss him."

"Yes, he was one of God's children. He accepted the Lord and was finally able to keep the Devil in the bottle out of his life."

"It was such a tragedy," said Lenny, "Fred dying after he'd been working the program so well."

"My loss is God's abundance. He has another beautiful soul in his house. I know my brother is at peace with the Lord." She saw the minister gesturing to her. "Excuse me. It's time for the service to begin."

As Lenny and his friends found seats, Florence went to the altar and waited for silence.

"Bless all who come to the house of the Lord," she said. "Welcome to this homecoming service."

"Amen!" sounded around the room.

"I am so happy here today, seeing all these wonderful people who loved Fred just as we did. Thank you all so very much for coming to our service. Let us pray."

She led the congregation in a prayer, calling on God to help them accept their loss. She said that she was happy for him, knowing he was home where he belonged.

After a teen choir led the faithful in a hymn, Florence read a selection from Scripture. Then she announced that a few close personal friends of her dear brother wished to speak about him. She gestured to Lenny, who rose and walked solemnly to the altar.

He looked out over the crowd, saw the many workers from every department and every floor of James Madison. He saw church members, family members, and neighbors, all looking at him expectantly.

"It might seem a little crazy to some of you, but I'm going to begin with a joke."

There was a look of uncertainty on several faces, especially the church members.

"Those of you who knew Fred would agree, if he were here today, he'd probably be telling a joke something like this." Lenny hesitated, saw a smile on Patience's face, then thought, *Fuck it.*

"It's a two-person joke, but I'll tell both parts.

"Knock, knock . . Who's there? . . . Rusty . . Rusty who? . . Rust in peace, old friend. Old friend."

Looking over the crowd, he saw that the earlier looks of doubt had turned to tearful looks of warmth and sympathy.

"I knew Fred for a lot of years. We walked shoulder to shoulder getting the first union contract at James Madison. He was always ready to go when we needed people to rally in front of the hospital, or to attend a meeting.

"Fred had a sense of humor that maybe wasn't everybody's cup of tea. Sometimes I wasn't in the mood for it, either. But I was always in the mood to spend a little time with him. He never had a bad word to say about anyone. Never, and that's quite rare. He always seemed to look on the bright side of things. Things were always getting better.

"He had his times of trial. He screwed up sometimes. But the only one who suffered from his mistakes was himself. He never hurt another person. Not once.

"When he was in the hospital the last time, he was really sick, we didn't now if he'd make it. He told me that he didn't regret anything that he'd done, he only wished he'd been sober enough to remember it all. That was our Fred.

"Well, he's gone now. We won't be seeing him making his rounds, telling his corny jokes, bringing a smile to our lips. Nobody can replace him. He was one of a kind."

Lenny stepped down from the podium. He grasped Florence's hand before returning to his place. As he settled back into his seat, Patience leaned over and kissed him on the cheek.

"What was that for?" he asked in a whisper.

Not answering him, she just leaned against him and wrapped an arm around his, as if she never wanted to let him go.

Dr. Fingers was called up to the altar. Standing in front of the crowd in a rumpled suit and a tie that didn't match his shirt, he coughed, grasped the lectern in two hands, and began.

"I have known many brilliant men in my time. Professors from medical school, physicians at James Madison, department chairs, administrators, politicians, and such. And I can honestly say that I have never known a finer, more honorable, more decent human being in all of my life than my friend Fred Gopie.

"He was a hard worker. Nobody ever put more into their work than he did. He was good at what he did, he didn't let the nature of our work get him down. No matter how busy we got, no matter how difficult the task, he always applied himself with enthusiasm.

"And now, if you will bear with me, I'd like to recite something from William Shakespeare."

In a rich, passionate voice, the doctor began to recite.

Fear no more the heat of the sun, Nor the furious Winter's rages.
Thou thy worldy task hast done, Home art gone, and tane thy wages.
Golden lads and girls all must, As Chimney-Sweepers come to dust.

He continued on through the poem, ending with the mournful words,

No Exerciser harm thee, Nor no witch-craft charm thee.
Ghost unlaid forbear thee. Nothing ill come near thee.
Quiet consummation have, And renownned be thy grave.

The doctor made a little bow and walked silently back to his seat.

The minister then took his place at the altar. A big man with an ample belly and a voice that rumbled and could shake the rafters, he spread his arms wide, lifted his face to the ceiling, and proclaimed, "Brothers and sisters in Christ, the Lord has called our Fred home. He is home in the bosom of the Lord, comforted and safe, free from pain and want, done with all his troubles."

"Hallelujah!" and "Praise God!" rang out among the faithful. The minister continued, extolling the beauty and wisdom and infinite kindness of God.

Lenny listened with one ear; with the other he heard the responses of the church members. He couldn't help thinking that Fred's knock-knock jokes made more sense.

—SEVENTY-ONE—

When all of the singing and the praying was over, and when the minister had invited all those who were not saved to come to the church on Sunday and join their congregation, Fred's sister invited everyone to join with the family for a simple meal of plain, home-cooked food contributed by friends and church members.

As the crowd filed down narrow wooden steps to the basement, Lenny took an envelope from his pocket and gave it to Florence, saying, "We collected around the hospital. For the funeral and all."

Florence put the envelope in her purse, kissed Lenny on the cheek, and sent him down to the basement, saying, "We have beer and wine and spirits for the men, if you care to enjoy them."

Downstairs, folding tables were set up with aluminum foil trays over flickering cans of Sterno. The trays were piled high with fried chicken, beans and rice, greens, turnips, biscuits and sweet soda breads. There was roast beef and a great big ham, sliced in thin spiral cuts waiting to be laid on a piece of bread. There were mashed potatoes, potato salad, and sweet potato pies. And salads, with bottles of low-fat dressing waiting to be poured.

Lenny filled a plate with food. On his way to the table, Regis handed him a plastic cup filled with beer.

"It's not real cold, but it goes down just as smooth," he said. "Hey, you haven't met my daughter, have you?" He pointed across the table, where his wife, Salina, was seated, holding a baby in her arm.

"We named her Olivia," said Regis. "I wanted to name her after you, Lenny, on account of all you did for me, but we had a girl."

"You're better off," said Lenny. "A little Lenny would have had a big nose and a bald spot on the back of his head."

"Listen," Regis said, "you think it would be disrespectful if I applied for Fred's job in the morgue? I got the experience."

"No, I think it would be great."

"Salina didn't like me coming home smelling like formaldehyde, but she thinks maybe I won't get in so much trouble, stuck down the morgue with the stiffs."

"Regis, I think your wife makes a lot of sense. Go for it."

Lenny settled into a seat beside Patience and tasted the beer. It was good, even warm. Patience and Birdie were sharing stories about their children, while Moose concentrated on his food, fried chicken in one hand, a biscuit dripping gravy in the other.

"Hey, Lenny!" called one of the men from Maintenance. "How long do you think we can stay?"

"Freely told us no more than an hour and a half away from the hospital, but I figure you have to allow for traffic. And parking."

"You can't rush a service, that's a sacrilege," said Lottie from Central Supply.

"Praise the Lord and pass the sweet potato!" called out Betty. "I ain't leavin' till my belly's full and my soul is at peace!"

"Amen!" rose up around the tables.

When Lenny had finished his food and drunk a second beer, he noticed Dr. Fingers standing to the side, looking at him. The doctor gestured to Lenny, who went over to him.

"Hey, Dr. Fingers, I liked what you read."

"I know that our old Fred was not a big Shakespeare fan, but you can't beat the Bard for eloquence."

"That's for sure." Lenny stood a moment surveying the crowd, then turned back to the doctor. "I wanted to tell you, I really appreciate what you did for Fred over the years. How you testified for him at the arbitration hearing and wrote the letters of support."

"He was a good man saddled with a bad addiction. When he was sober, he was the best man for the job."

"Drunk or sober, he still got the job done," said Lenny.

"True enough," said Fingers, who looked over Lenny's shoulder. "I wonder what sort of whiskey they're serving," he said, and walked off to find out.

As Lenny stood contemplating a third beer, he felt a tug on his arm. Turning, he looked into the kindly face of Alex Primeaux, family practice physician and director of the Employee Health Service.

"Hey, Alex, I'm glad you were able to make the service."

"You know I wouldn't miss it for the world, Fred and I go back a long way."

"You treated his liver more times than I'd like to remember. Have you eaten?"

"Yes, I ate my fill of their good home cooking," he said, patting his stomach. "Listen, I've got somebody special I want you to meet."

He led Lenny to a lovely, petite woman in a nurse's white uniform. Lenny recognized her from James Madison.

"Lenny, this is Abbie Stemple. She's taken into her lovely head the foolish notion that she'd like to be my wife."

"Hello, Lenny," she said, holding out a soft hand. "Alex has told me so much about you." She squeezed his hand an extra time, suggesting that she and Lenny shared a special knowledge about Alex.

"Congratulations, Alex, Abbie, this is wonderful news. Somehow it seems fitting that the word should be out on the day of Fred's funeral. It kind of takes some of the sadness out of the funeral."

"I'll miss the rascal, I surely will," said Alex. "He was a trial, but I loved him all the more. His was a bad addiction."

As Lenny turned to go, Alex said, "Oh, by the way, I looked up that information you wanted on cyanide. It does have some capability to induce changes in the DNA of a fetus. There aren't any human studies, but there have been animal tests, and the babies were deformed, some of them quite badly."

"Which means that the cyanide might have been aimed at the baby, not the mother," said Lenny. "Well, that adds to the funeral tone of the day."

"I'm sorry to be the bearer of bad news."

"It's okay, it is what it is."

"Are you getting close to finding the killer?" asked Primeaux.

"I'm not sure. Sometimes it seems like I'm spinning my wheels and going nowhere, other times I think I'm one step from the end."

"Well I have faith in you, Lenny Moss. A'hm sure you'll prevail."

He and his fiancée bid their farewells and left the church.

Lenny joined Abrahm, Moose, and several other housekeepers, who were drinking beer and telling stories about Fred. As he listened, he noticed Baby Love, the messenger who had snitched on him and his friends about the practical joke on Seven South. The young woman was sitting with a man from the church. She was leaning close to him, with one arm on his shoulder, looking into his eyes as if he were the most mesmerizing man she'd ever seen.

Moose saw where Lenny was looking, turned his head, scowled. "Lookit that little piece of trash. She's trying' to act like she's so righteous and pure. I got a mind to go over there and set him straight."

"I feel the same way," said Lenny, "but I think Baby Love is going to end up paying a price for her bullshit, and it's gonna happen sooner rather than later."

-SEVENTY-TWO-

Hector gestured to Lenny, indicating he wanted to speak with him alone. Leaving the little group, Lenny joined Hector beside a coat rack.

"Yeah, Hector, what's on your mind?"

"Oh, man, Lenny, I hope you won't be pissed at me this time."

"No chance, not on a day like this. What's up?"

"What it is, see, when you was asking me about Mike and telling' me it's better if the truth comes out, 'cause if I hold back from you, it's gonna come out later and bite you in the ass."

"I said that? I had not idea I could be so vulgar."

"Anyway, I didn't tell you absolutely *everything* that happened that morning the drug rep died."

"Okay," said Lenny, "what did you leave out?"

"I was going out with my cart delivering meds to the floors, just like always, and I saw this redhead going into the chemo room. I only saw the back of her head, I didn't see her face, but I'm pretty sure it was the sales rep, Colleen Creedon."

"This was the morning that she died?"

"Yeah, that's the day."

"And Mike was preparing chemotherapy drugs that day."

"He sure was." Hector took a bite of fried chicken. He licked his fingers, then asked Lenny, "You think the cops are gonna pick him up?"

"That's exactly what I'm afraid of," said Lenny. "I can't see Mike being a killer. It doesn't play."

"Normally I'd have to agree with you," said Hector, "but don't forget, he's taking a wicked drug for his migraines."

"Oh? What drug is that?"

"Ergotamine. It has a lot of nasty side effects, but the one that's got me most worried is, it can make you loco, big time."

Hector went off to refill his plate, leaving Lenny to wonder if he'd been wrong about Mike all along. He was almost sick imagining turning the sweet, gentle pharmacist over to the cops.

He looked at his watch, saw that the hour and a half Freely had allotted was past. He hated to break up the party, but he knew that Joe West would be counting the clock back at the hospital.

As he began to suggest that everybody start heading back to the hospital,

a guy from Maintenance called out, "Hey Lenny, don't you think we could have one more drink, for Fred's sake?"

He looked at his watch, looked at the crowd of workers. "I don't know, we're gonna get back late as it is."

Seeing the disappointment in the eyes of his coworkers, he said, "How about a quick drink for those whose throats are dry, and then everyone hits the road?"

A cheer rose from the crowd. As the drinks were poured, he made his way up the stairs. Slowly the others finished their drinks, grabbed a last piece of food, and followed him out of the church.

Nobody wanted to leave, especially knowing what was waiting for them back at James Madison. He could still hear people celebrating as he walked to the car.

As Lenny and his friends gathered outside the church, Moose said, "You know, it's a shame we can't give Fred a send-off that he deserves."

"Why can't we?" asked Celeste. "All we need is some good liquor and a bag of chips and dip. That's all old Freddie would expect. He was never into no fancy stuff."

"Why don't you come over to my place tonight?" said Lenny. "After you feed the kids. Say, seven. I'll pick up a case of beer and some snacks, and we can toast old Fred."

"That's a great idea," said Birdie. "I'll bring something to eat. I know I've got some frozen chicken wings I can pop in the oven."

"Spread the word," said Lenny, walking to his car. "We'll meet at my place at seven tonight."

—SEVENTY-THREE—

As Lenny parked his car in the employee parking lot, Birdie said, "You don't suppose we should go in through the loading dock, do you? We're powerful late."

"No way," said Moose. "We go in through the front door and don't take no bullshit from anyone. Joe West can kiss my sweet ass."

"I agree," said Lenny. "If there's a problem with our time, I'll talk to Freely."

As they approached the main entrance, Sandy rode up to them in a little electric Security cart. Grinning broadly, he said, "Man, I didn't think you was ever gonna come back. I'd have come with you, but West had all of us watching the entrances, keeping track of the time."

"I know you were with us in spirit," said Lenny. "Matter of fact, a few workers are coming over to my house tonight to toast Freddie. You've got to come."

"I'll be there, count on it. Old Freddie was never one to hang his head and moan, he was a good-time man. He'd want to see us drink and have a good time."

"Amen to that," said Moose.

"Uh-oh," said Sandy, glancing toward the hospital's main entrance. "Here comes the pit bull waiting to bite. I got to scoot. See you tonight."

Joe West walked down the marble steps, a clipboard in his hand, looking like the captain of a prison camp about to order several executions. As Lenny and his friends walked toward him, West announced in a loud voice, "I want everyone's name as they come in the door. You'll all be getting reprimands. Those of you with two disciplines this year will be suspended for three days. Those with prior suspensions will be terminated."

An uproar arose from the ranks.

"We had an agreement with Mr. Freely," said Lenny.

"The agreement was for an hour and a half, not two and a half. You're over your limit, I'm taking names."

Lenny said, "Mr. Freely didn't say we had to include the commuter time—"

"Don't even try it!" barked West, putting his face close to Lenny's. "You led your lambs to slaughter this time, Moss. I'm documenting every name and every minute of their absence. Tomorrow morning a lot of people are going to find their time cards missing. Too bad you won't be there to let them cry on your shoulder."

"What do you mean?"

"Dr. Kadish told me how you were impersonating a security guard. I'm terminating you as of today."

Lenny looked into the cold, humorless eyes of the security chief. As tempted as he was to argue in front of everyone, he knew that his best chance of warding off disciplinary action was to meet again with the head of Human Relations.

"You have things ass-backward," said Lenny as he walked nonchalantly to the door and opened it for Moose and Birdie. "You're the one in trouble. You sent Fred Gopie to his death when you threw a sick employee out of the hospital. I'm going in to see Mr. Freely to discuss the charges against you."

The workers behind him began shouting and jostling. Accusations of murder rang in the air as everyone tried to push past West without giving their names. West ordered another security guards to bar the door until all the names were recorded, but the crowd forced their way past him in the struggle to get into the building.

"You can piss and moan all you want!" West yelled at Lenny's back as he furiously tried to catch the names of the workers pushing past him. "Your people are dead meat!"

Once safely in the hospital, Lenny left the group and headed for the Human Relations office. He approached the secretary.

"Is he in?" he asked.

Looking past him to see if there were any more workers with him, she breathed a sigh of relief when she realized that he was alone.

"You'll have to make an appointment, Mr. Moss," he said.

"This really can't wait."

"I have strict instructions to—"

"Tell your boss if he doesn't see me *right now*, the Gopie family will be holding a press conference announcing their plan to sue the hospital for the wrongful death of Fred Gopie. They'll be naming Joe West as the murderer."

"I, uh . . . "

Leaning closer to her and lowering his voice almost to a whisper, he added, "If you let me speak to him, I may be able to save James Madison from a major public relations disaster."

Rising from her chair, she said, "Just a moment, sir," and hurried into her boss's office, being sure to close the door tightly behind her. A moment later, she opened it and gestured for him to enter.

Lenny found Freely sitting back in his chair, looking unhappy. His bow tie was askew, his hair untidy—unusual for the dapper director of Human Relations.

"Lenny, your people were supposed to be back to work an hour ago. I thought we had an agreement."

"I didn't plan it this way, Mr. Freely, it just happened. You know how funeral services are. They never start on time."

"That's not my concern. I was generous in giving the extra time, and now you've thrown it back in my face."

"I understand you're upset, and I'm sorry it ran so late, but what could we do? After Dr. Fingers spoke, the minister gave a long sermon. Nobody felt comfortable getting up in the middle of it; that would have been disrespectful."

"I appreciate the nature of the event. Still and all—"

"Everybody gave up their lunch break to get to the funeral. We had to take time to have something to eat. The family would have been insulted if we didn't."

"If there was any drinking—"

"The Gopie family is very devout. They don't even serve liquor, just fruit drinks."

"Well, that's one thing in your favor. Still, they *are* late returning to work." Leaning forward and resting his elbows on his polished desk, he said, "Now, what's this you told my secretary about the Gopie family bringing a wrongful-death suit against Joe West?"

"You know as well as me that Freddie wasn't drunk the day he died, he was suffering from diabetes. His blood sugar was sky high."

"His breath smelled of alcohol and he was staggering around. It isn't the hospital's fault that he concealed his illness."

"If Freddie *was* sick, it would have been criminal for West to let him get into his car and drive away, but he wasn't! Freddie didn't know he was sick; I checked with Dr. Primeaux. The doctor wanted him to come in for testing, his blood sugars had been a little high, but he kept putting it off because he was doing so much overtime."

"He should have told his supervisor that he was ill and reported to the emergency room. It's hospital policy. You know that."

"It's policy, fine, but when an employee is so sick that he isn't thinking straight, you can't expect him to follow the policy. That's unreasonable."

"Expecting an employee to state that he feels sick is unreasonable?"

"Maybe he did tell someone. We'll never know for certain, West buried the only witness to the conversation."

"If you are accusing Mr. West of falsifying a report—"

"West killed Freddie. He threw him out on his ear when he should have escorted him to the ER. Fred crashed his car because he didn't get the medical care he needed. The union has the right under the contract to file a grievance for failure to provide a safe work environment."

"That's the most ridiculous thing I've ever heard," said Freely.

"Ridiculous or not, when the family hears of our grievance, they'll be encouraged to file a civil suit of their own, and I will personally help them prepare their case."

"There is nothing we do can stop the family from suing," said Freely, looking more worried than his words suggested.

"True. Except that this is a very devout, Christian family. They feel that life's true rewards are in Heaven. My decision not to take any action would reinforce their spiritual approach to Fred's death."

Freely picked up a pen and doodled on a pad of paper, "What do you propose?" he asked. "Off the record."

"I propose that you okay all the time we took for the funeral. No discipline. Nothing in their file. In exchange, the union won't file any complaint over Fred's death."

"What if the family sues? I'm left with nothing."

"The contract gives you thirty days to bring charges for a work rule infraction. By then you should know of the family's intentions."

"That's an awfully short window," said Freely.

"I won't challenge a late discipline charge for up to sixty days; you won't bother with how I investigated the murder."

Freely scribbled over his doodle, frowned. "Very well, I'll accept it."

"One last thing," said Lenny, standing to leave. "Celeste Chambers, the Seven South unit secretary. I want her reinstated. And I want the letter removed from Gary Tuttle's file."

Freely started to object, thought better of it, nodded his head.

Lenny smiled. He actually felt sympathy for Freely, who would have to explain his decision to his boss, not to mention Joe West. As he left the office, he noted that for the first time since he escaped the morgue refrigerator, he felt quite warm and toasty.

-SEVENTY-FOUR-

Fielding his team of residents and students, Dr. Martin Kadish found Dr. Singh in the corridor, waiting for the elevator. Approaching him, Kadish said, "Allendale's progress notes are incomplete."

"That cannot be true, I wrote a summary of the code myself," said Singh. "I was in the unit at the time of the arrest."

"You didn't mention anything about the emergency reintubation," said Kadish.

"There is no need; it is documented in the notes from the day before."

"But that event is directly linked to his death," said Kadish.

"That is preposterous," said Singh. "His respiratory and cardiac failure were due to acute rejection of his organs. It had nothing to do with his mechanical ventilation."

"That diagnosis can only be made on histological analysis of tissue samples. Until we get the path report back, you can't make that diagnosis."

"But surely—"

"When Allendale bit through the endotracheal tube, your resident took too long to reintubate, and after *that* fiasco, they had to reposition it *again* because the tube was ventilating only one lung."

"Any hypoxia was due to the rejected lungs, not the breathing tube."

"He was oxygenating *fine* until your knucklehead residents screwed around with his tube."

Looking at the other hospital personnel gathering around, Singh said, "I do not believe a public area is the proper place to have this discussion."

"We're all family," said Kadish. "I just want you to know, I made out the death certificate. Under 'cause of death' I wrote, *Hypoxia secondary to failure of mechanical ventilation.*"

As Kadish turned and led his team away, Singh called after him, "I will write a note contesting your diagnosis. It will be part of the permanent record!"

Getting no reply from the surgeon, Singh added, "I will appeal to Dr. Slocum. The chief of staff will not let your charade remain in the record."

The transplant team continued on its path, like a warring army seeking higher ground and fresh ammunition.

Singh hated when a physician put his personal ambitions ahead of good medical practice. Nobody liked to have a death added to their monthly morbidity and mortality review, but it was part of the life of a physician.

Pushing the blame on another service was not.

Mae Yeung approached Lenny at the Seven South nursing station. "Oh, Lenny, I'm so glad I caught you, I know it's the end of your shift. I was up here earlier but I heard that you were at Fred's funeral. I'm sorry I couldn't make it."

"That's all right, Mae. What's up?"

"I just wanted you to know that the women's support group went very, very well this morning."

"Damn, I'm sorry, I'd forgotten it was today. Listen, that's great. Did Bridgette speak?"

"Yes, she did. She didn't say a whole lot, but it was a good start. I met with her afterward, and she's agreed to talk to me in private later in the week. I'm very encouraged."

"That's so great. I can't thank you enough, Mae."

"Oh, no, it is I who should thank you," she said, stepping close to him and putting a hand lightly on his shoulder. "It was your idea."

"Yeah, well . . . "

"I'll let you know how she does, without betraying any confidential communication, of course."

"Of course. Listen, thanks, I have to run, it's way past time for me to punch out."

"Good night, Lenny," she said, taking her hand off his shoulder but keeping her eyes riveted on his.

The social worker stood and watched Lenny walk to the stairs and leave the ward. Even as she made her way to the elevator, she couldn't get the image of this caring, gentle man out of her mind.

Martin Kadish sat alone in his office. He squeezed his hands into fists, felt a powerful urge to smash something . . . someone. He was confident that he could weather the death of his patient; it was that meddling guy in the blue work clothes who made him ready to kill. He picked up the phone, dialed the number for the page operator. At the sound of the operator's voice he barked at her to get him Joe West.

When West answered the page, Kadish barked at him, too. "I hope you've got rid of that pest Moss."

"Uh, no, not exactly," said West in an uncharacteristic tone of apology. "I had the termination order in my hand, but that wimp Freely over in Human Resources went over my head."

"How is that possible?"

"It's a long story. Freely's afraid of bad publicity. He cut a deal with the union. There was nothing I could do."

"Well you may be satisfied with the situation, but I am not," said Kadish, "and there is something I *can* do about it."

Kadish slammed down the receiver. He rose from his chair, put on his suit jacket, and stepped over to the secretary's office.

"Cindy, have Korwin take my pages, I'll be out of the hospital."

"Yes, Doctor." Picking up the phone to call the page operator, she added, "How long will you be gone?"

"Until I'm back!" he said and hurried down the hall.

Walking down the marble steps of the hospital on his way to the parking lot, Lenny found Moose talking to three members of the Dietary Department. They shook hands, clapped backs, and exchanged greetings.

"You want me to bring some beer tonight?" asked Moose.

"I was gonna pick up a case," said Lenny.

"A *case*," said one of Moose's coworkers. "That'll just get the four of us started."

Moose promised to bring more beer, saying, "and I'm not talking about that Belgian shit, either." The others promised to bring snacks and dips.

"Seven o'clock. Right?" said Moose.

"That's it. I'm going to take a little ride, but I'll be home in time to meet you," said Lenny.

"Where you going? You want some company?"

"Thanks, no, this is one of those interviews I should do alone. I don't have any idea how I'm going to get the guy to even open the door to me, let alone talk, but I feel like I really have to give it a try."

"Yeah?" said Moose, walking beside his friend toward the employee parking lot. "Who you going to see?"

"Colleen Creedon's fiancé."

—SEVENTY-FIVE—

As Dr. Wallace Slocum, the James Madison chief of staff, stepped up to the podium in the Alumni Auditorium, he reflected that he had reported on many cases in his long medical career, first, as a resident and fellow, then as an attending physician with privileges. Once he'd been made acting chief of staff, and later, official chief, he'd given up reporting on cases—something he dearly missed.

Looking out at the crowd, he saw a host of reporters mixed in with the usual medical students and physicians. There were video cameras with satellite feed, courtesy of the hospital's Information Services Department, as well as countless still cameras.

He waited a moment for all the lenses to get in focus, then he said, "Mr. Alfred Desmond Allendale expired today and was pronounced dead at ten thirty-five this morning. In attendance were Dr. Martin Kadish, Dr. Samir Singh, as well as numerous other physicians from various clinical specialties. Vigorous resuscitation efforts were attempted, but ultimately failed.

"The Department of Surgery of James Madison University Hospital is exceedingly proud of the pioneering work that our physicians have undertaken, especially Dr. Martin Kadish and his associate from the cardiothoracic area, Dr. Louis Defreres, and his team. We have learned a great deal about this difficult procedure, and we will continue to analyze the data in order to improve outcomes for future multiple organ transplants.

"And now I'm going to turn the microphone over to Dr. Kadish, who will speak about this enormously important case. Dr. Kadish."

Martin Kadish strode up to the microphone. A head taller than Slocum, he gave the senior physician's hand a cursory shake, then he took over the microphone. As camera flashes flared and video cameras advanced to close-up, he looked out over the audience.

"For the people of America and for the great people here at James Madison University Hospital, I want to announce to the world the giant strides we have made by undertaking this historic surgical procedure. I believe that history will show our efforts to be as groundbreaking and as precedent-setting as Dr. DeBakey's first heart transplant so many decades ago.

"In a single operation, our patient received four major organs from a carefully matched live donor. His body accepted those organs, and they functioned perfectly for two days. The efficacy of the antirejection medication which

293

we administered prevented his immune system from rejecting the new organs. We are satisfied that organ rejection was not the primary cause of death.

"While it is most unfortunate that the patient did not survive longer—we all hoped that he would have a full recovery—nevertheless, we are encouraged by his postoperative course. We have proven that a transplant procedure of unprecedented complexity can be performed safely. We have further proven that the human body is no more likely to reject four organs than it is to reject a single transplant. We are not discouraged by the negative outcome. Far from it, we look forward to performing more transplants of this type in the near future.

"Now, having said that, I will entertain a few questions from the press."

Voices and hands rose in unison, begging for recognition. Kadish pointed to a tall, willowy brunette reporter in the first row.

"Dr. Kadish, if your patient didn't die from organ rejection, what did he die from?"

"We will not have a complete answer to that question until a number of tissue samples are examined by the pathologist. The pathologist will not just look at cells from the transplanted organs, but he will examine all of the other organs. Once we have those reports, we will be able to give you a more thorough and accurate report."

He pointed to a local TV reporter.

"Doctor, we have heard unconfirmed reports about some problems with the respirator used to support the patient's breathing. There have been some vague references to inadequate oxygen delivery. Could you comment on these reports?"

"No, I'm sorry, I can't speak to that issue. The hospital's Quality Assurance Committee will conduct a full review of the case, as they do in every unanticipated death. The QA team will scrutinize every record and will interview every member of the team who cared for the patient. Once I have that report in my hand, along with the pathology report, I will be able to address any problems the patient may have experienced with regard to his ventilatory support."

Standing at the back of the room, Dr. Singh felt a stab in his heart at Kadish's comments. He had no doubt that someone on the transplant team had leaked a story about how Allendale bit through his airway and then had to have the new endotracheal tube repositioned. He was almost surprised that Kadish hadn't secretly released photos onto the Internet of the chest

X-ray showing the breathing tube in the right lung. But that would have brought a criminal investigation, and Kadish couldn't afford being scrutinized that closely.

Dr. Singh was certain of that point.

The transplant surgeon answered a few more questions, then he turned the microphone over to the CEO, Roger Lefferts. Lefferts spoke about the hospital's plan to expand the transplant service. They were going to offer an unprecedented array of procedures, from new limbs to a staggering array of internal organs. There was even talk of transposing human heads, a procedure that sounded ghoulish, he had to admit, but that promised to extend the life of a terminal patient indefinitely.

When the press conference was over and the news teams were making their way to their vans, Singh lingered a moment in the darkness of the auditorium. He dreaded having to go to Slocum, the chief of staff, and ask him to set the record straight about how the patient died. Once again he decided to wait and do nothing. It was likely that the medical examiner would be taking over the autopsy of Mr. Allendale. If the city agency did that, Kadish would find great difficulty in placing blame for the death on the Anesthesia Department.

Often it was better to wait and let others bring the truth to light.

Lenny aimed the Buick north, traveling out Washington Lane, past Chew, and on to Ogontz, on his way to Glenside.

He had a strong suspicion that he was on a fool's errand. How could he get Colleen Creedon's fiancé, a complete stranger, to talk to him? The man had no reason to answer Lenny's questions. He was in grief; he wouldn't want to speak about Colleen to some crazy man from the hospital.

Lenny didn't see any other way of getting the kind of information he needed. Detective Williams wasn't going to give it up, even with bartering information. Besides, Lenny wanted to know what kind of woman Colleen had been. He especially wanted to know more about her pregnancy. Like, was the fiancé sure that he was the father?

Pulling something like that out of a man he'd never met before was undoubtedly the dumbest stunt he would ever try. A fool's errand. Still, it wouldn't be the first time.

Cruising slowly up the street and pulling up to the curb, he pulled out the copy of Colleen Creedon's chart and checked the face sheet to be certain he had the right address. Looking up and down the block, he saw familiar landmarks.

What a small fucking world. He was just three blocks away from where he'd grown up. He and his brother used to cross this street on their way home from school. There was an empty lot where they used to play ball. Now it had a Wawa next to an A Plus gas station.

He didn't think that old memories of the neighborhood would be much of a basis of a conversation. Still, what else did he have?

Arriving at the house, he cut the engine and sat a moment studying the house. The trees were bigger and fuller than when he had lived nearby, the pavement more cracked and buckled.

He noted a Toyota Echo in the drive. *Eco-friendly*, he thought. A bumper sticker said READ A BOOK—SAVE A CHILD. The fellow was probably a teacher. Or a librarian. He walked up to the door and rang the doorbell. Footsteps sounded within. As he saw a dimly lit figure approaching the door, Lenny asked himself again what he was going to say to this complete stranger.

-SEVENTY-SIX-

After ringing the doorbell, Lenny took a step back so that the figure approaching the door could get a good look at him. He tried not to look like someone who was selling something.

The door opened. A young man with light brown hair, ruddy cheeks, freckles, and crooked teeth stuck his head out.

"Yes? Can I help you?"

"Hi. Mr. McBride? My name is Lenny Moss. I work at James Madison Hospital."

"Yes..."

"I, uh, I saw you at the hospital. You're Colleen Creedon's fiancée. Is that right?"

"Yes."

The young man eyed Lenny with suspicion.

"It's a little awkward trying to explain what I'm doing here, Mr. McBride. I was on duty when Colleen Creedon died, and I thought maybe—"

"You were *there*? You saw what happened to Collie? Come in, please."

Padric opened the door wide, allowing Lenny to enter the vestibule.

"I didn't exactly see everything, but I was there when they discovered her and the whole time that they tried to revive her."

"I hope you've come to tell me how she died. I've talked to a Dr. Singh. He seemed like an honest man, but he couldn't tell me very much. He said that they didn't know what the cause of her death was."

"Yeah, that's what I understand. Listen, I don't mean to mislead you, I'm not a medical person."

"What do you do there?"

"I'm a custodian, mainly, but I'm also a union steward. Over the years I've become a sort of jailhouse lawyer, investigating incidents and defending my coworkers against charges."

"I don't understand what that has to do with Colleen's dying."

Lenny peeked into the house. Seeing no one else around, he said, "Why don't we sit down and I'll tell you everything I know, which is a fair amount, considering how good people at James Madison are at hiding things. Okay?"

Hearing those last words, Padric ushered Lenny into the living room. They sat down on a leather coach.

"Can I get you something to drink? Coffee? A beer?"

"No, thank you. I was at a funeral this afternoon, I already had some beer."

"A funeral?"

"A coworker died in a car wreck. I've got friends coming over tonight, too, and I'll be putting down shots until well past midnight."

"I was hoping we could have Collie's funeral this Saturday, but I don't think that the medical examiner will release her body by then."

"That's tough. It's hard when you're in limbo and you can't make plans."

"Yes. It is." Padric looked at the mantel piece, focusing on a photo of himself and Colleen. He seemed to forget for a moment that he had a guest. Finally he turned back to Lenny.

"Tell me, Mr. Moss, what do you know about the death of my Colleen?"

Lenny looked into the pained eyes of Padric McBride. He was struck by the young man's earnest manner. He seemed genuine, not a bullshit artist. He decided that the only way to get the man to open up to him was to be as honest as he could be and tell him what he knew. Or most of it, at any rate.

"The way this thing started," said Lenny, "we had an admission to our ward that was canceled. We've been working under a lot of pressure for over a year. There's been a hiring freeze, we've been working short, and everybody's really stressed out."

"I can relate to that, I work for the Glenside library. We've had a hiring freeze for *two* years, but when the kids come in and need help finding material for their school, they don't want to hear that we're short-staffed. They want the service."

"It's the same with us. We take the heat if we don't satisfy the customer. Anyway, this admission was canceled, but different departments kept sending up trays of food and equipment and stuff, as if she was there, so I suggested as a joke that we act like there really was somebody in the room. That would keep the bed empty, at least until Admissions got wise to what was going on."

"That's brilliant! You were giving them back some of what they'd been shoveling on you for so long."

"That's it. So anyway, the joke was going pretty good until the nurse's aide went into the empty room to make a phone call. That's when she saw Colleen lying on the bed. She wasn't breathing. The aide told a doctor, and they called in the code team. They worked a long time trying to revive her, I can tell you that, because I was right outside the room the whole time, but it was hopeless. She never came back . . . I'm sorry."

"Do they really not know what made her so sick?"

"I don't think so. They don't think that the cyanide in her blood—"

"*Cyanide?* Perhaps we both better have that drink and you can tell me all about it."

Padric stood up and headed for the kitchen. Lenny decided that today was just going to be one long bar hop.

Coming home from work with a case of beer balanced on his shoulder, Moose found his son stretched out on the floor in front of the television.

"You do your homework yet, T.?"

"Its only four o'clock, Daddy."

"If you always put your work off till the last minute, you'll find yourself running to catch up, and everybody else is way ahead of you."

The boy rolled his eyes.

"Can I watch this one show?"

"No. I want to see your face in a book. You can watch TV after you do your work."

The child reluctantly turned off the set and slowly trod up the stairs, as if a terrible fate awaited him.

His daughter came bouncing down the stairs, carrying a report in her hand. She rushed up to show her father.

"Look at my project. It's beautiful!"

"Let me see it, baby," he said, setting the beer down. Moose looked at the title page: *THE CLOTHES OF MANY LANDS*. Several of the colorful letters were dressed in elaborate costumes. He opened the report and lovingly ran his fingers over the artwork.

"This is really fine," he said, turning a page. "I'm mighty proud of you, girl."

He turned the pages, reading the captions and studying the images. He was amazed at how quickly she had mastered the cut and paste commands for her bitmap images.

""See how I made the same face look different for different outfits, just like you showed me? I reversed it and stretched it and changed the tint."

"Wonderful," said Moose, "simply—"

He froze in midsentence. He recalled the digital images of the stomachs with the ulcers in the GI lab. He recalled several images that the computer had superimposed on the background: the date, the doctor's name, the caption.

He knew how Fox had faked the ulcers on his patients. It was a simple matter of programming a command to insert an image with a transparent background onto the current frame. Altering the image would have been done beforehand. Fox probably had a whole palette of images ready to insert, each altered just enough to conceal its origin.

"Is everything okay with my project, Daddy?" she asked, worried at Moose's sudden silence.

"Everything is fine, baby. I was just thinking of something I had to tell Lenny tonight."

He handed the project back to his daughter, saying, "You're gonna get an A-plus on this, I'm sure of it."

"Can I watch some TV before dinner?" she asked.

"Sure. Just keep the sound low, your brother's doing his homework."

"That'll be the day," she said, heading toward the remote and her favorite spot on the floor.

Moose chuckled, happy to have a part of the mystery solved. Now all they had to figure out was how Fox killed poor Colleen Creedon.

—SEVENTY-SEVEN—

Padric McBride reached into a cupboard and retrieved a bottle of Jameson, then he pulled a pair of cut crystal glasses from a shelf. He threw some ice cubes in the glasses and poured a stiff shot in each glass, saying, "I appreciate your telling me this, Mr. Moss."

"Call me, Lenny. Please."

"Lenny. I truly do. The doctors have been very close-lipped about the whole matter." He handed a glass to Lenny, took a long sip from his own, swirled the liquid around his mouth, then swallowed the whiskey.

"The medical people I've talked to aren't convinced that the cyanide they found in her blood was the cause of death, it was a very small amount. But it is curious."

"Do you have any idea who gave her cyanide, or why?"

"I'm sorry, I don't. I was considering some rather ugly thoughts about the poison . . . " He sipped his whiskey, unwilling to reveal the dark theory.

Padric put his glass down on the counter and stared at Lenny. "What could possibly be uglier than poisoning Colleen?"

"I was thinking that it might—this is just speculation, you understand—it might have been given to harm the baby. You did know she was pregnant, didn't you?"

"Yes, I knew. That was one of the things we fought about. She wanted to get rid of the baby, but we're Catholics, we don't believe in abortion. Hell, that's not even the main thing. The main thing is, I wanted our child. I wanted us to be together."

"But she was drifting away, is that it?"

"That's right. Colleen put off the wedding date twice, then she finally told me she couldn't set a date. She was leaving me. It was obvious. I saw it coming a ways back, I just didn't want to admit it."

"Why was she breaking it off?"

"It was the job. She'd had a sheltered life, really. Catholic school all the way through college. She went to La Salle. She studied art history, of all things. When she couldn't get a job in the field, she took a sales job with Falcon just to have some money coming in. Who would have thought she'd take to it like a duck to water?"

"It sounds like it opened up a whole new world to her," said Lenny.

"They sent her to Chicago to train. It was the first time she'd been away

301

from home except for a class trip. Once she started mixing with those sales-people, she started to change."

"It's understandable. They live a pretty fast lifestyle."

"That's what I told her! But she loved the travel and the hotels and the late nights. She liked getting to know the big-shot doctors in the hospitals. They flattered her, she flirted with them. It was a big tease. A game. The more she played—"

"The more she grew apart from you. I've seen it happen to a lot of cou-ples. One of them changes jobs, they meet new people, they change the way they dress and act. Pretty soon the old friends aren't good enough, and they're history."

"That's what happened to us, in a nutshell. Once she got a taste of the fast life, living with a simple librarian wasn't good enough. How could I compete with a world-famous surgeon?"

"She spent time with Martin Kadish?"

"That's one name she brought up several times. She said he was making medical history, and one of her company's drugs was involved in it." Draining the last of his whiskey, he offered a refill to Lenny, who declined. "But that wasn't the worst of it," he added.

"No?"

Padric refilled his glass, but held off drinking it. He looked into the golden liquid, measuring his words.

"The worst part of it all was when I found a vial of pills in her attaché case. I wasn't spying on her exactly, I was looking for her datebook. I wanted to be sure that she was going to be in town for my birthday, all the trips she was making."

"Was she going to?"

"No. She was scheduled to be in New York." He took a long sip of his whiskey. "I found the pills, and I was puzzled, because the samples that she sometimes had were always clearly labeled. You know, the trade name of the drug with the proviso 'Not for retail distribution.' That kind of thing."

"There was no prescription on them, either?" said Lenny.

"Nothing. I took a couple and showed them to our local pharmacist. I made up a story about finding them in the library. He told me he was pretty sure that they were   MDMA."

"What's that?" asked Lenny.

"Ecstasy."

Suddenly Lenny knew exactly why Mike had been so completely lovesick over Colleen. His one night of Heaven had been enhanced by chemicals.

"That's fucked up," said Lenny.

"I didn't want to know who she was sleeping with. I begged her to get some help, come back to the church, see a doctor. Anything. But she just laughed. She saw me as a simple soul who didn't know how to live. She was looking for an apartment in Center City just before she died."

"She was swimming with sharks," said Lenny. "It's a dangerous place to play."

"Then the police believe that my Collie was murdered?"

"That's the impression I get talking with one of the detectives. It was more of an interrogation, actually, but I was able to find out a few things about the case."

"Whatever light you can shed on her death, I'd be most appreciative."

"Right now I'm trying to understand how she was killed. Tell me: Did Colleen have any medical problems?"

"No, I don't believe so. As far as I know, she was healthy."

"No chronic things bothering her? She wasn't on medication?"

"No, only vitamins and herbs. And perfume. She had a big collection of fragrances."

"I know some people who drink gallons of herbal tea. They even bathe in herbs."

"Collie wasn't much for baths. She got dizzy if she soaked in a hot tub. She preferred long showers."

Lenny looked at his watch. "Geez, it's late. I've got to pick up some beer and chips, I have people coming over."

"Oh, yes, I'd forgotten, you've lost someone, too. Was it a close friend?"

"We went through a lot, Fred and me. He was a funny guy. He told terrible jokes, but that wasn't what was funny about him . . . I'll miss him."

He got up and stepped to the front door, which Padric opened for him. Lenny held out his hand. "Thanks for talking to me. I'm sorry I couldn't tell you more."

"On the contrary, you've told me more than anyone else. I'm grateful to you."

Standing in the doorway, Padric added, "If you find out who was responsible, will you tell me?"

"I'll call you. I promise."

As he walked down the steps and approached his car, Lenny thought about the odd couple that Colleen and Padric turned out to be. Doomed to split up. Better to do it before getting married and having kids, he thought.

He reflected for a moment on his own childless existence, his wife, Margaret, having died of cancer before bearing them any children. He was confident that they would have stayed together for the long haul; they both had been committed to the relationship.

Maybe it is time to try again, he thought. All the dying made him want more than ever before to raise children while he was young enough to enjoy them, and to give them the home they deserved.

−SEVENTY-EIGHT−

On the drive back to Germantown, Lenny pondered the information he'd gained from Padric McBride. He thought about what Padric had said about Colleen getting dizzy from a hot bath. Then he thought about what Dr. Fingers had told him about certain kinds of heart conditions: stress the heart, and it decompensated, like the athlete who collapses and dies on the practice field in hot weather.

He had no idea if heart patients were especially sensitive to cyanide, but he wondered if Colleen had a heart condition. Perhaps she never told her fiancé; she was known to keep secrets, that was for sure. He made a note to ask Alex Primeaux when the doctor came by later for the wake. He'd call Dr. Fingers in the morning, too, and run it by him.

Stopping at the beer distributor on Germantown Avenue for a case of Yuengling, Lenny wondered again how the cyanide had been administered. Did the fiancé secretly poison her because she was breaking off the engagement? The guy didn't seem to have an ounce of maliciousness in him.

Then there was Mike. He had the know-how to develop a slow poison, and that migraine medicine he was taking, the ergotamine, could make him crazy. "Plenty loco," Hector said. Lenny didn't want to believe that his friend was capable of such an act, but he had to keep an open mind.

As for Kadish, Dr. Arrogance was capable of a lot of self-serving actions, but murder? He just didn't have a handle on the guy. There was no motive, as far as he could tell. If they had an affair, he couldn't see how the young saleswoman was a threat to the big-shot surgeon.

And Fox had seen her at seven in the morning, almost three hours before she died. If he had given her poison, it would most likely have kicked in shortly after she left the GI lab.

He pulled up to his house, got out of the car, and carried the case of beer up to the front porch. He hoped he had enough glasses for everyone. He had some paper cups; they could use those in a pinch. Hell, most of his friends would be satisfied to drink out of a coffee mug, as long as the beer was cold and there was plenty of it.

He stepped onto the front porch, which was enclosed but never locked, and put his key in the lock of the front door, when he felt something cold and hard pressed against the back of his neck.

"Don't say a word, Moss," said a flat, modulated voice. "And don't turn

305

around. Just open the door slowly and step into the room."

"Dr. Fox, I presume," said Lenny, pushing the door open and crossing the threshold. "What an unpleasant surprise."

Once inside the living room, Fox closed and locked the door. He instructed Lenny to put the case of beer down on the coffee table, then ordered him to sit in the armchair.

"Can I get you something do drink?" asked Lenny. "A beer? Whiskey? An aperitif, perhaps?"

"Joke around if you want. They'll be the last words out of your mouth, I assure you."

Fox stood in the middle of the room, his pistol trained at Lenny's chest.

"I'm a first-class shot with pistol, rifle, and bow. Don't even think about doing something stupid."

"Like die, you mean?" said Lenny. "I wouldn't dream of it."

Lenny looked about the room, saw nothing that might help him escape the conundrum he was in. Nor did he think that he could talk himself out of this one. Unlike dealing with Joe West, this time the punishment was a more permanent kind of termination.

"The police are looking for you," Lenny lied. "You're a wanted man. How far do you think you're going to get?"

"Far enough. I have my bag packed, I have a fake ID and a plane ticket out of the country. Oh, I've planned for this day a long time. I've dreamed of it. You see, all the money I've earned from Falcon and other companies that I've helped, I squirreled it away in an offshore account. And the name on the account isn't Fox."

"So you're going to live the free and easy life on some Caribbean island, is that it?" said Lenny. "Or maybe the south of France. That would be more like you. More high-class."

"I do love Paris," said Fox. "Any time of the year."

The doctor picked up a pillow from the sofa, folded it in half, pressed the barrel of the gun into it. As Lenny watched the maneuver, he knew what was coming. The prospect of his imminent death did not paralyze him. Instead, to his surprise, it made him smile.

"What are you grinning at?" asked Fox.

"I know it's ridiculous," said Lenny, "but I'm so far behind in my credit card, I remortgaged the house when my wife was sick and we needed money for the care that the insurance wouldn't pay for. I was just thinking that my old man was right. He always told me the best plan was to die in debt. The bank will have to eat the loan."

"You are a sick individual," said Fox.

"So I've been told."

Fox took a step closer to Lenny, aimed the gun at his heart.

"Aren't you going to count to three?" said Lenny. "Or maybe, a thousand?"

"No, Mr. Moss, I'm just going to kill you."

On his way over to Lenny's for the wake, Gary Tuttle stopped at a Wawa to buy snacks. As he selected some spicy potato chips, he thought about his patient Mrs. Cavanaugh, and of her troubled relations with her daughter. He hoped that the two women would find the strength to reconcile their differences. Gary had no idea what issues kept them apart. The mother could be short-tempered at times, but she didn't seem particularly overbearing. She was certainly more agreeable than many of the patients he had cared for.

She was afraid of dying from the cancer, as any patient would be. He was glad that the chemotherapy hadn't been too tough on her. Her GI tract seemed to be holding up. The suppositories had done the trick. As long as the antiemetic was given enough time to get into the bloodstream and bind to receptors in the brain, it should hold down the vomiting.

He made a mental note to be sure and talk to the hospital's visiting nurse service about that before the woman was discharged.

His mind drifted back to the nursing notes from Colleen Creedon's chart. He recalled the vaginal discharge and the comments about her sex life. Then it hit him like a cardiac alarm sounding. It wasn't a *vaginal* discharge, it was a *rectal* discharge. All at once he knew how the killer had poisoned Colleen Creedon. More importantly, he knew *who* it was.

He wished he'd taken the cell phone with him. *Use the pay phone?* Somebody was on it, and she looked like she was taking her sweet time. He'd be at Lenny's in a few minutes; he would tell him then.

The one thing that eluded him was how such a small dose of the drug could put the young woman into cardiac arrest. But he was sure that once he and Lenny and Moose had compared notes, they would be able to figure the whole thing out.

They could bring Alex Primeaux in on the discussion, too; the Employee

Health physician was bound to be at the wake. He had stuck by Fred all through his years of drinking. The hospital admissions, the liver failure, the weeks of delirium, when nobody thought Fred would survive.

Yes, thought Gary. They would soon have all of the pieces of the puzzle assembled. They would call that detective, Bill Williams, explain their case in detail, and get the police to arrest the real killer.

The party at Lenny's was going to be one they would all be talking about for a long time. He went to the dairy section to select some dips.

-SEVENTY-NINE-

Elliot Fox stepped closer to Lenny, the pistol pointed at his intended victim's heart. Lenny closed his eyes. He was afraid that when the bullet struck his chest it would be painful, if only for a few seconds. Ever since he was a kid he'd never liked getting shots; he thought this might be even worse.

As he listened for the sound of the explosion, he thought he heard the sound of a door opening. And voices. Opening his eyes, he heard steps on the front porch, then a loud *knock, knock, knock.*

"Hey, Lenny, open up, you got company!" called Moose.

Never in his life had Lenny been so glad to have friends.

Fox's hand wavered in its bead on his chest.

"If you shoot, even with the pillow, they'll hear you. Then what will you do?"

Lenny had parried and thrust in many an arbitration hearing. He'd never had to talk his way out of dying.

"Shut up and let me think," said Fox. He took a single step toward the kitchen. "I can still make it out the back door and be away while they are trying to break down the door to find out what is happening."

Suddenly both men heard the sound of a key in the lock.

"Moose knows I keep a spare key under the mat," explained Lenny. "For the maid."

Just then Moose came in carrying a case of beer on his shoulder, Birdie and several other hospital workers behind him. As they tumbled into the living room, they saw Fox standing with the gun pointing at Lenny, and stopped in their tracks.

"Nobody move," yelled Fox, "or your friend is a dead man!"

Moose, holding the case of beer balanced on his shoulder, considered throwing it at Fox and jumping for the gun. He cast a quick glance at Lenny, who made the slightest shake of his head no.

As everyone stood as still as statues, there was the sound of car doors slamming and voices in the street. Fox realized his time was getting short.

"You can't shoot all of us," said Moose, "there's more of us coming up the steps. You best be turning tail and split."

"Not before I rid myself of this pesky custodian," said Fox, backing slowly into the dining room. "If it wasn't for him I'd be in the clear. I had the police snowed when they questioned me. They were even ready to call me in as a consultant on the case."

"I tell you one thing," said Moose. "You shoot my friend, you better be quick, cause I can get to you in two steps, and I swear I'll bring you down, even if I take a bullet doing it."

Fox took another step back. He stopped in the doorway leading to the kitchen, the gun still aimed at Lenny's chest.

"They can only execute me once," said Fox, "no matter how many of you I kill."

As Fox raised the gun to fire, an iron bar flew down with deadly force, striking his wrist with a fierce blow. The gun discharged, the bullet striking the floor harmlessly. A second blow struck Fox on the side of his head.

Moose came leaping forward. He pulled the gun out of Fox's paralyzed hand with one hand and grabbed him by the throat with the other. Squeezing his airway shut, Moose pushed the doctor against the wall hard and held him there.

Sandy, the old security guard, stood behind Fox, chuckling. He had a broad smile lifting his hound dog cheeks, looking as pleased with himself as the night he lost his virginity.

"I am arresting your sorry ass, motherfucker, for the murder of Colleen Creedon," said Sandy. "And I don't give a shit about no Miranda warning or anything else."

Taking a pair of handcuffs from his belt, he pulled Fox's hands behind his back and cuffed him, indifferent to the moan of pain that came when he squeezed the cuff tightly over the man's broken wrist.

Lenny sat in his chair, unable to stand. His heart was racing, his face was flushed. He couldn't believe that he had come so close to dying. He'd held his fear in check until it was all over, and now the anxiety was flooding over him.

Once his heart stopped pounding in his chest, he stood up and approached Sandy, saying, "Fucking A, you are my hero of heroes. Sandy, how did you know to come in the back door?"

"Wasn't no big thing," said Sandy. "When Moose found your door locked and I knew your car was out front, I asked myself why would you lock the door when you were expecting a passel of friends to come by any minute?"

"Always the true detective," said Lenny.

"And I knew that Fox had mysteriously disappeared, Tina told me when I made my rounds in the hospital. She thought you had him pegged as suspect number one, and with him being on the loose, and you holed up behind a locked door, I thought I better play it safe and cover the back door, just in case."

Moose dialed 911. As they waited for the police to arrive, Lenny suggested that they all have a drink. Nobody objecting, the case of beer was ripped open, a bottle of whiskey poured, and salutations offered.

"Somehow," said Moose, "I don't think a lot of hospital people are going to be surprised when they drive up and find police cars in front of your house."

"As long as they don't spoil the party, who cares?" said Lenny. He chugged a whole shot of whiskey, neat, then followed with a long pull on a bottle of beer. He belched loudly, and smiled as the alcohol began to soothe his frazzled nerves.

−EIGHTY−

As he surveyed the gaggle of hospital workers filling his house, Lenny turned to his best friend and said, "Moose, tell me the truth. Would you really have taken a bullet for me?"

"Heh, heh. Are you crazy? What kind of fool do you think I am?"

"You mean you wouldn't do it?"

"If I did, I'd be the biggest fool that ever lived."

"So you're not saying you *wouldn't*," said Lenny. "You just don't want to admit that you *would*."

"You're crazy," said Birdie. "Of course Moose would take a bullet for you. You men just don't want to admit how much you care about each other."

"I can think of somebody he *does* care about," said Moose.

"Shut up and have another drink," said Lenny, pouring a shot of whiskey for his friend. "What about you, Tuttle? Are you ready for the hard stuff?"

"I rather think I am," said Gary, holding out his cup of Coca-Cola.

"Whoa, Tuttle," said Lenny, "drinking with the grown-ups."

Gary took a sip of his whiskey and Coke, smacked his lips. "Did you realize that Fred's breath must have smelled like alcohol?" he said. "It's from acetone buildup when the blood sugar is out of control."

"What are you saying, that West made an honest mistake?" said Lenny.

"I'm just saying he wasn't completely out of line assuming that Fred had gone back to drinking."

"He still sent him out to his car," said Moose. "Drunk or sick, West killed him."

"Shoot," said Celeste. "I wish that bastard got what he deserved. Can't the union do something?"

"I wish we could, but I don't see how," said Lenny, keeping to himself his deal with Freely not to file a grievance in exchange for clearing Celeste and Gary. "It's up to the DA or the family to bring charges."

"How *did* Fox get the poison in her, anyway?" asked Birdie.

"He put nitroprussic acid in a rectal suppository," said Gary. "She must have waited until she'd made her other appointments in the hospital before taking it; it would work in about fifteen, twenty minutes."

"I had the idea it was something like that," said Lenny. "Dr. Fingers told me that Colleen had that 'slight' thickening of her ventricle."

"She had mitral valve stenosis," said Alex Primeaux, a glass of whiskey in

313

his hand. "She needed a full volume of blood filling her ventricles."

"Which was why she never took baths," said Lenny. "She got dizzy soaking in a hot tub. But I thought you could only give that drug right in the vein."

"A rectal suppository for the most part bypasses the liver," said Alex. "It's like giving a drug IV push. The nitroprussic acid dropped her pressure and put her in cardiac arrest."

"The one thing that I still don't understand," said Gary, "is why she came to Seven South and ended up in the empty room."

"Don't you remember?" said Celeste, holding out her cup for more whiskey. "Seven North is the transplant ward. She probably was looking for Dr. Kadish."

"I told you Kadish was the last one to see her alive," said Moose.

"Yeah, but you also said he was the killer," Lenny reminded him. "That business about the bad batch of drugs from their plant in India didn't pan out. I checked with Mike; the hospital's supply comes from a plant in Mexico."

He took a pull on his drink and continued. "The important thing is, Fox knew that we had an empty room on account of his admission was canceled. She probably called him to say she was feeling dizzy, and he told her to go lie down in seven-o-nine. He probably promised he'd meet her there."

"That would have been the phone call that he got in the GI lab," said Tina. "Myrna thought it was his wife; the woman asked for Elliot, not 'Dr. Fox,' but it was actually Colleen Creedon who called."

"Imagine that," said Moose. "Her last conversation was with her own killer."

"Tell them about how he faked the photos," said Lenny, turning to Moose.

"I figured that out when I was helping my daughter with a school project. She was making pictures of clothes from different countries. Since the people wear different colors, I showed her how to manipulate a face to change its shade and its shape. I realized Fox was doing the same thing."

"He's a smart son of a bitch," said Lenny. "Tina always said he was the best in the business. You wonder why somebody that smart would take a chance on a scheme that only brought in a few thousand dollars. It's not like he was going to get rich faking the reports in his drug study."

"He didn't do it for the money," said Patience, "He did it to pump up his male ego."

"How's that?" said Lenny. "I don't get you."

"You said before, Fox wasn't getting rich enrolling those patients in that drug study. Right?"

"Yeah."

"If money wasn't what made him cheat, it must have been something else, and it was. Ego. He wanted to look like the smartest doctor in the whole world. As long as he could fake the results, he was never wrong."

"That's rr-right!" said Gary. "He was like a poker player who was using a stacked deck. He could make a correct diagnosis one hundred percent of the time. He'd never be wrong."

"Careful, Tuttle, you're slurring your words," said Lenny.

"No I'm n-not," said Gary, swaying slightly. He held out his cup for more whiskey, a silly grin on his face.

Lenny added a drop more whiskey to Gary's cup, warning him to be sure and have his wife drive home.

Alex Primeaux, his wife-to-be beside him, said, "Did you hear, Allendale died?"

"Yeah," said Lenny. "A million dollars down the tube."

"From what I hear, the hospital is going to keep their million bucks, but Martin Kadish may have to return his fee."

"How come?" said Moose.

"Allendale's heirs have hired a lawyer. Actually, they have a team of them. They're contesting the contract. They feel that the old man was delirious from his liver failure and not in any condition to sign a contract."

"Say, Lenny," said Celeste. "Did you ever find out who the father is?"

"No. I didn't have the heart to ask Padric McBride what his blood type is, and he didn't volunteer it."

"I hope the baby was his," said Celeste. "It's bad enough losing the woman you're going to marry, but if her baby wasn't yours, that would really mess with your head."

"At least we know it wasn't Mike's," said Lenny. "He won't have *that* to deal with when he tries to get his wife to take him back."

"How can you be sure?" said Moose. "His blood type was right."

"I finally realized that the dates are all wrong. Even if he was bullshitting me and he *did* sleep with her at the conference in New Orleans, the baby was only about three months along. It had to be somebody else's."

"Thank Heaven for small favors," said Birdie.

"You got any more chips?" asked Moose, looking over at the dining room table.

"Why don't you get up off your lazy ass and see?" said Birdie.

"This detective is tired," he said.

Patience came up with a tray loaded with wings and dipping sauce. As everyone reached for the food at once, she held it out to Lenny, saying, "One at a time, there's plenty for everybody."

Moose held a piece of chicken in his hand, a drink in the other. Looking at Lenny, he said, "The girl can cook like nobody's business."

"Shut up," said Lenny. "I do all right in the kitchen."

"Yeah," said Celeste, "I've seen your peanut butter and jelly."

"Home cooking, that's what you need," said Moose. "Trust me."

"What I need is a week's vacation away from all of you," said Lenny.

Patience came over to Lenny and put her hand on his shoulder.

"My kids have been begging to go to Disney World,' she said. "I was thinking they might get to go as soon as school ends."

"That's not my idea of a vacation," said Lenny. "I need to rest, not run around Disney World."

"You wouldn't be doing any running," she said. "My sister said she'd take them with her kids. I was thinking about a week down the shore."

"Oh," said Lenny. "Well, in that case, I'll have another drink."

DEC 0 8 2010

POP

LaVergne, TN USA
18 October 2010
201281LV00003B/69/P